By Chuck Logan

SOUTH OF SHILOH

CHUCK LOGAN

HARPER

An Imprint of HarperCollins*Publishers*

HARPER

An Imprint of HarperCollins*Publishers*
10 East 53rd Street
New York, New York 10022-5299

Copyright © 2008 by Chuck Logan
ISBN 978-0-06-113670-2

First Harper paperback printing: April 2009
First Harper hardcover printing: April 2008

HarperCollins® and Harper® are registered trademarks of Harper-Collins Publishers.

Printed in the United States of America

Visit Harper paperbacks on the World Wide Web at
www.harpercollins.com

10 9 8 7 6 5 4 3 2 1

For the reenactors,
especially Company A,
1st Minnesota Volunteer Infantry

ACKNOWLEDGMENTS

Brit, for opening the door to Mississippi.

The members of Company A, 1st Minnesota Volunteer Infantry, especially John Taylor and Jim Moffet.

Dennis Landry, Kenny Knopp, and the troopers of Company D, 7th Tennessee Cavalry.

Del Horton, Executive Director, Corinth Area Tourism Promotion Council.

Kristy White, Director, Crossroads Museum, Corinth, Mississippi.

Chief David Lancaster, Corinth Police Department, Corinth, Mississippi.

Captain Mike Shipman, Patrol Division, Corinth Police Department, and his family, especially Butch, for good company.

Sheriff Jimmy Taylor, Alcorn County, Mississippi.

Mike Beckner, Investigator, Alcorn County Sheriff's Department, Alcorn County, Mississippi.

In Corinth: The Dinner Bell Lunch Bunch, Anne Thompson, Jerry Porter, Lee Ann Story Houry, Amy Sims, Bernard Toomer, Robert and Janet Krohn.

The readers of the Muses Book Club, Stillwater, Minnesota: Anne Bisgaard, Becky Clark, Becky Cummins, Mary Lynn Decarlo, Rose Grenell, Linda Livermore, Sue Payne, Jan Schueffner, Jody Vasilakes.

Dwight Cummins, Cummins Law Office, Bayport, Minnesota; Boris Beckert, M.D., Stillwater Medical Group,

Stillwater, Minnesota; Robin Eichleay, CAPthat Productions, Lakeland, Minnesota.

Don Schoff, Schoff Rifle and Hardware Company, Stillwater, Minnesota; Sergeant Wayne Johnson, Washington County Sheriff's Department; Jim Westberg, Muzzleloaders Etcetera, Inc., Bloomington, Minnesota; and Ron Cleveland, who did it for real on the Ho Chi Minh Trail.

Commander Pat Olson and retired Commander Denny Moriarty, Washington County Sheriff's Department, Washington County, Minnesota.

Jim Bradshaw, Director, Bradshaw Celebration of Life Center, Stillwater, Minnesota.

At Stonebridge Elementary, Stillwater, Minnesota: Megan Prom, Psychologist; Colony 3 Teacher Loretta Peterson; and special thanks to Colony 4 Teacher Denise Cote.

Kate Nelson, Guidance Counselor, Stillwater High School.

Penguin Group USA Inc. for permission to quote from *17 Kings and 42 Elephants* by Margaret Mahy.

Two shooters: Richard Sennott and Jean Pieri.

SOUTH OF SHILOH

PROLOGUE

Soon the man he plans to kill will tramp out from the woods with the other blue soldier boys.

For now he has fog and the smell of wet tree bark, rotting leaf fall, and his own sweat. These dews and damps are eerie enough without counting the minutes to a murder.

Mist cloaks the land, a memory of morning frost. This is how it looked for the real thing a hundred forty-odd years ago, when the two armies groped toward each other blind. After Shiloh, Halleck, the Union fuss budget, micromanaged his advance on Corinth. Beauregard, the cagey Rebel, played for time.

This is Banker Kirby's property and he has continued the family tradition of preserving the battle site. For the last ten years he has opened his fields and forests to the clamor of mock battle as reenactors from the North and South gather to replay the clash along the banks of Kirby Creek. Middle-aged men with the eager eyes of boys are drawn here to relive history, to wear blue and gray and touch off blanks in reproduction Civil War rifles.

Playing guns.

All that is about to change.

The match Enfield muzzleloader cradled in his lap is an original. The barrel has been re-sleeved and rifled by one of the best gunsmiths in America. The bore is charged with a precisely cast .577-caliber lead minié ball backed by load-tested black powder.

The fact is Alcorn deputy Kenny Beeman is going to get

way more authenticity than he bargained for this Saturday afternoon, once the Kirby Creek Civil War battle reenactment gets started.

He leans the rifle against the dead fall oak he's chosen as his shooting perch, raises his Zeiss binoculars, and nudges the focus knob. Waste of time. Just fog. He sets the glasses down.

The distance has been stepped off. Strands of unobtrusive brown yarn have been strung in the brush, tied to loose tatters of leaves for ballast. The yarn bundles mark the range at a hundred fifty, two hundred, and two hundred fifty yards and will provide an accurate reading of wind conditions in the target area.

He removes a tiny, palm-sized notebook from his pocket. The notebook catalogues the rifle's fall of rounds at twenty-yard intervals between one to three hundred yards in different weather conditions. He checks the notations for two hundred yards in high moisture. Under an inch low. He puts the notebook away, sits back, and stares at the wooden tampion plug inserted in the muzzle to keep the wet out.

Off to the left he hears the growl of motors. Chains rattle. The muffled shouts of men. They are unloading the cannons and caissons on the crest of the hill, manhandling them off the lowboys behind the trucks.

You have to make some allowances in the quest for authenticity. The cannons are expensive to maintain and cart around. The cost of a team of horses is prohibitive.

He leans back on the rubber poncho he's spread on the damp leaves. Except for the binoculars and the cell phone in his pocket, he's trucked very little modern gear through the woods this morning. On the remote chance of being challenged, he wants to look like a Confederate reenactor. So he wears gray wool trousers, matching sack coat, a pair of worn brogans, and a gray forage cap. A leather belt with a CSA brass buckle is cinched around his waist with a percussion cap box snugged next to the buckle. The larger leather cartridge box hangs on his right hip. He carries a holstered Colt Model 1851 Navy pistol primed with six live rounds. Just in case.

He withdraws a thermos from his haversack, unscrews the top, pours a cup of black coffee, then sniffs a hint of wood smoke. They've built a fire on the hill, so he figures he can get away with a cigarette. Cupping his hand, he lights a Pall Mall.

After another cup of coffee and two more cigarettes, a faint blade of sunlight stirs the mist. The first defined shape he sees is the head and shoulders of a brooding stone giant.

The dimensions of the granite figure slowly materialize atop the hill three hundred yards to his left. At the base of the monument the silhouettes of three cannon barrels and spoked wheels slowly darken in. Two shadowy figures stand among the cannons. One leans on a ramrod.

The statue commemorating the Confederate dead at Kirby Creek is so new it hasn't even been christened by its first drip of pigeon shit. The granite soldier towers ten feet tall atop a twelve-foot pedestal and stands at the "in place rest" position with his stone hands gripping his slanting rifle. He wears a slouch hat, and a bedroll is draped across his chest. In keeping with a long tradition, his stern face looks south and his rear end points north.

A rectangle of red earth is edged by twelve-pound cannonballs directly below the crest of the slope and defines the one officially recognized burial trench on the field. This mass grave is reputed to hold the remains of over a hundred Confederates. There are at least two other burial pits somewhere on the property; unrecorded, their location lost to memory.

Warmer now. The mist burns away like clouds of incense. Bathed in sudden sunlight, the chiseled statue loses its spectral power and becomes an oversized lawn ornament in the front yard of the white, pillared Kirby House.

Finally the rolling forests where Mississippi and Tennessee merge northwest of Corinth swirl into focus, all browns and green peeks of early spring. Dormant gray kudzu clogs the tree lines and drapes in smothering shrouds. White blooming dogwood haunts the dark thickets of hickory, oak, sweet gum, and ash like crippled angels crashed to earth.

Eight thousand men fought here in 1862. Today they'll be lucky to field eight hundred, three dozen horses, and six cannons. Most of the participants are Southerners, many of them putting on blue to balance out the Union side. Perhaps a hundred fifty Yankee reenactors have made the drive to Mississippi.

Kirby Creek is being billed as the premier "authentic" event of the season. What gives the battle special appeal is the fact that the land is virtually unchanged. The Kirby House, with its wraparound veranda, stands perfectly restored on the hill. Great care has been taken to preserve the pocked scars that, by actual count, four hundred and seventy-four Federal minié balls left impacted in the stucco walls and wooden columns. The snake rail fence where the rebels made their stand is reproduced in exact detail and stretches along the slope below the house.

And this year the Yankees are duplicating the famous swamp march that brought them in on the Confederate flank. His target, Beeman, is wearing blue, working security among the swamp marchers.

The outcome of the fight remains unclear. The North claimed a victory. The South would not admit a defeat.

Whatever.

A bugle call rouses him and then he hears the long roll of muffled drums. Twenty gray horsemen, two abreast, gallop onto the field, dismount, and form a thin line. Random muskets pop. Then the firing builds and white smoke blossoms over the thickets. Gray skirmishers trot from the far side of the hill.

His heart pounds as the cell phone vibrates in his pocket and he pulls it out and flips it open. "Can you hear me?" the spotter asks. The spotter wears a blue uniform and has spent the morning waiting in the woods.

"I can hear you."

"Gotta make this quick. They see me with a phone they'll run me off the field." The spotter's voice cracks, betraying his nervous reluctance with this day's work.

"You locate him?"

"Hard to see in all the fog and smoke and shit. But they're outta the swamp and sneaking in through the trees. Pretty soon they'll come out of the woods right in front of you."

Goddamn it. "Where in front of me? There's gonna be almost two hundred of them all dressed alike."

"Last I saw he's got a turkey tail feather sticking in his black slouch hat."

"I'm gonna need more than that."

"Well, last I saw, the guy right next to him was wearing a red bandanna wrapped around his head like a fuckin' do-rag. Best I can do."

The call ends. Less than pleased, he puts the phone back in his pocket and looks out over the field, where the cavalry have remounted their horses ahead of the retreating gray skirmish line. The first blue figures emerge from the cover of the trees; firing, reloading, advancing in rushes. He gets his first powerful whiff of black powder smoke.

He raises the binoculars and scans the blue skirmishers. He can see the flush of sweat on their faces in the tack-sharp optics, the dark drench of dew and burrs on their trousers. Slowly he shifts his focus to the curve of wood line behind the skirmish line, where the blue companies will spill out of the trees.

He pans the binocs in tighter, fixes on one of the subtle yarn dangles, focuses, and sees the brown bundle shiver so slightly it's hard to tell if it's a puff of breeze or the transparent ripple of mirage rising off the warming ground.

Then, through pauses in the skirmish fire, he hears a muted tambourine jingle of tin cups and canteens on rifle stocks; the steady tread of hobnails beating down the brush. The main body emerges from the trees, wading through lingering fog, and forms, shoulder to shoulder, two deep, into one long battle line.

His binoculars explore the blue line but smoke drifts in and combines with the fog and the wavy ground mirage. All he sees is blurred bands of identical sky-blue trousers, dark blue jackets and caps. Waiting, he studies the U.S. flag that juts above the smoke. Sees it shiver in a gust of wind. Bites his lip. A strong breeze can play hell with the shot. Then the wind dissipates and the flag hangs limp.

He scopes the foliage and grass for signs of the lurking wind. He checks his yarn dangles. Finally the mass of blue clears the smoke and halts to dress the ranks.

Then he spots the red smudge on the extreme right, standing out in the front rank. Carefully he focuses, and there is Kenny Beeman with a feather in his hat, standing to the right of the man with the red headgear.

Okay.

He sets the binocs aside, reaches for the rifle, pulls the wooden plug from the muzzle, and rests the rifle in a notch on the tree trunk. Elevation two hundred yards. He aligns the notched rear sight and gently nudges the front blade from blue chest to leather-crossed blue chest. After the intense resolution of the Zeiss, Beeman swims blurry, tiny in his naked eye. But he's always had good eyes; has always been able to read the bottom line on the eye chart. He blinks away sweat and the sight picture improves.

His index finger caresses the trigger.

Jesus!

He gasps and jerks his hand from the trigger when a man in the rear rank pitches forward. What the hell? The guy tumbles down, hits the ground, and lies still between the legs of the man capped with the red scarf.

Crazy moment. Did I shoot?

No. Hammer still at half-cock. Wait. Panting, squinting, he sees that other men are falling along the line. Okay. Calm down. They're just acting; part of the scenario, playing wounded and dead. Goddamn, man. Had me going there. Yes you did.

Steadier, he looks down, checks that the percussion cap is fitted to the nipple cone. As he pulls the hammer to full-cock, he notices that his right hand is trembling slightly. Damn guy falling broke his concentration. He wills his skin into a rigid body stocking to contain the thundering of his heart, leans back to the sights, snugs the rifle stock into his shoulder, and sights down the heavy barrel.

The blue line emerges from the dissolving smoke, reloading and priming their rifles. That's him, definitely him in a heavc of white smoke, standing toy-soldier-stiff and serious.

Two hundred yards almost exactly.

Make a decision. Excitement, the roar of cannons and muskets and the clouds of smoke, is challenging the amateur discipline of these play soldiers.

Companies drift in the confusion. The blue line is now uneven, canted slightly away on the broken ground. Wait until they are more full-front? Or take him now?

He pauses, debating, as the black powder cloud melts away from the blue ranks and slowly leaks straight up, evaporating. No wind. The shot is clear. No more waiting. DO IT NOW. He nestles the front blade in the iron notch. Remembering the notation about humidity, he settles the aiming point toward the top of the dull brass twinkle on the intersecting leather straps. Exhale. Make it happen. Squeeze the trigger. In that fraction of a second he sees it all in exploding clarity . . . how it unfolded over the last three days . . .

1 **"JENNY, ANY LUCK?" PAUL EDIN CALLED** out as he stooped over the duffel bag he'd just torn apart by the front door and pawed through a pile of blue wool clothing. He set aside a tangle of leather belts and pouches. A silver bayonet in a black scabbard clattered on the floor.

At the other end of the house, in the mud porch off the kitchen, Jennifer Edin turned her head in a slow toss that was old habit from when her hair was longer. Thirty-five last October, she had learned to put little faith in luck as an eleventh-hour solution. "When's the last time you remember seeing them?" she called back.

"I don't know."

"Them" referred to his reenactor spectacles without which he could not embark on his Mississippi Civil War adventure. When Jenny narrowed her eyes, the sprinkle of cinnamon freckles across the bridge of her straight nose and wide cheeks tightened. Her fifth-grade students understood that this quiet, alert look signaled a prelude to intense scrutiny.

A blue-eyed brunette, hair in a tidy bob, she stood five seven and kept the needle on the bathroom scale planted dead on one twenty-four. Willowy and athletic, she stayed a few calculated pounds shy of curvaceous.

Something held in check there.

Methodically, she began to sort through the mound of workday debris her husband and daughter regularly tossed on the long table on the porch: books, magazines, clothing, newspapers, a bicycle pump. The mud porch was her triage station, where she stemmed the casual chaos of his garage from invading the order of her house.

"Mom?" Molly Edin appeared in the kitchen doorway with a cordless phone in her hand. "Rachel wants to know if I can come over."

They'd rushed home from school to see Paul off, so Jenny gave her daughter the Look, followed by the Voice; a no-nonsense tone she had perfected teaching special ed to inner-city kids in St. Paul. "Not now, you will help me look for Dad's glasses."

"He's *wearing* his glasses." Molly, just turned eleven, with her first pimple on her chin, was indignant at being ignored. She waved the phone, insisting. The sweet malleable Gumby years of nine and ten were gone forever. Molly was becoming a prepubescent "me."

"His *reenactor* glasses, you know; the old ones," Jenny said. "Now hang up the phone and check the kitchen counters."

"Nobody says hang up the phone anymore," Molly said, then she retreated from the doorway and was replaced by her father.

"They won't let me in without those glasses, says right on the printout. Kirby Creek is a semi-immersion event. No modern eyewear of any kind allowed," Paul said.

Jenny took a deep breath and concentrated, raising her hands, arms floating out like wands of a divining rod. She closed her eyes and recalled seeing the glasses . . . turning, moving . . . to the shelves next to the table, and opened a fishing tackle box that was full of old buttons, bits of cloth, and various old brass insignias.

"There you are." Jenny plucked up the battered gray case containing the errant spectacles.

Paul exhaled and gratefully squeezed her arm. Then he took the glasses case and hurried off through the kitchen to repack his bag. Jenny turned briefly to the flotsam covering the table. Automatically, her hands reached out to sort the mess. Then she paused, seeing the newspaper section on top of the recycling pile.

The Metro section of yesterday's *St. Paul Pioneer Press* was folded to an inside page, where a news brief announced: "*Pioneer Press* Photographer Suspended." She glanced out into the empty kitchen, faintly heard the boops and chimes of Molly logging on to Club Penguin in the den; the scuffs of Paul sorting his gear. She read the short paragraph that she and her husband had discussed last night.

> Pioneer Press *photographer John Rane was suspended for two weeks yesterday, following a complaint from St. Paul Police Chief, Oscar Talbot. Chief Talbot charged that Rane violated a SWAT team cordon and endangered officers and civilians during a tense standoff last week in West St. Paul . . .*

But people were still talking about it. *"Did'ya see the picture that guy took . . . ?"*

"Hey Jenny," Paul yelled, "we gotta go."

"Coming," Jenny said, dropping the paper back on the pile. Paul was in the den, saying good-bye to Molly. After giving her dad two kisses and a hug, Molly sighed dramatically: "Have *fun* in the *war*, Dad."

"We all set?" Jenny asked, following him to the foyer, where he'd repacked his gear.

"Yep."

"You sure?"

Paul nodded and rattled off the checklist: "Forage cap, sack coat, flannel shirt, wool trousers with straps, brogans, wool socks, muslin underwear, gloves, gum blanket, wool blanket, greatcoat, field pack and canteen." He paused to take a breath. "Combo knife fork and spoon, mucket cup." He held up a square black bag with a strap and stuffed it in the duffel. "Haversack."

"What about food?"

"Davey's in charge of the hardtack and slab bacon. Coffee, veggies, stuff like that."

Jenny made a face. "Rifle?"

Paul hefted the 1861 Springfield rifled musket in a canvas case. Then he shoved in a tangle of black leather: belt and straps to which his cartridge box, cap box, and bayonet and scabbard were fastened.

"Cartridges?" Jenny asked, remembering the time her dad went deer hunting without his bullets.

"Eighty," Paul grinned. He'd spent three days in the basement, rolling paper cylinders off a pattern with a half-inch wooden dowel, tying them off with kite string, insisting on explaining the process to her. The way he put in a wad of Kleenex as a substitute for a .58-caliber lead minié bullet. Then he filled the paper tubes with fifty-eight grains of carefully measured black powder and methodically creased and folded the open end with a distinctive flourish, like nineteenth-century origami. Jenny didn't approve of keeping the can of black powder in the house after she'd heard that the stuff could ignite around plastic. Something about friction. She made him keep it in an olive-drab surplus steel box in the utility shed in the backyard.

"Glasses," he finished up, tapping the glasses case stuck in his jeans front pocket. The optometrist had refitted lenses from an old prescription into the cramped period-accurate frames.

"I'll put this stuff in the car," he said, dragging the large duffel and the rifle out the front door. As he walked back in, first his, then her cell rang. They attended to the calls; Paul talking to Davey Manning, who was already waiting in the parking lot of historic Fort Snelling in St. Paul. She took a call from her mother, Lois, who was running late on her way to look after Molly.

"Okay," Jenny said, ducking into the den. "Gram's coming in ten minutes. Don't answer the door till she gets here. After I drop Dad off I'm going to do some shopping and stop at the club . . ."

"Rachel—" Molly began.

"No Rachel tonight. And I want you to get in half an hour on the piano. And go over your spelling sorts before any television. Clear?"

"Claro." Molly nodded and never moved her eyes off the video screen.

"I mean it," Jenny said.

"Jenny, honey . . ." Paul said.

Jenny backed the Subaru Forester out of the drive and got underway. Paul was on his cell again, talking to his insurance office, scheduling a client for next Wednesday. He ended the call and perused the row of houses on their street. As they passed the *for sale* sign at the end of the block, he mumbled: "Two months, nobody's biting."

"Sally said they came down in price," Jenny said.

"Hmmm."

Jenny ran her eyes over the ranks of new roofs that crowded the horizon as she threaded her way out the Croix Ridge Development. No trees yet to break up the regimented dollhouse cul-de-sacs. She had wanted an old Stillwater house on the north hill, so Molly could walk to school. Paul, who evaluated homes in his business, worried about boobytrap repairs that lurked in nineteenth-century Victorians. The new house in the new development would appreciate before they'd have to spend anything on maintenance; or so he thought two years ago, when they'd moved from St. Paul. That was before the stucco fiasco, when most of the houses in Croix Ridge came down with terminal mold infestations.

"Is Molly wearing a bra?" he asked suddenly.

Jenny smiled and wondered if she should tell him she had noticed Molly's first pubic hair. "Just a bra top," she said.

"We're going to have to talk to her about it, before she's a teenager," he said in the resigned voice of a man who kept moving an item from one to-do list to another.

"It," Jenny said. Not a reference to the birds and bees. He meant the newspaper brief. He meant John Rane.

"We'll talk about it, first thing when I get back," Paul said.

Jenny changed the subject. "You guys still going to drive all night?"

Paul shrugged. "Three of us, we'll trade off." He looked out the window at the obstinate grime of late March: yellow, frost-stunted lawns, bare gray branches. "It'll be greener in Mississippi."

"You'll be careful," Jenny said.

"Jenny, honey, I go the speed limit. I don't run stop signs. I sell insurance, for Christ's sake." Paul grinned.

They traveled in silence and Jenny was thinking how her husband was a risk-assessment machine. He watched his diet and stayed trim and fit; he'd never smoked and seldom drank. And now his passion for accurate detail had found an outlet in his historical focus on being a Civil War reenactor. The unit he joined was based at Fort Snelling, their destination on this cool early-spring afternoon. Paul was on his way with two "pards" to a battle event in Mississippi. Over the last year he had scrupulously researched and accumulated a full set of equipment off the Internet. He had attended the bimonthly drills, learning to march with and fire his Springfield musket. During a three-day encampment in southern Minnesota he'd honed his skills at marching in the arcane formations and firing blanks from the clunky rifle. Now he was ready to test himself in the fine print of an authentic battle so he could pass "muster" and be judged a field-worthy member of Company A of the First Minnesota Volunteers.

Jenny worked the road grid toward the city, taking Highway 36 to 694, then turning west on 94 and jumping off to catch 61, then Warner Road that turned into Sheppard Road. The sweep of the city where she'd grown up was getting less familiar; the capital, the cathedral, the high bridge, the new waterfront along the river. Ten minutes later, she negotiated the tricky freeway interchanges and finally pulled into the parking lot at the old fort that overlooked the confluence of the Minnesota and Mississippi Rivers.

A red Toyota 4Runner waited in the parking lot with bags lashed to the roof rack. Two men, Tom Dalton and Davey Manning, greeted them. Dalton was travel-casual in jeans and cross trainers. Manning was in character, wearing a battered blue forage cap, a blue tie-dyed T-shirt, pale wool trousers, and scuffed brogans. Pigtailed, mustachioed, and goateed, his pale face was eerily reminiscent to Jenny of an old tintype of John Wilkes Booth.

Jenny got out and took a closer look at Manning's shirt, which had a Civil War vintage photo printed on the front. It was the famous picture of a member of the real First Minnesota, Pvt. Marshall Sherman, standing next to the Twenty-eighth Virginia Regiment's Rebel battle flag he'd captured during the high watermark of Pickett's Charge at Gettysburg. The flag, the object of a long-standing tug-of-war between the state of Virginia and the state of Minnesota, now resided in a vault in the Minnesota Historical Society. The caption under the picture proclaimed: *i survived the battle of gettysburg and all i got was this crummy flag.*

"Jesus, Davey. That's like a skinhead walking into a black bar and yelling the N-word. If you're going to wear that Down South I'm putting Paul back in the car," Jenny said with a discernible edge in her voice.

Manning twirled his mustache, struck a pose, and furrowed his brow. Dalton cleared his throat. Paul, the new guy, stared straight ahead.

Jenny persisted, raising one eyebrow. "My fifth-grade boys have more sense."

Now Manning cleared his throat. "I'll wear it as far south as Cairo, Illinois, and reevaluate."

"Fair," Jenny said. "No sense in getting killed at a truck stop before you get to the battle, eh?"

"We should take her with," Dalton said diplomatically, "she'd be worth a platoon of skirmishers."

Jenny grinned and threw up her hands. "The Lost Boys, I swear . . ."

They continued kidding as they transferred Paul's gear to Davey's 4Runner.

"You got everything?" Manning asked Paul.

Paul and Manning went through the duffel, ticking off the inventory. Satisfied that Paul was properly equipped, they prepared to leave. Jenny and Paul embraced and she elicited another promise that he'd be careful. Then they kissed and she left him to the excitement of his extended weekend adventure. She wheeled the Forester out of the parking lot and raised an arm out the window in languid farewell. He'd be gone five days.

As she retraced her route, she slowed to a stop at Randolph Avenue. Easing up to the light, she coasted into the left-turn lane with her arms extended on the wheel, tingling a little, tugging her into a left turn. As she backtracked on Randolph, then turned north on Lexington and drove past blocks of tidy houses, she started the bargaining.

After dropping Paul off, she was just taking a shortcut up to I-94. Besides, if they were going to deal with IT, might be a good idea to see if he was still there.

Not like she was going to get out of the car. Her workout bag was in the backseat. She *was* on her way to the club. Shopping, she told Molly. A teeny lie.

The pressure in her extended arms guided the car off Lexington onto Laurel Street. This was Summit University, near Central High. Now she saw fewer moms pushing strollers and more black kids on the streets, some of them slouching in baggy carpenter jeans riding low over their boxer shorts. Paul would say, lock the doors. A few subtle, lidded stares came her way.

The boys reminded her of Andre.

Jenny concentrated on driving. Andre was the last one she'd tried to save before moving to the suburbs and switching to general ed.

The house was still there, just like it had been six months

ago. That time she'd dropped Paul off at the airport for a business trip to Cleveland. Peeling paint, Paul would say. The small green bungalow needed some attention . . .

Then, *oh cripes*! She stabbed the brakes when she saw him sitting on his front porch steps, talking to another man.

"SO YOU JUST HAPPENED TO HAVE THE 500, HUH, running through backyards, scaling a fence?" asked Perry MacNeil, acting photo editor of the *Pioneer Press*.

"What's your point?" John Rane said.

"One of the cops who ordered you to stop said he drew his gun because he mistook the lens for a weapon."

"Oh c'mon, I identified myself," Rane said.

"But you didn't stop, you kept going. Except you dropped the 500 . . ."

"I didn't *drop* it, Perry. I set it down, carefully," Rane said.

"Right. And somebody swiped it. The only 500-millimeter lens the staff has. That's what got you suspended, losing that lens."

Rane shrugged. "I had to strip down to get in tight with the 80–200; you know what Capa said . . ."

Perry knew Robert Capa's maxim: if your pictures aren't good enough you're not close enough. Capa's penchant for getting in close got him killed in Indochina before it became Vietnam.

They were sitting on Rane's stoop halfway through their cans of Bud Lite. MacNeil had dropped in to check on the usual rumors. The *Star Trib* across the river was interested in cherry-picking the best spot news shooter in the state.

Again.

He could go anywhere, set his own terms; but he stayed based in the Twin Cities. He was a funny guy.

To MacNeil, Rane resembled a 9/11 hijacker who didn't care about landings and takeoffs. He just wanted to fly the plane. In Rane's case, he just wanted to make the shot. The more difficult the better. And it had to be the exact perfect shot. If he decided the picture wasn't there, he'd blow off the assignment.

This inattention to the basic requirements of his job made him impossible to supervise. Rane was a maverick perfectionist who could always fall back on a cushion of independent income from the books: photo essays augmented by substantial narrative.

Perry appraised the braid of scar tissue around Rane's right eye. His method was controversial: to immerse himself in a subject before shooting it. His latest book, *Cage*, an inside look at Ultimate Fighting, could have blinded him. Plain dumb. A man on the downside of thirty-five, with 20/10 vision in both eyes, training six months in a gym, getting in the octagon ring, and fighting no-holds-barred, bare-knuckle.

And winning the bout.

Perry shook his head. "I heard Magnum approached you to do a tour in Iraq . . ."

"C'mon, Perry. I was in the original movie in '91. Watching my country march off a cliff doesn't grab me, know what I mean," Rane said.

Perry didn't know what he meant. Iraq would be perfect for him. The picture that resulted in Rane's latest suspension had run on network and cable news and most front pages in the country. The *Pioneer Press* had sold a slug of them and was not displeased with the attention Rane had generated.

"You really yelled at the guy?" Perry asked.

"Seemed like a good idea at the time," Rane said.

After slipping through a police cordon and ignoring warnings to stop, Rane had documented a tense SWAT situation with the big handheld lens. Then he set the 500 aside and worked in close enough to surprise and distract the erratic, barricaded shooter. In the split second before the shooter turned his shotgun on himself, he had aimed it directly at Rane. Hell of a picture: the mad, hopeless eyes; the muzzle thrusting forward, veins corded on the guy's neck. Furious that Rane had put himself and several officers in extra jeopardy, a number of cops deeply regretted the guy didn't punch a deer slug through Rane's face before he stuck the muzzle in his mouth.

"The *Chicago Tribune* . . ." Perry said.

"I ain't going anywhere," Rane said.

"Yeah, I know. If you were going to make a move you would have done it already, when you were younger," Perry said.

They finished their beers and Rane asked, "So, you want to slap my hands, take my gear and ID?"

"Naw, keep it. You kidding? You've scored another unpaid vacation. In fact, it wouldn't break my heart if you nosed around and maybe found something we can use later."

Ranc was nodding to Perry when he caught the peripheral movement two houses down the street; a red Subaru Forester jerked to a stop then accelerated. As he watched the car go past his house, he marked the profile of the female driver and his chest tightened.

"What?" Perry asked, seeing Rane frown.

"Nothing."

After a few more snippets of small talk, they stood up and shook hands. "Stay in touch," Perry said. Rane watched him get in his car and drive away. Then his eyes traveled down the street in the direction the red Subaru had turned and disappeared.

JENNY STARED STRAIGHT AHEAD, BOTH HANDS ON the wheel, reining in her runaway heart. After a dozen blocks she rationalized that he hadn't seen her.

Don't kid yourself. Never could have worked. The man was the pure opposite of careful.

You did the right thing. For Molly.

But, then, as always, came the echo. *But did I do the right thing for me?*

She hurried from the neighborhood and accelerated down the ramp onto I-94, swung north on 35E, and was soon on her route home. On surer ground, her breathing returning to normal, she joined the commuter stream racing east on Highway 36. Finally she saw the king stack of the Excel plant jut like a beacon on the horizon, marking the St. Croix River. The car tires fell into familiar grooves, the predictable tracks of her life that took her from her home to Stonebridge Elementary—Molly rode the bus—to Cub Foods, Kowalski's, and the health club.

She turned off 36 onto Greeley, took another left, and passed Happy's Garage, took another left and parked in the health club lot. She got out from the car, slung her bag, went in, chatted with the receptionist, turned over her membership card, and received a towel and locker key. She waved at several women and paused to talk with one of them, who had a girl in her class. Then she entered the locker room, changed into her suit, walked to the pool, pulled on her cap and her goggles.

Jenny had been a swimmer; pretty good but not great, at the U of M on a swim scholarship. Since the move from St. Paul, she'd returned to the pool, pushing herself through grueling sets that left her a lean replica of her younger self. Her mom had been a swimmer, and she always remembered her dad telling a friend, with a satisfied grin, "Marry a woman who swims and you'll always be happy."

Molly broke the pattern and recoiled from the water. Molly played soccer with a flock of friends, studied the piano, and danced at the Phipps. Jenny remembered a T-shirt she'd seen on a swim kid, *if swimming was easy they'd call it soccer.* Running back and forth, following the herd. Can't blame her, Jenny mused as she lowered herself into the water and pushed off the wall in a tight streamline, for doing what I did.

An hour later, standing under a hot shower, she stared at a grid of gray-green tile. The tile was the color of John Rane's eyes. Probably he'd seen her.

He missed nothing, saw everything, always.

2 THE WEST ALCORN THURSDAY-night Alcoholics Anonymous group met at six p.m. in the back room of a Baptist church on the outskirts of Theo, Mississippi, located off Highway 72 about midway between Corinth and the Tippah County line. Alcorn was a Baptist-majority dry county, except for beer in the Corinth city limits, and you had to be serious about staying sober to be seen walking into an AA meeting there.

The tall stranger showed up six months ago with a court-ordered voucher in his pocket, which had to be signed as proof of attendance. He'd sat quietly self-conscious on the margin of the group, surrounded by a cloud of gossip and drama.

Now, finally, he was ready to break his silence. He looked around at the pale pine-paneled walls, and then dropped his eyes to the scuffed linoleum. He avoided eye contact with the other eight people, who sat on gray metal folding chairs arranged in a circle. The style of the meeting was informal. After they joined hands and said the Lord's Prayer, they read the Twelve Steps of Alcoholics Anonymous.

"Not sure if I'm ready to start on this," the stranger said in a halting baritone.

The other members of the group were not quite ready for him, either. A whiff of cheap cosmetics, sweat, and even a touch of manure circulated in the close room. In an attempt to fit in he wore faded jeans and a T-shirt, but his boots were of good leather and buffed to a low gloss. His fingernails were manicured and his dark, curly hair had recently been styled. Despite his humble posture he radiated a sleek, muscular health, and the tan that colored his face and forearms was clearly not a working-blister tan. Looked more like easy vacation. Looked like golf.

Two women in the group had decided after he first showed up that he looked like one of those mournful, too-handsome preachers who get in trouble with the married gals in their congregations.

The men noticed his soft hands and were prepared not to trust him. But they were all here for a reason and the fact was, their perceptions had tended to serve, not temper, their addiction before they washed up in AA.

"I need some time," the stranger said. "An' I'll take feedback. My name is Mitchell Lee and I'm an alcoholic. I did court-ordered treatment at Timber Hills and I been sober now for almost six months."

One of the women raised her hand and wagged her finger. "You're the boy who started the radio show over in Corinth. I recognize your voice."

"Yes ma'am," Mitch said. "I am."

"You raised the money to build that monument for the Confederate dead at Kirby Creek," she said.

"Well," Mitch said, eyes lowered. "Fact is, I had some powerful incentive, like two hundred hours of court-ordered community service."

"You grew up around here, didn't you?" a weathered older man in overalls, sitting across from Mitch, queried, studying him carefully.

"Yes sir, I did," Mitch answered.

"Tommy Lee's boy, ain'tcha?"

"Yes sir," Mitch said.

"I knew your daddy back in my white-lightning days. Him and Towhead White, Pusser too. Never thought we'd see you again after you married Banker Kirby's daughter." The old man, named Marlon, scratched his whiskered chin. "Yeah, we all know who you are and what you're going through."

One of the women gently stirred the pot. "We read the stories in the *Daily Corinthian*—how Hiram Kirby suffered the stroke driving back to Corinth from his estate."

"Yes ma'am. What I want to talk about."

People set their faces, composed themselves in their chairs, and waited.

"The old man has taken a downturn," Mitch said slowly, leaning forward in his chair, elbows resting on his knees, eyes fixed on his clasped hands. "Now they got him on a machine, doing the breathing for him."

"What do the docs say?" Marlon asked quietly.

"Well, it's, ah, not good. When they found him on the road too much time had passed. Way the body works in a crisis, it protects the wheelhouse, the heart and lungs." Mitch sighed. "Blood gets diverted from the brain. Now they're saying he's in this . . ." Mitch pursed his lips, ". . . persistent vegetative state."

"Let go and let God . . ." one of the women whispered, more to herself than to Mitch.

"I was up there to see him at Magnolia Regional today. They got him laying in a bed all snarled in these tubes like this astronaut; got this big one stuck down his throat. Machines . . ." Mitch's deep voice broke and the tears that welled in his eyes were genuine. "That old man changed my life, was like a father . . ."

"Times like this," Marlon said gently, "it's important to keep things in perspective; remember this is happening to him, not you."

Mitch squashed a tear from his cheek with his palm, inhaled, and let it out. "I know. Just that the goddamn monument was put up today out there in front of his house and now it looks like he ain't going to see it."

One of the women leaned forward. "How's Miss Kirby doing with it all?"

Mitch sat up straighter. "Ellie's at the hospital most of the day." He shook his head. "Been rough on her. First her brother, now her dad. Then she runs. Guess that's the way she's handling it. Goes out and trains for her marathon. Kinda worries me, her out on the back roads like that."

For the first time Mitch raised his eyes and directly engaged the circle of faces. "Thing that gets to me is there's people who still say I been out to take advantage of the old man's kindness. Gets almost like I feel guilty going to the hospital."

Now Marlon, the old moonshiner, spoke up. "Folks know all about that, Mitchell Lee; how Deputy Kenny Beeman got that subpoena to go through the monument bank account you set up. How he implied you was skimming money."

"And how nothing come of it," one of the women sniffed.

Marlon raised an index finger. "People on this side of the county gonna remember that, if Beeman gets a mind to run for sheriff like some folks think he might."

"'Appreciate that, Marlon," Mitch said. Just then his cell phone jingled in his back pocket and his imagination leaped.

Christ, was it the old man? Already?

"Excuse me," he mumbled as he quickly whipped out the phone. But it wasn't Ellie. He saw his cousin Darl's number on the display and thumbed the pad to end the call. He replaced the phone and finished up: "Whatever else, I still have almost six months sober, so I thank God for this program."

Then he sat back in his seat and kept an attentive look on his face as he listened to several other people recount the difficulties they'd traversed during the week, thinking, Man, these are some white-knuckle bubbas just making it hand-over-hand one day at a time across the snake pit.

After the group ended, they all stood in a circle, holding hands, and recited the Serenity Prayer. Mitch stayed behind with Marlon, folded the chairs, and volunteered to sweep out the room. Then he said good-night, went out, and got in his truck.

Marlon stood in the parking lot with another man, named Luke. He inserted a pinch of Skoal in his lower lip and watched Mitch's taillights recede in the dark.

"So whattya think?" Luke asked.

"Ladies' man," Marlon shrugged. "The gals go for the smile and his voice like a radio commercial. But you look in his eyes, it gets kinda cold and slippery."

"Uh-huh. What I heard was, when he married that banker's daughter she kept her own name," Luke said.

Marlon spit on the gravel and said, "The way I heard it, Mitchell Lee was always a demon for work, never did drink much before he pulled that drunk stunt. Had him a hot-shit Corinth lawyer got him throwed in treatment to beat jail time."

"Uh-huh," Luke said.

"The way I heard it," Marlon continued, "his little drinking spree got him out of going to Eye-rack with the National Guard. Yep," Marlon stroked his chin, "that boy's way smarter than his daddy."

MITCHELL LEE NICKELS GREW UP WEST OF CORINTH, Mississippi, near the small town of Theo, sweating like hell in Liberty overalls, cutting pulp wood for his keep on the Reverend Leets's farm. He was three when his grandpa on his momma's side came into his life. Mitch didn't remember his mother. What he remembered was the smell.

On the hot August afternoon when the McNairy County deputy found him in the back-road shack outside of Selmer, Tennessee, Pearl Leets was swelled up on the bare mattress, hatching bluebottle flies. She had a hypodermic needle protruding from her tied-off, puffed-up arm, and the deputy figured Mitch had been in there two days wearing the same diaper, living off stale potato chips and warm Dr Pepper.

The reverend, being the white sheep of the outlaw Leets clan, did his best to steer his grandson clear of trouble. Mitch kept busy working on the farm, going to school, and regularly attending church. He was sixteen when two events altered his life. First, he discovered that girls really liked what he did for them. The downside of this revelation was that his grandpa caught him behind the tractor shed, minus his pants, with the older neighbor girl's heels banging around his ears. Mitch expected a beating but instead the reverend thrust him into the old Chevy truck and drove him through a rainstorm to the ruins of a honky-tonk on old Highway 45 going south of Corinth. Leets, a Primitive Baptist minister, was famous in two counties for his powerful pulpit presence, so, in lieu of the beating, he delivered a single scathing sentence:

"Mitchell Lee, you got bad blood like your daddy."

After the rebuke, the preacher left him alone in the rain to think about it. Which is what Mitch did, hugging himself, meditating on that oil-slicked cement slab where his father's blood had leaked out on another rainy night, two months before Mitch was born.

According to the local lore, this was where Tommy Lee Nickels, a bootlegger and murderer, had been mysteriously gunned down. The authorities attributed the shooting to another of the fatal squabbles among the state-line mobsters who'd infested the region. But everyone agreed it was Alcorn deputy Clarence Beeman who'd killed Tommy Lee for reasons that would never be known. Old Clarence had gone to his grave neither confirming nor denying the allegation.

The second event was much drier and more positive. The FFA oration banquet was held that year in the Corinth Coliseum. When Mitch's turn came, he got up to the podium and recited a long passage from Faulkner. Even back then he had a great voice and could string out words soft and sly as clear water trickling over pretty-rock bottoms. Effortlessly, he captured the rhythms Mississippians remembered from their childhoods. And that night the perfect acoustics in that old hall showcased his precocious baritone.

Sitting in the audience, banker Hiram Kirby had noticed the roughneck kid with the great speaking voice and the notorious family pedigree. The banker was given to quirky streaks and took an interest. That summer he gave Mitch work clearing brush to maintain the old battlefield on his Kirby Creek estate. The downside to this fortuitous turn of events came in the form of the banker's son, Robert, who resented this smooth-talking redneck intruding on his summer and on his father's affections. Mitch had acquired his first lifelong enemy.

The banker's vivid tomboy daughter, Ellender, however, had an opposite and more hormonal reaction to the interloper. She had inherited her father's long jaw but also his earthy sense of humor. She initiated Mitch into the mysteries of shooting her dad's antique Civil War rifles, so he returned the favor with a few mysteries of his own. When she gave it up, Ellender surmised that every Southern princess had to kiss at least one nasty old bullfrog to see if it would turn into a prince. "Ellie," Mitch had replied in all sincerity, "this ain't no frog."

"Don't say 'ain't,' " Ellie had sighed tartly, "you aren't in Theo anymore . . ."

That was for sure. When Mitch peeled her pants off, it was on the heirloom horsehair couch in the library of the fine old antebellum house. But after that one time, just like a slumming princess in a fairy tale, Ellie Kirby danced beyond his reach.

The banker arranged for Mitch to attend Corinth High School, where Mitch encountered his second lifelong enemy, who was Kenny Beeman, the son of the county cop Clarence Beeman who everyone said killed his daddy. Robert Kirby tended to fight with words he stuck in Mitch's back. But Kenny Beeman and Mitch were destined to collide by events that occurred before either of them was born. They fought regularly to a draw, with their fists.

So Mitch commenced on his twenty-year battle with gravity. Everybody in town was saying Hiram Kirby better watch himself sponsoring Mitchell Lee, that the apple don't fall far from the tree. The constant drip of gossip only made Mitch more determined to fly that apple all the way to the big house on the hill at Kirby Creek.

And that is exactly what he did by dint of hard work and after-hours schooling. He had risen to loan officer in the bank when he eloped with Hiram Kirby's daughter, Ellender.

Couple years back, his cousin Darl put it this way: "Hey, Mitch, I seen you and your trust-fund wife in *Southern Living* magazine." The only reason Darl had occasion to read *Southern Living* was because the magazine was opened to the article about Mitch and Ellie's remodeled antebellum Corinth house when Darl found it on the coffee table in the McMansion he was ripping off in a posh Memphis neighborhood.

And so, finally it occurred to Mitch that if enough people tell you the same damn thing long enough, you just might wind up believing them. He probably did have bad blood like his father. Once he accepted that fact, the rest came easy.

DRIVING EAST ON HIGHWAY 72, BACK TOWARD CORINTH, Mitch was a little pissed that Darl would call him during his group. They were supposed to be exercising a modicum of caution. Like the saying goes, you can't choose your family. With a sigh, Mitch flipped open his cell and called Darl, who answered on the second ring.

"Darl, man, I told you never call me during that meeting."

"Sorry. Got excited, I guess."

Darl thought AA was a hard sell in West Alcorn, where some folks were convinced the air was still part moonshine and part gunpowder. And there it was; the conflicted reluctance in his voice.

"Keep a lid on it, okay? Where are you?" Mitch asked.

"Coming back from my mom's, I just dropped the kids off. I'm heading west on 72."

"I'm coming east. Keep coming past the farm and we'll touch base at the 604 turnoff."

"See ya," Darl said, ending the call.

Mitch shook his head. Darl was getting cold feet, was trying to change his stripes and reinvent himself as a dad.

It's not that he had avoided Darl after he started riding the Kirby escalator. More like they existed in different circles; Mitch attended First Presbyterian, maintained a membership in the Shiloh Ridge Country Club, worked on his golf game, and got his picture in *Southern Living*. Darl struggled as an entry-level dope dealer in Memphis under his older brother Dwayne's stern tutelage. Then he met and married an icy-hot confection of brains and glands named Marcy. Together they'd anticipated the crack boom, then doubled up and hit it big in meth. Smart enough to leave when the well-armed and very murderous Mexican gangs moved in, they took their bankroll to Alcorn County and laundered it in land speculation. Darl had a sentimental side, so, out of nostalgia, he'd bought and reopened an abandoned Tennessee honky-tonk just over the state line north of Corinth. Darl was living fairly straight, running XTC, his beer joint, and doing his land deals. On the side he provided a smattering of coke and designer drugs for the recreational use of the local gentry.

Fairly straight, that is, until Mitch took him aside and made known his intention to migrate back to the outlaw side of the family. Mitch found it kinda exciting, rubbing up against his hoodlum kin.

Especially Darl's wife.

He weighed the cell phone in his palm. What the hell. Go for it. He punched in Darl's home number.

"It's you," said Marcy Leets in her standard bored idle.

"You're free tonight," Mitch said.

"Just so happens," she said.

"I'm thinking of taking one of my walks. Say eleven thirty?"

"Meet you at the end of the block. If I ain't there, don't wait." She ended the call. That was Marcy for you. Always liked to keep you dangling.

Mitch slowed, hit his turn indicator, wheeled right on

County 604, then swung left in a U-turn, parked along the side of the road, and switched off his lights. He zipped down the window and fingered a Marlboro Light from the pack in his pocket. Flat fallow soybean fields stretched to either side. You could almost hear the dirt yawn, emerging from its winter rest. He flicked his lighter and thought: Land. Like they say, they ain't making any more of it.

A few drags into the cigarette, Darl's gray Ram Charger with its distinctive vanity plate—OJDIDIT—turned off 72 and stopped across from Mitch's truck. Two vehicles pulled off on a country road, pointing opposite directions, one man getting out to talk. Most normal thing in the world.

Baby-faced Darl Leets got out, walking in his brisk, small-footed shuffle. The man was built like a razorback pig—thick in the trunk; short, powerful, hairy arms and legs; moving with a rooting intensity. Mitch really wondered what Marcy saw in him. Had, in fact, asked her on one occasion. Marcy had just rolled over in the motel bed, arched an eyebrow, and told him he sure knew how to wreck a mood.

"Hey," Darl said, leaning his heavy forearms on the open truck window.

"So, are we on track for tomorrow?" Mitch said.

"It's confirmed. He's working security on the blue side," Darl said. "And I'll go in and hang the stuff early in the morning, do the measure like you said." Darl grimaced and ground his teeth. "After I do all that I don't s'pose there's any way I could duck this one, huh?"

"You getting cold feet?" Mitch asked slowly.

"Well." Darl screwed up his lips. "Marcy ain't real hot for it, know what I mean?"

"Can't do it without you, Darl," Mitch said.

"Yeah, I guess. Family reunion time, huh Cuz?" Darl managed a weak grin. He held up a slim half-pint glass bottle. "A toast. Vodka, so's not to tell on your breath." He took a swig and handed the bottle to Mitch, who took a small sip for ceremony's sake. "Keep it," Darl said. "You gotta unwind a little, huh?"

Mitch placed the bottle on the seat and said, "Yeah, I suppose I do."

"Okay, we're all set. Dwayne's driving in, gonna stop by Mom's, then come out to the farm. He's looking forward to seeing you . . ." Then Darl forced a jerky grin, working out his nervous kinks. ". . . We'll have some fun. You know, like when we were kids . . ."

Mitch studied the stupid expression on Darl's face. Fun? "All right, then," Mitch said. "I better get going to the station."

Darl reached in and punched Mitch halfheartedly on the shoulder. "Tomorrow," he said.

Mitch watched his cousin get in his truck, start it up, and drive away. Fun? They were going to kill a man. And that was just for starters. For all his reservations, it was amazing how casually Darl talked about it, grinning and cackling, like he was going over a play in a baseball game on TV. Mitch whistled softly into the dark. Man, that's a criminal mind for you. Some of the human parts were missing.

Before he pulled back on the highway, he idled on the shoulder, upended the half-pint of vodka out the window, and tossed the empty over the top of his truck into the ditch. Then he got back on the road.

A few minutes later, he sat bolt upright, electrified when a red flasher pulsed the empty stretch of blacktop. The unmarked cruiser came up fast behind him. No headlights, Musta been tailing him with his lights off. Mitch pulled over, watching in the rearview as the black Crown Vic eased up and stopped at his rear bumper.

Now that was downright spooky. Mitch knew the car and the man getting out of it. Alcorn County deputy Kenny Beeman had attached himself to Mitch like a shadow since Mitch had resigned from the bank following his drinking indiscretion. Mitch prepared to have his buttons pushed.

How long's he been hanging back there? Probably saw him with Darl. Damn. Mitch unclipped his seat belt, pushed open the door, and got out as Beeman walked up wearing dark slacks, charcoal shirt, badge on his belt in a black leather cuff, and a black SIG Sauer .40 on his hip in a black holster. Beeman was still full of himself, since he'd shot Darl's little brother, Donny, in the knee after pulling another one of his specialties: running Donny's car off the road into the ditch. True, Donny had gunned down a clerk and a customer in a Texaco during a sloppy robbery just off the Iuka exit. The customer had died, and now Donny was limping around the state penitentiary, filing appeals. Word was out that Dwayne Leets had come down from his cocaine tower in Memphis and put a contract out on Kenny Beeman.

And a lot of people were waiting for that cap to bust.

Okay. Take a deep breath. So here was Kenny Beeman dressed in black, driving his black car. He had worked his way up in the world all the way to being a two-bit investigator for the Alcorn County Sheriff's Department.

Mitch smiled and shook his head. "Bee, you gotta stop dressing like a Johnny Cash song. Bet you didn't know that Cash auditioned for a radio job in Corinth when he was starting out . . . he didn't get it."

"Didn't know that," Beeman said as he held up the vodka half-pint Mitch had thrown out the window. "You dropped something. I know you didn't just throw it out the window, 'cause littering is against the law. And we don't want broken glass on the road, do we?"

Mitch laughed softly. "You know what they say. If we could figure out a way to make money off kudzu and broken glass, Mississippi would be the richest state in the Union." He took the pint bottle, upended it, and shook out the last few drops, then tossed it into the front seat of his truck. "A leftover. Found it under the floor mat. Poured it out. No law against not taking a drink, is there?" he asked.

"After going to an AA meeting, guess not," Beeman said carefully.

"So you been following me, huh, Bee?"

Like always when they met, the distance between them

crackled with dry fuses. One wrong word could flame the air. But Mitch couldn't help toying a little with the edge of risk. "Instead of creeping around with your lights out following me you should be catching bad guys, like we pay you for," he said.

Mitch smiled and Beeman smiled back. "You watch yourself, Mitchell Lee," Beeman said. "There's drunks on the road."

Mitch carefully did not reply as Beeman spun on his heel and walked back to his car. As the cop drove away, Mitch was more certain than ever. The guy never quit.

And that's why, among other things, Beeman had less than forty-eight hours left to live.

3 WITH PAUL OUT OF TOWN, JENNY decided to take her mother and Molly out to dinner. After she showered at the club, she called her mom and proposed they go to the Dock Café in downtown Stillwater.

Jenny and her mother, Lois, ordered salads; Molly always had the macaroni and cheese. They sat at a booth next to the broad plate-glass windows overlooking the historic iron railroad lift bridge that spanned the St. Croix River.

Molly was telling her grandma about a fifth-grade drama that involved a girl who acted friendly to her face but spread gossip about her with the other girls she played with. Jenny stared out the window at the Wisconsin bluffs across the river, where the bare maples and oaks bunched like mangy porcupines. She caught herself drifting, overheard her daughter's dilemma, and said, "I spy a new word, Molly."

Molly cocked her head. Attentive. It was a vocabulary game they played.

"Fickle," Jenny said. "What do you suppose it means?"

Molly furrowed her brow. "Rhymes with 'tickle.'" She asked, "Use it in a sentence?"

Jenny continued to peer out the window and said, "The weather in March is fickle."

"Cold?" Molly wondered.

"Was it cold yesterday? What did you wear out at recess?" Jenny prompted.

"Just a T-shirt. It was real warm yesterday." Molly scrunched up her lips, chewing on a thought.

"So the weather in March is . . . ?"

"Hot and cold," Molly said. "Hot one day, cold the next . . ."

"Kind of like your friend at school," Lois suggested.

Jenny circled her index finger in a tight cuing gesture, "And . . . so fickle is . . . ?"

Molly conjured with her gray-green eyes, rolling them back and forth. "Not the same?"

"Close," Jenny said. "Think changeable, not constant. As it applies to people, we could say a fickle person is change-able, not loyal."

"Ha," Molly snorted. "So Mary is fickle."

"Perhaps," Jenny said. "Now spell it."

As Molly used "tickle" as a basis for spelling "fickle," Jenny's eyes drifted back out the window; thinking of other relevant definitions that exceeded grade-school perfidies. Words like "deceive" or "treacherous," which reminded her how her husband's presence tended to exercise a governing influence on her . . . well . . . fantasies.

Jenny turned back to the table and found her mother's eyes studying her over a forkful of romaine, poised in mid-air. Lois said, "You're distracted. Penny for your thoughts."

"That's a cliché, we studied them in Mr. Magnan's class," Molly piped up.

Jenny reached over and tousled her daughter's unruly dark hair. So unlike her own, or Paul's. Recovering briskly, she said, "I was thinking the weather in March is fickle. That winter is warmer and comes later."

Her mother continued to appraise her; then said, "It's a fact. Minnesota is turning into southern Iowa."

Back home, they put on sweaters and sat on the deck off the kitchen, watching Molly and her friend Rachel kick a soccer ball. After one of those long silences full of invisible maneuvers, Lois asked casually, "Have you thought more about getting that medical history?"

Jenny let the question slide by, staring across the back-yard. Not really a yard, more a grassy gully, a low common area hemmed by ranks of new houses that resembled a beige quilt pattern of dollhouses. Then, down in the yard, Molly decided to impress Rachel with her ability to sneak up on a squirrel.

"Look at her," Lois said, "the way she stands statue-still, then creeps . . ."

Jenny nodded. "I saw her actually get close enough to touch one."

"A squirrel? Is that a good idea?" Lois wrinkled her nose. "A squirrel could have rabies." Since Jenny's father died suddenly three years ago from an aneurysm, her mom had become a collector of exotic medical stories. Of possible scenarios. Hence, the current discussion that Lois wanted to initiate.

Below the deck, the girls squealed as the alerted squirrel ran for the sanctuary of a spindly tree. As they darted around the corner of the house, Lois turned to Jenny, patiently.

"So it's time, don't you think?" Lois said.

"Paul and I have talked about how to break it to her," Jenny said.

"No telling what's in his family background," Lois said.

"His parents died in a small-plane crash, Mom," Jenny said pointedly.

"Doesn't mean there wasn't heart disease, cancer, diabetes. You haven't talked to him since . . . ?"

Jenny took a breath, held it until it started to hurt, and exhaled. "Five years ago, just before Molly started kindergarten, he called and asked if there was anything I wanted him to do. You know, with her starting school . . . I thanked him for calling and said I'd just as soon leave things the way they were." Jenny narrowed her eyes. "He was never there, Ma. Now what? We spring him on Molly out of thin air?"

"He's never approached her, you're sure?"

"Positive. We've drilled her about strangers. She's good at sneaking up on things. But she's not sneaky."

"So, you don't have to meet him face-to-face. Do it on the phone, to break the ice. It's a legitimate request."

Jenny shivered slightly. "Now's probably not a good time."

"The thing in the paper?" Lois arched an eyebrow and studied her daughter. "That's just doing his job. That's not real trouble."

Jenny smiled tightly. "You mean, not like the other time."

"Let me do it," Lois said. "He'll remember me. I'll just call him up and explain it's time to fill in a blank. All he has to do is provide a basic medical history; him, his parents. Just swab his mouth with a Q-tip, pop it in a baggie. No sense in having half a picture."

"Okay, Mom. Enough. I'll think about it," Jenny said with rising sharpness.

Lois put up her hands in a mollifying gesture. "You're right. 'Nuff said." She stood up. "It's starting to get chilly. Molly should get a coat on."

Jenny warned her with a direct look. Back off, Ma. Lois smiled and pulled on her own light jacket. "Got to run. I have a class in town." After Dad died, Lois sold the St. Paul house and moved into a tidy condo behind the Menard's on Highway 36. She had lost weight and dressed more stylishly as a widow; now she filled her nights with cooking classes and yoga.

"Say good-bye to Molly," Lois said as she took out her car keys, leaned over, and kissed her daughter on the forehead. Then she opened the patio door, went through the kitchen, and left Jenny alone on the deck with the setting sun and a nip of goose bumps on her arms.

Mom was right, of course. And Paul, in his reasonable, calm way, agreed. Sooner rather than later, they'd have to tell Molly about her biological father.

After homework, Paul called from a truck stop. They had driven the width of Wisconsin and made their turn south. He sounded tired but excited, off with the boys. After he said good-night to Molly, they exchanged their own brief good-night. A standard "Love you, Jenny." As he ended the call, she heard the foreign clatter of country-western on a jukebox in the background.

As Jenny loaded the dishwasher, Molly practiced the piano, a Chopin piece she was preparing for a school recital. Music defeated Jenny. Paul had never played an instrument. They were indifferent dancers. The piano teacher came once a week. "Oh well," Paul quipped, "it's a gift that skips a generation."

Jenny paused and caught a distorted flash of her face reflected up from a plate she'd just wiped off and was holding in both hands. The tingle was back in her arms, almost an ache.

Paul had always known, of course.

She thrust the plate between the plastic uprights of the washer rack. One of the main reasons she loved him was the poised, tolerant way he took things in stride. Never stored them up. Never obsessed.

They had tried for two years to have another child. Then he had the tests done. Sperm counts didn't skip. They just were. It had been like having another piano in the middle of the living room.

They'd been dating steady for two years when Jenny swerved into her fling with John Rane.

Methodically, she removed the heavy grates from the stove, stacked them aside, and worried dots of grease off the circular plates around the burners with a 3M scrub.

She'd got as far as the first call to Planned Parenthood and knew she couldn't go through with it. "It's okay," Paul had said without a tremor of jealousy or censure, stepping in. Their marriage evolved into an intricate gravitational field revolving around an unspoken core.

She replaced the grates, wiping each one in turn.

After the Indian Ocean tsunami hit Sri Lanka, Thailand, and Indonesia, Paul had helped Molly build a water model for a science project. They selected a huge transparent storage tub from Target and Paul spent a week in the garage, converting it into a likeness of the ocean floor. He layered Styrofoam and odd bits of insulation, built it up with glue into the shoreline of a continent, and sprinkled it with sand, gravel, and limestone shards. Then he spray-painted it and used Liquid Nails to fasten it to the bottom of the tub. Molly tucked little palm trees in the Styrofoam beach. Tiny houses and plastic people they found at Michaels. Then he created a movable piece of ocean floor with a handle attached: so you could raise and lower it, like a plunger. Then they filled the tub with water. When the plate was lifted, it shoved the displaced water onto the model shoreline. As a teacher, Jenny pointed out there was too much Dad in the project, but Paul would not be deterred. They took the tub to the science fair at school, and a gang of exuberant fourth-grade boys demolished the ambitious project in two minutes flat.

Jenny took a deep breath. Sometimes she felt like that ruined science project, like she was one seismic shift away from a catastrophic wave.

She added detergent, hit the start button, and looked up to find that Molly had approached silently and was standing next to her. She held up a book from the school library. Every night after supper they read for an hour. The script on the front of the book proclaimed: *myths and legends*.

"What are we reading?" Jenny asked.

Molly flipped open the book and pointed to an illustrated page showing Athena erupting full-grown from Zeus's forehead. "Creation stories," she said, oblivious to the psychic bullet she'd drilled dead-center into her mother's heart.

4 **MITCH DISCOVERED HIS SMOOTH** baritone was made for radio not long after he launched the monument project in the Timber Hills Treatment Center. Ostensibly, the project was inspired by the Alcoholics Anonymous requirement to make amends to those he'd harmed, which he interpreted to mean his mentor and father-in-law, Hiram Kirby. And, with his lawyer's help, the project satisfied the judge's community-service recommendation.

Ellie, relieved to see Mitch actually get excited about something, encouraged him to pursue the project full-time. Glad to have him out of the office, the board of directors at the bank accepted his resignation. And, like Mitch figured, Old Man Kirby approved. His son, Robert, had never taken such an interest in the family battlefield. When Robert deployed to Iraq as a second lieutenant with the guard, Mitch, a sergeant in the unit, had to forgo the challenge of sand fleas, 120-degree heat, and improvised explosive devices. He was stuck in court-ordered group therapy.

He'd started with small promotional radio spots. In a few months, with the backing of the United Daughters of the Confederacy and the Sons of Confederate Veterans' camps across Mississippi and Tennessee, he'd expanded the format into a weekly evening radio show he called *Southern Almanac*. The show's original emphasis on preserving Southern battlefields from development attracted regional attention. A reporter at the Memphis paper had mixed his states up and termed Mitchell Lee Nickels the "Bluegrass Garrison Keil-lor," and then ended his piece with speculation that Nickels was good enough to move up to a bigger market.

Mitch turned off Highway 72 on Corinth's east side and parked on the trap rock apron of the small station behind the White Trolley restaurant. Powered by twenty-five thousand watts, WXRZ broadcast over a fifty-mile radius. Five hundred dollars in advertising bought Mitch half an hour a week. Tapes of the show went out to other stations in the region.

He sat for several moments, calming down after his encounter with Beeman. Carefully, he checked the surrounding street to see if the cop was still dogging him. Then he picked a portfolio up off the passenger seat, leafed through his program notes, and selected one slim sheet. Tonight he didn't really need the notes, because he'd be talking primarily about the Kirby Creek event and the monument dedication. He set the portfolio aside, swung out of his truck, went into the station, and waved at the engineer sitting behind the console in the one-room studio.

As the minute hand moved toward the bottom of the hour, Mitch sat down, arranged his mike, and took a sip of water from the bottle that had been set out. Then the engineer cued him and cracked his mike.

"Good evening Alcorn. This is Mitchell Lee bringing you another *Southern Almanac* from the studios of WXRZ right here behind the White Trolley in Corinth where we can actually smell the slug burgers sizzlin' on the griddle.

"Our show tonight is going to be less me and more you doing the talking because I know you have questions about the event at Kirby Creek this Saturday. But first I have the announcement you've been waiting for. Because of your support and contributions the monument is a reality. Special thanks go to the Heritage Development Corporation in Nashville for their very generous donation. The monument was put in place out in front of the Kirby House today. But we're going to wait on the landscaping until the reenactors get through tramping around. Once they finish up we'll get it all spiffed up for the dedication right after the Shiloh Living History. Okay folks. The mikes are open and I see the calls are stacking up.

"Hello, you're on *Southern Almanac*."

"Hey Mitchell Lee, this is Jimmy Tobin calling from Hatchie, and some of us over here are not real clear on how they got the dates all mixed around with the battle event and the dedication. Kirby Creek was after Shiloh, not before. I thought getting history accurate was still important around here."

"Well, Jimmy, I hear you. But this year the Sons of Confederate Veterans decided to sponsor this super-hardcore authentic battle scenario and that means no spectators. We'll still be doing an event on the anniversary but it's gonna be more dedication ceremony and celebration than a reenactment. So's not to conflict with the dedication, the SCV moved their reenactment up."

Mitch punched another button. "Good evening, you're on *Southern Almanac*."

"Yeah, Mitchell, some of the boys I know are complaining about the way they cut off registration for Kirby Creek. It's gonna cause a stink in some SCV camps. It's discrimination."

"It's a problem, I agree," Mitch said. "But you gotta see their side. Don't get me wrong, these hardcore types do tend to roll their grits in little balls. On the other hand they expect a level of commitment most mainstream reenactors don't, well, want to put up with."

"Who thought this up anyway?"

"Way I heard it, a local boy went out to West Virginia last year for Rich Mountain. That's the one where a couple hundred Yankees grounded their packs then hiked six miles up a mountain in the rain. Then they slept up there without their packs, blankets, ponchos, and most of their food."

"Not my idea of reenacting."

"Look at it this way, maybe somebody figured if you could get Yankees to march up a mountain you could get them to pollywog five miles through Cross State Swamp. Which is what they're gonna do."

The caller laughed. "Bleep that," he said.

Mitch went to the next call. "Howdy, you're on *Southern Almanac*."

"So Mitchell Lee, you gonna be at Kirby Creek?"

"Not me. I never was into dress-up reenacting. I was in the shooting end. My father-in-law, Hiram Kirby, God bless him, we were on the Forrest Rifles until . . ." Mitch's voice caught slightly.

"You got our prayers, you and your wife. Damn shame what your family is going through."

"Thank you, sir." Mitch paused for a moment before hitting the next call. "*Southern Almanac*, come on."

"Talking about Forrest Rifles—where'd you learn to shoot?"

"Well now . . ." Mitch let his voice ruminate. "'Suspect I did just like most of you all out there. You see, my grandpa who raised me always had two squirrels for breakfast. Every morning from the time I was twelve till I started high school he'd get me up at dawn, hand me this old single-shot .22 and two long cartridges. Then he'd push me toward the woods and not let me back in till I had two skinned squirrels. And Grandpa, he didn't like the meat shot up. Grandpa, he insisted on head shots."

Mitch switched to the next call.

"Got a monument question. Now, the new Tennessee memorial they put up at Shiloh is cast bronze, am I right?"

"Yes sir, cast in Wyoming."

"But the statue you put up is granite."

"Southern gray, out of Georgia."

"How come granite and not bronze?"

"Well, we had meetings on this and I figured we should

honor those sleeping heroes with an old-fashioned flavor. Fact is, granite sculpture is a dying art. As the old sculptors retire there's no new blood stepping up. Had to look all over the South till we found a hand-carver in Spartanburg, South Carolina."

"'Appreciate what you done, Mitchell Lee."

"Thank you, see you at the dedication. Now we gotta pause to pay the rent."

After a commercial break, Mitch took a few more calls and then gave a weather report.

"So all you hardcore reenactors out there, you better double up on your blankets and gum rolls for Kirby Creek. According to the weather report, it'll be rain all day tomorrow and into Saturday morning.

"And a special Alcorn County welcome to the Union boys from Illinois and Ohio coming down to join in our event. You fellas best pack some Deet in case some of our quarter-pounder skeeters hatch out early. And down here, fellas, the ticks never die. You been warned."

Then he gave times for scheduled activities for the Living History event coming up on the anniversary of the Shiloh battle next Saturday. He sat back while the engineer ran a public service announcement about a church bake sale.

Mitch exhaled, looked at the clock, and ruminated how that media writer in Memphis was prescient when he coined the description "Bluegrass Garrison Keillor." Mitch had completely stolen the format from the National Public Radio celebrity's show.

He had studied Keillor's tapes with special attention to his folksy, ironic delivery. He appreciated how Keillor got mileage out of his gentle mocking of his Scandinavian roots. Mitch used the same technique, telling humorous tales about the foibles of antebellum Mississippi. He made a point to sprinkle in factoids about local blacks who had contributed to the history of the area.

After another taped commercial, he cleared his throat,

keyed the mike, and reread the temperature and tomorrow's forecast for northern Mississippi and southwestern Tennessee. Thunderstorms through Saturday morning, then clearing and a high of seventy-five.

He looked up at the clock. It was time to wind it down.

He paused to allow his listeners an interval of preparatory silence. As the seconds ticked away, he floated to the familiar subdued whir of the almost-empty studio; just him and the engineer walled off in a glass aquarium stacked with flickering machines.

Then, just when the meditative silence verged on suspense, he slowly recited the signature quote from Faulkner with which he ended his broadcast; the same passage that had brought him to Hiram Kirby's attention almost twenty years ago . . .

For every Southern boy fourteen years old, not once but whenever he wants it, there is the instant when it's still not yet two o'clock on that July afternoon, the brigades are in position behind the rail fence, the guns are loaded and ready in the woods and the furled flags are already loosened to break out and Pickett himself with his long oiled ringlets and his hat in one hand probably and his sword in the other looking up the hill waiting for Longstreet to give the word and it's all in the balance . . .

Some shows, Mitch gave them the whole long passage. Tonight he stopped here, knowing that many of his listeners would shut their eyes, concentrate, and fill in the remainder. Older folks, mainly.

Mitch exhaled, pushed back from the desk, stood up, and stretched. Like the Great Man said, It's all in the balance.

On the other side of the console, the engineer motioned to Mitch and held up the telephone. Mitch looked down, saw the red light flash on his phone console, and picked up.

Billie Watts, his attorney. Not an unexpected call.

"Hey, Billie, what's up?" Mitch said casually.

"You know what's up. Can we talk?" Billie's voice sounded like cocaine jitters in an echo chamber.

Mitch took it in stride. "Sure. Say the parking lot at the Interpretive Center. Should be deserted. Be there in ten minutes."

Then Mitch replaced the phone in its cradle. Patience, stay on task. So he shook hands with the engineer and spent a few moments of small talk before he said good-night. Then he left the station, got in his Ford, turned the key, zipped down the windows, and lit a Marlboro Light.

The night air was delicately crisp, with a damp tang of far-off wood smoke and green whisperings of spring. A smell of coming rain.

He opened his cell and called Ellie. No answer; the call went to the machine. Mitch left a message that he was leaving the station and would be home shortly.

Then he drove west on Highway 72 toward downtown Corinth. As he passed a gas station, he noticed a caravan of reenactors that had pulled over. He turned in to cruise the trucks, raising his hand in easy greeting to several men, who returned the gesture. The plates on the pickups identified Tennessee and Alabama. Bubba's rust-bucket, back-road pickup with the shotgun hanging in the rack was passing from the scene. Now Bubba was naming his kids Windsor and Meredith and had a permanent cramp in his neck from talking on a cell phone and balancing his latte while he piloted a pimped-out 150 with plush leather seats. Like Mitch drove.

A knot of men quietly sipped coffee and chatted among the vehicles; they were dressed in well-cut Confederate sack coats and slouch hats. Serious living historians, the men were headed for Kirby Creek. The reenactment season had begun and the summer would be one long Confederate Halloween.

He left the reenactors behind, continued down 72 through the strip-mall alley that lined the highway, then, just past the Holiday Inn at the west end of town, he turned north onto Galyean Road. Moments later, he took a right on Linden Street, then turned right again and pulled into the empty parking lot. Mitch switched off the truck and lit another Marlboro.

Smoking too much. Darl wasn't the only one getting nervous.

His eyes cautiously tracked the empty open area around the center, looking for the black shadow of Beeman's car. Satisfied he was alone, he peered at the zigzag sidewalk that led up the gentle slope to the long, low, brick History Center operated by the Federal Park Service. The parking lot lights caught a gleam of metal in the walkway. They'd bronzed pieces of soldiers' gear—haversacks, crumpled forage caps, shards of broken rifles—and embedded them in the concrete. "Battle detritus" they called it. On the left end of the building the ground swelled into a revetment, and through the embrasures he glimpsed the shadow of a barrel and the spokes on a cannon wheel.

A squeal of tires on asphalt announced Billie's arrival as his silvery Mercedes-Benz SLK swerved into the lot and stopped in a lurch of trembling suspension. Billie Watts, Ole Miss, Law Review, sure to make partner in his daddy's firm, heaved up and out of the low, sleek car. He wore designer jeans, handmade leather boots, a silk shirt open three buttons—so his tanned, hairy chest and gold chain hung out. Billie looked around and darted his frog-like tongue to lick up a faint trace of white powder on the left side of his sweaty upper lip.

Mitch did not get out to meet him.

It was Billie's loose lips that had set all this in motion. And Billie Watts understood utterly how Mississippi's Conspiracy Statute could be liberally interpreted to constitute a mere meeting of the minds. So Billie knew just enough to be real fuckin' scared; which, since he couldn't really be trusted, was the only way to control him.

Mitch started right off, feeding the fear. "Hey, Billie. Wanna hear something spooky? Beeman pulled me over tonight west of town. Musta followed me to my AA meeting."

"Jesus," Billie muttered as he turned his head and scanned the dark lawn around the center, like he expected Beeman to pop out from behind a tree like Wile E. Coyote. "You think he suspects . . ."

"Hell, he always suspects. Hounded mc all through the monument project, didn't he . . ."

"You came out of that clean," Billie said, knitting his brow.

"Yes I did. So what's on your mind?"

"Your cousin Darl. Is he watching me? He showed up at my son's Little League game last night . . ."

"Billie," Mitch said patiently. "Darl's oldest boy, Toby, is in Little League. Darl's an assistant coach. Could it be your kid's team was playing his kid's team?"

"I just don't want him around my wife and boy," Billie said.

"Uh-huh. You just want him on twenty-four-hour call to deliver toot to your condo at Harbor Springs, when you're banging those teenyboppers two at a time . . ."

Billie stood flatfooted, his face working; a snapshot of intelligence and breeding losing big-time to unregulated appetite. "It's just . . . everything's happening so fast," Billie finally said.

"And it don't concern you, does it? Go home, Billie. Keep your head down and your mouth shut."

5 **EVERYTHING *WAS* HAPPENING FAST.**
That was the point. When Hiram Kirby suffered his disabling stroke, the people around him froze in place like abandoned pawns on a chessboard. Not Mitch; he started scooting around like Pac-Man.

But he was driving slowly now, along Waldron, into the downtown section of Corinth; killing time with one eye out for Kenny Beeman. He was not real keen on going home and dragging through a conversation with Ellie, all the time counting the minutes till he could get free and meet with Marcy.

As he cruised past the county courthouse, he glanced up at the statue standing vigil over the quiet streets. Colonel Rogers, hero of the failed attempt to storm Battery Robinett during the Battle of Corinth.

My statue's better, taller, more detailed, he thought.

Obscure in darkness behind the courthouse loomed the Crossroads State Bank. Mitch averted his eyes from the shadowy pillars. *I tried it your way, old man; I really did.*

Working like a frickin' hamster running a treadmill in his cubicle. When the old man retired after cancer claimed his wife, Robert took over and had Mitch scrambling like hell just to stay in place.

Year after year he'd played the line from *The Godfather* over and over; another scenario in which a sister had married beneath her in the eyes of a powerful brother. "*Give him a living," Sonny Corleone said, "but keep him away from the family business."*

Mitch correctly believed that the old man had allowed his marriage to Ellie to stand because the Kirby family needed an infusion of new blood to produce an heir. Bachelor son, Robert, had neglected the task. The Kirby family tree had thinned out to a last fork with Robert on one spindly branch and Ellie on the other. Despite Mitch's best efforts, Ellie suffered three miscarriages. Robert privately quipped that the Kirby DNA rejected Mitch's gold-digger seed.

Mitch circled around the courthouse, headed west on Foote, and turned north on Fillmore. He came up on the white, two-story, wood-frame house behind a screen of magnolia, plum, and flowering dogwood. The street directory by the curb stated that General Pierre G. T. Beauregard had sheltered in the "Kirby House" during the Siege of Corinth.

Way too much house, people said, for a run-in-place loan officer.

He turned into the driveway.

It was her goddamned fault, really; there should have been tricycles in this driveway, a basketball hoop. Ellie and her damned tipped uterus like a broken egg-basket.

He thumbed the garage opener, saw that she was home, and slid the Ford in beside her Lexus. He closed the door behind him, shut off the truck, and sat through a moment of quiet rage, listening to the hot tick of the cooling engine.

Marcy Leets called Ellie the "titless mouse," but that crack had more to do with Ellie giving up on her hair and cosmetics. Aside from not having much on top, she was tough as a wasp; deadly fast from the hips on down; the fastest white girl ever at Corinth High. All-state track three years running.

At Ole Miss she'd been a standout on the archery team. Small tits evidently gave her an Amazon advantage when it came to pulling the bowstring.

Mitch heaved from the truck, took a deep breath, and

padded in through the sun porch, past dust-covered furniture and plants turning to brittle crepe. He wondered if she was consciously letting all the plants die; slowly, they were shriveling, inch by inch, going brown to gray to dust. She'd given the plants a do-not-resuscitate order. No extra measures. Practicing for the decision she had to make about her daddy.

He entered the remodeled living room that had looked so elegant in the photograph for *Southern Living*. Now it was heaped with stacks of paper, plastic shopping bags tossed haphazardly on the Oriental carpet. Her cast-off clothes littered the couch. A pile of unfolded towels occupied a chair.

Distracted, Ellie had let the cleaning lady go.

Mitch was a fastidious man; he ironed his own shirts and shined his own shoes. Coming through the dining room, he spied a stack of magazines and books teetering on the table in an inverted pyramid. It drove him insane, the way she piled little items on the bottom, bigger things on the top.

He had heard of the "Twinkie defense." He wondered if there was a "clutter defense."

A metallic grinding came from the kitchen, sounding like a dentist's drill, but it was just Ellie whipping up one of her damn veggie drinks in the Osterizer.

He walked into the kitchen and stared at his wife of seven years.

Ellender Jane Kirby, Corinth's premier charity-czarina, leaned against the kitchen counter between stacks of unwashed dishes, dripping copper-freckled sweat. She wore road-blasted Nikes, red running shorts, and a purple halter. Her somewhat long face had the unnerving quality of looking really attractive only when you were groveling and looking up at her. Most people would say, diplomatically, that Ellie was a striking redhead. She was certainly excessively fit and gaunt now from the constant running.

Her blue Kirby eyes, patrician nose, and full lips were underslung by half an inch too much jaw. This piranha-like set to her features enabled her, Mitch suspected, to detect one part of Marcy Leets in a million parts of air. And at such times, Ellie's jaw muscles bunched and she looked like she could bite through a steel bar.

"Hi honey, I'm home," Mitch said, coming through the door, watching a trickle of sweat ooze down the defined muscles of her tight stomach and disappear into the waistband of her shorts. He imagined the tart sweat pooling down between her salmon-colored thighs. Seven years he'd labored after roses in that super-uptight briar patch.

Just trying to figure a way to get her to . . . unclench.

Might as well just forget the sex and stuff a lump of coal up there. See if she could bear down and piss diamonds.

After they buried Robert with full military honors in the family plot out at Kirby Creek, Ellie had cut her coppery hair short and started living in the gym like a crazed aerobic nun. After her dad had the stroke, the one that cut off the oxygen to his brain, she took to the roads.

"Where you been?" he asked softly. "I called from the station."

She drowned out his question with a flick of the juicer switch and gave him the dentist drill again. Then she removed the glass beaker from the stainless steel contraption and poured the frothy orange mess into a tumbler.

"Running," she said, raising the glass and taking a drink.

Mitch showed his teeth in a faint grimace. "At night? Where?"

She shrugged. "Out old 45, north of town."

"Jesus, Ellie, that stretch is full of drunks at night." He took a step forward. "I wish you'd cut back on the running. And eat more . . ."

She smiled tightly, held the glass aloft.

"Eat some real food, you're too thin," he said, thinking he should take the extra two steps and kiss her on the forehead. But he couldn't bear the thought of ever touching her again. So he stood there as she placed the glass on the counter and turned to him and said, "I've employed LaSalle Ector to work full-time out at the house. He's back from the hospital and, the way he is, they're not going to give him his old job."

Mitch nodded patiently but did a double take behind his eyes. LaSalle. Big nigger EMT drove an ambulance out of Magnolia Regional before he went to Iraq as a medic in the guard. Robert Kirby's last gesture on earth had been to drag LaSalle out of an ambush kill zone.

"Before his stroke, Daddy remarked we should look after him, considering how he got wounded and all," Ellie said.

"Fine," Mitch said. Lot he had to say about it. She managed the finances from her trust fund and paid the bills. After he quit the bank, she gave him a monthly allowance.

After a pause, she went on.

"Mitchell Lee," she said frankly, "they brought in another expert this morning. He's the one who did the brain scan when they had Daddy down in Jackson. I confess, the tests he conducted were not exactly what you'd call scientific. They do this painful sternum rub and this thing called 'doll's eyes.' You know how Daddy's eyes kind of roll from side to side? Well, they move his head and check to see if his eyes normally adjust with the movement. He doesn't appear to be able to acquire and track movement, an object." To illustrate, she moved an upright finger back and forth.

She shook her head. "They say he's in this sensitive gray area; a range between minimally conscious and a persistent vegetative state. And now he's contracted pneumonia and they've pumped him full of antibiotics . . ."

Mitch narrowed his eyes. "Did Bob Watts bring in the expert?" The senior Watts, Billie Watts's father, was the Kirby family lawyer.

"Well, yes."

"He still have that lawyer with a notary stamp standing vigil round the clock outside Hiram's room?"

Ellie nodded. "If Daddy wakes up just a little all he has to do is nod to transfer power of attorney to me. Daddy wanted to donate part of the estate to a research hospital for veterans. In Robert's name . . . but he never got around to putting it in writing . . ."

Mitch nodded. "You mean Bob Watts wants to reduce the size of the estate before Hiram dies, to ease the tax bite."

"That too," Ellie said frankly.

Mitch pursed his lips, lowered his eyes, and nodded. Her fingers floated out and rested on his forearm. Inside, he cringed at her touch. Really wish you wouldn't do that . . .

She said, "Cornel Wight at the bank says I have to prepare to make a decision about Daddy. He's suggesting we convene a meeting with the board of directors. Mitch, look at me . . ."

He raised his head and engaged the full intensity of her driven blue eyes.

". . . Cornel canvassed the board and says it would be all right for you to attend." She tightened her grip, and for one almost sweet moment her blue eyes reached out to him. "I'd like it if you'd agree to ease back . . . into things."

Startled by the sudden gesture of intimacy, Mitch started to pull away.

"Mitchell, honey, listen to me, they're coming around. They know how Robert was always hard on you. No one's surprised you started drinking. It's different now; after all the work you've done. They know the monument is for Daddy."

Gently, Mitch disengaged her grip. "Ellie, don't give up on Hiram so quick. Give him a fighting chance. He could still pull out of this. No," he shook his head with slow finality, "out of respect, I can't go near this. You know what people say about me. It's best I finish what I started, so I'm driving to Memphis in the morning. I reserved a room in a Holiday Inn. Might take two days to finalize the paperwork on the monument, pick up the last check from the Heritage Group, and see to the dedication plaque."

"Really wish you'd stay home," she said, the plea still in

her eyes. "I'd like you to be out at Kirby Creek when the reenactors show up, so they don't tear up the grounds again dragging in their cannons."

Mitch averted his eyes from her watchful gaze. Shook his head. "Look, I'll stop at the hospital in the morning on my way out of town and look in on Hiram."

Then he opened the cabinet beneath the sink, stooped, took out a tall plastic juice container, straightened up, placed it in the sink, and twisted the tap.

"What are you doing?" she asked.

Eyes still downcast, he watched the water fill the container. "Going to water the plants out yonder," he jerked his head toward the sun porch, "otherwise they're going to die."

6 MOLLY WAS ASLEEP IN HER ROOM down the hall and Jenny leaned back in the king-size bed, rubbing African Shea Butter into her arms and legs. As she smoothed the emollient into her skin, she studied the precarious stack of books leaning on Paul's nightstand. Shelby Foote's three huge volumes dominated the pile; so bulky, Paul joked they amounted to a public works project and took about as long to finish as the interminable road improvements on I-494. Then there was McPherson's *Battle Cry of Freedom*, *Confederates in the Attic*, *The Killer Angels*, and, perched on top, a slim, fifty-year-old paperback Pocketbook edition of the *Red Badge of Courage*. A Union soldier was portrayed in raw watercolor on the cover, dashing past a ruined cannon. The style reminded her of the noirish paperbacks unearthed from an old trunk and laid out on a card table at the garage sale her mom held after her dad died. Except the cover art on those books all seemed to be variations of a tough Barbara Stanwyck–type babe with a Chesterfield jammed in her painted lips as her slip draped off her shoulders on top and hitched up her thighs on the bottom.

Paul read Stephen Crane's classic over and over, as if it was a relic—a splinter from a purer time.

She understood that her husband was smart and sensitive and moving in emotional retreat from the twenty-first century. He'd concluded that he'd grown up in the last stages of a stable ahistorical bubble that existed between the end of World War II and the fall of the Berlin Wall. Now, he believed, the true forces of history were reasserting themselves, namely ancient religious and ethnic hatreds. He worried that Molly would grow up in a world full of shadowy suicide bombers stalking the malls alongside child molesters and computer-game-addled teens planning school shootings.

So he'd found refuge in the Civil War, where he believed what individual men did on a given day had determined the course of history.

Paul wanted to make a difference. He just hadn't figured out how yet. They'd met as Wellstone volunteers, had intended to join the Peace Corps together and save the world. Molly changed their plans. Paul went into insurance to make some money so she could stay home until Molly started preschool. She studied nights to get her special ed degree, then set a more modest goal to save just part of the world in one inner-city school.

After four years of failing to make a dent in a reluctant parade of broken kids, she scaled her expectations down to saving just one of them from the streets. She wound up leaving to save herself. They moved to the "quieter demographics" of Stillwater, where she taught general ed to mostly white kids from intact families.

Starting to drift, Jenny stared at the cover of the *Red Badge of Courage*. Perhaps Paul would look like the illustration on Saturday, crossing a field in his accurate getup. She had the powerful impression that Paul was grabbing hard at a second chance for the boyhood adventure he'd missed growing up. That's what the reenactors called their emulations of Civil War soldiers . . .

Impressions.

Maybe this was his way of making up for never having been in the military. In fact, none of the men in their new neighborhood had worn uniforms. Unlike her dad and her uncles, who, after a few beers in the backyard, would send the women away when the strange place names from Vietnam and Korea started cropping up.

She pursed her lips in a tight smile. The neighbor gals were mostly corporate housewives whose husbands worked at 3M; they gave Jenny decent marks for having good legs and subtracted points when her blue-collar petticoat showed. Her dad had been a wood-and-steel kind of guy down from the Iron Range, a business agent for the Typographical Union until the advent of cold type gutted the trade.

Abruptly, she was seeing Rane sitting on his front steps; his skin pale, his dark hair cropped close. Quiet. Self-contained. He took on careers as research projects. When she met him, he was a veteran back from the Gulf War, experimenting with being a St. Paul cop.

Then he took a side trip to research, falling in love.

Stay focused on Paul.

She could go months without thinking about Rane. But then she'd see Molly walk through a room in her loose-limbed amble. Or see a photo on the front page of the paper. Or turn on the TV.

Public TV's Friday night news magazine; the same lean pale face, the tight mop of dark hair, the standard jeans and T-shirt augmented by a sports coat.

Rane sitting next to a coiffed female interviewer with her anchor voice so earnest . . . Christ, didn't they watch tapes of themselves and see how pompous they sounded? This blonde with an Hermès scarf tucked to her throat and her smile pumped from holding up about two pounds of cosmetics. By comparison, Rane leaned back totally relaxed and bland.

"Tonight our guest is the always controversial Pulitzer-winning photographer, and sometimes writer, John Rane, who changes jobs the way the rest of us change socks. Really, John, at last count you've been fired by both the Pioneer Press *and the* Star Tribune.

And you've quit the Pioneer Press *twice. So why do they keep hiring you back?"*

And Jenny watched Rane go into his famous Just Plain John Rane Act. With a slackening of his spare features and a skew to his eyebrows, he sloughed off his wiry handsome presence and became mild, blank, and totally nonthreatening. This innate mannerism reminded Jenny of the Australian phasmid, the stick insect who, when challenged, could imitate a dead leaf or twig swaying in the breeze. This quality of changing shape to avoid detection was prized by undercover cops, con artists, and men faced with a woman delivering an ultimatum about commitment.

Rane had blinked innocuously at his interrogator and smiled politely.

Jenny understood him completely. Rane was controversial because he simply did what he wanted to do. Period. If his current employer got in his way, he quit or got fired and pursued a story on his own. They kept taking him back because he was good and won them prizes.

"You're a difficult man to categorize," the interviewer had said, trying to keep the interview going, "you're a photographer, but sometimes the writing takes over in the books. What's the secret to going back and forth between mediums?"

Rane replied in his steady, slightly hushed voice: "Whether you're using words or a camera the idea is not to tamper with the subject, not to leave fingerprints . . ."

Fingerprints.

Jenny hugged herself and felt the rash of goose bumps circle her arms. Why you hypocrite . . . You sure as hell left some fingerprints on me.

Rane had written three modestly successful books illustrated with his photos. He'd followed an ounce of cocaine from its inception in the Colombian jungles, through the twists of processing and smuggling, until it was cooked into crack and consumed in south Minneapolis. Then he'd put himself through smoke-jumper training in Montana and spent a whole summer in the mountains fighting fires. His last book was about mixed martial arts.

A bio on his publisher's Web site noted that Rane was born into a musical St. Paul family. His mother and father, both concert pianists, died in a small-plane accident when he was twelve. Then he was raised by his aunt and uncle in rural Wisconsin. He became interested in writing and photography while attending the University of Minnesota as a music major. He dropped out his sophomore year, enlisted in the army, and was trained as a combat photographer. Following service in the Gulf War, he briefly joined the St. Paul Police Department before settling down to writing and photography. He was single and lived in St. Paul, Minnesota.

Heady stuff: following your dreams, living your first choice.

Jenny caught herself: from a few idle thoughts, she had started down the road of wondering what if . . .

So she set aside the moisturizing cream, stretched out, and smoothed her hands on the sheets. Exploring the cotton texture, she found a straight brown hair, plucked it up, and rubbed it between her thumb and forefinger. Light brown, dry, straight, and fine. Paul's hair. Her own hair was deeper brown. And Molly's was a dark, comb-mocking tangle verging on black.

"Nice," she said aloud. Nice was an apt description for the intimacy contained within the four corners of this bed. She aimed a puff of breath at the strand of hair but it stayed on her fingertip. The shea butter reminding her that life gets sticky.

Nothing nice about the nagging, visceral thought: *I'm still young enough to have another child.* Molly had wondered more than once when she'd have a baby sister or brother.

They had discussed adoption; Paul had determined that the risk of taking on someone else's wild-card genetics outweighed the benefits.

Jenny wiped off the hair on the T-shirt she wore to bed, lay back, and studied the pebble-beige ceiling, so subdued and easy on the eye. She and Paul had an upper-medium income and upper-medium expectations. Her life was set on medium cruise control. The scenery going by was a slow, comfortable smother in medium beige. Abruptly, she composed a vision of another ceiling. Older, yellowed like the thumbed pages of Paul's paperback, stained with watermarks and fissures intersecting like the lines on an open palm.

For one instant, she could feel and taste the tickle of their cooling sweat and the taboo smell of the cigarette smoke rising in sinuous curls.

This was where her daydreams degraded into a version of *Crossfire.*

Forget it. He walked out on you.

You let him walk away. You weren't willing to take a chance . . .

He was kinda a mess at the time, you'll recall; back from the war, in trouble with his police job . . .

I thought that was your thing, wanting to deal with hard cases. You could have tried to get through to him . . .

Enough.

She switched off the light and reclined in the dark, listening to her heartbeat, to her lungs take in air, then let it out. She imagined parking the Subaru on Laurel Street, getting out, and walking up the cracked concrete steps. Raising her hand. Knocking on the door.

A teeter-totter of anticipation in the dark.

She pictured herself parking the car, getting out, and walking up those steps, over and over, until she fell asleep.

7

IT WAS MITCH'S HABIT TO STAY UP later than his wife, so it wasn't unusual for him to escape the house at eleven thirty for a walk around the neighborhood to have a last smoke before turning in. These days, he slept on a narrow bed he kept in the scrupulously clean downstairs den that served as his office.

After packing his travel bag for tomorrow, he eased out the front door and walked slowly down the darkened street. Promptly at half past eleven, the white Escalade slowed and pulled to the curb.

She'd turned the dome light off, so when he opened the passenger-side door, her bold eyes were concealed in shadow. And that's how he thought of her, this irresistible shadow out of mythology almost: half Sphinx, half bitch in heat.

She cut hair in Corinth.

Marcy had learned her basic haircutting skills in jail, when she was barely out of her teens. Since then she'd put a lot of distance between the women's correctional facility in Jackson and her spotless, airy beauty shop with ferns in the windows. It started normal enough, just making eyes at the few Leets' family affairs he'd attended, their arms and hips grazing when they met. Then he'd stopped into her shop to buy some shampoo at closing time and next thing they were tearing each other's clothes off in her back storeroom.

"Jesus, I don't know. Darl's gonna catch us," Mitch had muttered, liking the combination of being more scared and turned on than he'd ever been in his life.

"Me and Darl's got an arrangement," she'd said in that deceptively bored, passive-aggressive voice. "Like the army and the faggots. Don't ask don't tell."

". . . gonna put a gun to my head."

"Darl don't put a gun on nobody unless I say so," Marcy had said, slightly annoyed, like she didn't care to repeat herself for the benefit of slow listeners. "We got two rules: no diseases and come home in time for breakfast, for the kids."

For over a year they'd been meeting like this. Mitch found it a maddening joke, the way she could steer a man into sex that practically bent the laws of physics. And both of them married to people they hardly slept with anymore.

"When this is over we should go off together," he said.

"Won't work," she said.

"Why the hell not?" he wanted to know.

"You ever watch flypaper," she said.

"What?"

"They put scent on it to attract the flies. The smart fly's gonna get close enough to catch a buzz off the lure, then keep going. The ones who venture in too close get stuck," she said.

Mitch shook his head and placed his hand on her lap. "Flypaper," he said.

"Sweet and sticky. Where to," Marcy Leets said.

"Let's drive down to the depot," he said.

A few minutes later they were standing in the deserted parking lot next to the Crossroads Museum in the warehouse district. Mitch lit a cigarette, passed it to her, and then looked up. The night had flipped warm, with an errant south wind driving black, stringy clouds.

As he scanned the empty streets past an old red railroad car, he thought to tell her about Beeman stopping him on the road, then decided not to. Somewhere he heard kids running on skateboards, the rattle of wheels echoing off the old brick buildings. The breeze carried a whiff of something pungent. Marijuana maybe? Or the keen scent Marcy dabbed behind her ears, on her wrists, and the cleavage of her breasts, which always managed to be on display?

"What's that you're wearing?" he asked.

"You always ask that. Patchouli." Spill from a streetlight caught on the whites of her eyes, her teeth, and described a nimbus in her tawny-blond hair. Fast nights like this she wore a loose cotton dress. When she dragged on the cigarette, the coal flared and he saw her clean, even features briefly illuminated. She'd pearl-dived in the sewage of Memphis and come up as coldly beautiful as carved ivory . . .

. . . and just as hard.

"It's cold," she said simply, handing back the cigarette.

Mitch, thinking it was warm out, cocked his head. "Huh . . . ?"

"What you're doing. You and Dwayne. I think you're making a *big* mistake," she said.

"How's that again?"

"You want to destroy Beeman you should corrupt him, buy him, bankroll his run for sheriff down the line. That way you kill his Boy Scout heart and make him keep walking around with it gone bad in his chest," she said.

"Jesus." Mitch shook his head. Once, he had heard Darl describe Marcy with pained awe, how when she got riled she was so damn mean that black widows carried her likeness on their stomachs. Well, I guess . . .

"C'mon, walk with me," Mitch said, wanting to change the subject. He flipped the smoke away, watched it skitter on the asphalt in a tiny shower of sparks. He took her hand and led her into the dark, around the side of the building.

"Where we going?"

"Out to the tracks."

"I'll mess up my shoes."

"No you won't."

He put his arm around her shoulders, pulling her in so their hips glided together.

"What are you up to, Mitchell Lee?" she asked, watching her step.

"Symbolic deal-making gestures, asking for a blessing," Mitch said. He nuzzled her hair and savored the patchouli

like a lingering whiff of the life she'd lived on the Memphis
streets, where the sex came with a boost of drugs and murder. "You listen to blues?" he asked.

"I guess."

They'd stepped over the railroad tracks and now stood
face-to-face, in front of the depot. He whispered in her ear:
"You know how down in the Delta the old black blues singers tell it? How you trade your soul for success? You gotta
take your guitar down to the crossroads at midnight?"

"You ain't exactly got a guitar, honey," Marcy said, toying with his belt buckle. She moved her hand. "'Bout now I
suspect you're praying for a harmonica . . ."

Mitch sighed. "And for a crossroads, look where we're
standing."

"In a bunch of nasty old railroad tracks coming together."

"Exactly. X marks the spot, where the rails of the Memphis & Charleston and the Mobile & Ohio railroads inter-
sect, in front of the old depot. Marcy, we are standing right
on the fabled crossroads of the Western Confederacy."

"You lost me, sport," Marcy said.

"All we need now is for the devil to open shop," Mitch said.

"Don't go complicating a thing, Mitchell Lee," Marcy
said with an edge coming into her tone. "And don't expect
my blessing . . ."

His hands eased down the sides of her hips. "If I can't
find me a proper devil to initial a contract, I figure you're
the next best thing . . ." Gathering and sliding up the loose
cotton, searching for the band of the panties. ". . . Once you
hike your dress up in the dark . . ." He felt her belly dry up,
tighten, and pull away.

"Just humor me," Mitch said.

"Maybe I ain't in the mood to humor you," she said.

"Aw c'mon," he whispered as he moved his hands to her
shoulders and pressed down, insisting, guiding her.

Marcy resisted, flung off his hands, and stepped back,
tripping on a rail, catching her balance.

"I've had about enough of this. Being taken for fuckin'

granted. You and Dwayne dragging Darl into this bullshit," she said evenly, straightening her dress.

"Whoa, wait a minute," Mitch protested. "We talked . . ."

"We talked about things changing. But this now—it's way over the line," she said firmly. There was just enough light off the street lamps to see the cold witchery come into her eyes.

Damn, but Marcy's moods and her favors balanced on greased-lightning divots and could turn on you quick.

"Mitchell Lee," she jabbed her finger at him, "I am not exactly pleased with you bringing in Dwayne and his Memphis crowd. I been there. They eat the cripples and the strays. I spent half my life getting Darl and the kids away from that bastard brother of his. We was just about living *normal*."

Mitch's mouth dropped open. "This? You and me is normal?"

"Best I can do," she said doggedly. "My boys need a father."

It occurred to Mitch she could be dangerous, going off like this. He fished another fact from memory: how black widows mate, then sting the male to death and wrap him up so the babies can eat him.

"C'mon, Marcy, don't be like that," he said, his voice reasonable, soothing. He reached for her. She parried his hand.

"Knock it off. Truth is, I think what you're doing is pretty damn shitty. I told Darl as much."

"Oh right. And you never did anything shitty?" Mitch came back at her.

Marcy sniffed, looked away. "Whatever I might have done was when we were in the game. We all took our chances. And we had to learn it step by step; not all of a sudden overnight like you."

Mitch took a moment to control himself, to lower his voice. "Damn it girl, whose side you on?"

Marcy raised her chin and the witch was back, looking

him right in the eye. "I told Darl he goes through with this, I just might leave him. Something trips weird I got two kids to raise; that's whose side I'm on."

Mitch stared at her, momentarily confused. Like she'd dumped a basket full of pink mice at his feet and now they were scurrying all over. What the hell's going on here; phases of the moon, the tides, PMS? Who do you ask about this, the perils of a woman being a career criminal? What do you do? Hide the guns once a month?

"You're in one of your moods," he said finally.

"I'm telling you one last time, Mitchell Lee. Call it off and just walk away," she said, drawing herself up.

When he didn't respond, she said, "Okay, that's it."

And then she walked away; striding away in the darkness, back to her car, getting in, starting it, and leaving him alone on the tracks. He looked down and saw his belt buckle dangle, half unfastened, like the leavings of folly. Nobody was getting laid at the crossroads tonight. He exhaled, tidied up his belt, thought to curse, and finally just muttered, "Women."

Then he began the long walk home.

8 JENNIFER EDIN WOKE UP FEELING cross and foolish, showered, and then stared in the bathroom mirror. The light coming off the bank of forty-watt vanity bulbs, while not harsh, was not exactly kind either. Jenny saw a thirty-five-year-old elementary-school teacher with tidy but slightly sagging boobs and suggestions of stretch marks on her flat tummy. Not exactly an airbrushed desperate house-wife, are you, girl?

Over breakfast she admonished Molly for not finishing her orange juice and then reprimanded her for not clearing her plate. By the time Jenny was positioned at her desk at school and had finished her second cup of coffee, she had made up her mind.

Molly was out of sight, behind a partition in another homeroom. Jenny's fifth-graders were starting to assemble; the girls talking, heads close, the boys plunging with more explosive energy.

Spring weather. Short sleeves. Out of old habit, she checked their arms for signs of bruising and remembered her last bunch of city kids. The day she quit. Just three of them; one rode the bus from a homeless shelter, one was happy because he'd visited his dad the night before in Stillwater prison. The third, Andre, came to school hungry, so Jenny fixed an extra lunch every morning.

She thought she might actually be getting through to An-dre, gaining his trust, and so left him alone for just a minute with the bagged lunch. When she came back he was gone. So was her purse. She called the cops, who told her to call her credit card companies.

She'd handled a lot worse: fistfights, knives pulled. Blood. But she'd reached her tipping point.

Now she surveyed the bright eyes and ruddy faces assembling around her desk. Like a clot of ants joined by a shared-antennae wavelength, they sensed that Mrs. Edin was looking more serious than usual this morning.

She could purge the daydreams with a simple, direct plan: sit down with Rane and propose setting up a meeting with Paul when he returned. They'd figure out an equitable way to structure breaking the news to Molly. Paul was good at stuff like that.

No more drive-bys. Play it straight.

Sitting erect at her desk before class began, she opened her cell, tapped in directory assistance, requested Rane's number on Laurel in St. Paul, and selected the connect option.

ONCE, AT AN AWARDS CEREMONY, THIS FULSOME professor from the University of Missouri had compared John Rane, with a camera in his hands, to Odysseus: a man who was never at a loss. Rane picked up the phone on the second ring, heard the voice on the other end, and immediately sagged.

I'm not ready for this.

"John," Jenny repeated, "it's Jenny Edin."

"Yes," Rane said, keeping his voice level.

"It's time we talked. About Molly. I'm in St. Paul tomorrow afternoon. I could drop by your house at, say, two. Would that be convenient for you?"

"That would be fine," Rane said, blinking through a bout of dizziness.

"Good. See you then," Jenny said in her best crisp Voice.

What was yesterday, he wondered, a practice run? "Good-bye," he said, but she had already ended the call. He sat at his kitchen table, wearing his old silk bathrobe, unshaven, unshowered, halfway through his first cup of coffee. He stared at the telephone like it was hot and still potent with Jenny Edin's voice.

And where'd she get that voice? Deeper than he remembered. With an unself-conscious authority that reminded him of an IRS collection agent who'd once interrogated him about a misapplied estimated-tax payment.

Rane ran his fingers across his bare chest. They came away dotted with nervous sweat.

Jesus.

HER DECISION MADE, JENNY GLANCED AT THE WALL clock. Nine thirty. Mississippi was in the same time zone. Dutifully, before the school day began, she wondered where Paul was and if they'd really driven all night.

9 MITCH DIDN'T NEED THE ALARM. HE woke up covered in sweat, seeing Marcy's hex eyes peering into him, felt them throb behind his forehead like a dull metal wedge.

Goddamn her anyway.

He eased from bed, taking care not to wake Ellie sleeping in the master bedroom upstairs, took a fast shower in the downstairs bath, shaved, and dressed quickly. Then he grabbed the bag he'd packed last night and quietly slipped from the house into the rain. Darl would be out in the Kirby woods about now, stringing the wind dangles, sighting with his range finder.

On the way out of town, he stopped at KCs Espresso to pick up a large dark roast with a shot of espresso. By the time he turned off West 72 onto the access road to the Magnolia Regional Health Center, the jolt of caffeine had softened the headache.

He entered the building, padded down the corridors, and, approaching the intensive care unit, smelled the cloud of orchids, lilies, tulips, carnations, and roses drifting from Hiram's room half a ward away.

"Immediate family," Mitch said to the nurse at the desk.

Like he'd told the AA group, Hiram Kirby had the outward aspect of a frail astronaut geared up in medical countdown for launch to inner space. One gnarled, liver-spotted hand marked with IV tape jutted from the soft, green sheets. And just a corner of his gaunt cheek showed above more tape

that held the intubation tube inserted in his throat. Under a
fluff of white hair, his watery blue eyes moved to and fro
in wrinkled sockets pointed up toward, but not seeing, the
fluorescent ceiling lights.

The funeral scent of carnations and roses combined with
the electronic beep of a Dash 4000, twelve-lead heart monitor, and the bubbly whoosh of the square gray respirator beside the bed.

Two people kept vigil on chairs along the wall. The nurse
had to stay, but Mitch glowered at the attorney from the
Watts firm. The slick young vampire with a notary stamp
and power of attorney request was ready to leap forward the
moment Hiram regained consciousness.

"Do you mind?" Mitch growled at the lawyer.

The young guy folded a page to mark his John Grisham
novel, shrugged, stood up, stretched, and walked into the
hall. The nurse smiled and also stepped out, giving him a
private moment.

Mitch turned back to the bed where, amid the snarls of
tubing, digital readouts, and graphing trace lines, it seemed
that Hiram was being sent off by a chorus of blinking R2D2s.
Mitch stared down into the wandering blue jelly of Hiram's
eyes.

Mitch had tried to love this man. But the fact was, he had
a permanent crick in his neck from all the looking up that effort required. For years, sequestered in his bank cubicle, he'd
thought Robert Kirby shooting down his efforts to bring in
outside business to invest in Alcorn was personal spite. Then
he realized the son was just following the father's lead. The
Kirbys didn't want outsiders coming in, rocking the boat with
new ideas and stirring up the natives with higher pay scales.

"Well," Mitch said, not unkindly, to the comatose old man,
"I'm gonna rock the boat." *Only way you all will let me.*

*Thank you. Good-bye. You tried. I tried. You brought me
in like a stud horse to fertilize your played-out herd and it
just didn't take . . . so go to Plan B.*

Mitch bent over and gently kissed the dry, brown-spotted skin of the old man's forehead. Then he turned and walked from the room, shouldering past the lawyer in the doorway. As he walked swiftly down the corridor, he wondered if he'd ever meet a grown man anywhere, especially in the South, who could claim a clear goddamn conscience.

Low-beam weather. The road west out of Corinth was thick with ground fog turning to drizzle. Darl's farm rental property was just outside of town. Tires hissing, turning over curds of red clay, he rolled his Ford up the rutted track to the farmhouse. He didn't see Darl's truck or Dwayne's Caddy. He parked, climbed the porch steps, and knocked on the door. When no one answered, he entered the house, which was furnished in early Dogpatch with a heavy under-scent of bacon grease and gasoline. Darl's tenant had a coffee can full of gas sitting inside the door, soaking some machine parts. An amber Stonehenge of empty beer bottles on the table suggested that Darl and Dwayne had been here. Mitch made a quick tour of the house. Nobody was home.

So he sat down on the swayback couch, leaned back, shut his eyes, and dozed off.

He blinked awake with somebody shaking him. He opened one eye and saw Marcy looking down on him like she'd popped full-grown from the knot of pain in the middle of his forehead.

Marcy, with all her sassy war paint on, for Dwayne probably, scarlet lipstick and blue eye shadow and poured into a scoop-neck, pastel blue cotton summer dress. As she sat on the side of the couch, the dress pulled up when she crossed her knees, so he could see the smooth, curved fit of inner thigh on calf, pressing flesh on flesh; same action as was going on in that low-cut bodice. She wore open-toe sandals with her toenails painted blue. Splashed mud dotted her bare ankles.

Like always, she smelled good. Not clean, but good; trailing this faintly unwashed, silky scent of lazy, fondling, waking arousal. Her blue eyes watched him, the witch hiding beneath a mild contempt.

"What?" he blurted.

"I just wanted to remind you how dumb it is what you're doing, is all." She lowered her eyes. "I kinda hoped you and Darl would see the light and take a pass."

Mitch blinked at her and said, "We already had this conversation."

Marcy looked up. "Dumb," she repeated, "too many moving parts." She cocked her head one way, then the other. "This has gotta happen so the next thing can happen."

"Aw for Christ's sake," Mitch mumbled. He scratched his chin, then checked his wristwatch. "It's nine thirty in the fuckin' morning . . ." Mitch sat up, now fully awake. "Marcy, you scare me. What is it with you?"

Marcy gave him one last-chance look, then, when she got no response, her expression told him she had wearied of the conversation. She shook his arm hard. "Get up, Darl's waiting out back and Dwayne's with him. You gotta audition. Remember, your cousin Dwayne's all growed up now and he's a King Crook. He don't miss nothing." She stood up, smoothed her dress, and walked out the front door.

Mitch followed her onto the porch. She sat down on the swing and extracted a copy of *Entertainment Weekly* from her purse, turned to a story on Tom Cruise, looked up once, and gave him the bored look.

."Where are they?" Mitch asked.

She jerked a thumb toward the back of the house, then said, "Hear that?"

. Mitch listened, heard a hammer striking wood. "What?" he said.

"Boys playing," Marcy said, not raising her eyes from her magazine.

10 THE RAIN HAD PAUSED AND NOW THE land seemed to jump with green. Going down the porch steps, Mitch glanced over the property, which consisted of a weathered gray barn, a chicken coop, and some fenced pasture in which a dozen black cows grazed. His last gesture in the world of banking was arranging a loan to underwrite the sale of these four hundred swampy acres that skirted a potholed stretch of 72 to Darl. Mitch grinned, remembering how the other loan officers took it as a sign of his downward spiral, unloading this bog on his cousin.

Darl told people he had this notion to open a Civil War paintball range. Figured he'd piggyback on the Kirby Creek reenactment, get all these people lined up shoulder-to-shoulder in cheap blue and gray smocks and hats, march them at each other. When they were a hundred yards apart, they'd blast paint. The Rebs would fire red paint. The Yanks would load blue. Kinda like the red-state, blue-state thing, Darl said, half-serious until his patrons laughed him out of his beer joint.

The real fact was, Marcy knew somebody in the highway department, who gave her an inside track on the Corinth bypass scheduled eventually along this road.

Mitch walked around the back of the house and saw Darl and a taller man, who was Dwayne Leets, standing about three hundred yards away. They were nailing a four-by-eight piece of plywood up against a post along the fence line. Then he saw Darl's truck parked closer in and spotted a compact black object on the hood. Curious, he detoured toward the truck and identified the shape as Darl's Bushnell rangefinder.

"What the hell you guys up to?" he called out, quickening his step. Seeing him, Darl grinned. He had a bucket of red barn paint in one hand and a small brush in the other. He had sketched a crude, man-size silhouette with an exaggerated stovepipe hat atop the head on the plywood.

"Hey there, Mitchell Lee, how the hell you doing?" Dwayne Leets said, extending his hand, which, unlike Darl's, was free of paint. They shook. "Caught you telling tall tales on that radio show last night when I was driving in," Dwayne said, with a droll raise to his eyebrows. "I don't recall Grandpa Leets eating *that* many squirrels? Maybe a couple on the weekend?"

Mitch shrugged, grinned, and said, "Shucks, Cuz; gotta keep Bubba entertained."

Until the last two weeks, Mitch hadn't seen Dwayne much to talk to since his childhood. What he remembered was a cruel sneer and early leadership ability. Dwayne organized his brothers and cousins into lynching parties to string cats up by the neck with slip-knotted bailing twine. Then they'd line up and shoot them with .22s. Finally, they'd set them on fire with lighter fluid as they flopped around.

Mitch knit his eyebrows and pointed at the plywood.

"We, ah, figured you needed some target practice," Darl said.

"Kinda with a little pressure thrown in," Dwayne said.

"Uh-huh," Mitch said. Then he turned to Darl. "You been out to the Kirby place?"

"It's all set up," Darl said.

Mitch nodded, then jerked his thumb back toward the house. "Is Marcy on the rag or what? She just gave me an earful about leaving you over this thing."

"Ah," Darl gave a shaky grin and waved his hand in a

dismissive gesture. "She knows the score, man; she's already in up to her neck. She'll be just fine."

"So where's the rifle?" Dwayne asked.

"In Darl's truck, didn't want anybody seeing me hauling it around," Mitch said, looking around. "We secure out here?"

"Don't sweat it; we're alone. I sent my renter into town to pick up fencing material and gave him a few bucks to stay overnight. He'll be gone most of the day," Darl said.

"Where's your Caddy?" Mitch asked Dwayne.

"Jimmy dropped me off." Jimmy Beal was a Memphis hood, Dwayne's driver.

"So what's this," Mitch asked, indicating the plywood.

Darl and Dwayne exchanged conspiratorial grins. "Well now," Dwayne said, putting his hands together, lacing his fingers, and cracking his knuckles. His cat-killing days behind him, he'd lost the sneer. An easy-smiling man now, with blond, razor-cut hair and an accountant, a lawyer, and a personal trainer. His slurred drawl was not quite skin-deep, like his hotel-swimming-pool tan. The jeans, orange ostrich-quill boots, and Western shirt he wore could not change the faint white line that ringed his ruddy throat. Country-born, he had become a city boy. When Dwayne wasn't slumming with his country kin, he wore a gold chain. Dwayne Leets had been born in Selmer, Tennessee, and found his way back by way of Chicago and Detroit. He owned a half dozen used-car lots in Memphis, along with a string of pizza joints and dry cleaners. The businesses were useful laundries for the proceeds from the drug trade.

"Give you a hint," Darl said. Then he dipped his brush into the paint and sketched a lopsided smiley face on the silhouette head, swirling the brush to make an exaggerated left eye about four inches in diameter. Then he scrawled *abe* across the target's chest. "See," he continued, "I was telling Dwayne how people call in to you on the radio with questions about The War. How you ain't been stumped yet."

"Yeah," Dwayne said. "So I been doing some reading and I got a Civil War question."

"Really," Mitch said, shaking his head, starting to grin. Their infectious nonsense was easing his headache. The Leets boys.

"You ready? Here's my question," Dwayne said. "In October 1861 Hiram Berdan shot Jefferson Davis through the right eye, firing offhand at six hundred yards—true or false?"

"Bullshit, I told him nobody ever shot Jeff Davis." Darl grinned.

"And," Dwayne said, making a flourish with his hand, "Ole Abe Lincoln was watching."

"True, sorta, figuratively speaking," Mitch said, chewing the inside of his cheek, mulling it.

"Give you a hint, it was in the nature of a contest," Dwayne said.

Mitch cleared his throat. "Okay, what happened was Lincoln and McClellan were touring army camps in Virginia and had dropped in on Berdan's Sharpshooters to see a demonstration . . . fact was, the War Department was resisting Berdan's request for the pricey Sharps breechloader . . ."

"Yankee piece-of-shit rifle," Darl offered.

Mitch continued. "The assistant secretary of war, Thomas Scott, was along and Scott dared Berdan to take a shot. So they set up a man-sized silhouette with JEFF DAVIS painted on it. Scott instructed Berdan to shoot offhand at the right eye." Mitch shrugged. "He made the shot. Lincoln got such a kick out of it he assured Berdan he would get his breechloaders."

"Damn, thought he had you," Darl said.

Mitch fingered a cigarette out of his chest pocket, popped a Bic, lit up, and blew a stream of smoke. "Fact is, you got your facts a little skewed . . ."

"Skewed?" Dwayne rolled the word, like he didn't hear it every day.

"Yeah," Mitch said, loosening his shoulders. "Most sources put the range at six hundred feet, so two hundred yards."

"Just so happens," Dwayne said, looking at Darl, "it's two hundred yards back to the truck. Darl bet me twenty bucks you could make a similar shot."

Darl pointed to the target. "Left eye, sorry. And ah," Darl nodded down the fenced pasture, "try not to hit the cows."

Laughing, they strolled back toward the truck.

"You nervous?" Dwayne asked.

"Nope," Mitch said.

"Got a lot riding on this shot, huh?" Dwayne needled.

"Ain't gonna work, Dwayne; you trying to fuck with me."

"Okay then, let's see if you're really Tommy Lee's boy," Dwayne said.

"Comin' right up," Mitch said.

Darl opened the diamond plate locker in the bed of his truck and removed the rifle case along with the duffel that contained Mitch's shooting paraphernalia. Mitch opened the case, withdrew the Enfield, and carefully set it on the soft, corrugated rubber interior of the case. Then he zipped open his satchel and set up the tripod for the spotting scope. Several slender pieces of cardboard were attached by threads to the tripod legs along with a few lengths of light yarn.

A faint eddy of breeze kicked up. Mitch immediately checked the tripod, to see the wind's effect on the dangles.

Then, from the corner of his eye, he noticed Marcy walk around the house and approach halfway to the truck. Her curiosity had apparently got the better of her high-and-mighty snit. But he wasn't watching the sway of her hips or the flash of her shins. He observed the way the thin material of her dress hung limp, moved only by the motion of her legs.

No-wind day. Dead still. But the air was a long rain shadow; lots of moisture.

Marcy called out, irritated, "This is bullshit what you're up to. No-brain redneck bullshit, Darl; I'm telling you."

"For Chrissake, Marcy. Don't be like that. Dwayne's here," Darl protested.

Dwayne laughed, "Get-r-done, Darl, bring that woman to heel."

Marcy gave Dwayne her best Medusa glare, extended a pointed finger, like a curse, and declared, "I'm serious, god-damn it; I ain't having this."

"Then get your holier-than-thou little ass back behind the house and let the men be," Dwayne shouted back, less than amused. When Marcy spun on her heel and stomped out of sight, Dwayne gave Darl a reproving sidelong glance. "What the fuck, Darl?"

Darl gritted his teeth and suffered Dwayne's disapproval with a pained expression.

Mitch kept his eyes lowered and ignored Marcy's attempt to hex him. He took a tack cloth from his satchel, wiped down the barrel and the wooden stock. It was one of Hiram's fa-vorite rifles. Mitch had quietly borrowed it from the spacious gun cabinet at Kirby Creek.

Shooting was a bonding hobby he'd shared with the old man. On a no-wind day, from a bench rest, he could reli-ably shoot the Enfield into a three-inch bull at two hundred yards.

Then he removed from the satchel a tray containing wrapped paper cartridges; old Hiram's private stock. He'd measured out the powder and made the rounds in a custom bullet mold, then ran it through a sizing die to achieve the absolute correct diameter.

As he puttered with a cartridge, he thought out loud. "El-lie's hired LaSalle Ector to stay out at the Kirby House."

Darl shrugged. "I heard LaSalle came back from Iraq so fucked up they didn't give him his job back driving the am-bulance. Maybe all that big jig is good for anymore is empty-ing bedpans . . ."

"That ain't it. She's got a soft spot for LaSalle because of Robert. The old man'll never leave the hospital. She's getting ready to pull the plug. Sign one of those do-not-resuscitate orders," Mitch said.

"Woman is depressed. Her brother got killed in Iraq, her dad is stuck full of tubes . . ."

Mitch thought about it and shook his head. "She don't get depressed, she broods and then she gets mad."

"C'mon, she's depressed," Darl said. "No offense to Aunt Pearl, but all Miss Kirby's sorority sisters from Ole Miss are gossiping behind her back, saying 'I told you so,' marrying some state-line redneck out of a roadhouse whore in Selmer, Tennessee . . . Poor woman's probably standing in the bathroom right now staring at the pills in the cabinet."

"I doubt it," Mitch said. Then, abruptly, he emptied his mind and stared at the target. "So what are we doing here?"

"You're going to shoot at two hundred, right?" Darl asked, gnawing his lip.

"Yep," Mitch said.

"Okay then. Cold shot, supported," Darl said, "you can snap in over the hood of the truck." He closed the gun case and plopped down several sandbags on the hood.

"Okay," Mitch said. More serious now, he looked downrange at the target, leaned back to his rifle. Then, all business, he bit the end off the cartridge, poured powder and ball down the muzzle, then tucked in the paper. Ramrod in, then out, and returned to the pipe along the barrel.

He bent over the rifle, chest and elbows on the warm hood of the truck, adjusting the sandbags on the case. Then he slipped on a percussion cap, clicked back the hammer, flipped up his elevation crossbar, got his eye relief, and got tled the sights on the almost invisible dot.

He took a deep breath, let it out, steadied over the warm hood, and rested the rifle barrel on a sandbag, snugged the stock along his cheek, raised the sights imperceptibly, found the magic moment, and squeezed the trigger.

With a loud, familiar bang, the rifle heaved against his shoulder. As the cloud of sulfurous smoke dissipated, he counted under his breath, one thousand . . . and heard the whack of cast lead tearing wood as the low-velocity round smacked home.

"Aw right," Darl crowed, looking up from the spotting

scope. "You owe me twenty bucks, 'cause Mitch just blew a wad of splinters through 'Abe Lincoln's' friggin eye."

So much for auditions.

Mitch set the rifle on the hood of the truck, looked back over his shoulder, and saw Marcy watching from the side of the house. She shook her head and turned away.

"Hold out your hands," Dwayne said.

Mitch did.

Dwayne took Mitch's outstretched hands in his own, gently pressed his fingers into the hollow of Mitch's wrist, then released them, and said, "Not bad. You were under some pressure and made your shot. Your hands are dry and your pulse's practically normal. What about tomorrow? Think you'll be sweating and your heart banging?"

Mitch said, "You really believed that you wouldn't be here talking."

"Pretty sure of yourself, ain'tcha." The way Dwayne said it, it didn't come out like a question. "Okay." He glanced at the rifle lying on the case across the hood of the truck. "So a fuckin' Civil War rifle."

"Yep," Mitch said. "That's the original wood, the original lock and action. Go on, touch the barrel and feel the dead Yankees. Hiram sent it up to Bobby Hoyt in Pennsylvania and he retooled the barrel. No one does it better."

"I thought the Whitworth was the big sniper gun for our side," Dwayne pondered.

Darl shook his head. "Whitworth fires a distinctive six-sided bolt."

"Plus," Mitch added, "in addition to being rare as hell, they kick like a mule. They used to be able to identify a Whitworth shooter by his black eye from the scope clocking back and busting him in the face. Enfield shoots as good as a Whitworth out to five hundred yards."

Mitch looked downrange at the rectangle of plywood, turned back to Dwayne. "Tomorrow they'll be more'n four hundred cheap-ass repros of this rifle on the field pointed at the Yankees. All of 'em capable of firing the same kind of round. The cops are gonna go nuts trying to secure four hundred rifles."

Then they talked Dwayne through how'd they get in and out, Darl working the blue side to spot Beeman, talking Mitch in on him with the stolen cell that he'd ditch later.

"You put a contract on Kenny Beeman for laming Donny—well, tomorrow you're gonna watch it come due," Mitch said.

"Like an accident. No money changing hands. Keep it in the family. You do me a favor and I reciprocate. And you want that done when?" Dwayne asked.

"Right after the old man dies," Mitch said.

"What if she quits running the roads after her daddy passes?"

"She won't, she'll run more," Mitch said. "And then you and me will sit down, have a beer, and look over a plat map of the Kirby Estate."

"Okay, Cousin, we got a deal," Dwayne said. "You deliver on your part and I'll give it to Jimmy Beal. Too bad we ain't got Donny. He always liked to drive fast." Dwayne paused, and for the first time Mitch observed the young cat-killer gleam in his eyes. "Thing with Donny, he had a vicious damn streak I never could break. Fuckin' kid. Just as well he ain't here to run her down. Wouldn't put it past him to drag his dick in some roadkill pussy."

11 **THEY'D TURNED HARD RIGHT AT MADI-**
son and entered a long, dark tunnel of rainy
freeways that coursed down the length of Illinois. At dawn, they rolled down the windows to the shock
of soft spring air. Whooping, they crossed the Mississippi
near Cairo and entered THE SOUTH.

"'I do not know what lies before me,'" Manning dra-
matically intoned, mimicking Martin Sheen playing Robert
E. Lee in the movie *Gettysburg*, "'it could be the ENTIRE
FEDERAL ARMY . . .'"

Then, briefly, they discussed some pages Manning had
downloaded about Mississippi cypress swamps. "Okay, we
got poisonous water moccasins and copperheads native to
the swamp we have to march through. Plus there's bears and
Florida panthers, whatever they are."

"And Rebs," added Dalton.

They rode I-57 down a corner of Missouri that skirted the
river, and then merged with I-55. After Arkansas streaked
by in the rain, the open road plunged into a maze of interchanges and bridges when they turned east, crossed the big
river again, and sped into storm-blurred Memphis. Intent on
navigation, Paul studied the road map.

"Get this," he said, "Minnesota and Mississippi are front
to back in the atlas."

They found the exit sign for Mississippi State 72, veered
south and east, left Tennessee, and emerged into a foggy rural landscape. Mississippi. Warm and wet and green.

An hour later they arrived at the Corinth city limits and turned off the highway to search for the historic downtown. Dalton pushed the 4Runner between old brick warehouses and hit the brakes. Wow—check it out, right there—a Rebel battle flag rippling in the rain, lashed to the wheel of a cannon chained on a lowboy behind a pickup.

"That's a Napoleon, Paul," Dalton said. "A twelve-pounder gun Howitzer, model 1857. Smoothbore bronze tube. Range two thousand yards . . ."

"Not exactly your shotgun in the old gun rack," Manning quipped.

They stopped briefly to see the famous railroad crossing the Battle of Shiloh had been fought to defend, and to eat a rushed takeout lunch. Then the rain moderated and, squinting in the drizzle, they headed north out of Corinth. Following their event map, they drove into the Tennessee border country, where, finally, they found the Union encampment.

They parked next to vehicles with license plates from Illinois and Ohio in a field where men wandered in various stages of uniform dress. In the distance, a wall of dense hardwood forest was freckled with green buds.

"Christ," Paul said, grinning, "it looks like a cross between Woodstock and a powwow for middle-aged white guys."

Quickly, they changed into their uniforms.

"Lose the corps badge," Manning told Paul, "we'll be playing an Ohio regiment. Western war."

Paul removed the silver First Minnesota cloverleaf Second Corps badge from his coat, then took off his glasses and tucked them into the glove compartment. Gingerly, he fitted the tiny nineteenth-century wire frames to his face; his peripheral vision fell away as he squinted experimentally through the narrow lenses. The road leading into the parking area was obscure in drizzle, already a memory. So this was it. The moment he'd been waiting for. Good-bye, twenty-first century.

And he couldn't help wondering: Had I lived a hundred forty years ago, would I have been a different man?

After buckling on their leathers, they hoisted full packs, shouldered their rifles, and slogged toward a broad tent pitched at the edge of the trees. Several banquet tables set up on a plank floor were manned by vendors in period dress, who displayed clothing and accoutrements: Daley, Fall Creek, and the local sutler, C & D Jarnagin.

Paul sat at a picnic table and filled out a liability waiver, grinning when he read BLACK POWDER IS DANGEROUS in bold print, and then they lined up at the table marked with a registration sign, where Paul signed in on an old-fashioned ledger. The man behind the desk checked Paul's registration, thumbed through a file, and then handed him a folded three-by-four-inch manila card sealed along the bottom edge. The front of the card was addressed with antique black script.

Paul read aloud: "Pvt. Amos T. Mauldon, Co. C, 7th Ohio Vols." He paused, then asked, "What's this?"

"Fate card," the registrar drawled. "They'll let you know when to open it. On the inside it tells you what happened to the soldier you're portraying in the actual battle."

Paul stared at the suddenly portentous card; then he turned to Manning. "You mean . . . ?"

"Neat, huh," Manning grinned. "You could be walking worm-food. But you gotta march five miles through snake-infested swamps to find out."

Paul balanced the card in his open palm, struck by the notion of carrying a man's life in the hollow of his hand. Manning tugged on his sleeve. "C'mon, we gotta find our company," Manning said.

Paul inserted the card into his jacket's inner pocket and they were directed to a muddy trail. Trudging in search of C Company, they hadn't traveled far down the trail when the drizzle stopped and the moisture in the air plumped to billowing mist.

Paul struggled for footing, fighting his bayonet hilt that

tangled with the tin cup dangling on the strap of his haver-sack; his cartridge box caught on the stock of his ten-pound rifle and the mire threatened to slop over the uppers of his leather shoes.

"It'll get easier, don't worry." Davey Manning slapped him on the back. "You're doing just fine."

The slick black trees and brush closed in, walling off the parking area and, up ahead, Paul smelled fitful wood smoke mingled with a fruity drift of pipe tobacco. Then the trail widened and he saw forty or so men in blue uniforms lounging and squatting to either side, taking shelter under the trees.

He stopped and his heart speeded up.

So here it began; his first step through the looking glass into a Matthew Brady tintype. He found himself among Union soldiers hunkered down, sipping coffee from big tin cups. With startled fascination he stared at the gaunt, whis-kered men mangy with the rain, strapped in leather, and everywhere the hard glint of period-accurate metal. Here and there an overweight guy, but mostly they were lean and weathered. Damn, he marveled. *Damn.* Like that time in the Superior National Forest, when he had his first look at a wolf in the wild.

He blinked and noted a tall, triangular white-canvas Sibley tent erected next to the smoldering cook fire. A wet gleam of interlocked silver bayonets crowned a row of pre-cisely stacked rifles.

They spied a hand-lettered sign marked *C Co* jammed in the mud, and headed for it. A red-bearded soldier wearing a diamond and chevrons on his sleeve waved to them from under a gum blanket strung between two trees. The sergeant maneuvered a wad of chewing tobacco in his cheek, spit a stream of brown juice, and greeted them. "Fresh fish. Where ya from?"

"First Minnesota," Dalton said. They gave their names and the sergeant checked a roster.

"Thought we'd be late," Dalton said.

"All you missed was the rain," the sergeant said. "Besides, we're on Reb time. Everything is bass-ackwards. Kirby Creek happened a week *after* Shiloh and here we are more'n a week before. They're dedicating a memorial on the actual date, so they scheduled the battle early. You sticking around for Shiloh?"

"Nah, we gotta get back," Dalton said. "So, you seen the other side?"

"There's a Tennessee Regiment and, ah, some snappy guys from the Stonewall Brigade. A regiment from Alabama. Saw the Fifty-first Tennessee yesterday. Their drill looked . . . okay. There's a pretty sharp Tennessee cavalry unit—this is Bedford Forrest country, you know. And lesse, there's an artillery battery." He jerked his thumb off toward the right. "Over thataway, there's about a hundred fifty galvanized locals, wearing blue. So we'll have maybe three hundred infantry if all our guys show up, half a dozen cavalry, and two cannons. A hundred sixty-six of us Yankees signed up, so far a hundred thirty-some have registered on site. The Rebs'll have over four hundred infantry, maybe twenty horses, and a four cannons. You seen the field yet?"

Dalton shook his head and, as the sergeant talked, Paul's hand floated to his breast and fingered the stiff shape of the card under the damp wool. He was tempted to take a peek.

"It's pretty cool," the sergeant said. "When we cross into Mississippi and hit the swamp, we'll be on private land that's been in the same family since the actual war. They keep it absolutely untouched. There's this restored house on a hill overlooking the field that still has all the original minié ball scars in the walls." The sergeant smiled and looked directly at Paul. "This is as close to 1862 as you can get without a time machine."

Paul dropped his hand from his chest and let it fall to his side.

Then Dalton asked, "What's the support situation like?"

"They're modeling on Rich Mountain last year; same caliber of troops and support." The sergeant shrugged. "They'll have water points in the woods, Tennessee highway patrol troopers are mounted in blue to provide our side with cavalry. Officers all have cell phones. Anything happens, they call 911. There's EMTs in the ranks, an ambulance on standby at a command post, and four-wheelers positioned in the woods. Plus a couple local cops blended through the ranks on both sides. They'll have police radios and first-aid kits."

Then the sergeant looked back to his roster. "Okay. I have Edin here in Company C." He squinted at his paperwork, then looked up at Dalton and Manning. "Got a note that says you two been in contact with Colonel Burns, the battalion commander?"

Dalton nodded. "Burns and I have been on e-mail. He suggested we bring spare uniforms with chevrons and stripes just in case. We left them in the car."

"Probably have to put them on. We got some no-show NCOs. We can use some more veteran sergeants who know their Hardees. You guys best go talk to Burns's adjutant, Lieutenant Eichleay; he might stick you up front with Company A."

"Ah," Dalton said, "this is Edin's first event. I wanted to keep an eye on him."

The sergeant made a face. "He sure picked a doozy. Okay. When we form up for inspection I'll put him between two veterans. You two go find the adjutant, I'll settle Edin in."

Dalton and Manning assured Paul they'd be back to check on him, then they walked toward the group of men around the campfire. The sergeant got to his feet, directed Paul off the trail, and pointed to an open patch of muddy grass among the trees.

"Okay, Edin, drop your pack here. I'll get you squared away when we muster." Then the sergeant turned and walked back to his shelter half on the trail.

Paul looked around for a place to sit and spotted a mostly

dry rubberized gum blanket spread out at the base of a tree. A soldier napped, knees drawn up, leaning back against the trunk with his wide-brimmed slouch hat tipped forward over his face. A long brown-and-black feather protruded from the seam along the crown. Paul first thought to ask him for permission to sit on the blanket, then, deciding not to disturb him, he leaned his rifle against the tree, put his forage cap over the muzzle to keep the bore dry, took off his pack, and sat down on the far edge of the ground cloth.

As he mopped sweat from his face with a kerchief, he noticed how his fingers trembled. He grinned, unable to shake off a giddy, being-on-stage sensation of floating adrift in this strange costume party; part Outward Bound, part midlife crisis. Carefully, he removed his steamed spectacles, cleaned them, and put them back on.

Then he fished a brown leather-bound journal from his haversack, opened it, and stared at the empty lined page of the small notebook. Fumbling with his crude jackknife, he sharpened a brown pencil. A drop of sweat fell off his eyebrow and splashed on the page, swelling the blue ruled lines.

So here I am; it's 1862 and I'm a Union private on the eve of my first battle. Self-consciously, he worked the fate card from the pocket of his sack coat and studied the spidery penned name. *Amos Mauldon.* Was this *his* first battle?

Paul toyed briefly with the glued edge of the card. Then he placed it on the notebook, bore down with his pencil, and signed his name in clear, legible script below Mauldon's.

There.

He tucked the card away and found himself inspecting his hands. Telephone hands, keyboard hands. Pink. Private Mauldon's hands would be filthy, toughened, and calloused from farm work, then hardened further by countless hours of drill with a heavy rifle and by digging entrenchments. Would he be a cautious man? Would he have a sense of humor?

Paul took a sharp breath and peered into the fog-shrouded

trees. Without rancor he recalled the conversation with Jenny. The inevitable moment when he'd have to tell Molly he wasn't her biological father. *I wonder.* Would Mauldon be raising another man's daughter?

He shook off the personal twinge and in a sudden rush of imagination found himself trying to visualize what they'd called "seeing the elephant," being in battle for the first time. As opposed, say, to watching it acted out in segments on a TV screen between Cialis commercials?

Stephen Crane had allotted a lot of space to his untried youth's apprehension in *The Red Badge of Courage*. Paul could summon up bits of narrative from memory: *The youth perceived his time had come. He was about to be measured. For a moment he felt in the face of the great trial like a babe, and the flesh over his heart seemed very thin.*

No military tradition in Paul's family; no war stories after holiday dinners. His mother and father had both been bureaucrats; two "Minnesota Normals" burrowed lifelong in the State Highway Department. They'd stressed education and job security.

Suddenly, he recalled a tense office meeting with a prospective client. Years ago. The guy was judged ineligible for insurance because he had some run-ins with the law and had been hospitalized twice for drug dependency. The man, a Ranger veteran, had served with distinction in Somalia.

Wincing, he cast his eyes around the dank clearing. During the day he insured people and property against loss or harm. At night, his imagination embraced violent panoramas where men marched shoulder-to-shoulder into massed rifle and cannon fire. He bridged the contradiction between his bloodthirsty reading habits and his quiet work and personal life with an ironic sense of humor.

But now that he was here, with mud on his brogans, he couldn't help wondering . . . would Private Mauldon have read Lincoln's First Inaugural? Would he have been stirred by the line about the mystic chords of memory reaching back to every patriot grave? Would he have abolitionist tendencies or would he be a racist who would desert at the first mention of the Emancipation Proclamation? Was he in uniform to preserve the Union or because he'd collected a twenty-five-dollar bounty to enlist? Then Paul smiled and put the brakes on. Slow down, man. For starters, could Mauldon even read?

Get real. It's cold and wet. The woods are full of hostile Rebels. Mauldon would be concerned with staying warm, dry, fed . . . and alive. If the bullets spared him, he'd have all the other subparagraphs on his fate card to ponder: dysentery, cholera, malaria, and the plain old running shits they called the "Tennessee two-step." His main impression of Abraham Lincoln would be the certain knowledge that, he, Amos Mauldon, would be sleeping in the mud tonight and Lincoln would not.

Paul leaned back and looked up through the dripping branches that tangled skyward, black and barren of leaves, like crooked fingers.

Mauldon may have fought at Shiloh and survived, so his immediate world would have been gloomy enough. Would he suspect, this early in the war, that Lincoln would design modern America on the foundation of a million corpses?

Paul twirled the pencil in his fingers and dropped his eyes back to the empty journal page. So, what would Private Mauldon write to his wife and daughter? Slowly, carefully, Paul began to put pencil to paper. He'd barely filled the first page when he looked up and saw that the napping soldier had sat up and tilted his wide-brimmed black hat back from his face.

"Howdy," the man said, his voice coming soft and slow as if half the breath stayed vibrating in his throat and sinuses. "Where you from?"

Paul cocked his head and grinned. Sonofagun. The guy was a Southerner wearing a blue uniform. "Minnesota," he said, intrigued.

"Damn," the guy said, sitting up and stretching. "You affiliated with a unit up there?"

"Company A, First Minnesota," Paul said.

"No shit," the guy said with interest. "When'd you leave?"

"Thursday afternoon. We drove straight through. Just got in. We stopped in Corinth to see the railroad crossing and eat lunch."

"Smart move. I just had some hardtack tastes like soggy cardboard."

"I have to ask," Paul said. "You're in blue and you sound . . ."

"Like I'm from around here, huh," the guy frowned.

He looked to be just under six foot and rangy lean with slow, amused brown eyes, dark eyebrows, and a four o'clock shadow bristling on his chin and cheeks. Paul noticed that the Southerner's lazy aspect of voice and manner shook out deceptively, like the loose coils of a braided lariat.

"This your first trip Down South?" the Southerner asked.

"I was in Atlanta last year at a convention," Paul said in his defense.

"Oh bullshit, Atlanta's just a big goddamn strip mall. Could be anywhere and probably is." The guy screwed up his lips and rolled his eyes with mock drama. "What have I done, Lord, to deserve this Yankee pilgrim?"

Paul laughed out loud, delighted that his first Southerner appeared to have a sense of humor.

"What's so damn funny," the guy glowered.

Paul held up his hands. "Hey. It's just that I'm surprised, that's all."

"Hmmm. Well, we get two basic kinds of Yankee pilgrims. The first kind, being the more numerous kind, comes down here highly opinionated. They get off the main roads, hear a Mississippi accent, and the theme music from *Deliverance* starts playing in their heads. Would that be you?"

"Not me, I'm here to learn," Paul protested.

"You say? Well, maybe I'll give you the benefit of the doubt and provide you some insight into the dread secret of what's goin' on," the guy said. He leaned forward, placed his finger conspiratorially to his lips, and whispered, "Shhh." He looked around and lowered his voice. "The first thing you gotta know is, I ain't like the others."

Paul nodded, going along with the tongue-in-cheek conversation. "Ah, is that why you're wearing blue?"

The guy gazed solemn-faced for several seconds before his lean face split into a grin.

"You're putting me on, right?" Paul said.

"Yep, just fuckin' with you. But the truth is, the way people talk is the first stumbling block now ain't it. Like George Bernard Shaw said: the English and the Americans are two peoples separated by a common language. It appears we got the same kinda situation here. Since you brought it up, try an' look at it from my end. See, you sound sorta like factory work to me. Flat words being stacked up fast, know what I mean?"

"That's fair." Paul had to smile.

The guy reached between the buttons of his jacket and withdrew a tin case from an inner breast pocket. He opened the case and selected a long, crumbling cigar. "You, ah, care for one of these?"

Paul made a face. "I'll pass. You go ahead."

The Southerner placed the stogie in his mouth, took a Lucifer wooden match from the case, and popped the tip with his thumbnail. Paul smelled the flare of sulfur from the match, then the stink of burning tobacco. After several puffs the guy removed the cigar and studied it. "Your second smart move, this cigar tastes like month-old camel shit."

"So, ah, what are you . . . ?" Paul fumbled.

"Doing out here in Bumfuck, Egypt, gettin' rained on, huh?" The Southerner grinned.

Paul nodded. "Yeah? We were told there's locals wearing blue to round out the numbers."

"Nah," the Southerner waved his cigar. "My reenactor days are pretty much over. I was heavy into it when it peaked, oh, mor'n ten years ago. You see *Gettysburg*?"

"The movie? Sure."

"I was in it. Pickett's Charge. I was a November."

"Huh?"

The Southerner took another puff on the cigar. "The way they set it up they had phase lines. Like, we're going across the field, say five thousand of us shoulder-to-shoulder in line of battle. You hit a phase line and they call over the PA, 'everybody born in January take a hit.' So guys knew when to fall and play dead. I was a November so I made it almost all the way to the stone wall."

The stark rattle of drumsticks interrupted their conversation. Paul saw a picture-perfect young drummer boy standing in front of the row of stacked rifles, beating the long roll. Men were rising, slinging coffee from tin cups, stowing the cups, pulling on their leathers.

Manning and Dalton came trotting from the assembling mass of blue. "Paul," Dalton said, "we've been detailed to the lead company. We're going to deploy as skirmishers in front of the battalion tomorrow . . ." Paul blinked at the urgent chop of Dalton's words. Things were starting to speed up. ". . . So we have to bed down with Company A. Remind that sergeant you're new, so he'll put you between some old hands."

"No sweat," the Southerner said, standing up, wiping wet leaves from his trousers. "We got us a little dialogue going," he said with a slow smile. "And I need a spot in line. So I'll fall in with him. Show him the ropes. We're about the same height. Should work out."

Dalton and Manning paused briefly to peer at the stranger.

The Southerner grinned, extended his hand. "Name's Beeman. Deputy Kenny Beeman, Alcorn County Sheriff's Department." He reached in his haversack and discreetly produced the top of a police radio. "Y'all are playing; I'm working security. I asked for blue to do the swamp," Beeman winked, "and stack up pooped-out Yankees."

"Paul. Paul Edin," Paul said. Beeman snuck the radio back in his sack and they shook hands. More formally, Dalton and Manning introduced themselves.

"Fall in for inspection, full marching order," bellowed a sergeant near the campfire.

"It's just a formation to count noses, inspection, maybe some drill," Manning said. He hoisted his rifle to shoulder arms and wished Paul good luck, then he and Dalton trotted back toward the other end of the clearing.

Then it was all happening too fast. Men were shouting, some eyed the grumbling overcast and unrolled the heavy wool greatcoats from the top of their packs and pulled them on. A gust of damp wind blew a cloud of acrid cook-fire smoke in Paul's face. Coughing, he reached for his overcoat. Beeman stayed his hand. "Best wait on that. Need it tonight though."

As the three companies started to form to the long roll of the drum, Paul experienced a mixed rush of acute awareness and extreme awkwardness. Dry-mouthed, clumsy, and sweating, he hoisted his pack and then struggled with the hook that secured the right shoulder strap. Beeman deftly fastened the clip, then handed Paul his rifle and took his own.

Standing face-to-face, their rifles resting side by side with the butt plates on the ground, Paul observed slyly, "Mine's longer."

"Don't go gettin' familiar, we just been introduced," Beeman said. "But since you brought it up. This here's a three-band Enfield; English manufacture, far superior to that Yankee piece-of-shit Springfield."

Paul grinned, excited and nervous and grateful for Beeman's company, for the odd musical way he used the language, like he grew up reciting the lyrics to an epic song.

"Now, let's see," Beeman said, fussing with Paul's gear. He rearranged the strap on his cartridge box, moving it back on his right hip. Like a parent dressing a child for the first day of school, he slid the bayonet scabbard to the left, straightened out Paul's collar, and pulled the visor of his cap lower over his eyes. Then he stepped back and evaluated. "You look reasonable, I guess, for a mindless fuckin' Northern robot. You know who your sergeant is?" Beeman asked.

Paul gestured with the heavy rifle. "The guy there, with the red beard and the lump of chewing tobacco in his cheek."

Beeman took a last brave puff on his ghastly cigar, made a face, dropped it, and ground it under his heel. "Well, c'mon. You're in the Yankee army now, Private Edin."

No, Paul thought, briefly touching his wool-and-leather-covered chest, where the fate card nestled in his sack coat pocket. Private Mauldon, actually.

BEEMAN QUIETLY TOOK THE FIRST SERGEANT ASIDE, produced a badge, and they held a brief conference. Then he joined Paul as the company arranged itself; taller men in the rear rank, shorter in the front. When the pushing and shoving ended, Beeman stood his ground in the jostling and made sure Paul was on his immediate left in the front rank. The sergeant consulted a small leather notebook and barked out roll call. Paul yelled "here" when his name—Edin, not Mauldon—was called. They counted off and Paul was a two. After a cursory inspection in ranks, Red Beard addressed Company C. "Build up the fires and wear your greatcoats tonight. There was frost on the grass this morning. And get some food and some sleep. We won't post pickets tonight because registration doesn't officially close till midnight. Reveille will be at four a.m." Then the company was dismissed.

Beeman selected a campsite in the lee of a limestone outcropping a little ways from the Ohio men who composed the bulk of the company. He motioned to Paul to follow him over to the horses tethered on a rope line along the trees. Paul stood aside as Beeman and the blue-dressed Tennessee troopers recounted war stories from their deployment during Katrina.

". . . Still can't believe those lame-ass Chicago cops coming into New Orleans and sayin', 'We've come to take back your city.' . . ."

"But those deputies from Maricopa County, Arizona, man, they was some fierce boys . . ."

Then Beeman bummed some hay, which they carried back to their campsite and spread on the wet ground. Paul learned how to poncho-camp, laying his rubberized gum blanket on the bed of hay, spreading their blankets, and covering them with Beeman's poncho. Paul followed Beeman's example, folding his rifle under a flap of the poncho to protect it from the weather.

As Beeman started arranging stones in a fire circle, he sent Paul into the damp thickets to collect deadfall. Returning with a drag load of kindling, Paul discovered Beeman still struggling with a mound of smoldering twigs. Paul retrieved his haversack and removed a stash of lint he'd squirreled away from the clothes dryer at home for just such a contingency. Moving Beeman aside, he used the tinder to jump-start a fire and broke off small branches to feed it. He stacked wood around the struggling flame to dry out.

"Canoe camping in the Boundary Waters; tends to get wet up on the Canadian border," Paul explained.

Beeman grunted as he warmed his hands over the building flames and grudgingly admitted that "One thing Yankees are good at is starting fires."

Paul peered into the chilly twilight, tapped his teeth together. "Don't look like my pards are coming back. And they have the food. All I have is jerky and hardtack in my haver."

"No biggie, I always bring a little extra." Beeman shrugged

as he produced a blackened skillet from his pack along with potatoes, onions, a slab of salt pork, and several evil-looking peppers. He pulled an antique jackknife from his pocket, opened it, and sliced the bacon. When it was sizzling over the fire, he carved up the vegetables and tossed them in. As the meal cooked, he showed Paul how to fold coffee beans in a bandanna, put them on a rock, and grind them with his rifle butt plate.

A cold drizzle filtered down and sharpened a nip in the twilight. Huddled now in his greatcoat, Paul licked his fingers, grateful for the kind of greasy meal he'd never eat at home. Then they set their tin cups in the embers of the fire to heat water. When it boiled, they added spoonfuls of the crushed beans, some brown sugar, and brewed camp coffee.

"Usually don't drink this stuff at night," Paul said, straining the coffee grounds through his teeth.

"This ain't a usual night," Beeman said.

After they finished their coffee, they buttoned their greatcoats, crawled under their blankets, and draped the other rubber ground cloth on top. With their packs for pillows, they peered up into the cloud cover that ebbed and glowed with distant lightning. Beeman said, "Suppose to quit raining tomorrow morning. They say." Then he propped on one elbow and asked, "So what's your wife think of you comin' down here and playing soldier?"

Paul chuckled. "Jenny's a teacher. In Minnesota they have a zero tolerance for violence in the fifth grade. She makes me keep my musket in the garage. What about yours?"

"Hell, we did the reenactor thing as a family. Margie had the bonnet and hoop skirt, made outfits for the kids . . ."

Curled next to their campfire, they compared background notes: kids' names, their jobs, activities. Paul learned that Beeman had served in the Gulf War after college, had returned home, and wound up in law enforcement.

Then they agreed that, with a four a.m. wake-up, they should get some sleep. Carefully, Paul removed his flimsy spectacles, folded them into their antique case, and tucked them in the inner pocket of his sack coat. After a moment's hesitation, he withdrew the fate card.

"You get one of these?" he asked.

"Nah. No fate card for the hired help. Nice touch, though. Means the organizers went the extra mile. You gonna open it? Most guys have," Beeman said.

"I'll wait," Paul said, experiencing a stab of thrill as he tucked the card back into his breast pocket. Then he peered nearsighted into the murky woods, making out a blur of fires and the shapes of men hunched to the warmth. Inhaling, he smelled a chilly broth of wet wool, tobacco, damp hay, and wood smoke. Then he shoved up on his elbows and strained his ears into the night. Was that the wind playing tricks? Or was it music?

"You hear that?" Paul asked.

"Yep. Confederate psychological warfare. They sent their band forward to tramp around in the woods and serenade us. Their main body ain't gotta hike six, seven miles tomorrow."

"I thought it was five?" Paul said.

"Yankee disinformation," Beeman retorted. "You think you're gonna walk a straight line through a fuckin' swamp?"

"So is the band in the swamp?" Paul asked.

"Hell no. They're probably sitting in a pickup truck," Beeman said. "Suckin' down Rebel Yell and harassing us, trying to keep us up all night."

Paul snuggled back down under his blanket and edged closer to Beeman for warmth. He imagined Jenny and Molly, finishing supper, doing the dishes. And here he was, curled next to a stranger in a strange dark land.

Paul found himself listening to a discussion at the nearest campfire, where two men were having a heated exchange about the lax dress code in the three companies; some men were in period-specific dark blue shell jackets, pants, and

Hardee hats. Most of the others, like Paul, wore the common uniform: four-button sacks, sky blue trousers, and forage caps.

When the conversation persisted and rose in volume, Beeman threw off his blanket, sat up, and barked a gruff drawl in the direction of the fireside debate: "Gay bars and *authentic* reenactors—gotta be the only time men dress up for other men. I swear, some of you guys are fussy as stamp collectors who wear the fuckin' stamps . . ."

The talk at the campfire sputtered out abruptly, followed by a chorus of snickers that tittered off into silence. Then, faintly at first, coming in on a fold of mist, Paul heard the music building into an eerie, almost medieval mix of fifes and drums and banjos getting louder, getting closer.

Playing "Dixie."

12 OKAY. IT WAS ON SCHEDULE. HE'D sealed his pact with Dwayne. He'd cleaned his rifle and then left it with Darl. Marcy had driven separately and had stormed off, so he didn't have to deal with any more of her goddamn naysaying.

Dumb bitch, better watch herself. Not the time to flirt with incurring Dwayne's wrath.

"Or mine," Mitch muttered as he drove west on 72 through squalls of rain.

He arrived in West Memphis and checked into a Holiday Inn next to Highway 55. Over a late lunch at the Peabody Hotel he received a cashier's check for $33,000 from a representative of Heritage Group of Nashville, the final contribution for the monument. He returned to the motel and tucked the check in the side pouch of his travel bag. Then he called and confirmed his Saturday supper date with the manager of the Memphis stone company that was finishing up work on the dedication plaque. After a hot shower he went outside to have a smoke and watched the trucks roar past on 55. He counted fifty-two trucks go by in less than a minute: going by as fast as his thoughts.

He went back inside, ordered *War of the Worlds* from the TV menu, and lay on the bed, watching the alien tripods squash and zap mankind until germs saved the world. Then he ate supper in the Perkins that adjoined the motel and paid with a credit card so there'd be a record. Back in his room, he set the alarm for 3:30 a.m. and fell into a dreamless sleep.

At five thirty in the morning, Mitch was nursing his Ford at five miles an hour inside a bale of cotton. With his low beams blunted, he crept down a soggy, narrow fire trail at the edge of the Kirby property. Then his headlights lit up Darl standing next to his truck. Mitch backed off the trail, got out, and they shared a fast cup of thermos coffee.

"I talked to Billie Watts Thursday night. Had to calm him down. He's got a tendency to get nervous," Mitch said.

"Don't worry about Billie," Darl said. "I'll shut off his coke retainer he gets too antsy. That don't work we'll put Dwayne in his life . . ."

"That'd do it," Mitch agreed.

"I been thinking about what you said, how LaSalle Ector's out at the Kirby House," Darl said. "People might could talk about that."

"Talk how?" Mitch remembered the guy; quiet, clean-cut, big, and scary serious. Ector was an Easom High School success story after a rough start in the Combs Court projects.

"You know," Darl said offhand, "how Robert Kirby got himself killed in that ambush saving a nigger's life. And nobody remembers Robert dating anybody. You think him and old LaSalle had a knocking-boots kind of thing?"

Mitch thought about it. Was Robert Kirby gay? It was a tired gossip theme. Mitch, who remembered his former boss as a sickly, brittle, socially maladroit prick, didn't think so. Didn't matter now. Whatever. But LaSalle didn't feel right, him showing up now.

Then it was time to get down to business. Darl removed the gear and rifle from his truck and Mitch stripped off his street clothes and changed into a beat-up Confederate wool uniform and worn brogans. He stowed his clothes in the Ford, set his cell phone on vibrate, slipped it in his pocket and buckled on the gear. Then he hefted the Enfield. Expecting rain, after cleaning the rifle at the farm, he'd tucked it in a black rubber-covered canvas case.

"How do I look?" Mitch asked as Darl looped a folded gum blanket over his belt in the back.

Darl gave him thumbs-up. "Anybody sees you from a distance, you'll blend right in. This is it, huh?" He looked around. "Christ, hope this fog clears out. Can't see shit. You gonna be able to find your way?"

"I grew up working in these woods; I know every trail." Mitch nodded vaguely, getting past small talk now, starting to concentrate. "But it'll be slow going. Give me close to noon to get in place. Then call to make sure the phones work." Suddenly, he patted his chest. "Shit, forgot my smokes."

Darl handed him his pack of Pall Malls. Mitch stuffed them in the haversack. It was time. Mitch and Darl embraced awkwardly.

"You going to be all right?" Mitch asked, peering at his cousin's shadowed face.

"Sure. Gotta be. Get'r done," Darl said gamely.

Mitch nodded, then picked up a branch and wedged it in the fork of a tree just off the trail. "On my way out I'll ditch the rifle and clothes behind this tree. When things quiet down you'll collect them, right?"

"Like we said," Darl bobbed his head.

Mitch wished he could see Darl's eyes but he couldn't and it was time to go. He shrugged, turned, padded down the muddy trail, and disappeared into the tangle of trees. In a few minutes he was raising a sweat, breathing harder.

Damn, this was turning into *work*. He was already sweltering in the wool uniform and his feet started to swell in the cramped shoes. And every step took him closer to killing his first man. *Thou Shalt Not* . . . Mitch shook it off. Dwayne and his psycho little brother, Donnie, talked casually about putting people down. Darl had killed more than once. Even Marcy, if you believed the stories.

He'd asked her about it once, and she'd appraised him and said slowly, "There's people with violent fantasies and people with violent memories and it ain't smart to have those two meet up in a violent altercation."

Bible Belt–raised, Mitch was lip-service religious. Social.

Not a believer. But the visceral Southern Baptist scale of weights and measures—sin, salvation, redemption or hellfire punishment—were hardwired in his DNA and could not entirely be ignored. His vices were vanity and women . . .

His forehead started to throb. Damn you, Marcy, putting a hex on me. All I wanted was a piece of ass down at the crossroads to kick things off . . .

His sin was ambition.

He knew his Bible and employed understated snippets on the radio show. The Sunday-school words from St. Luke still burned in his memory.

And the devil, taking him up into a high mountain, showed unto him all the kingdoms of the world in a moment of time.

And the devil said unto him, All this power will I give thee . . . if thou therefore wilt worship me, all shall be thine . . .

People would tolerate his vices.

But would they tolerate his sin?

Still, deeper and thicker than Jesus, or the bluesman's voodoo, was the local priority of blood kin. There were some who'd say the shot that killed Beeman had been loaded in a feud before either of them had been born and had been hanging fire all Mitch's life.

"State-line rules," Billie Watts had quipped.

Billie. Bright and flawed and talking loose with his nose full of Darl's cocaine—Billie saying, "Shit, man, if you dropped Beeman in broad daylight on Waldron in front of the courthouse, chances are fifty-fifty a grand jury with enough old-timers from West Alcorn would return a 'no' bill."

But it wasn't really about Beeman. Not really. Beeman was just one of those moving parts Marcy had mentioned.

Walking easier now, warming to the work, he silently threaded in on the muddy trails. He wasn't kidding Darl; he did know the trails by heart. And they never changed, because the old man wouldn't let anybody come in, even to log it off.

He pictured the long parcel of land along the Tennessee border, which held enough oak and hickory to timber a whole suburb. The Kirbys owned two thousand acres wrapped around a spring-fed lake jumping with bass.

In his father's day it was about bootleg whiskey and road-house hustles.

Now it was all about the land. Christ, look what they did with Pickwick over on the Tennessee River.

Like most of the established families who ruled Corinth, Old Man Kirby was committed to slowing down the clock, to preserving the past. While Corinth gloried in its quaint storefronts and museums, all the fuckin' jobs went to Tupelo.

Fact was, if Beeman did get elected sheriff, he would be their paid, loyal temple dog, guarding their moldering Civil War mausoleum. He'd use the sheriff's office to block Mitch at every turn.

So Beeman had to go. And then Dwayne would owe him the favor.

For one piercing moment he pictured Ellie lying asleep in bed. Getting up, driving out to the estate, worried about the cannons tearing up the flower beds . . .

Not now. Bust up your concentration.

Think positive.

When it all worked out and Mitch had his way with the land, he'd line the bulldozers up, tread to tread. And those machines would belong to the construction company he and Dwayne would put together. They'd have plenty of time, maybe two years for it all to settle down. First they'd have to weather a public outcry. The state of Mississippi would initially stay plans to break ground near or on the battlefield. Citing historical preservation protocols on the books since 1966, the state would have to satisfy its mandate that no archaeological or human remains would be disturbed.

But, in the end, it was private land. Billy Watts would be on top of that.

Mitch would detour around the battlefield, in respect to the old man's memory, and then dig up and build on everything all the way to the waterfront lots on the lake. The construction boom would bring hundreds of well-paying jobs to the county. Memphis commuters would be willing to accept the drive time to live in a tastefully designed development adjacent to a pristine battlefield. Heritage had conducted discreet surveys and had run the numbers.

Hell. In another generation you could probably plow under the battlefield proper. The Boomers and the iPod-brain X-ers moving in wouldn't give a shit. Serve 'em right for teaching history-lite in the schools. In the end it was like the man said in the movie. It ain't personal. It's strictly business.

You had to get real.

The land had been stolen and re-stolen over and over for the last three hundred years. The first white settlers had chased out the Chickasaws, who stole it from another bunch of Indians, and so on, going back to Cain knocking Abel's brains out. All he was doing was adding a modest footnote to a long ledger of crimes.

Mitch shifted the cased muzzleloader from his left to his right shoulder and mused.

Face it, man. What I am is *Progress*.

Saturday, 4 a.m.

---

13 **PAUL'S EYES JOLTED OPEN WHEN A** bugle stuttered a spitty, off-tune version of reveille. Coughs and groans all around as stiff men stirred in soggy blankets. More grumbling as they sat up and faced the icy predawn air. Paul felt beside him—no Beeman. His fingers probed whiskers of frost on the grass. Sitting up, pawing for his glasses case, he saw a shadow turn from the embers of their campfire. Beeman knelt and handed him a steaming cup.

"Careful. It's hot," Beeman said, and Paul was amazed to see his words strike faint white commas in the air. He put his glasses on and took the cup in both hands, gratefully pressing his palms to the tin warmth. As he sipped the wonderful coffee, he heard Red Beard, the sergeant, yell, "Roll call in fifteen minutes. Pack your gear and grab something to eat. Drink some water. Formation in fifteen minutes."

The warning prompted a scramble in the dark as a bright tendril of lightning illuminated the clearing. Paul blinked. An electric flicker. A hobo-camp scurry of disheveled men with pale, sleepy expressions. On all fours, stooping, they gathered up their bedding and saw to their knapsacks.

Beeman assembled his knapsack, set it aside, and then instructed Paul as he packed. Fold the overcoat inside to keep it dry. Roll the blanket inside the poncho and strap it on top of the pack. When Paul's fingers fumbled on the new stiff leather straps, Beeman moved in and cinched them tight. Paul used the last of the coffee to wash down a mouthful of dry hardtack and beef jerky from his haversack. As he chewed, his teeth crunched a residue of grit off his fingers, making him aware how *dirty* he was from a night in the rain and muddy straw.

He looked around. Christ, he'd be lost without Beeman. Where the hell were Manning and Dalton? It was impossible to see. Someone held a candle in a tin holder that cast a meager light.

All so strange and fast. At home, Jenny and Molly would still be asleep. Saturday was a leisurely wake-up, waffle-breakfast kind of day. Rattles of tin and steel brought him back to the sounds of equipment being hoisted, cinched, buckled.

"Mother*fucker*," a man nearby muttered as he dropped his musket.

"Don't think they used 'motherfucker' in 1862," another man commented dryly. "I downloaded a nineteenth-century slang dictionary off the *Camp Chase Gazette* Web site and didn't find it under M."

"Bullshit," the first man said as he retrieved his rifle, "they say it on *Deadwood* ten times a minute . . ."

Paul grinned, trying to get traction on the day as he struggled to arrange his belt and the crisscross of leather straps. Every surface he touched was slippery, gritty, and cold; steel, wood, rubber-coated canvas, leather, and tin. Shivering without his overcoat, he shouldered his pack and lifted his rifle.

Beeman made him take off the pack, pointing out, "Your canteen strap is under your pack strap; fix it the other way around." Paul straightened out the straps, re-shouldered his pack.

"C Company. Fall in," Red Beard shouted.

Paul joined the shadows stumbling on the pitch-black trail, where he was manhandled by rough veteran hands, shoved bodily into his slot as the mob rejiggered itself into two ordered lines. He wound up magically in place, with

Beeman on his right, an Ohio man on his left, and more Ohioans to the rear. He was grateful for the darkness that hid his confusion at being so swiftly sorted and mechanically aligned. His grin faded. He swallowed and registered the full weight of the pack and the corseting straps. Paul Edin had been transformed into a "two" toting a ten-pound Model 1861 Springfield .58-caliber rifled musket in the front rank of C Company.

From the wry compendium of Civil War facts at the back of his mind, he selected Lincoln's somber phrase: "Facing the arithmetic."

Men as numbers. The evolutions of Civil War drill were based on soldiers being designated ones and twos. Paul visualized a tapestry of glowing computer code, ones and twos, flowing in various combinations in the foggy, dripping Tennessee forest. For instance, at the order "right flank," the two lines would double to the right. Paul would step right and forward and tuck in on Beeman's right side and be in a file of four men abreast. At the order "front," he would un-double back and be on Beeman's left in a two-line company front again.

A two. He extended two fingers of his left hand at his side to remind himself.

There was no preview of what waited for them. Red Beard bawled the roll. Satisfied that all his men were present, he gave the order, "In each rank, count twos," to verify that the same men were ranked left and right and behind from the previous night. Then Red Beard stepped back, and a shadow with a wide-brimmed hat and a sword appeared.

"Captain Sayles," someone whispered in the rear rank.

Then the rippling orders: "Attention company, shoulder arms, in two ranks, right face." Then, "Forward march."

Paul pivoted and plunged his left brogan almost ankle-deep in the sucking mud. Just like that, the hunched shapes lurched off, the front of the file dissolving in the dark. And in the unified motion of that first step, it struck Paul that—

this is what they looked like—sounded like—the muted clatter of three shadowy companies of Civil War soldiers, accurate down to every stitch, material, and pattern. All that was missing were the actual minié balls in their cartridge boxes.

After a few minutes they veered off the muddy trail and started uphill on a drier narrow path. Men muttered and cursed as they slipped on loose rocks and slick shale that made for more treacherous footing.

"Route step, march," yelled Red Beard.

The ranks relaxed from marching cadence, the men now at liberty to step and carry the muskets however they wished. Beeman did a side step and negotiated an exchange of positions with the Ohioan on Paul's right. Now they walked side by side, file buddies.

"Most of the march will be in double file," Beeman said as he took Paul's musket, loosened the sling, and handed it back. "Sling it over your shoulder. This here part, the uphill, it's the easy part," Beeman said. "Take a drink," he finished.

Paul took a few swallows of water from his canteen and then walked in silence, shrugging his shoulders to ease the cut of the pack straps and the rifle sling. The upward grade stabbed his shins; he exhaled clouds of crystallized breath. No longer cold, now he was flushed and suffocating in a blue plaster of sweaty wool.

Over a hundred fifty men struggled up the rocky trail but Paul felt isolated, walled off in darkness. He lurched for footing, ducked the wet slap of overhanging branches. Then, slowly, the surrounding pattern of underbrush floated into focus as dawn fuzzed through the trees. With the coming of the light, Paul felt the claustrophobic isolation loosen its hold. Up and down the line men were beginning to talk.

"So why's it the easy part?" Paul panted.

"'Cause it's more or less dry. Once we get down the other side of this high ground we hit the swamp," Beeman said. They slogged past an overweight soldier who sat breathing heavily on a fallen tree trunk, wiping his dripping face with a kerchief. "Got him on my list," Beeman said, "him and another whale up ahead. Both officers. If those boys hadda carry more'n a fuckin' sword they'd be bear bait."

Half an hour later, they took a break on an intersecting trail with tire treads mashed in the leaves. Two large, circular, plastic water containers had been positioned by men in period civilian clothes. As the battalion fell out and water details collected canteens, Beeman pointed out an approaching soldier. "He's one of my trail contacts, an EMT from Illinois. Gotta have a quick conference about our whales."

As Beeman talked to the blended EMT, Paul saw Tom Dalton, moving fast back down the column; spiked black beard, sergeant-serious in chevrons and striped trousers. "How you holding up?" Dalton asked.

"Fine," Paul said. "A lot easier than I thought so far."

Dalton nodded. "We probably won't see you until tonight. They're pushing Davey and me out front. You get paired up with that secesh cop?"

Paul grinned. "He had hot java waiting when I woke up."

"Fuuaack. Marry him. We'll convert him later." Dalton was impressed. "I chewed coffee beans." The conversation was cut short by shouts of "fall in" up ahead. Dalton bared his teeth, excited, "This is great, huh? Doing a swamp in the fog. Gotta go." He cuffed Paul on the shoulder and jogged back toward the head of the column. Paul watched him disappear into the blue ranks and wondered if he'd opened his fate card.

Beeman returned and explained, "We're sending one of the whales back on the four-wheeler that brought in the water. He's got severe dehydration and an elevated pulse won't slow down." Then the company fell in, Red Beard called roll, and the march continued.

An hour later, Paul's shoes, socks, and trouser legs were soaked as he waded cautiously through murky, knee-deep water. Just before they entered the swamp, Paul and a number of other soldiers had followed Beeman's example and found sturdy branches to use as walking sticks. Now he carried his rifle on his left shoulder and probed with the stick in his right hand for footing. The muddy bottom sucked at his shoes every step. Ahead, ghostly figures waded, shifting their weight from foot to foot, dissembling into the mist. Dawn had transformed the swamp into a muddy steam room, and Paul missed the cool rain.

After this, the Civil War would be forever linked in his mind to a memory of mist, of fog, of endless vapor.

The tall trunks of cypress trees loomed in the filmy air like pillars of ancient ruins, then faded away. Dormant kudzu vine spun in the brush and hung the blurry trees with shaggy Druidic sculptures.

"Blair Witch Project South," one of the Ohio soldiers quipped.

Paul's fascination with historical accuracy now seemed a quaint, academic memory that melted away with the morning heat. His whole body cooked and ached, bisected by tight leather straps. It had all come down to a practical ordeal of making it from one step to the next. He cast an eye at the kudzu-choked dry ground they were skirting, twenty-five yards to the left. "How come we don't walk over there where it's dry?" he asked.

"Mister No-shoulders," Beeman said cryptically. "Cottonmouths are aggressive territorial little fuckers, like to curl up along the water's edge. The organizers figured it'd be safer out aways in the water. Plus, we're walking in the channel. This moving water'll come out in the creek."

"Great," Paul muttered, looking more suspiciously at the ripples in the murky brown water.

"Hey, it's what the Yankees did back when," Beeman added. "Was all flooded in here, lot worse than this. Feature the water's up to your chest, you got your rifle and cartridges held over your head and you meet up with Mister No-shoulders sorta eye to eye . . ."

"So what do I do if I see a snake?" Paul wondered.

"Give him the right of way, be my advice."

The sergeants called a halt and bellowed the roll to count noses. Up and down the line, disembodied voices answered in the mist. Then they were ordered to drink some water. Beeman excused himself and waded off to check in with the command center.

After the break, back to the mud-sucking slosh, Paul finally asked, "So why are you out here, Beeman? For the overtime?"

"Well now." Beeman shifted his rifle and walking stick from one hand to the other. "Part is I wanted to see it. All you guys doing the march. See. This is the first authentic treatment of Kirby Creek. Usually it's an afternoon picnic kind of thing up by the Kirby House. Boys burn some powder, the cavalry rides around, the artillery shoots off their stuff, and everybody fires up the grill and has a party. Lots of spectators. This is different. Might actually get a feel of what it was like."

Paul nodded. "I read a lot and went to Civil War round-tables and the thing is, it's always about the generals. Like a couple dozen big-name guys fought the whole war . . ."

"Yeah," Beeman agreed. "The Big Bugs, they called them."

Paul nodded again. "So I wanted to get an idea of what it was like for the ordinary privates."

"Finding out it was hard, ain'tcha?" Beeman grinned. "Probably harder on them. Average guy back then weighed under one fifty. Five foot seven, eight was typical. Rifles had less steel in them, so they were lighter too. But I'm impressed so far. This is a pretty well turned-out bunch of Yankees. 'Cept for my remaining whale. You can really tell. They just let in real serious folks on both sides . . ."

"The guys I'm with, Manning and Dalton, they're kind of down on regular reenactments," Paul said. After a pause, he added carefully, "They say the mainstream crowd can get a little wild. Especially this far South."

Beeman squinted at him, weighing his response. Now some of the Ohio solders front and back were paying attention to the conversation. Noting the interest, Beeman cleared his throat and said with his slow, casual smile, "Hmmm. Gotta watch what I say here, being as I'm seriously outnumbered and cut off from my kin."

An eavesdropping Ohio soldier slogging in front of Beeman turned with a sidelong grin. Several of the Ohio soldiers had slowed or speeded up to form a knot around Beeman.

Beeman surveyed his audience and said, "I *suppose* it is fair to say that the average hardcore Union reenactor here present is more of an objective historian, especially when it comes to stitch-counting and such. May I?" he asked Paul, reaching over and unsnapping Paul's cartridge box.

He withdrew a brown-paper cartridge and turned it in his fingers for inspection. The cylinder of paper was meticulously folded and seamed.

"For instance," Beeman said, "your average Confederate ain't going to put hospital corners on his cartridges." He handed the tube of paper back to Paul.

"Thing is," Beeman went on, "your Reb hardcore tends to be a bit more edgy. Might say he has some of the traits of a neighborhood gang member. Got turf issues . . ." Beeman narrowed his eyes and then let some edge insinuate into his voice. "Seeing's how, ah, this is our turf."

After a moment, one of the more rugged-looking Ohio guys executed an exaggerated pantomime of urban gang signs with his fingers. Grinning, he finished his show by thumping his chest with two fingers of one hand, then tapping his forehead with the index finger of the other.

"Double tap to the chest, one in the head," the guy said with a broad smile and a wink. "Tell you what, Dixie—in my other life I'm a copper in Cleveland. That's how we signal back the homeboys when they lay their gang shit on us."

The gesture broke the tension. Beeman rolled his eyes and they all laughed and then splashed back into file.

Paul and Beeman slogged side by side for several moments, then Paul lowered his voice and asked, "What you said back there, you serious?"

Beeman treated Paul to an inscrutable smile and said, "'Bout half."

14

PAUL LURCHED, STRAINED HIS EYES up ahead at a sudden bedlam of thrashing water and alarmed voices. Sergeants shouted. The double file splashed to a halt. Beeman slogged forward and disappeared in the cottony air. He returned a few minutes later and Paul and the Ohio men gathered around him. "A guy up front stepped into water over his head. Was touch-and-go for a minute there," Beeman explained. "The crew that scouted this line of march didn't have to deal with this fog. Way it is we could lose somebody in this soup."

"Are we lost?" an Ohioan asked.

Beeman grinned. "No mor'n your Yankee ancestors were. Okay, here's the deal. We're gonna leave the channel and bushwhack through the woods. Be slower but less chance of drowning."

"What about . . . snakes?" someone asked.

"We come here to live the history, huh?" Beeman said.

The bedraggled Ohioans grumbled their assent. "Fuckin' A," one of them said.

Red Beard appeared bearlike in the mist, recapped what Beeman had said, took out his sergeant's journal, and called the roll. Assured that he had everybody, he guided the company into the marshy shallows. Soon they were on more solid footing, tripping single-file now along the boggy shore. They tossed away their walking sticks and traded the suction of mud for a tangle of matted vegetation. Thick clumps of tall reeds concealed foot traps of mossy deadfall. The constant webs of kudzu fouled their path.

And now they had bugs flitting in their faces.

"Watch it there," Beeman muttered, pointing to a squirm of activity on the ground. "Don't be disturbing the fire ants."

Fighting through the brush and clouds of pesky gnats, Paul sensed a new seriousness driving the men. He felt it himself. Despite the bone-jarring terrain, his equipment seemed to ride easier, his step was becoming surer.

So this was Espirit. Generated in men's chests and moving down the line. Not young men either. The more he studied the flushed faces of the Ohioans, the more he saw the set jaws of men in their forties and fifties. All of them determined to gut it through the march.

Now Paul stumbled on his second revelation: the rigors of the swamp were merely a *prelude*.

In mid-thought, like an object lesson in pride going before the fall, Paul felt his hobnailed sole slip on a green, moss-greased branch, and he pitched forward. Beeman turned to put out a quick hand to catch him. Too late. Paul thrust out his musket with both hands to break his awkward plunge. His rifle came up fast and the steel lock slammed his forehead; his glasses skewed and the sharp hammer spur gashed into flesh and bone above his left eyebrow.

"Ow shit."

Stunned, tangled in brush and broken branches, Paul was pulled to a sitting position. Amazed, he felt the hot drip down the side of his face and into the corner of his mouth. His own blood. A coppery, hot meat taste, salted with sweat and dirt. He reached up and gingerly removed his sprung glasses, and saw the lenses and his fingers smeared muddy red.

"We got a man down," Beeman yelled. Voices rippled up ahead in the mist and the column halted. Red Beard came at a clumsy trot.

Beeman doused canteen water on a bandanna and cleaned the gash. "Ain't bad, Paul. Head cuts bleed a lot, all the capillaries." While a knot of men gathered, Beeman applied pressure to stop the bleeding. He took his first-aid kit from his bag, dabbed on antiseptic cream, and closed the cut with a butterfly bandage.

Paul was standing now, blinking at the numb throb of pain, testing the side of his face with his fingertips. Beeman grinned and took out a clean red bandanna. He folded it over Paul's head and knotted it in the back. "This'll work better than your cap. Looks cool too." Beeman shook four liver-colored pills from a plastic vial, dropped them in Paul's grubby hand, held up his canteen. "Ibu. Go on. Take 'em."

Paul swallowed the pills with a gulp of Beeman's water, then splashed a little on his glasses to rinse them off. He stowed his cap in his haver and carefully put the glasses back on. Then, cautiously, he tested the bulge of swelling bandage with his fingertips. His skull had elongated, like a nubbin horn jutting out, overlapping his eye. But it wasn't that painful. Not really. One of the Ohioans handed him his rifle. Several of the men grinned, admiring.

"Cool."

"Way k-ewl," one of them enunciated, stressing the k-sound.

A wound.

Red Beard asked Paul if he felt good enough to continue. Then he looked around and laughed absurdly at his own remark, as if there was a choice out here. Paul nodded, adjusted his gear, shouldered his rifle, and the column moved forward in single file.

Now Paul experienced an almost embarrassing surge of joy. In addition to being drenched in sweat, mud, and slime, he was bleeding and bandaged. A grime of blood was etched into the dirty whorls of his palms. Dots of it shone dully on the rifle hammer: terra cotta bumps drying around red rosette centers.

He framed a foreign thought that was suddenly appropriate. It was sloppy . . . unmilitary . . . going messy like this.

Quickly he removed his own kerchief from his pocket, wiped his dirty hands, and rubbed the drying blood from his rifle.

Soon it was evident that the painful swelling on his head was an ironic source of strength that magnified his energy. He'd stopped sightseeing. The exotic, mist-shrouded landscape was now merely an obstacle course to be negotiated to get to the fight waiting ahead.

He accepted the soggy mash of his socks in his mud-filled shoes and the wet drag of his trouser legs. The strict leather straps that spliced his chest now rose and fell with his breathing like a new web of muscles. He sipped from his canteen, rationing his water. He keyed on Beeman's swaying pack and shoulders and watched the placement of his own feet. His breath dug deeper; he was getting used to it. *Shit, man, I can do this all day.*

The sun rose, a pale blur in the fog, and they fought tangled brush and pools of swamp for more than three hours.

Then, up ahead, Paul heard a patter of conversation start again. After barging through a last muddy thicket, the ground firmed. They left the margin of the swamp and entered open forest. "Double file," called out Red Beard.

The single file sorted back into a double line and Beeman was back, walking beside him on a silent mattress of wet leaves. The suffocating mist was thinning.

"Hear that?" Beeman asked.

Paul strained his ears above the muted clatter of marching men and detected a fresh sound of rushing water up ahead.

"Kirby Creek," Beeman said, cuffing Paul on the shoulder. "We made it around the lake, through the swamp."

A few moments later the column halted at a water point. Canteens were collected and water details were sent to the large plastic jugs. Paul and Beeman cast off their packs and sprawled on the spongy leaf cover. They removed their sodden shoes, yanked off their wet, filthy socks and wrung them out. Up and down the line men were peeling off their wet shoes and pulling dry stockings from their packs.

An Ohio soldier passed a metal container of talc among his buddies. They shook the white powder into dry socks, unbuttoned their trousers and dusted it into their shorts. "The sacred order of the white palm," someone quipped. Another soldier produced an antique watch and muttered in an awed voice, "We spent five hours in that goddamn swamp."

The water detail returned and the canteens were distributed. Sergeants walked the line. "We'll be here for an hour and a half. Get some fires going and try'n dry out your footwear. Careful, though; don't get them too close to the flame."

Soon wood smoke mingled with the fog. Paul and Beeman brewed coffee in their tin cups, peeled open their shoes and placed them on upright sticks by the fire. One of the Ohioans came over and asked Beeman, "You know where we are?"

Beeman scraped off a layer of leaves and sketched a long kidney shape in the damp earth with a stick. "We just skirted Cross State Lake off to our left." He marked an X on the left, below the kidney. "I figure we're about here, where the creek runs out of the swamp."

"Have you been in here before?" Paul asked.

Beeman shook his head. "Old Man Kirby don't let anybody on the land. Not even to hunt." He looked up at the Ohio soldiers, who now formed a semicircle around him. "The fight started on the opposite side of the lake." Beeman drew lines of force around the bottom right side of his diagram. "The Rebs figured they'd lure the Yanks through the thick stuff onto an entrenched position, here. Have 'em hemmed in, lake on their right, the creek to their left." He marked another X south of the lake. "They dug in on the hill below the Kirby House with the swamp behind them to protect their rear."

Paul sipped his coffee, studying the circle of men intent on Beeman's scratching. The word "bonded" came to mind. Except "bonded" was Minnesota therapy-speak and it didn't fit. This was more than a bunch of adhering particles. The shared ordeal of the swamp had beaten them into a unit.

Beeman was saying, "See, they never figured on the Yankees sneaking a regiment through the swamp. That's us. We break out of these woods and hit their works end-on. Had 'em trapped, except starting that night and through the next morning it rained like hell. The Rebs were able to slip out under cover of the storm and withdraw toward Corinth."

The group disbanded back to their campfires. Beeman and Paul took off their trousers and attempted to dry them along with their shoes. Barefoot in flannel drawers, they munched hardtack and jerky next to their small fire.

"How's your noggin?" Beeman asked.

Paul lightly touched the red bandanna where dried blood had formed a stiff patch over the swelling. "I'll survive," Paul said.

Beeman smiled. "You know, with that do-rag on your head—you was a little shorter you'd look like Audie Murphy in the old *Red Badge of Courage*."

Paul almost blushed. He'd been toying with the exact self-dramatic connection. "You know the battle pretty good," he said, changing the subject.

"Wasn't a battle. What you call an engagement. But yeah. I heard about it all my life." Beeman propped up on an elbow, tossed a few sticks on the fire. "See, my great-great-granddaddy, Matthew Beeman, was from Brandon, Mississippi, down in Rankin County. They had this militia company, the Rankin Guards. When the war come along, they were reorganized into the Rankin Greys as part of the Sixth Mississippi . . ."

His voice trailed off for a moment. "The Sixth fought at Shiloh in Cleburne's Corps, pushing against Sherman's division the first day and he come through it unscathed." Beeman jerked his head toward the sound of the rushing creek water. "Way it worked out he wound up on that hill up ahead, probably shitting his pants when the Ohio boys busted out of the swamp."

"Turf," Paul said, picking up a damp handful of leaves and dirt and letting it trickle from his fingers. "My dad's people came over from England before the First World War. Mom's came from Sweden around 1900."

"An' you discovered the Civil War on TV when Ken Burns made his documentary, huh?" Beeman observed.

Paul chewed his lip, flashed briefly on the Civil War statue in front of the old courthouse in Stillwater. Then he reached over and gathered a pinch of Beeman's blue sleeve between his thumb and forefinger. Let it go. "So why're you out here playing a Yankee who was shooting at your ancestor?"

Beeman shrugged. "You gotta understand, I work in a small department, we ain't got but ten deputies for the whole county. And I been on stakeouts where it was hard getting four guys coordinated. So I wanted to be part of a hundred fifty men trying to come through the swamp in some kind of order. And they did it. Didn't lose anybody. Not even my last whale. He huffed and puffed his way all the way through."

Paul sat up and swirled the last of his coffee in the bottom of the cup. "I think I know what you mean. Now, myself, I was never in the army. But it seems to me marching now is different from then."

Beeman nodded. "You got that right. It was all about drill, how you move these jam-packed hedgehogs of men around on a battlefield and get 'em in range of one another. I mean, the mechanics of doin' that with thousands and thousands . . ."

Paul cocked his head. "I think I get it; the attention to detail, uniforms and equipment and drill. Respecting what they went through. And I know it's a hobby. But I just can't help thinking it was about something . . ."

"Uh-oh." Beeman scrubbed his fingers in his sweat-frazzled hair. His spare features nimbly worked the tension between the prescient light in his eyes and the unrepentant set of his jaw.

"Well, it was," Paul said flatly.

"Ah Jesus." Beeman sighed. "Here comes the Public Radio sermon." He sat up, placed his tin cup carefully on the ground, and said, "Was about something, huh?"

"Damn straight . . ." Paul felt his own jaw tense.

Beeman held up a hand diplomatically and looked directly into Paul's eyes. "Paul," he said frankly, "you got black folks for neighbors up there in Minnesota, live right next door or down the block; your kids walk to school together?"

Paul furrowed his brow. "Well, no . . ."

"Thing is, Paul, down here—win, lose, or draw with all the ugly and we still got plenty ugly to go around—we're still neighbors. Not like up there where you look down your noses on the South and talk *diversity* . . . and then get in your cars and drive like hell to get to the suburbs."

15

AFTER DELIVERING HIS CONVERSA-tion stopper, Beeman politely excused himself, reached for his police radio, and padded off barefoot into the woods to make a radio check. Paul chewed his lip, doubting things were all that hunky-dory in Mississippi. But no missing the message: whatever Beeman might be, he was saying, he wasn't a hypocrite.

Which left Paul wondering how far under the genial etiquette the bare knuckles were cocked and ready to go. But before he could phrase a reply, the sergeants were on their feet, going up and down the line, giving the fifteen-minute warning. All around, men were putting out the fires and getting ready to resume the march. Paul busied himself with getting into dry socks, half-dry trousers, and still-wet brogans. Seeing the Ohioans wipe down their muskets, he followed suit, trying to retard the stain of pumpkin-colored rust that spread over the Springfield's exposed metal.

Beeman returned and saw to his clothing. Sergeants were bawling now, shaking the men out of their lethargy after the long break. Slowly, the three companies fell in on an overgrown path. Beeman turned to him and said, "Don't get me wrong. We'll talk later . . ."

That was as far as he got, because Red Beard called the roll. Then he ordered them to attention, had them assume the ready position, prime their unloaded muskets with percussion caps, and cock the hammers. Then he ordered them to aim their muskets in the air and fire the caps. After the volley of muted pops, Beeman, his old self again, explained, "To dry out the chamber, also as a safety precaution. Make sure nobody brought a loaded piece by accident."

Then they were ordered right-flank. At the route step, four abreast, they started down the path.

The sound of rushing water was louder now, and up ahead Paul heard men bitch about putting on dry socks and now they were wading in a goddamn creek.

They came to the stream and it was not as bad as it sounded. Paul sized up the ford of slick rocks and skipped across without getting his feet too wet. Ten minutes after crossing the creek, the men cheered when a beam of sunlight poked for the first time through the churning mist. But soon everything that was wet turned to clammy steam. The mist lost the last cool spoor of rain and became a compost stew seeping up from the ground. Paul simmered in his itchy wool. Up ahead, the lead company appeared and disappeared in the peekaboo fog.

Trudging through the woods, hearing the weary clink of equipment and the tired voices, Paul now thought the long break was a mistake. With the challenge of the swamp behind him, he'd lost his earlier edge and now floated, drowsy with the heat. There were moments of dappled sunshine, and, briefly, Paul could see the U.S. flag and the blue standard of the Ohio regiment hanging exhausted in the center of Company B. Then the mist closed in again and it felt like they were marching through a moldy basement with dark tree trunks jutting up like posts holding up a fog ceiling.

A weary shudder passed down the line when a spooked deer jumped from cover and sprinted down the side of the trail and crashed through the brush. Paul tried to blink himself alert. It didn't work. Then . . .

"Halt." Not Red Beard. A stocky man appeared, with a pistol and saber and eagles on his shoulder straps.

The column lurched to a sluggish stop.

"Front."

A lackadaisical blue shuffle as they undoubled back into two ranks.

Abruptly, the colonel bawled the order:

"Load."

Holy shit!

That did it. Paul's eyes darted into the foggy wall of brush and trees that suddenly jerked into pin-tight focus. Were *they* out there? Already? He placed the rifle butt on the ground between his feet, turned so the trigger guard faced him.

With shaking fingers, he tore at the flap of his cartridge box, removed a brown-paper cartridge, held it to his mouth and tore the folded end away with his teeth, spit away the paper, and poured the black powder down the muzzle.

He tasted a chemical grit of sulfur and charcoal and nitrate on his lips, crunched it in his clamped teeth.

"Ram paper, go ahead, use the rammers, boys," Colonel Burns ordered. Mutters sounded up and down the ranks. "Rammers?"

Beeman, who had not loaded his rifle, said, "Usually you don't use rammers: safety issue."

Paul stuffed the paper into the muzzle and drew his ramrod. A metal hiss slithered along the ranks as a hundred fifty rammers were pulled from the "pipes." The rammers twirled like slim batons and jammed down the muzzles, were withdrawn, then another choreographed twirl and they returned to the slots along the barrel. Paul remembered to hook the little finger of the right hand atop the tulip bulge of the rod, shoving down—to keep his hand clear of the muzzle.

They brought their rifles up to the ready position.

"Prime," Colonel Burns called out. Trembling with excitement, Paul raised the heavy rifle to his waist. The muzzle tilted up to eye level. The muzzles of rifles in the rear rank projected to either side. He balanced the rifle in his left hand and reached down with his right and unsnapped the cap pouch, plucked out a shiny copper percussion cap and was placing it on the touch hole cone when an officer jogged up, making a waving motion with his hand. After conferring briefly with the officer, Colonel Burns ordered, "Remove caps."

Huh? Paul plucked off the cap, let it fall.

"Fix bayonets," Burns ordered.

Paul lowered the rifle butt back to the ground between his shoes and steadied it with his right hand. There was another dull swirl of metal as the bayonets were drawn from scabbards with the left hand and turned in the air. A steel jangle rattled down the line as the bayonets were fitted over and locked down on the muzzle rings.

"Stack arms."

On surer ground here from much practice, Paul took Beeman's musket, crossed the bayonets, and leaned the rifles out, steadying them with his left hand on his, then reached behind and took a rifle being passed forward from the rear rank, slid the bayonet into the angle of crossed hilts, positioned the rifle butt to form a stable triangle. The fourth musket, the "leaner," was passed through and placed against the other three.

"Break ranks, march. Rest."

Men stepped away from the stacked rifles, drank from their canteens, stuffed pipes, lit them. Some went to the edge of the trail and peed.

"What's going on?" Paul asked Beeman.

Beeman pointed to the officers, who stood in a huddle, heads close, talking. "Officers," he said simply. Then he stared down the row of precisely stacked rifles. "Not real smart, stacking loaded muskets."

"Look," Paul said, "back there it got a little touchy when we were talking . . ."

Beeman smiled. "I said don't get me wrong. It's just, the way trouble starts in these things is when one side steamrolls the other for openers . . ."

Bang. Bang-bang. BANGBANGBANG!

One-two-three-many distinct explosions punched ahead in the mist.

Paul's and Beeman's eyes widened, mirroring each other. Those were . . .

Shots!

The reports played tricks in the shrouded forest, rippling, echoing. A long, delicious shiver corkscrewed up Paul's back. The confab of officers scattered, running to their companies.

"FALL IN!" a lieutenant bellowed.

Paul joined the blue scramble; pumping arms and legs, crisscrossed black leather, swinging canteens and pouches. Down the road, the companies formed on the rifle pyramids and jockeyed to get in proper order.

"TAKE ARMS."

A clatter of untangling steel and wood counterpointed the rising crackle ahead.

"UNFIX BAYONETS."

With a rattle and a clink, Paul unfastened his bayonet, rotated the slender silver knife in his left hand, and returned it to his scabbard in a hiss of leather.

"SHOULDER ARMS."

Then—

"PRIME."

Really trembling now, Paul lowered the Springfield to his hip and dug another cap from his pouch. All butterfingers; it slipped away. With urgent care, he plucked another, placed it on the cone, and started to yank back the hammer. "Not yet," Beeman cautioned. His slow voice had speeded up, animated with the contagious excitement. "Make sure you get the wings on that cap bent down so it don't fall off."

As Paul squeezed down on the thin cap flanges with his thumb, Red Beard's shout echoed the orders rippling down the line: "SHOULDER ARMS. RIGHT FACE. ROUTE STEP—FORWARD—MARCH."

Men moving machine-like, Paul thought. Me too.

A shimmer of wood and steel as the double lines of blue shouldered the rifles, reshuffled into four abreast, and lurched forward, down the road.

Dizzy and out of breath, Paul felt a flush surge from his throat and flood his cheeks. This tingle started between his sweat-drenched shoulder blades and stitched up the back of his neck and pecked at his scalp.

A palpable current now harnessed the close-packed bodies, and Paul half-expected it to arc where he rubbed elbows with Beeman and the man on his right.

Up ahead, in a fold in the mist, Paul saw the flag swirl in a flourish of red barber-pole stripes, and it was like he was seeing it for the first time.

Maybe the way it's supposed to be seen . . .

Gaps were opening and closing overhead in the mist, and sprays of sunlight poked down through the trees like the turning spokes of a giant yellow wheel. Just as suddenly, the sunlight was gone and the gloom closed in again on the urgent muffled tramp of hobnailed shoes. Birdcalls made tiny shrieks amid the increasingly loud bang of gunfire.

Paul and Beeman exchanged sidelong glances.

"You think this is how it was for them?" Paul asked, dry-mouthed.

"Gotta be close, don'tcha think?" Beeman said, raising his eyebrows.

Paul watched Beeman's lean face. *He's excited, too.* Then he adjusted his rifle on his shoulder and glanced over to make sure the hammer was at half-cock, that the frail copper cap was still nestled on the cone.

The firing louder now, massed volleys off to the right. Men were going turtle, tugging their heads instinctively down between their hunched shoulders. Beeman elbowed Paul's arm, inclined his head toward a man in the next file, who'd switched his rifle to his left hand and was making the sign of the cross on his chest with his right hand. Shouts now and the ripping sound of crashing brush. Paul made out a scramble of activity up ahead. Men in blue held their rifles high in both hands and sprinted out to either side of the road.

"They've put out flankers," Beeman said, face alight. "Oh, lookit that."

Paul swallowed to clear his hearing, thought to take his canteen, decided not to. He had this red jackhammer going in his chest. The faces were bleached gray around him; streamlined, eyes bulged forward.

Like a tattered curtain pierced by gunfire, the mist was coming apart, fluttering down and pooling in low places. Men in blue fanned out up there, dashing off the road in open interval. They floated, bobbed, then sunk in the mist; their heads and shoulders and chests gliding in a chalky wave, their black rifles slanting forward.

The mist dissipated, the trees opened to a blur of a field. Paul squinted through a sheet of sweat. To the right, he saw rising ground.

"COMPANY. COMPANY INTO LINE."

The marching thicket of rifles and blue caps immediately surged to the left as men stampeded off the trail.

"QUICKLY MEN. DO IT. GO!"

Paul's eyes and mouth were stuck wide open as he automatically plunged, his legs stretching out. A jagged wicker wall loomed up; gray, rust, bits of green, brambles, dead branches, and knee-deep brush.

Stinging barbs lashed his cheeks, his hands, caught his rifle and snared his feet. Some kind of nettles. A sergeant bawled, "Extend to the left, goddamn it. *Line of battle.*" Paul tried to sprint, clumsy with swinging equipment, slipping off-balance in a struggle to keep up with Beeman. *Gotta fill my slot. Gotta keep Beeman on my right.* Shoulders, rifles, packs, canteens, and bayonets askew, Company C collided in a frantic, shoving tussle to form two lines.

His life had been reduced to one simple task. *Gotta claim my place in line!*

The stocky colonel—Burns, was it?—Burns was in front

now, waving a sword, barking orders. Unintelligible. Too fast for Paul to comprehend.

"FORWARD INTO LINE. BY COMPANY, LEFT HALF-WHEEL, *MARCH*!"

"What?" Paul blurted. "WHAT?"

Beeman's hand firmly grasped his elbow, propelling him.

"FORWARD MARCH. GUIDE RIGHT!"

"C'mon," Beeman said, "it's a left wheel, follow along with me."

Paul stuck to Beeman as each company in the battalion swung to the left. At the command "Forward march," they plowed straight ahead through the brush, hurrying to join the line formed by Companies A and B.

"THIRD COMPANY, RIGHT TURN, MARCH!" an officer near the ranks yelled. Beeman maintained steady pressure on Paul's elbow, yanking him forward and to the right at a run. The clattering confusion of bodies and equipment slowed to a walk, Beeman released his hold on Paul's elbow, and Paul found himself in his proper place. The headlong rush of men off the forest path into the dense underbrush was now three companies advancing in a line of battle.

Looking ahead, Paul saw a strobe-like snapshot. The skirmishers aimed and fired their rifles. Puffs of white smoke. Paul inhaled the exploding scent of fire on sulfur. Felt the sting in the eyes and tasted the grit of nitrates on the tongue. Loud booms of musket fire slammed his eardrums, rang in the trees. The volume of rifle fire squeezed his vision, and the air itself seemed to go powdery and visibly shake.

The ground dipped and then rose up, crowding the formation. Paul stumbled on a pile of slippery deadfall strewn over a limestone outcrop. His left foot and leg plunged through the branches into a rocky crevasse and he went down, his right leg spraddled akimbo. Flailing for balance, he couldn't extract his wedged ankle. He was stuck.

"Keep it moving, extend to the left, goddamn you . . . make room for Company B . . ."

Paul felt Beeman's strong grip under his right arm, bodily lifting him from the crevasse, and he was careening forward again. A sergeant's angry face ahead, rifle held horizontal across his chest, roughly herding men to the left. From the corner of his eye, Paul saw the color-bearers stumbling through dense undergrowth off to the right, flags swaying, clumps of men struggling in the thickets. Company B. Company A funneling in after them.

Gasping, trembling, swinging his elbows, he bulled in between Beeman and an Ohioan, teeth clenched, breath coming in rasps.

"RIGHT DRESS GODDAMN IT! DRESS IS RIGHT!"

Banging shoulders. Curses. The line did an accordion rumba, then rammed together, closing up, elbow to elbow. One moment Paul was panting for breath, the next the loudest shock he'd ever heard, felt, seemed to erupt up out of the very ground, and his muscles spasmed. Christ! The trees were shaking. Involuntarily, he turned. Beeman seized his arm. "Steady down there."

Trembling, everyone instinctively stooping now, white-faced, crouching. Eyes glancing, clicking audibly, it seemed, like fat cue balls up and down the line. The great sound happened again, and Paul felt the concussion on his face, saw the branches recoil. "That's cannon fire," an officer yelled. "Lie down, men."

"Hot load," someone muttered, "they must have double-charged it."

Paul fell to his knees, jerked forward by Beeman's grip on his arm. He thrust his rifle out in front of him to clear away the brush and landed heavily on his elbows. He shot a look down the squirming line of wide-eyed men who kneeled, lay prostrate, with knuckles blanched white, clutching the long rifles. A drifting, stinking haze of smoke floated over them and, for an instant, Paul was alone, isolated in black-powder limbo.

No more looking in. He was all the way inside, looking out.

The smoke cleared and he saw Beeman's grinning face, down in the mashed bushes just inches away. They shared a moment of muddy-cheeked exhilaration. Then Paul stared at his own dirty hands, cut by brush: stripes of red, a little ooze of blood. All that mattered now was the tiny copper cap on the rifle cone. He checked to make sure and found it still miraculously in place.

So the damn gun would shoot.

The skirmishers were moving forward now, shouting. Other yells, a yipping howling yell. Beeman pounded his arm, pulled him up to his knees, pointed through the trees. "There, see 'em."

Gray-brown shadows slipped in the brush ahead of the skirmish line. The yelling general now. Officers waved their swords. Sergeants bellowed from the back of the line. They were getting up out of the brush, dressing right, shouldering arms, going forward. Paul lurched, his ears plugged; not sure if he was hearing a rolling drumbeat or his own heart in his chest. Hoarse, spontaneous growls erupted down the line.

From Paul's own throat.

And right there, facedown and motionless in a patch of green ferns and moss, sprawled a blue soldier. His hat and rifle flung away. Paul watched the line of muddy shoes ripple over and past the body like an onrushing tide.

Fate card, Paul thought as the long blue double line flowed into a wooded clearing and he saw four more rag-doll shapes, one blue, three brown-gray, scattered in the low brush. A group of blue skirmishers had taken cover behind a long mound of freshly dug earth, loading and firing. One of them writhed in pain on his back. He had a bandanna wrapped around his knee and was holding the knee in both hands, his face contorted in an all-too-believable grimace of pain.

"Halt. In place rest," Red Beard called out. "If you ain't already, now's the time to open those fate cards, boys."

Paul panted, momentarily snatched back to the twenty-first century. He reached in his pocket, pulled his card out, bit the wrinkled corner and tore it open like a paper cartridge, and read quickly, his heart pounding: *"Pvt. Amos T. Mauldon survived Kirby Creek as well as Chickamauga and Missionary Ridge. He went home when his enlistment expired and did not return to the army."*

Paul grinned, showed the card to Beeman.

"Aw shit, says here ole Abner Massey is a goner," somebody intoned right behind Paul, in the rear rank.

"Kin I have yer boots."

"Don't fret, Abner old boy, I will go home after this fuss and comfort the missus."

Red Beard walked the line, extending one arm toward the tree line across the clearing. "We'll follow the skirmish line through the trees ahead; when we come to the edge of the woods we'll see their entrenchments. A Reb regiment will contest our advance. That's when people taking hits will go facedown. Pick your time and don't move. Support will escort you off the field once the battle moves on."

"What if you're wounded?"

"Act wounded, groan and roll around," Red Beard answered. "Support will collect you. The fallen and the wounded will not return to the unit until the event is finished."

"Makes it more real, I guess," someone said.

After the momentary lull, firing had started again on the right, beyond the screen of trees. Officers and sergeants now worked up and down the line like border collies, snapping orders. As the gunfire swelled on the right, the skirmishers rose and stalked toward the next line of trees. The three companies lurched forward in line, stamping through the knee-high brush.

Then more shouts and another halt to dress the ranks. Paul used a kerchief to wipe moisture from his spectacles. He toed his shoes in the thick grass, trying to ungunk the red gumbo clotted to the soles. His wool trousers were soaked to the knees from the wet brush and knotted with burrs. Grass-hoppers darted in the weeds.

"Jesus." Sound of a hand slapping a neck. "Can you believe this shit? A mosquito."

The slap echoed away in a startling moment of quiet. Paul heard the tick of insects, the drip of condensed mist draining from the leaves overhead, and the distant cry of birds. Then he jerked alert as a ragged pop of muskets and the deeper boom of more cannons sounded beyond the woods to the right. Like a tangible echo of the gunfire, a cloud of white smoke combined with the fog and flowed through the trees. Plump with humidity, the white tide drifted no higher than a man's waist.

"Check them out. On the right, two o'clock, about two hundred yards," Beeman said.

Paul squinted into the smoke. A blur of movement congealed into three Confederates, who waded hip-deep in the pooling mist. Rifles at port arms, they scrambled through the trees to a swell of higher ground, so their bodies came into full view. They wore a mélange of hobo color, mismatched gray, brown, and green, with blanket rolls across their chests and beehive slouch hats on their heads. A shudder of anticipation snaked down the line. Men instinctively raised their muskets.

Paul's heart pounded as he saw the Rebels clearly for the first time. He squeezed his rifle, raised it to his shoulder, and was astounded at how easily he had come to see other men as targets.

"Reb scouts, that's their picket line," Beeman said.

At about a hundred fifty yards, the three Rebs knelt behind a log and fired their muskets at the advancing blue skirmishers. Paul, getting into the mood of the thing, aimed his musket at the three soldiers. An odd sensation tickled up his spine when he tried to steady the notch in his rear sight on a man in a gray jacket and brown slouch hat.

"Bang," Paul said. When he lowered the heavy rifle, his breath came in excited gasps and a flush of sweat damped his hands. He turned to Beeman. "Do you think I could have hit that guy?"

Beeman shrugged. "The leaf sights on the '61 Springfield range out to five hundred yards, suppose to be lethal out to a thousand."

"I think I could have hit that guy," Paul said under his breath, turning away from Beeman's quiet gaze.

The Rebs retreated as the skirmish line plunged into the trees. "At the route step, MARCH," an officer yelled, swinging his sword. The three companies trudged forward, crossed the clearing, stamped through the last stand of trees, and stopped at the edge of the woods. A cheer broke out to the left, where figures in blue shook their rifles triumphantly around a cannon and Reb prisoners on a gravel road.

Through gaps in the foliage, Paul could see it all in one dizzy sweep. Just like Beeman described it: a long slope with three cannons on the crest, toy-size in the distance. Rebel flags waved in the smoke next to a low white house with slim pillars. Below the house, a rail fence curved across the slope, with men massed thick behind it. Then clusters of other men were running around the end of the fence, forming into line up the slope from where Paul now stood hidden. Atop the hill, in front of the house, Paul saw a monumental figure in white granite catch a flash of sunlight.

"See, over on the right," Beeman said, pointing to several dozen gray-clad men running back toward the slope. Some of them dashed for groups of horses being held by mounted men and hoisted themselves into the saddles. "Their skirmishers and cavalry are falling back from the creek. Luring the main Yankee body forward. 'Cept now we're gonna pop out of the woods to the rear of their flank."

Cheers, a clatter of equipment, and a persistent roll of drums mingled with the gunfire as the main Union force emerged from the thickets across the field.

"Lookit those fellas, taking their blue suits pretty serious," Beeman observed as the ranks of "galvanized" Southerners in blue uniforms marched out from the thick brush in
tight formation, shoulder to shoulder. At the edge of the trees
a group of men maneuvered an artillery caisson into place,
wheeled a cannon. Then several horsemen in blue cantered
into the pasture. One of them rode a prancing black horse and
held a fluttering American flag. Never, until this moment,
had Paul really felt the sorcerer's tug of that bit of cloth.

He touched the red bandanna wrapping his head, the pain
totally forgotten as he felt his thoughts quicken. He tried to
summon Stephen Crane's words he knew by heart, describ-
ing the youthful protagonist in his story reacting to men
assembled for battle. Henry Fleming in *The Red Badge of
Courage* had been wide-eyed—he was *going to look at war,
the red animal—war—the blood-swollen god . . .*

Paul shook his head. It didn't work like that. No room
here for flowery talk. All you could think about now was not
screwing up, keeping your place in line, getting the gun up,
and pulling the trigger when the time came.

Doing your job.

He glanced left and right. Probably how it had actually
looked. The officers conferred; the sergeants paced, hound-
ing the ranks, tightening the companies.

"It's really something," he said to Beeman, raising his
voice because the Yanks across the field had stopped to fire
a long, crashing volley to send the Reb skirmishers on their
way. The blue lines vanished in a cloud of white smoke. "I
mean, no plastic. No cell phones. No fucking traffic jams."

He looked up into a sultry gray sky uncut by wires. Mer-
cifully empty of aircraft. Only a few starlings wheeled above
the treetops. The air was a dank brew of sweat and filthy
wool, wet leather, black powder smoke, and a barn odor of
horses and wet grass. He gripped the heavy rifle tighter and
took a deep breath.

"The air must have been different back then," he said.
"Imagine breathing air with no radio or television signals in

it. No electronics. No PCBs. No millions of internal combustion engines dumping exhaust. No nuclear bomb had ever exploded . . ."

Beeman cuffed him on the shoulder with his forearm. "Slow down, boy, you're gonna OD on the period rush."

Paul said happily, "Christ, think of it. Thousands of men who never thumbed a remote to escape a TV commercial."

It occurred to him that the men who had stood shoulder to shoulder in this pasture, presenting a wall of living flesh to shot and steel . . . had never considered purchasing life insurance.

A bugle sounded like a cheerful summons to mass suicide.

"They're formin' up there, boys," an officer shouted. "I do believe they're coming this way. We're gonna surprise their Reb asses."

How many, Paul couldn't be sure. A double line of yellowish gray . . .

So that's . . . butternut, he thought.

The advancing ranks were partially obscured by the foliage at the edge of the woods. A hundred men, maybe more, tramping down the hill, skirting a copse of trees to the left. A red flag waved in the center of the line.

"SHOULDER ARMS. DRESS THE LINE," Red Beard bellowed.

The blue lines coiled tighter, connected at the shoulders.

"FORWARD . . . MARCH."

No route step now. They set off at a measured tread. Metronome men, crisscrossed with black leather straps, joined at the shoulders in a trundling, steel-quilled blue porcupine. Paul flinched when the cannon shattered the heavy air. He did better when the second cannon fired, and he didn't even blink when the third one let go.

They cleared the last of obscuring trees, coming out at an angle a little to the left of the approaching Reb formation.

"AT THE RIGHT OBLIQUE, MARCH," the colonel shouted.

In unison, the blue line shifted direction forty-five degrees.

"Cool," someone said in the rear rank. "We're gonna catch them on the end before they can adjust."

"STEADY BOYS," an officer shouted.

Paul marched forward, trying to maintain elbow contact with Beeman on the right, the Ohioan on the left. Somewhere in back a drummer banged a rolling cadence.

Paul thought, in real life they would have fixed bayonets. Men would be falling now, hit by musket fire. The haze hovering around the base of the slope bristled with rifle barrels of the advancing Confederates. Now, off in the smoke, the damn band started up, playing "The Bonnie Blue Flag." On the hill, a shudder of flame and smoke erupted along the fence.

The Reb formation was starting to turn toward them. Not more than a hundred yards away. Paul could make out their faces.

"HALT. RIGHT DRESS."

The moving rows of upright musket barrels stopped. Tense, controlled sidestepping, drawing up elbow-tight.

"FIRE BY BATTALION," Colonel Burns bellowed.

Paul's right foot moved back, instep snugged to left heel, and formed a right angle. Up and down the line, hammers clicked back to full-cock. On either side, rifle barrels appeared tilted up at eye level as the rear rank took the ready position. Paul checked the percussion cap. Still there.

Looking over his barrel, he saw the gray line scrambling to face them, raising their own rifles.

"AIM."

Paul smoothly raised the heavy rifle and stuffed the butt into his shoulder. Now the barrels to either side of his head extended into full firing position. The man in back of Paul rested his left forearm on Paul's right shoulder. Paul put his sights on the red-blue flutter of the rebel flag, then lowered the sight picture to the chest of the color-bearer. Christ, aiming a rifle at a man and I never shot a rifle for real in my life, he thought. This is going to be *loud*.

"FIRE!"

Paul yanked the trigger and flinched as the gray line of men disappeared in a blast of flame-laced white smoke.

I did it. He grinned, ears ringing. I didn't screw up. I shot my gun. Suddenly, he had the sensation of almost being alone. The battlefield had constricted down to a tiny tunnel of smoke containing the men on either side. Then . . . hey! He pitched forward, jolted from the rear as the man in back of him took a hit, dropped his rifle, and tumbled, bouncing roughly off Paul's side and collapsing heavily to the matted vegetation at Paul's feet.

"LOAD."

With the fallen man crowding his feet, Paul moved reflexively to reload. As he drew his rammer, plunged it down the muzzle, and returned it, he saw several other soldiers tumble forward and sprawl facedown on the ground. Through an opening in the smoke he saw that four or five Rebs had also flopped down.

He turned to Beeman, who was not loading, just going through the motions. "You're not shooting?"

Beeman smiled amiably. "Outta respect to my great-great-grandpa Matthew, I'll pass. You go on, don't mind me."

As he lifted the rifle to the ready position, Paul nodded at the casualty at their feet and widened his eyes.

Then he reached for another percussion cap. Fingers surer this time, he seated it and crimped down the wings with his thumb. Just then the "dead man" shifted position, and his bayonet scabbard jabbed into Paul's ankle and got caught in the uppers of his brogan.

Paul grimaced and turned, lowering his rifle with his right hand, starting to bend forward to reach down with his left, to free the bayonet. He paused and stared at his flushed left hand, the veins plumped up thick in a grime of sweat, streaks of dirt. He saw the yellow wedding band circling his finger in startling detail and reflected: *I guess I did bring one thing on the field that's not period-accurate . . .*

"FIRE."

The roar of musket fire boomeranged into onrushing black that slammed into the left side of Paul Edin's neck and tore through the carotid artery and wrenched the image of his wedding ring from his eyes. He didn't feel his body smash sideways into Beeman. His eyes took a few last pictures going down.

Tilt of gray sky and blur of green grass; porous blue wool, black muddy leather. Red dirt.

"I thought you didn't get hit . . ." Beeman started to say. Then he recoiled, his eyes going wide as the spray of bright arterial blood splashed across his chest, hands, face.

"JESUSFUCKINCHRIST!"

For a moment nothing happened. Smoke obscured the blue line, the Rebs had fired another volley, and more men whose fate cards had come up were dropping.

"MAN DOWN. WE GOT A MAN DOWN. *MEDIC UP,*" Beeman screamed.

"What? *WHAT?*" Red Beard lurched frantic through the numb formation, flinging men and rifle barrels aside.

Beeman dropped to his knees, clawing his police radio from his haversack, and yelled into it. "SHUT IT DOWN. We got a man down for real . . . fuck do I know . . . hit by gunfire. Yeah, *hit bad.* In the throat. Deputy Beeman, I'm with the casualty at the far left end of the Union line. Start an ambulance."

Beeman's eyes locked on Paul's.

"Hang in there, Paul, we got help coming," Beeman shouted in a shaky voice, grimacing at the awful gurgle coming from Paul's throat. Eyes fluttering, whole body fluttering, his breath hollow, feathery. Jesus there's a lot of blood.

Beeman's hands were slippery with it as he tore packs of compresses from his haversack, ripping through the plastic covers, pressing the pads of white gauze down on the blood welling from the ragged neck. Pressure point? Where, for a throat wound? Collarbone?

The sun had come out, because Red Beard's shadow fell across Paul's shrunken white face.

"Get an EMT, goddamn it," Beeman yelled at the sergeant with pointed fury. Red Beard stumbled off. Fingers fumbling, Beeman gripped Paul's limp hand.

"Hold on there, buddy . . ."

Beeman watched the light leak slowly from Paul's eyes, the bloody bubbles turn to faint slush on his slack lips. No more air. *I'm losing him.* His eyes scoured up the slope to the reloading Rebs, then left, to the edge of the copse of woods, instinctively looking for the source of the fire. *Where are you, fucker?* Then, leaning over the bloody compress with one hand, holding Paul's hand with the other, he noticed that the man from the rear rank, who had taken a hit, was on his hands and knees, vomiting into the grass. Jesus, everybody was just standing around numb, in shock. So Beeman bellowed a reflex command never given on an early Civil War battlefield. But he'd yelled it a couple of times for real, as a young army sergeant in Kuwait in '91:

"SPREAD OUT, GODDAMN IT! HIT THE DECK, TAKE COVER!"

16 CANNONS STILL FIRING UP ON THE hill drowned out the loud pounding of Mitch's heart. *Can't see. Did I get him?* Breathing heavily, he strained to see into the drifting clouds of smoke. The extreme right end of the blue formation, where he had fired on Beeman, had come apart and now milled in confusion. The chaos rippled through the blue uniforms from right to left, stalling the center. Officers and sergeants waved their arms as if trying to stop the din of musketry and cannons. Others raced up and down the ranks.

Then, after a last crash of muskets, he could hear muffled shouts. Several officers had their hands cupped to their ears, yelling in cell phones.

"C'mon, c'mon," Mitch mouthed impatiently as he crouched, groggy with excitement, sliding the rifle into the protective canvas sleeve. Then he got down on his hands and knees, folding the poncho, tucking it away, and checked the ground to make sure he didn't leave anything behind. He plucked up a cigarette butt, pulled a loop of yarn from a branch he'd hung it on to test the wind.

Finally the smoke cleared enough for him to make out four or five blue uniforms stoop over, then hoist a flopping burden. The playact panorama was shattered by a wailing siren. A blue-and-white ambulance, lights flashing, started bumping across the field. Closer in, Mitch saw the gray reenactors rise from behind the fence, craning their necks forward. A last doleful musket popped. The siren tocsin froze hundreds of men in place as they looked around for information.

Several mounted men galloped across the field, followed by a man in a blue police uniform racing a four-wheeler. They converged with the ambulance toward the right end of the line where men sat, their heads in their hands. Some stood like statues in the tatters of smoke. Others wandered. Near the scrum of blue gathered around the casualty, some men had started with clubbed rifles toward the now-confused gray line that had come out to challenge the flank attack. Other men in blue restrained them.

Mitch took no great pleasure from the mayhem. Necessity, he thought, and then, with fleeting cynicism, What y'all come down here for, to experience the Civil War . . . Now you'll have something to talk about.

Men dressed in gray were now climbing over the snake-rail fence, descending the slope. Some of them assumed the familiar twenty-first century posture, hands raised to their ears, hunched to their cell phones.

Okay. It's time to get out of here.

He backed out of the nest, using a fallen branch to smooth out the tramped leaves and erase his imprint in the muddy earth. After he tossed the branch aside, he slung the cased rifle over his shoulder, then turned his back and quickly walked away. The trees closed in, walling off the scene below. A minute into the woods, and even the alarm of the siren started to recede.

He had a three-hour walk to get back to his truck on the fire trail. Up on the hill Dwayne would be watching through binoculars from the artillery position. Darl would take his time, then thread through the confusion to the Reb camp parking area. It was going to work. In mid-thought, he froze at a scurry in the brush. Squirrel maybe?

After a few more steps he stopped and heard it again. Something was out here, pacing him.

Mitch unsnapped the leather holster and jerked out the Colt Navy. His sweat-slick thumb poised on the hammer.

So damn thick out here, hard to tell.

When he turned to continue, it lunged out from behind a tree; fast and silent and massive. Mitch's hands swung up defensively as he tried to pull the Colt on target. His left fist caught hard, painfully, on something sharp, scrape of dry bark, a spike of dead branch. Just before a stiff right-arm punch stunned his face, he caught a nightmare glimpse of his attacker: white of eye, swollen in anger, a bunched brow of purple-black pigment under wooly black hair. In that second of blindness, the pistol was stripped from his grasp.

Powerful hands spun him, then a thick, muscular, dark-skinned arm snaked around his throat. Mitch scrambled, trying to plant his feet for leverage, but his attacker had now clamped Mitch's neck in a vice formed by biceps and forearm squeezing together. Gasping, Mitch pawed, trying to break the inexorable pressure. Fucker was leaning into him, pushing his throat deeper into the crook of the elbow. Eyes bulging, he saw sweaty pores in dark skin overlaid with a pattern of fresh scars, like purple worms. Struggling more feebly now, losing air, losing light in some kind of strangle hold. Blacking out . . . just the sharp muscle odor smothering him, like burning compost, armpit-scented fear.

Fuckin' nigger . . .

. . . jumped him . . .

Mitch's knees buckled and he lost consciousness.

A ripping sound brought him back. Duct tape tearing. The sticky adhesive cut off light, covering his eyes. Then another strip wrapped his mouth.

Sheer panic. Struggle to breathe through his nose. Fight back. But the attacker was too strong, had twisted his arms behind him. More ripping sounds as the tape wrapped his wrists.

Roughly, Mitch was pulled to a kneeling position.

Blind, mute, bound, he strained to hear. And what he

heard coming through the vast silence of the forest was this loopy electronic chiming of the cell phone in his pocket. Ring tone must have been activated during the fight.

He felt the guy dig the cell from his trousers, heard him speak, a garbled "Wha?"

Mitch could only hear a miniature buzz imprisoned inside the slender metal device, no words. Then the sound ended abruptly as the guy clamped the phone shut and spoke in his wheezing, disgusted voice.

"Dumb," he said.

The powerful hands wrenched Mitch to his feet, seized his arm with a bruising grip.

"Now what have you done, you dumb motherfucker?"

Mitch heard the blubber of his own terror and frustration, blocked by the tape. The grip on his arm propelled him forward, stumbling on the leaves, snapping dead branches.

"You were set for life, man. Now what have you done?" the guy repeated.

Mitch tripped. The powerful guiding hand on his shoulder steadied him and shoved him onward.

"Dumb," the guy said again.

17 SATURDAY AFTERNOON, AT 1:55 P.M., John Rane paced his living space, which was tidy, sparsely furnished, and—he glanced at the wall clock—about to be entered by Jenny Hatton, married name, Edin.

He had trained his mind not to entertain thoughts about Jenny. His visual memory was too acute. When she crossed his mind he visualized a blindfold . . .

Blindfold. Firing squad. For desertion in the face of paternity.

Shorthand for Jenny. You did her wrong. Moreover, on making her exit, she had explained at great length just exactly what a mistake he was making.

Right in this room, sitting there on the couch. *You'll never find another woman like me.*

For eleven years, not unlike an addict searching to recreate the magic of his first high, he'd tried to prove her wrong with a parade of women.

Well, shit.

Rane sagged and did what he did best; let his thoughts drift off like bubbles and observed the physical world in front of his eyes. His living room was a functional studio; bookshelves floor to ceiling over a computer/writing desk. An old-style light table remained out of nostalgia for the pre-digital world of negatives and darkroom dodging; gone now in the mouse clicks of Photoshop. The same swayback couch. An upright piano.

An enigmatic Modigliani nude hung on the wall over the couch, his sole personal touch since he'd removed the Henri Cartier-Bresson print of the classic 1932 shot behind the Gare Saint-Lazare: man leaping from a plank over a wide puddle, perfectly suspended above his reflection.

The Decisive Moment.

Letting her walk out that door.

Item by item, he'd stripped the bungalow down to a bare-bones staging area for his work, and the no-frills theme carried through to his appearance. Six feet tall, slat-lean; his regular features were dominated by deep, watchful eyes. A pale man who preferred shadow to sunlight, who kept switchblade reflexes spring-loaded in unobtrusive stillness.

Indifferent to clothing, he lived in jeans and T-shirts. In winter he added a layer of fleece and a pair of dog-eared Sorels. When an assignment required different coloration to infiltrate a story, he could turn himself out with the virtuosity of a character actor.

Standing in the living room, he combed his long fingers through his dark, short-cropped hair and tracked his eyes across the room to the upright piano. He walked over, picked a plastic bottle of water off the bench, and took a swig. Then he glanced at the clock again. Two minutes. He sat down.

Like Ansel Adams, he honored the artistic link between the keyboard and the camera; his taste in music and the composition of his shots reflected the moody minor keys. With a lazy flip of his wrists he let his fingers wander over the keys and, automatically, like a default setting, he began to pick at the sweet piece by Debussy. A selection from the *Children's Corner* the composer had written as a present to his daughter . . .

Punctual as a planned barrage, three sharp knocks rapped on the door. Rane exhaled, stared at his hands on the keyboard, then got up and walked to the door. He pulled it open and stared into Jennifer Edin's steady, unforgettable blue eyes.

She wore faded jeans, tennis shoes, a white cotton blouse, and a loose unzipped fleece the color of poppies. Rane automatically stored details, so he noted the same leather saddlebag purse slung over her shoulder; a little more worn . . .

In that instant, the whole predictable momentum of his life swerved. He experienced a falling sensation in his chest. His heart raced, his mouth dried up, and, even though he knew it was coming, he couldn't put sound to his surprise.

Jenny was more composed or, at least, more ready. She had prepared for this moment, yielding to it by fractions.

But she didn't speak either. They stared at each other across three feet of space and eleven years. Images flooded in: he looked the same; the room had changed slightly, with the addition of the computer desk and more bookshelves. The famous picture by the French photographer was missing above the light table.

Maybe, she thought, Rane had outgrown the Master.

The same solitary Modigliani nude hung over the same brown couch like Rane's Dorian Gray soul; distorted beauty complicated by hunger. Looking past him into the kitchen, she saw the plastic glitter of stacked twenty-four-packs of bottled water. Used to be gallon jugs. Rane had always surrounded himself with water. Hoarded it. Weird. It's like Rane and the place where he lived had been frozen in time.

Crazy moment, like she'd walked into her imagination.

Long seconds passed in complicated silence. Where to start? Rane backed up, formally, courteously, to give her space to enter the house.

She took a step closer, then another, and saw that he wasn't an entirely preserved fantasy. The sunless skin of his face fit tighter. His eyes had matured and hardened. A starfish of scar split his right eyebrow.

Rane held his breath and stared.

The trill of the cell phone in her purse broke the awkward tension.

They both laughed too loud, grateful for the trivial intervention. She reached for the phone and flipped it open. "Yes . . ."

Rane studied her face, which looked a mite fuller—no, it was the shorter hair. She still had little use for makeup or lipstick. *What you see is what you get*. And what you got was still pretty good. A clean, tart scent spooled in her hair. Chlorine. Swimming . . .

"Who?" Jenny's voice broke.

Rane tensed as the bottom dropped out of her tone and instinctively went up on the balls of his feet.

"What do you mean, *something happened*?" she gasped, and Rane watched her eyes go slick and ugly.

He started forward as she jockeyed for balance; nostrils wide, pupils dilated, then contracted. Saw shock suck the color from her cheeks.

Jenny put one hand out to brace on the door jam. "What? *No!*" She hunched over the phone in the other hand, drawing it in tight as her voice rasped. Then the whites of her eyes swelled suddenly and Rane identified the exploding mortal pain he'd seen up close too many times, burned into the optics of a lens.

The phone slipped from her fingers and clattered on the oak floor. Her knees buckled and her eyes fluttered and she pitched sideways against the side of the foyer doorway.

Rane moved in fast and supported her with one hand as he snatched the phone in mid-spin off the floor with the other. It was still connected, so he raised it to his ear and demanded, "Who is this?" His other hand pressed the hollow of her throat and shoulder, propping her. Her skin was clammy, cold, and he could distinctly feel the big vein throb in his palm.

"Mrs. Edin, ma'am . . . ?" A male voice lashed down in a steel twang. Rane knew immediately. Cop's voice. Not from around here.

"She can't talk," Rane said quickly, as a straight-edge shiver razored down the back of his neck. Rane could just tell, it was gonna be bad, so he improvised. "Damn it, I'm her neighbor. Who is this?"

"Sir? This is Deputy Kenny Beeman. I'm with the Alcorn County Sheriff, we're in Corinth . . ."

"Corinth?"

"Yes sir. Corinth, Mississippi; we're down here a little ways south of Shiloh."

"What the hell's going on?" Rane shouted as his own control slipped. *Jesus, where's Molly?*

"It's real bad, sir. Been a wrongful death. Paul. Her husband. Ain't no easy way to put it. See to her. Got me a similar situation with a friend of her husband's who started this call. I was with the man . . . with Paul . . . right next to him when it happened. Hang tight. I'll call you back in ten at this number," the cop said.

"What happened, what do I tell her?" Rane blurted.

"Her husband just got killed in some crazy accident. At this Civil War reenactment we got down here. Could be somebody accidentally put a live round in a muzzleloader. If it was an accident . . ." the voice was labored, conflicted. Rane heard anger, remorse; the tone off for a cop, like he was taking it personally. "Ain't real clear; I'm at the hospital right now. Sir, you better see to the woman. I'll try'n get more information. Call you back in ten." The Mississippi cop broke the connection.

An utter failure in the small gestures of ordinary life, Rane excelled in crisis. Automatically, he lifted her and she fought his arms, her eyes struggling to focus. Jesus. *In my arms. Smelling her, gathering the warm, loose weight of her.* Then he crossed the room and lowered her to the couch. Swiftly, he unsnapped the button on her jeans, removed her tennis shoes, and went to the kitchen, where he uncapped a bottle of water, tilted it into a glass, reached for a clean towel, soaked it under the cool tap, and wrung it out.

Back at the couch, he folded the damp towel on her forehead. Then he retrieved the cell phone, came back to the couch, and bent over her.

"Jenny."

Her eyes were locked open now and she surged to get up. When he steadied her, she threw her arms around his neck and pulled him close, so he felt the hot flush of tears on his throat. He firmly eased her back down.

More alert now, she cringed and made a terrible sound in her throat, and her hands came up fists and flailed. "No," she insisted. "No."

Rane captured her hands and pushed them to her sides. "Breathe," he said gently. "Breathe through your nose." His tone seemed to calm her, and her chest heaved as she took a deep, shuddering breath. "I'm going to let your hands go," Rane said. "I want you to drink some water. Okay?"

She nodded with great deliberation as if a sudden move would break the fragile dam that contained her tears. As he handed her the glass, she scooted her back up the arm of the couch and drew up her knees. Elbows tight to her sides, she accepted the glass with both hands and took a sip. As she handed back the glass, she took in her unfastened jeans, her shoes on the floor, the cloth that had slipped from her face, the way he continued to hover as he set the glass aside.

From first aid classes, she understood he was monitoring her for shock.

"Cripes," she said with empty mirth, blinking as she saw a stocky gray cat strut into the living room from the kitchen. "Hajji. You've got the same cat." Her eyes traveled the room and she muttered, "My husband went to Mississippi, see, to this Civil War . . ." her voice trailed off and she looked him level in the eyes and asked frankly, "That really happened? What the cop said?"

"He's going to call back in a few minutes," Rane said softly.

Jenny nodded. Numb. Vacant. Couldn't talk. Something filled her chest, something big and inert that crowded her throat and made it hard to breathe. And then she could talk, from a practical, metal part of her mind: "Paul went out of town and I drove in from the valley to knock on your door and now they say he's dead." She grimaced, and it hit her.

"Oh my God, Molly. Jesus, what do I do?"

Rane waited a moment, then said in a flat, practical tone, "Triage. Take care of the living, starting with you."

The Mississippi cop called back promptly in ten minutes. Rane handed the phone to Jenny and retreated. He fetched a pad and pen when she made a scribbling motion with her hand. After five hard minutes talking through tears, she ended the call and stared at two pages of notes and numbers. Rane offered her a towel he'd grabbed from the kitchen, and she blotted the tears from her face. Then she shook her head and spoke in a deliberate, blood-drained voice: "Paul was wounded in the throat and bled to death almost instantly. It doesn't make sense. The cop, Beeman, couldn't give me a straight answer. He said accidents can happen with those rifles they use."

Rane reigned in his curiosity at the whole reenactor scenario and the way the cop's voice had sounded. Stay on the present. "First things first. Where's Molly?" he asked.

"My mom's with her. They were going to a movie. That's why the cop called my cell. No one answered at home."

"How'd he get the numbers?"

"Paul's friend, Davey. He was going to call but I guess they had a rough time trying to get Paul some medical help and he needed some attention himself. The cop picked up the phone, like you did." She narrowed her eyes, studying his expression; like he was waiting on her permission. "What? Go on, talk."

"Maybe you should call and have your mom send Molly over to a friend's. Molly should hear this from you, not from her grandmother. I wouldn't tell your mom on the phone."

Jenny bit her lip. "Don't tell Mom?"

"Better face-to-face. Then tell Molly." He thought for a moment. "Is there a minister? I mean . . ."

Jenny shook her head. "We don't go to church. Just on Christmas." She stared at the piano. "For the music." She pushed off the couch and tested her balance. Important to stay in control here. "I gotta go home."

Rane moved in fast to steady her. "I don't think you should drive right now." After a pause, he said, "Put on your shoes."

Jenny blinked and lowered herself back to the couch, leaned forward, slowly pulled on the sneakers, and stared at her fingers busy with the laces. Paul was dead and she had to tie her shoes. Paul was dead and soon she'd be hungry and have to remember to eat. Paul was dead and eventually she'd have to go to the bathroom. Enough.

Need to be strong. For Molly. Something Dad said once. My turn.

Her eyes tilted up, still tear-bright but some strength returning. She flashed on the famous photograph in the paper last week: the guy killing himself while Rane took his picture. "You're good at this. People dying." Saying it, she felt stronger.

Then she stood up and noticed the unfastened top button of her jeans and did it up. Rane handed her the cell phone and her purse. She plunged in her hand, fished out her keys, took a deep breath, looked around the room. "I shouldn't be here. I gotta go home."

He blocked the door. "Not a good idea, you driving right now," he said patiently.

She pushed against him, he resisted. She pushed again. Just before it became a physical struggle, he raised his hands and stepped back. She exited the door and managed to reach the sidewalk before all the normal street sounds curdled in her stomach. She looked up once and was stunned by the immensity of the sky. Then, in a lurch of nausea, she walked stiffly to the car. Muscle memory. Open the door.

Trembling, she felt bile ripple up in her throat and push more tears from her eyes. A whole shelf of grief collapsed her to her knees and she vomited on the pavement.

Rane was standing there as she shuddered against the side of the car. When the spasm passed, Rane took her arms and helped her to her feet. He handed her a blue bandanna to wipe the vomitus from her face. Then he handed her one of his ubiquitous bottles of water to rinse her mouth.

They were alone.

In the shadow of Paul's death.

And they had a daughter.

"I'm going to drive you home," Rane said firmly.

This time Jenny did not protest. She let him lead her to the passenger seat. Saw him for what he was: hard-edged and extremely competent. Right, for now.

She sat trying to marshal her thoughts as he got in and strapped the seat belt. As he put the car in gear, she said, "I want a cigarette."

"I quit," Rane said.

"Me too. Everybody did. I want a cigarette."

Before they reached the freeway, Rane stopped at a Holiday station, went in, and bought a pack of American Spirits and a lighter. When he returned, Jenny lowered her cell phone and said she'd called her mother and that Molly was going over to her friend Rachel's house.

"You tell her?" Rane asked.

"No, but she could tell from my voice, something's wrong."

Rane nodded, brought the memory out of storage, meeting her folks. The mother had been fit, animated. But the father, who was tall and lanky, and projected brooding quiet, had peered into Rane's eyes and, seeing something familiar, had warned him away with one somber look.

He handed Jenny the pack of cigarettes. Her fingers fumbled with the cellophane, so Rane took the pack, opened it, put one in his mouth, flicked the lighter, and inhaled tobacco smoke for the first time in what, five years? He handed the cigarette to her.

Jenny took it from his fingers and put it to her lips. The burning tobacco hissed in her throat like a fuse that was going to blow open a vault full of memories. Already had. Lying side by side, passing a smoke. Had to be shock, denial, an out-of-body joke. Mindless libido trying to face down sudden death?

When she started to tremble, Rane said, "Delayed reaction. Just keep breathing."

When he said "breathing," she stared at the cigarette, then tossed it out the window with an icky reaction, like she'd discovered a spider in her hand. But she tucked the pack in her purse and then gave him directions to the house.

Had to be shock. Paul was dead and she was watching the familiar landmarks stream by as they drove east out of the city, toward the St. Croix River. She tried to remember the last time she and Molly had talked about human death. Not a cat, not a hamster, not a goldfish. Okay. Her dad. But that was three years ago. Molly was eight and she and Mom had stage-managed the funeral. Had Dad cremated so Molly wouldn't see . . .

She watched Rane in profile as he concentrated on the road, staring straight ahead, steady behind the wheel. Neither spoke. Words were too flimsy, and her thoughts lost their sync, inappropriate. Damning.

I had thoughts about this man, adulterous thoughts.

They threaded into the cul-de-sacs. She pointed at the house, Rane pulled into the driveway and parked the Forester, and they got out.

"I better go grab a cab," Rane said; low-key, respectful, handing her the keys.

Jenny nodded, but when he started to turn away she touched his arm. "No, wait," she said. "Stay."

18 MOTIONLESS AS WAX FIGURINES, Rane and Jenny watched a smiling woman push a stroller along the street; this beaming, ruddy-cheeked new mother, as plump as her bundled baby.

Rane looked after her. "No sidewalks," he wondered in a detached voice, then he turned to Jenny.

"Have to tell her," Jenny thought out loud.

"Tell her the truth. It'll hurt now but she'll remember all her life if you give it to her sideways," Rane said with conviction.

Jenny pursed her lips. "I might need help."

Before he could respond, she turned away and walked stiffly up the drive and went into the house. Rane watched her go and realized he was counting under his breath: one thousand one, one thousand two. It was an old bracing reflex from the army, exiting the jump door, waiting for the chute to open.

Except he didn't have a parachute or a net under him; not in this scene. Jesus. He should leave. *Trespassing here.* More than that, it was a dilemma. This eerie sensation drifted through his chest, that he was on personally dangerous ground, that he was way too close and naked without his camera. If he didn't leave he would be in trouble.

Then he saw Jenny emerge from the front door with her mother, a trim woman with short salt-and-pepper hair. They moved in slow motion, walking underwater, fixed stares.

Rane followed the direction of their eyes, and a moment later he saw a girl skip from the open garage of a house across and down the block. She wore jeans, a blue striped T-shirt, and largish tennis shoes. Rane noticed that her shoelaces were not securely tied and trailed along the street. But she was light on her feet, lean and graceful. He recalled observing over time that girls stopped skipping when they were eleven.

Molly was eleven.

Then Jenny's mother's knees misfired and she stumbled. Jenny put her arms around her to steady her. Molly had broken into a jog, and as she came closer, Rane saw a frown crease her clear forehead. Her mother and grandma didn't look right. She shot one fast look at Rane standing at the foot of the driveway; a stranger out of place in her yard.

Molly slowed her pace to a tentative walk.

Jenny summoned Molly with a curt jerk of her hand, a teacher's reflex. Molly's walk slowed to a wary, loose-limbed amble, and she called out, "Mom?" Rane could see her physically tense as her body stepped into the radius of the pain coming off Mom and Grandma. Her mind hadn't caught up.

Jenny put one hand on Molly's shoulder, said something, then reached fast with her other hand as Molly pulled away. More words. Faces getting terrible. And Rane knew they were talking around it.

By instinct and experience, he absolutely knew that the kid would resent sugarcoating and evasion all her life . . . at this moment she needed to know the truth.

The truth.

He rocked back at the invisible barrier of complicity in the large lie he and Jenny had nurtured.

Screw all that.

Rane started forward. The kid should know.

Molly shook her head, hugged herself with both arms, and jumped back, dancing away down the driveway. Jenny and her mom slowed down with the weight of it. The girl . . . his mind grinding, could feel the gears move, teeth engaging. *Molly*. His daughter, not his daughter. Molly went the other way and bolted.

"Molly! Stop!" Rane's voice reached out, the sound as foreign as a naming ceremony in his mouth. But his clear, hard voice caught her up and she halted, frightened now. As Rane walked toward her, he saw that her wide green eyes were angry. Good, he thought, better pissed than cowed.

But then she shook her head again, and Rane could hear Jenny and her mother coming up behind him. Molly began to cry. Then she turned and broke into a dead run.

Rane dashed after her. Damn, the kid was *fast*. They darted between the houses, doubled back across the street and up a slope toward a tiny stand of trees in the sea of new houses. Rane overtook her, worried that she'd trip on the bad footing, snaked an arm around her waist, and hoisted her, kicking and pummeling him. "Let me go," she screamed.

He firmly pinned her arms and carried her to a walking trail, where he saw a bench. He placed her on the bench and knelt before her. From the corner of his eye he saw Jenny jogging up the hill.

"Let me go. Who are you?" Molly blurted.

"I'm Uncle John," Rane said.

"I don't have an uncle John."

"Yes you do," Rane said in an even voice. "Now listen to me."

"What?"

"Your father is dead."

"Is not," she insisted.

"He died in an accident in Mississippi," Rane said firmly.

"The reenactor thing?" Molly sniffed and looked away.

"Yes. Now listen to me," he repeated, waiting for her eyes to return. When they did, he went on. "There's no right way to say this. Usually bad stuff happens to other people . . . but today it happened to you and your mom."

"Uh-uh," she sniffed, staring into his eyes.

"You won't see him again alive," he said as he held her, firm but steady, a hand cupped on each of her shoulders. In an attempt to contain the spasm roiling in her body, his grip tightened and he himself trembled at the sensation. Like a transfusion, the pain coming off her was an open wound bleeding into his hands.

He was holding his own flesh and blood, and nothing would be the same again.

"Why?" Anger raged through her tears, demanding an explanation.

Rane was unsure, trying to calibrate his words for an eleven-year-old mind. "Molly, listen to me: maybe there's a reason, maybe there isn't. That's for later. Right now all you have is other people, like your mom and grandma, you all need each other now."

He watched the words slash at her eyes. When her eyes began to roll up and away, he repeated, "Listen to me."

She responded to his tone, faced him, and leveled her eyes.

"You need to be with your mother now," Rane said. "She's coming up the hill. When I let you go, walk down to meet her."

Molly nodded, raised her forearm, and wiped it across her nose. Rane released his hands. She rose from the bench and walked, stiff-kneed, from the path, through the stretch of brush to the edge of the trees. Rane followed her at a distance. When she got into the open, she looked back once. He nodded encouragement. Molly walked down the slope. When Rane cleared the trees, he saw Molly and Jenny arm in arm, turning and walking slowly down the hill, supporting each other like walking wounded.

Rane followed, and the grandmother came up to meet him. The woman extended her hand. "I'm Lois, Jenny's mother."

"Yes. Lois and Greg Hatton. We've met," Rane said.

"Years ago, when Jenny was pregnant with Molly," Lois said pointedly, with a touch of frost coming briefly to her damp eyes. The edgy moment passed. "Greg, my husband, Jenny's father, died . . ."

"Three years ago," Rane said.

Lois cocked an eyebrow over a watery eye.

"I read the obits in the paper," Rane said. He shook her hand. "Lois, I don't have my cell. I'd appreciate it if you called me a cab."

"Of course."

Rane waited awkwardly at the curb, pacing. Lois came out with a cup of coffee and the pack of cigarettes and the lighter he'd bought at the Holiday.

"Jenny thought you might want these," Lois said.

Rane refused the cigarettes but took the cup.

"It's my fault she went to see you," Lois said.

Rane cocked his head.

Lois continued. "I've been after her to approach you and get a basic medical history, you, your parents. You know, to have on file in case anything came up with Molly."

"Okay, I see," Rane said. Then he motioned at the house with the coffee cup. "I think you better go back in with them."

Lois said, "Right."

But she stood watching him for several seconds, waiting for more of a response. When she didn't get it, she said, "Just, ah, leave the cup on the curb." She turned and left him at the foot of the driveway waiting for the cab.

In the living room Molly had stymied Jenny with a single word.

"Why?"

Jenny saw her mom come back in the house. She saw a thousand words, a hyper video stream behind her eyes. They were moving too fast and she needed to grab the right one.

"Why Dad? Why not somebody else?" Molly demanded. She shuddered and clamped her arms across her chest. "I never even said good-bye . . ."

Molly's face was going as pale and cold as dry ice. She sat on the couch with her knees pressed together, her elbows rigid at her sides, arms crossed, fists clenched. No tears. They'd retracted, been sucked inside. Tears purged pain, washed it out. But her daughter was turning it inward. Like when heat-stroke victims stop sweating; it's a signal that the process inside was busted.

"There was an accident," Jenny said.

"A car accident?"

"No honey, they think an accident with a gun."

Molly's face receded, getting paler. She pulled her knees up and drew her elbows in tighter. Jenny watched her daughter try to physically disappear inside herself.

Jenny felt panic fill the house, ready to explode the air. It smelled like the lemon-scented disinfectant she'd used this afternoon, after lunch, to wipe down the granite counters in the kitchen . . .

To hell with this! She gritted her teeth at a surge of anger. Both of the significant men in her life had left her alone to deal with this: Paul by dying and Rane by standing outside waiting for a fucking cab.

She stood up, walked to the door, opened it, and called down the driveway to Rane.

"Get in here, I shouldn't have to do this by myself. You're *involved*, goddamn it!"

John Rane walked up the driveway, lowered his head, and entered the house. The first thing he saw was the jumble of shoes just inside the door; a larger pair of running Nikes alongside the smaller shoes were worn and comfortable. And empty. He ventured deeper into the house, past the piano room, to the kitchen, which was to the right of the family area. Jenny, Lois, and Molly were in a mannequin tableau among the cozy couch and chairs that now looked as cold and remote as moon rocks. A lifeless vacancy filled the room.

Lois sat on the couch next to Molly. Jenny stood hugging herself; her eyes grabbing at Molly without traction.

Rane took it in and adapted fast. Talk won't work here. Do something.

As he turned his back, he caught a glimpse of Jenny's raw eyes; a damning, resigned look at his leaving. He kept walking down the hall to the alcove that contained the upright Kawai piano. He opened the French doors, went in, sat down on the bench, and opened the keyboard. His fingers poised over the keys but then he knew intuitively where to go. His left hand spread, little finger and thumb extended to gently press the C-sharp octave whole note. The fingers of his right hand settled softly on G-sharp, C-sharp, E.

The slow, melancholy first movement of Beethoven's Sonata No. 14 must be played very softly, *adagio sustenuto*. The "Moonlight Sonata" had always impressed Rane as somber and mysterious but also rooted in reality.

Toward the end of the piece, he felt Molly slide onto the seat beside him. He finished playing and stared at his hands.

"You're not really my uncle John are you?" Molly said in a wrung-out voice.

Rane looked up, saw Jenny standing, eyes brimming, behind Molly. Like an adept shortstop plucking up a fast ground ball, Jenny said, "It's an expression, honey. It means he's an old friend."

Molly sniffed, stared at the keyboard.

Rane shifted to the side. "You play the piano?" he asked.

"Uh-huh," Molly said in a shaky voice.

Rane waited patiently as she began to cry. Then he said, "Sometimes, when I'm down, I find it helps better than trying to talk. Sometimes," he said gently, "you can go somewhere else . . ."

After a moment, Molly sniffed again and then experimented with a finger, touching the keyboard. Then she wiped the back of her hand across her nose, sat straighter, opened a music book, and started to play.

Rane eased from the seat. When Jenny started to speak, he shook his head once with finality. Lois moved next to Jenny and put her hands on her arms. Rane walked to the front door and let himself out. As he walked down the driveway to the waiting cab, he heard the tentative music pushing back against the emptiness in the house behind him.

19   C'MON RANE, DO THE TRICKS.

Triage, compartmentalize; bring on that reliable mental body armor to protect you from the unexpected . . .

. . . so you can function in tight spots, man . . .

Except his gimmicks weren't working, because he kept looking at his hands and right now Molly was in his hands and he couldn't get her out. So he tried to concentrate on the road going by as the Somali driver piloted the cab back to St. Paul.

For one instant, a string of negatives—blacks and whites reversed—streamed in back of his eyes. Bulging dark eyes wrapped in a desert Shemagh headdress . . . Just a flash that was quickly gone. He had taken thousands of pictures. Only seven of them stayed perfectly preserved . . .

Suddenly he became very thirsty and asked the driver to pull off the freeway at a gas station. Rane went in and bought a liter of water and returned to the cab.

As the car entered his neighborhood, a gut instinct told him he should get out and walk, so he had the cab drop him three blocks from his house. Rane tried walking. A trio of kids raced by on bikes. There was enough chill in the afternoon air to float their breath like exuberant scarves.

Walking didn't work. Now his gut told him he should eat. He arrived home and spent indecisive minutes walking his small yard. He'd dated a woman once who talked him into planting perennials. After she'd given up on him, he made an attempt to keep up with the plants. Now every spring only a few obstinate hostas peeked up through the weeds, like stealthy, knife-edged periscopes.

He ran his hand along the bubbling, peeling paint on his wood siding, searching for a seam in time that would allow him to find his way back to the moment before Jenny knocked on his door . . .

Kept seeing Molly sitting on the couch, locked up; heard Jenny's angry, grieving accusation.

You're involved, goddamn it!

John Rane never got involved. He kept a crisp 200-millimeter lens between him and other people's problems.

He went inside, sat down at his kitchen table, and stared at the front door. Heard the frustration in that Southern cop's voice. *If it was an accident?*

What the hell did that mean?

He got up, went into his bedroom, and emptied his pockets. As he dumped his change and a fold of bills on his dresser top, he stared at his keys. A quarter was fixed to the snap ring by a chain inserted through a drilled hole. A bigger, jagged-edged puncture about the diameter of a pencil ripped George Washington's head wide open. He nudged the pierced coin back and forth with his finger.

C'mon, Rane. Do something.

And finally he was back to food and understood his impulse to eat. His uncle Mike had schooled him in the tricks; pointing out how certain people needed survival tactics. People, say, who had too much baggage and could go off half-cocked and make bad decisions and wind up back on the bus to hell. Mike had struggled through a rocky transition from legendary hellion to responsible husband to Aunt Karen. One of the main tricks Mike used to air out tension was cooking.

Rane snatched his wallet and keys off the dresser. What you had to do was go shopping. Stay busy. Create some space to think in.

He drove to the nearest grocery store, went in, and roamed brightly lit aisles. Mike was a big advocate of one-pot meals: venison chili, stew, spaghetti, cabbage soup. The cabbage soup sounded like a good antidote to the gray weather, so he dropped carrots, celery, onions, and a large head of cabbage into his cart. Then he added some Italian sausage and onion soup mix. On the way out of the store, he stopped at the convenience counter and bought two packs of American Spirits.

Back home, he loaded his coffeemaker with the concentration of a monk performing a Zen ritual: a filter, some water, and the heady French roast. As the machine brewed, he wiped down his kitchen counter, set a large pot on the stove, laid out his ingredients, and withdrew a knife from the wall rack. His thumb flicked along the edge of the blade, testing the sharpness. Midway through slicing vegetables and sausage, he collided with the very thought he was working to avoid. He'd regularly tucked money away in an education account. Always assumed he'd meet his daughter when she was more grown—which was a way of putting it off.

Should have been there from the beginning. Should have been paying child support, something. Tried to call that one time. Jenny froze him out.

He shook olive oil into the pot and turned on the gas burner. When the oil started to sizzle, he shoveled in the sectioned sausage, then he dusted the browning meat with paprika and added a pinch of pepper. He tipped in the bowl of sliced onions, carrots, and celery. Keep busy. Stir the pot. Now measure the water and add the soup mix. Finishing up, he sectioned the head of cabbage and dumped in shredded handfuls. There. Let it simmer. He washed his hands, poured a cup of coffee, and lit a cigarette.

But the taste of caffeine and nicotine inside these four walls took him straight back to the last tense face-to-face conversation he'd had with Jenny, eleven years ago, right out in the living room. He found himself there now, pacing up and down in front of the couch, smoking to cover a twinge of nerves, just like on that day long ago.

A young Jenny Hatton had leaned forward, her color up, her eyes bright; expectant in all ways. So she came at him all straight-ahead righteous, like a figurehead on a war galley. And, of course, he could imagine all the jetsam in her wake: the diapers, the mortgage, the deadening cadence of the mallet setting the pace for the galley slaves. But that wasn't it.

"I'm going to keep the baby," she'd said.

"I'm not ready for this" was all Rane could honestly say.

So she'd called him a coward and said if that was his answer she never wanted to see him again. No half-measures. No calls, no child support. Nothing. Then she stood up and walked out of his life, carrying his baby in her belly.

Rane stood in the empty living room a long time, until the cigarette built up an inch of ash.

"Coward" still hurt.

So he told himself he was a pragmatic man who didn't waste time with imprecise notions like irony. He dumped the cigarette in the kitchen sink, left the coffee cup, and walked into the bedroom.

Do the exercise.

He opened the closet, reached behind the hangers, and found the long leather case. He placed the gun case on the bed, unzipped it, and eased out the old 30.06 Remington with the battered Redfield scope. The date of manufacture was stamped on the breech: 1942.

Mike had taught him to hunt with the old rifle; had started him shooting with a .22 when he was twelve.

Rane fired the rifle ceremonially every November, when he accompanied Mike to hunt whitetail in Northern Wisconsin. His uncle's eyes were graying with cataracts and Rane would patiently work the tree lines and thickets to find a fat buck for Mike and Karen's freezer. But he kept the rifle scrupulously clean year-round; the pitted wood stock stayed shiny from the oils of his hands. He opened the blinds to the bedroom window, raised the rifle, and wrapped his elbow into the sling. Mike had taught him to shoot using an off-hand formula: no sense shooting supported. You ain't gonna have a bench to lean on when you jump the whitetail.

The late afternoon light was hazy, failing, but he could still make out the knothole in a telephone pole exactly a hundred ten yards down the alley. He knew every whirl and twist of that knothole better than the faces of his few acquaintances. He acquired the tiny, puckered wood genie in the scope and tickled it with the crosshairs.

Dry-firing was an exercise in holding on a target and trigger pull. Rane used it as a form of meditation half an hour most days. His Nikon had shutter speeds that could take multiple shots per second. But you still had to intuit the precise nanosecond to pull the trigger.

Composition. Tempo. The piano flowed into the camera and they both informed the rifle. He exhaled, attuned to the pulse in his hands as he let the crosshairs float in a tightening figure eight. Pattern of timing, a felt thing. In between heartbeats, he brought the trigger pressure and sight picture into balance.

He smelled the cabbage soup simmering in the kitchen. He saw Molly's eyes the moment the fact of sudden death was shoved in her face.

Gently, he pressed the trigger straight back with the tip of his finger.

In the crisp metal snap of bolt on steel he heard the minor key rhythm of his life: a simple, elegantly designed machine clicking on an empty chamber.

20

MITCH LOST TRACK.

He'd been pushed and dragged through thickets, forced to crouch down in the bushes, and stuffed into the front seat of a vehicle that sounded like a truck. Then the truck door opened and he was slung over his attacker's shoulder and hauled into someplace tight, because his feet kept hitting the sides.

He passed out again.

When he woke up, the tape wrapping his eyes was mashed over his ears and made it hard to hear, so the voices sounded far off, garbled, like underwater, but angry.

"What the hell is he doing dressed like *that*? *He's supposed to be in Memphis.*" And that was one mad woman.

"When I saw him he was hiding up the woods, shooting toward the reenactors. Check the bag. He's got real rounds in those cartridges."

Same voice from the woods. The black guy.

"Christ. You know what happened down there?" the woman yelled, and when she hit the shrill high notes it sounded like Ellie.

Then the voices were lower and he couldn't hear.

Shit.

Panting, blind, he realized they'd removed the tape from his mouth. He could breathe better and taste the air, which was close and musty with mineral damp.

He kept his eyes shut tight behind the sticky tape. Aware of his body now, huddled in a fetal cringe, he realized his hands were free, so he moved his fingers and felt raw earth. His left hand hurt something fierce. Okay. It's gonna be bad. How do you open your eyes on something real bad when you can't remember . . .

"Take off the tape," the woman ordered, the voice getting more familiar with every syllable.

"Shoulda left him in the woods, fucker pulled a pistol on me," said the black guy, breathing heavily from exertion. Some of it was coming back now.

With an excruciating jerk, the tape ripped off his eyes, tearing his hair and eyebrows.

"Ow damn."

The strong hand gripped his shoulder, shook him. "C'mon, Mitch, wake up, you dumb motherfucker."

Mitch cringed deeper into himself, keeping his eyes clamped shut, shying away from the patient hostility in that voice. Like a nightmare. Keep your eyes shut. Maybe it'll pass. Worked sometimes. The hand released his shoulder. A moment later, a slap jarred his left cheek. Hey.

The blow unstuck his eyelids. And it hadda be a bad dream, because he was staring at LaSalle Ector's blacker 'an shit face just inches from his own. A grime of sweat, dirt, and bits of brush stuck to LaSalle's cheeks, neck, and shoulders. The debris formed a pattern with the wormy purple scars streaking his face and neck.

So it was Ellie's paid boy who jumped him in the woods. Damn.

Mitch grimaced, trying to make sense of it. LaSalle stood up and stepped back and the dream got worse, because Ellie was standing there next to him, looking madder than he'd ever seen her, with eyes glittering as hard as ball bearings. She wore Levi's and a peasant blouse and hiking shoes, and her freckles blazed in the bad light like copper nails pounded into her long face.

"You sonofabitch," she seethed. "This is the last time you lie to me."

Mitch avoided her eyes, looked around to get oriented. He was sprawled on a dirt floor in a narrow chamber of raw, sloping limestone. A wide, urn-shaped chamber pot gleamed in the emergency harshness of a heavy-duty utility light wedged up in a rock crevasse. A long extension cord snaked off into the gloom.

Jesus, special-effects weird? They had him back in some kinda cave.

When he tried to shift his weight, he heard a rattle. This rusty iron cuff surrounded his ankle, clamped over his trousers. A shiny Yale lock pinned the cuff's eyelets together.

The shackle was attached to an ancient chain, the other end cemented in the stone wall. Several of these long, anchored chains coiled in a rusty jumble on the dirt floor, like a pile of snakes.

"His hand's cut pretty bad. Should I see to it?" LaSalle asked.

"Go ahead," she said.

A plastic flicker appeared in LaSalle's hand, a water bottle. He unscrewed the cap and thrust the bottle at Mitch. "You should drink some water." Mitch craned his neck and drank greedily. Then LaSalle dribbled water on Mitch's injured left hand to see the gash better. "I need to clean that up," he said.

LaSalle had a medical bag; he pulled the Velcro flap and selected a bottle of disinfectant, gauze, a tube of ointment, and tape. Mitch's eyes now bulged, sheer animal alert. Still, it took several heartbeats to notice that LaSalle had frozen in mid-motion.

LaSalle went around six one. One ninety. Real black, smoky black, cold reserve black; like his people got the haughty North African features on the other side and kept them pure.

He was lithe-muscled. Had all that graceful shit going. Like he kept up basketball. Weights.

But right now his hands fluttered in the air and his serious brown eyes blinked. Like he'd become stuck and appeared to be momentarily confused by the simple first-aid items he had laid out on the bag just inches from his fingers.

"Are you all right?" Ellie said, coming closer, and Mitch marked the concern in her voice, so suddenly off her anger.

Something funny here?

LaSalle shook his head and refocused. "I'm good. You stay back from him. Let me tend to this." Now his fingers flew, certain, as he cleaned the wound with orange stinging Betadine, dabbed on the ointment, and taped on a bandage.

"I want to talk to him, alone," Ellie said emphatically.

"You sure?" LaSalle said.

"I'm sure," she said.

"Okay. Just stay back by this line I marked in the dirt. Be out of his reach that way." Then LaSalle placed the water bottle next to Mitch's leg, turned, and retreated down the crypt-like chamber to another pool of light.

Mitch grabbed the bottle, drank, gagged, kept it down. Drank some more. The water helped some. Squinting, getting used to the light, he saw the rifle leaning against the cave wall along with his haversack, leathers, and the holstered Colt. Flashed on the shot, the smoke and confusion.

They know something? What?

Ellie stooped to the haversack, removed the pack of Pall Malls and the lighter, and tossed them to Mitch. He plucked them up, got one going, and took a drag. And that helped more than the water. What was this, bad cop, good cop?

Ellie put her toes on the line marked in the dirt, watched him for several seconds, then said, "Mitchell Lee, you got some explaining to do."

Mitch gritted his teeth and scooted on his side, got his knees under him, then shifted over on his butt and leaned his back against the cool stone.

"Where am I?" he asked, rattling the chain on his foot.

"Looks like you finally made it to the big time; like you

always wanted," Ellie said. Her voice was more under control now. Her eyes were still pretty terrible.

Mitch chewed his lip. What you had to do with Ellie was first get her calmed down. "I mean where exactly?"

"The old potting shed down by the lake, built into the caves. The caves go deeper than most people know. This part was walled off."

Mitch shook his head. "The hell . . ."

Ellie smiled tightly. "LaSalle knocked down the wall and strung electric in from the shed. This is the old slave quarters from back in like 1820; before the family bought the place. I originally thought the Black Historical Society in town might want a look in here."

Mitch took a shaky pull on the cigarette, exhaled, then shook his leg chain, indignant. He blinked several times and attempted to fathom her, standing there, her eyes getting harder and harder. "You let that sonofabitch put me in these?"

"Watch your mouth. It's a miracle he managed to drag you in here during all the confusion."

"Confusion?"

"Yes, Mitchell Lee. The confusion still going on outside, along Kirby Creek after that Union boy got shot in the neck."

Shit.

Mitch slumped back against the wall, shut his eyes, tried to work it back. Not now. Think. He opened his eyes and said, "No idea what you're talking about."

"Really," Ellie said. She turned, scooped up the leather cartridge box, and opened the flap. She fingered one of the cartridges and felt the bulk and weight. She pinched the weighted end, peeling it open. For a moment she held the lead bullet and the black powder in her open palm, then she turned her hand and let them fall to the dirt floor.

Then she pointed to the rifle leaning down the passage. Out of the case. "You're supposed to be in Memphis but you

were carrying Daddy's Enfield when LaSalle found you in the
woods. The barrel is fouled. It's been fired, Mitchell Lee."

"Bullshit. I been attacked. You're making this up," Mitch
said.

Ellie planted her hands on her hips. "Am I? That boy died
before the ambulance even got to him. They have all the police in two counties out there, questioning the reenactors,
looking through the woods."

How, Mitch wondered? I was dead on Beeman. Dead on.

He took a moment to order his thoughts, then wondered,
"So if you know so much, how come I'm not out there? Why
am I wearing leg irons in a hole in the ground?"

"Because I'm not sure what to do with you until I get an
answer."

Infuriated, Mitch lurched to his knees. "Fuck me dead,
Ellender Jane! *What is the question?*"

She clenched her arms across her chest. "LaSalle said,
just after he took you down you received a call on your cell.
He answered the call." She reached down and withdrew his
cell phone from the haversack. "LaSalle said the person who
called said you 'missed Beeman.' " She cocked her head. "So
you were trying to shoot Bee and now I want to know why.
All of it. Exactly."

Mitch mimicked her voice contemptuously. " '*LaSalle
said.*' C'mon Ellie, you gonna believe LaSalle? What I heard
his head is mush from getting blowed up." Mitch knew he
should button up. But this was Ellie and he just might be able
to talk her down. Worked before.

"So what about the cell phone call?" she insisted.

"Weren't no cell phone call," Mitch muttered. He glanced
past her to where LaSalle was stooped in a narrow part of
passage, sorting through what looked like a pile of bricks.
Lowering his voice, he leaned forward and hissed, "That's a
lyin' nigger you got workin' for you is what."

"Listen to you," she said with a disgusted curl to her lower
lip. "You're regressing to Theo."

Situation like this, you gotta think positive. Reason with her. Mitch set the cigarette aside, slowly rose to his feet, and took a moment to order his thoughts. He tested his balance, estimated the length of chain.

He cleared his throat. Gave her the smile, then the voice. "C'mon, Ellie, somebody's got to be the adult here. How's it gonna look? One minute I'm in my motel room in Memphis, the next I'm chained up in a hole underground. No idea how I got into these clothes. Who're people going to believe, me or him? Shit, everybody knows they wouldn't let him back on the ambulance. That's why you got him out here doing manual labor."

Mitch edged forward, uncoiling the chain. Encouraged by Ellie's frown, he pressed on, improvising, "Think, Ellie, how's it going to look when Billie Watts gets through tearing LaSalle a new asshole in court. Gonna look like he staged all this." He tugged at a dirty gray woolen sleeve. "How do you know he didn't steal this getup and the rifle and take a shot at Beeman. Shit, I'll bet Beeman arrested him back before he cleaned up." Mitch paused for effect, then said, "And here you are aiding and abetting."

Ellie was unimpressed. "Forget Billie Watts," she said, jaw set. "This is between you, me, and LaSalle. Courts got nothing to do with it." She showed her perfect piranha teeth in a demure snarl. "What do folks say on your side of the county? State-line rules."

Mitch grimaced and tried to get his mind around what she was saying. Just you, huh? Tell you what.

If he could just get his hands around her skinny neck, then they'd let him go.

With a growl he leaped forward, thrusting his arms, clawing for her throat. Just before the slack ran taut on the leg chain, she skipped back almost casually, upper body steady, arms folded.

Mitch gasped when the chain caught him, and for a fraction of a second he was jerked, his rear leg extended straight back, torso and arms stretched forward, balanced on his un-shackled foot. His fingers stopped just inches from the cold, merry anger in her eyes.

"Why Mitchell Lee," Ellie purred, studying his extended posture. "I believe you've performed a yoga position called Warrior Two."

"Fuckin' bitch," he snarled, losing his balance, toppling sideways, and falling heavily to the dirt floor.

Ellie raised a hand to quiet LaSalle, who had started back down the corridor. "Listen up, Mitchell Lee," she said. "Much as I like Bee, and bad as I feel about that poor Yankee boy, that is not where we're at, you and me."

She paused and then Mitch heard her icy voice echo along the stone.

"You better tell me the whole truth, you hear? If you don't it's going to be like that Edgar Allan Poe story we read in high school."

Mitch hated it; sprawled in the dirt, looking up, seeing her draw herself erect and clamp her damn Kirby jaw and point down the passage to the narrow part where LaSalle stood watching in his pile of rubble.

"As God is my witness, Mitchell Lee, I will brick you up in here with my own hands and leave you to the dark."

21

ON SUNDAY PAUL EDIN'S DEATH received two minutes on CNN. A spokesman for the Alcorn County, Mississippi, Coroner's Office appeared briefly and read from a prepared statement:

> *"A Minnesota reenactor has died in an unfortunate accident at the Kirby Creek tactical event. The results of an autopsy just completed in Jackson found that Paul Edin, of Stillwater, Minnesota, died as a result of an unidentified projectile passing through his throat. The wound ballistics are consistent with trauma caused by a low-velocity lead bullet, but no weapon or bullet has been found, and no one has determined who might have fired the shot. The Alcorn County Sheriff's Department has made a preliminary finding that this regrettable incident was an accident until witnesses or new evidence indicate otherwise . . ."*

Rane watched an establishing shot of a white one-story house with a wraparound veranda on a hill overlooking a wooded field. Then they showed some file footage of Civil War reenactors firing muskets, while a serious-faced reenactor in a gray uniform was interviewed and listed a catalogue of reenactors' deaths and injuries during the mock battles. For instance, a man had survived a shot in the neck at Gettysburg several years ago. In that case, someone had accidentally left a live charge in a pistol. A few questions were devoted to safety precautions. Yes, there were risks associated with the hobby; you had all these guys with functioning weapons, and black powder was dangerous, especially with artillery. A live round could have been fired by accident. A piece of ramrod could have broken off, debris could have lodged in the barrel . . .

Accidents happen.

The *Star Tribune*, *Pioneer Press*, and local TV recapped the story and interviewed members of the First Minnesota in front of Fort Snelling. Both papers ran a portrait of Paul Edin, a smiling, conventionally handsome man "whose interest in Civil War history had taken a fatal turn." The article went on to say that Edin was survived by his wife and daughter. His death ran its course in less than twelve hours; a one-day story crowded off TV and the printed page by a vicious string of Baghdad bombings.

Rane avoided the piano and went for a ten-mile run along River Road; he ate his cabbage soup and drank too much coffee. He smoked too many cigarettes, then went down to his basement, where he pushed himself on the free weights, then the heavy bag, and ended the workout with the jump rope. Lungs burning, dripping sweat; he trudged back up the stairs finally exhausted enough to get to sleep.

Late on Monday morning, Jenny called and said straight away, "Tom Dalton and Davey Manning, the two guys Paul went down there with, are coming by to drop off his . . . things. They're on the road right now, driving back. They'll be here around six . . ."

Rane waited.

"They have new information about what happened, like maybe Paul's death wasn't an accident. I'd like you to hear it, to advise me if I should go to the cops." She sounded lost in a thicket, reaching for a handy machete.

Rane exhaled audibly, remembering the Mississippi cop's voice on the phone. *If it was an accident . . .*

Jenny continued quickly, "That piece you played? Molly wants the sheet music. She asked if you'd help her learn it . . ."

Rane shut his eyes, thinking, She's grabbing at straws.

When he didn't respond, Jenny said, "She's been asking questions about you . . ."

"Christ, Jenny," Rane breathed.

"Slow down. I just told her what you did for a living and she's looking through back issues of newspapers for your pictures. She's found three so far."

"Sure, okay, I'll listen to what those guys have to say," he said cautiously. "About the music, it's a little beyond her. She probably hasn't played pieces in C#-minor yet. Maybe I could help her memorize the right hand . . ."

"I'd appreciate it," Jenny said tightly.

"Jenny, how you doing?" He immediately regretted the intimacy of his tone.

"Not so hot. I spent the morning talking to a funeral director, signing forms to have Paul's body embalmed so they can ship it back. Did you know they fly bodies back in these containers they call air trays?"

Rane remained silent.

"Sorry," Jenny said. Her attempt at laughter came out in a sputter of nerves. "One of my neighbors brought over a lasagna and a bottle of Valium. I'm asking you, John . . ." The request dangled in awkward silence.

"Six," Rane said finally.

"You remember how to get here?"

"I'll be there at six."

At five that evening, after a shower and a shave, Rane rifled through his closet and came up with a pair of gray cords and a black turtleneck. Then he applied polish to a pair of dark loafers and buffed them to a low gloss. Heading for the door, he thumbed through the sheet music in his piano bench and found the Beethoven piece; a yellowed relic bearing a coffee stain, left over from college.

Rane took the long way, down Lexington then east on Sheppard Road, under a late March sky that threatened to spit freezing rain. To his right, plates of gray ice wallowed in the river, and on the left, dirty snow scabbed the brown grass.

He arrived a few minutes before six, parked on the street, walked up the drive, and knocked. A tallish woman in an apron opened the door. Rane noted a resemblance to Jenny in her rangy build and her older, lively, wide blue eyes.

"You must be John," she said. "I'm Vicky, Jenny's sister. I came down from Bemidji to help out." She extended her hand. "Relax honey," she said with a weary frown, "I know all about you. C'mon in. Give me your coat."

Rane slipped off his leather jacket, which Vicky hung in the hall closet while he removed his loafers by the door. Paul Edin's running shoes had been taken away.

"Okay," Vicky said, "just warning you, it could get crazy if Paul's parents call again. They're in Kyoto, Japan, visiting their . . ." she hooked two fingers of each hand and struck quote marks in the air ". . . successful son, Paul's brother, Toby. Toby suggested that Jenny find a funeral service that has real-time Internet capacity so they can attend online. That way the parents don't have to interrupt their trip and fly back . . ."

"You're putting me on," Rane said.

"Nope. And they got a place like that right in town. It's a busy world, huh?" Vicky said.

Rane walked down the hall into a house that now had the feel of circled wagons. The heat was turned up, he supposed, because it could be; a comfort factor they could control. Delivered flower arrangements lined the fireplace mantel, giving off the damp scent of thoughtful tears. A hot dish warmed in the oven. Vicky pointed him to the den off the living room. Jenny, her face a drawn practical mask, looked up from a desk covered with notes and official-looking forms. Molly sat cross-legged in shorts and an oversized T-shirt on a couch opposite the TV. Seeing Rane, she unplugged her earphones, clicked off the TV remote, and pushed off the couch.

Rane held out the sheet of music as she approached, relieved he had a piece of paper to interpose between them. Molly took it and quietly left the room. His eyes followed her out of the den, then he turned to Jenny. "How's it going?" he asked quietly.

She pursed her lips and nodded at the scatter of paper on the desk. "People in and out. Paul's partner is helping a lot, with the insurance, dealing with the funeral, planning the service. Mom's picking up some paperwork at the funeral home so I could be here when they show up."

"How's Molly handling it?" Rane asked.

Jenny's head jerked mechanically, and Rane thought of an old-fashioned typewriter carriage being slapped to a new line. "The school psychologist, Patti Halvorsen, is a friend. She's getting Molly into a grief group they have at Lakeview, for kids . . ."

They maintained a strict physical distance and did not make direct eye contact. Rane had occasion to be caught in several minefields in his life, and that's how he felt now. Jenny's defenses were down and the naked grief made her, frankly, beautiful.

So he excused himself and joined Molly in the piano room. Stiff and formal, he sat down beside her on the bench. Christ, he thought, I'm acting like my old Russian piano instructor, when I was twelve; using his stories and metaphors. As they settled in, he noticed Molly's long fingers resting on the keyboard next to his own long fingers, and her dark, unruly hair, so like his mother's. Patiently, he led her into the music and held her hand to help her span the wide first chord. Then he played along with his left hand. Experimentally, Molly, forehead furrowed with concentration, began to pick at the keys.

The doorbell rang. "They're here," Vicky called from the kitchen.

From the corner of his eye, Rane watched Jenny go toward the door, told Molly to keep playing, and got up from the bench. The bell rang again. Rane walked swiftly to the door and opened it.

The two men he let in had their arms full. The taller one held a cardboard box under one arm, a heavy duffel in the other. The second carried a bundled thick blue wool coat and a long canvas case that obviously contained a rifle. Their faces were a determined fix of road fatigue and duty.

Rane stepped back as Jenny hugged them both. Heads close in a rush of tears, they tried to comfort each other. "He was having such a good time, Jenny. You should have seen him," one of the men said in a husky voice.

"It's okay," Jenny said, squeezing their arms. Then she wiped her eyes and turned to Rane. "This is a friend, John Rane. He used to be a St. Paul cop and I wanted him to hear what you told me on the phone."

As Jenny introduced them and they shook hands, Dalton, the tall one, said, "I've talked to more cops in the last couple days than in my whole life." He exhaled, then indicated the box in his arms. "Sorry Jenny. We didn't have time to clean . . ."

"Let's put that in the basement," Jenny said quickly.

Rane offered to help but the men briskly moved past him, knowing the way to the basement stairs. When they came back up, Jenny led them to the kitchen table, where Vicky had set out four coffee cups and a carafe. Jenny asked Dalton and Manning to sit down.

Rane hesitated, balancing on eggshells of taboo and trespass. Jenny pointed to an empty chair. Rane sat. Vicky, wiping her hands on a towel, walked toward the alcove.

Jenny poured coffee, then sat at the fourth chair in front of an empty notepad and pen. Rane quickly studied the two reenactors. Dalton sported a spiked beard and Manning had a twirled mustache, goatee, and longish hair pulled tight back in a pigtail. He'd covered a Memorial Day parade once, to shoot the First Minnesota placing flags on Civil War graves, then they'd put on a drill exhibition. The seriousness of the hobbyists had surprised him. Despite the hobnailed cadence of their step, Rane recalled a flicker of ritual: pilgrims drawn to tending a flame. Although dressed casually in jeans and T-shirts, an iron touch of those blue uniforms clung to Manning and Dalton.

As Molly picked awkwardly at the slow, sad notes muffled behind the closed French doors, Dalton produced a business card and placed it in front of Jenny. "This is the county cop who was standing right next to Paul. He was blended in the ranks, dressed in blue, on a security detail. He went all out to . . . help."

Jenny stared at the card. "Beeman. We've talked twice. He said he and Paul got to know each other on the long hike before the battle." She smiled briefly and her eyes softened. "He said he liked Paul."

Like a good NCO reporting, Dalton cleared his throat and ticked off: "He helped waive next-of-kin identification of Paul's body to allow us to do it. He helped smooth things with the coroner during the autopsy, expedited the death certificate and release of the . . . remains."

"He was pretty decent, actually. For a Southerner," Manning said. "Not like the rednecks at Raymond a couple years back . . ."

"Raymond?" Jenny asked with a twitch of an attentive smile.

"Another sniper situation," Manning said in a clipped voice.

Rane sat up straighter. Jenny bit her lower lip and turned to him. "See?" she asked.

"Tell me about Raymond?" Rane asked.

Manning shrugged. "Six, seven years ago at Champion Hill, near Raymond, Mississippi. A guy wearing blue was shot in the groin and nearly bled to death before we got him to the medics. No thanks to the locals. They didn't find a bullet that time either. But figured it was .36-caliber, from a pistol," he said, shaking his head. "You go down there you never know what to expect; some of those guys will look you in the eye and tell you Gettysburg was just the Army of the Potomac narrowly avoiding another defeat . . ."

Rane held up his hand, putting an edge of the old cop control in his tone. "Tell me about Saturday in Mississippi, minus the editorializing."

"A lot of people down there think it was a sniper," Manning said directly. He pointed to the card on the table. "Including him."

"The newspapers and TV said it was an accident. The death certificate the coroner faxed me listed 'accident' under cause of death," Jenny stated, looking at Rane.

"You think someone shot Paul Edin deliberately?" Rane asked.

It became very quiet in the house. The furnace fan in the basement whirred on. A muted click; Vicky opened and closed the refrigerator door. The silence elongated as she poured a glass of milk, placed some cookies on a plate, and put the glass and plate on a tray.

Rane noticed the piano had stopped. He scanned the living room and spied Molly, who had crept in unobserved and was crouched, listening, big-eyed, behind the couch. He touched Jenny on the arm and pointed.

Immediately, Jenny stood up. "Excuse me a moment," she said, then collected Molly and aimed her down the hall off the kitchen, telling Vicky to put her in the shower and make sure she washed her hair. Vicky and Molly went down the hall. Jenny returned to the table and sat down. The shower started to run, the bathroom door closed.

Jenny turned to Dalton. "Tell him."

Dalton exchanged glances with Manning. "Now this is hearsay, not official . . ." he said.

Rane kept his face expressionless, but he was leaning forward as if exerting sheer gravitational pull would tug the words from Dalton's lips.

"Tell him," Jenny insisted.

Dalton shrugged and said, "There's a specific rumor we heard. This Confederate contacted me by cell phone and made a point of meeting me at the hospital. He's a Virginian with the Stonewall Brigade. A reliable guy. We met at Antietam years back and have kept in touch. He was incensed about the incident and thought I should know what the local reenactors were saying . . ."

"Which was?" Rane asked quietly.

Dalton held up his palm and pursed his lips. "According to the locals, the shooting wasn't an accident. Beeman, the cop, has a running feud with a family around Corinth. He was standing shoulder to shoulder with Paul in line. The locals think somebody was trying to settle scores with Beeman and hit Paul."

22 RANE REACHED FOR THE NOTEPAD and pen in front of Jenny, then pushed them to Dalton. "What did Beeman actually say?" he asked.

Dalton stared at the blank paper, then tongued the inside of his cheek. "We asked him about the rumor. He showed us a text message on his phone, daring him to show his face at Shiloh next weekend."

Manning screwed up his lips. "He *did* say that could just be harassment piggybacking on the shooting . . ."

Dalton shook his head. "Nah, he said that strictly CYA, ain't what his eyes said. Gut read—he thinks somebody tried to kill him. He said, and I quote, 'a reenactment's the perfect place to shoot somebody, with all the noise and smoke.'"

Manning nodded and leaned forward. "Beeman sat us down when we identified the body, and he was pissed. First thing he said was they, meaning the local politicos, weren't real interested in looking too hard at this."

Dalton said, "Corinth's a big tourist destination, see? They can damage-control an accident. But if word gets out you have a sniper? There's half a dozen reenactments in Mississippi and Tennessee over the next three, four months."

"Show me how it happened," Rane said, nodding at the notepad.

"Okay," Dalton said. He picked up the pen and talked quickly as he sketched. "See, like Jenny said, Beeman and Paul got to know each other before the battle. When they

got in line Paul was standing on Beeman's left . . ." Dalton
drew a double line of circles representing men in formation.
He X-ed one of the circles in the front rank near the left end
of the line. "Beeman's here." Then he drew a little counter-
clockwise arc coming off the circle to the immediate left
of the X. "Beeman said Paul stepped to avoid tripping, like
this, to his left front when it happened."

"Like maybe the sudden movement threw off the shot,"
Manning speculated.

"What's the ground like? Where's the other guys, the
Rebels?" Rane asked.

"Open field in front, woods to the left and rear. A Reb
formation was about a hundred yards out here." He scribbled
wavy lines to represent tree lines, and some more circles to
show the relative position of the Rebel reenactors. He raised
his fingers to the left side of his neck, looked at Jenny.

"Go on, I want to know everything," she said.

Dalton nodded. "Paul was hit here. Beeman figures if
there was a deliberate shot it had to come from these trees on
the left. He doesn't think it came from the Reb formation."

"Too chaotic in the ranks for an aimed shot," Manning
added.

"How far to the trees?" Rane asked.

Dalton and Manning exchanged measured glances. Dalton shrugged. "Depends, anywhere from a hundred to two
hundred yards?"

"About that," Manning agreed. Then he looked at Dalton
and gritted his teeth. "We're kinda breaking a promise here.
Beeman asked us for a favor, kind of, seeing's how he expedited things."

Jenny spoke up. "I don't have a lot of faith in Mississippi
promises right now."

Rane gently cautioned Jenny with an upraised hand.
"What kind of favor?"

Dalton explained: "He asked us not to discuss the sniper
rumors until after Shiloh."

"Shiloh?" Rane rolled the two syllables on his tongue.

Manning nodded. "The battlefield is just over the state line, half an hour's drive from Corinth. They have this Living History coming up on the anniversary next weekend. Beeman said cops from Tennessee were going to be all over that event in case this guy shows again."

Rane cocked his head slightly. "He said that? 'This guy'?"

Manning nodded again. "Yeah, like he had someone in mind. So they want to stake out Shiloh, quietly."

"You trust this Beeman?" Jenny asked Dalton.

Dalton shrugged. "Don't know for sure. Like Davey says, it's different down there. But he sounded pretty sincere. Like he got to know Paul and was taking it personal."

"Could you write a number down where I can reach you?" Rane asked.

"Anything I can do to help, let me know," Dalton said, signing his name and telephone number on the notepad under his diagram. Rane tore off the sheet of paper, folded it, and put it in his pocket.

Jenny reached across the table with both hands and covered Dalton's and Manning's hands with her own. "That's enough. Tom, Davey, thanks, I know this has been hard and you two are really tired."

Dalton nodded, cued Manning with a sideways look, and the two men rose from the table. "We better get on the road," Dalton said. They each accepted a last grateful hug from Jenny. Then, after a round of condolences and proffers of help, Dalton and Manning shook good-bye with Rane and left the house.

Rane and Jenny resumed their seats at the table, listening to the muffled sound of a car starting in the driveway, backing out, then seeing the play of lights in the windows.

"Damn it, I'm not going to let a bunch of rednecks sweep Paul's death under the rug," Jenny vowed.

"Molly," Rane said.

She had appeared in front of the table almost magically,

pink-faced and steaming, wearing one large yellow towel around her middle, another turbaned around her hair. She trailed distinct wet footprints across the tile kitchen floor.

"Mom," she said, big-eyed, "are we going to die?"

Jenny stood up fast and wrapped the girl in her arms, "No, honey. No."

Molly pulled back and Rane watched the thoughts work with blank, innocent logic on her face, as if death was a normal adult mechanism into which she had suddenly stumbled and now needed explained. "I heard what they said. Is the man who shot Dad going to kill us?"

Rane stared at the child and it was all very simple. He stood up, placed one hand on her shoulder, and said, "No one's going to hurt you anymore. Promise."

Jenny's eyes went bright with cracked-diamond grief— as, instinctively, she pulled Molly back from Rane and held her protectively. Vicky came down the hall and Jenny said, "Get Molly dressed for bed, I'll be there in a minute." As Vicky led Molly toward the hall, the girl turned to Rane. "Cross your heart?"

Without irony, Rane drew his finger twice across his chest just as the front door opened and Lois came in. She cocked her head. "You again?"

"Not now, Mom," Jenny said between clenched teeth, her voice sliding like wreckage on a tilted deck. "Do you believe this shit? I don't believe this shit."

"Jennifer," Lois reprimanded, "Molly will . . ."

"I heard that Mom, you owe me two bucks," Molly called from the hall.

Jenny turned, plucked a sweater off the back of a chair, pulled it on, walked to the patio door, and pulled it open. Rane immediately followed her onto the deck. Across a grassy dip of lawn, a house loomed in shadow except for a giant TV pulsing color in an upstairs window.

"So, what do you think?" she asked, calmer, looking into the dark.

What he thought was she had trailed the lure of an irresistible story in front of him. What he said was, "Did Beeman tell you anything like Dalton and Manning said, when you talked to him?"

"No. He said it was a terrible accident."

"Then it's rumors until somebody goes on the record. I know a lieutenant in St. Paul Homicide. I could ask him to call the Mississippi sheriff's office . . ."

Jenny turned and engaged the thing she'd always wondered about, the scary thing behind his quiet eyes. "This isn't something you figure out on the phone, is it? There's only one way to find out for sure. Somebody has to go down there and look them in the eye."

They realized they were standing facing each other. Eyes locked.

Again it was simple. You don't debate the decisive moments. The puzzle pieces of his life could fit. He just had to put out his hand. "I can do that; it's a hell of a story," John Rane said softly.

"And make sure they don't get away with this," she said.

From decision to plan in half a blink, he said, "I'll need those things in the basement, the clothes and gear."

"Why?" Jenny narrowed her eyes, suddenly catching herself. "What are you going to do?"

"You have to trust me, Jenny," Rane said.

She stared at him, standing there lean and crisp and coldly determined. But good with Molly. Showing human parts she didn't think . . . *Cross my heart.*

"I need you to trust me," Rane repeated.

Jenny couldn't stop the words that slipped out. "You don't get it, John. Most of us don't get what we want or need. We settle . . ." She bit off the thought and hugged herself. Control, damn it. This is verging on . . . deranged. "Jesus, what are we doing? My husband's body is in a funeral home in Mississippi being *fucking embalmed for shipment.*"

"I'll be in touch," Rane said. Then she watched him go

through the patio door, walk across the kitchen, trail his hand on the table, and pick up the Mississippi cop's card.

Jenny stood on the deck for a few moments, looking at the dark slumbering shapes of the houses full of young prosperous people who had never done anything wrong in their lives. She turned again when she heard Rane come up from the basement with his arms full, cross the kitchen, and disappear down the hall. Faintly, through the patio glass, she heard the front door shut.

Christ, is this the way I'm going to find out, finally, what makes him tick?

Not quite ready to go back in, she rummaged in her sweater pocket, withdrew the crumpled pack of cigarettes and a lighter. She lit one, took one drag, grimaced, and flipped it away. Then she squared her shoulders, went into the warm house, padded down the hall, and opened the door to Molly's room.

Molly lay facedown in the covers, hugging her dilapidated blue-and-white-striped bunny. Vicky and Lois sat on the edge of the bed, drying and combing Molly's hair. They rose, gave up their place to Jenny, and tiptoed from the room.

"You smell like smoke," Molly said, making a face.

"Sorry, I should brush my teeth."

"It's okay. Will you rub my back?" Molly asked.

Jenny eased up Molly's oversized sleep T-shirt and began to knead at the trim muscles of her daughter's back.

"Mom?" Molly asked.

"What, honey?"

"Can John Rane really stop the bad guy from hurting us?"

Jenny pressed the heels of her palms along Molly's spine. "If there is a bad guy he's a long way from here and I don't know what John Rane can do."

"I know he promised. But can he do that? I mean, he takes pictures?"

Jenny took a deep breath, held it, bit her lip, and let it out. "Mom?"

"He didn't always take pictures for the paper, honey," Jenny said. Then she noticed the children's picture book next to Molly under the covers. She eased into the bed, arranged the pillows, picked up the book, and opened it to the first splashy, colorful page. Molly curled in beside her and chanted under her breath as Jenny started to recite the singsong verse that Paul had read as a nightly lullaby for so many safe, happy years.

"Seventeen kings on forty-two elephants
Going on a journey through a wild wet night . . ."

23 **RANE RACED WEST DOWN I-94 WITH** the windows open to feel the cold wind on his face, thinking how his old Russian piano instructor made him practice Bach fugues backward. The teacher insisted it was the only way to appreciate their depth.

Now here he was, backing into his life.

He stepped on the gas going past the 3M building, flipped open his cell phone, and punched in a number with a Wisconsin 715 area code. A man answered in a gruff, abrupt voice, "Morse."

"Mike, it's John."

"Johnny, well, well. We read about you in the paper. How you stepped in do-do again and got suspended."

"Yeah, yeah, look, I need some help."

"We agreed: I gave up on counseling your sorry lost ass."

"A special kind of help," Rane said.

"Hmmm. Not likely," Mike said, the barest hint of curiosity creeping into his voice. "But run it by me."

"You still have that Sharps?"

"The one you got me for my big six-oh birthday and took me two years to get so'd shoot right?" Mike said. "Oh yeah. Haven't fired it for a while . . ."

"Got any rounds loaded for it?"

"Probably."

"Maybe you could get me up to speed on it and let me borrow it for a couple weeks?" Rane asked mildly.

"What happened? You get over your aversion to gunpowder?" When Rane didn't respond, Mike asked, "Borrow it when?"

"Like in the morning," Rane said.

"This another of your projects?" Mike asked.

"Tell you in the morning, say hi to Aunt Karen," Rane said, ending the call. Then he thumbed through his directory and selected HC, for Lieutenant Harry Cantrell at St. Paul Homicide.

Cantrell's cell went to voice mail. "Harry, it's Rane. I need a favor." Three minutes later Cantrell called back. "Rane you deviant, what do you want?"

"I need a letter of introduction faxed on police stationery to a cop in Mississippi."

"Mississippi, huh," Cantrell drawled. He'd wound up in the Twin Cities out of New Orleans by way of Dee-troit. "After your latest stunt you might get a collection for a one-way ticket with an Al Sharpton button pinned to your forehead."

"C'mon, I'm jammed up, I need some help. Where are you?"

"You might try Alary's but I ain't promising nothing."

Rane weighed it. Alary's was a St. Paul cop hangout. "I thought you quit drinking."

"I did, most people wish I'd start again. The troopies say drinking humanized me. Now I just sip ginger ale and breathe the fumes."

"Give me ten minutes."

Rane switched off the phone, gunned the engine, and listened to the Cherokee. Need to get it tuned up, change the oil, and throw on new tires. He rounded a bend, and the lights of the state capitol dome sparkled like a chilly tiara. He swung around the curve coming into town, took the exit at Fifth, and worked the streets, looking for a parking spot near Alary's. Found one. Don't think about it. Just keep moving.

He got out, squared his shoulders coming up the street,

pushed open the door, and entered the barroom. Waitresses in tight shorts and halters worked the horseshoe counter, serving cops in various states of alcohol-assisted relaxation. The walls were a collage of shoulder patches from police departments from all over the country. Side doors from cop cars were suspended on wires from the ceiling, Fargo-Chicago-Minneapolis PD like a mobile hanging over a steroidal street monster's crib. Rane preferred Alary's in the old days, when it was a seedy strip joint.

He didn't make six steps before he was challenged.

A stout middle-aged man in a bulging gray suit pushed off a stool. "Rane," the man enunciated with flushed, ornate distaste. "You got some balls showing your face in here."

"Hiya Frank," Rane said. "See you're still keeping Krispy Kreme in business . . ."

Another guy pushed off the bar, took Frank by the arm. "C'mon, Frank, let it be," the guy said.

"He's no fucking good," Frank pronounced, blinking at Rane.

The second guy interposed himself between Rane and Frank. "What's up, Johnny?"

"Looking for Cantrell."

The cop jerked a thumb. "In the back, last booth on the right."

Rane walked deeper into the bar and saw Harry Cantrell sitting alone in a booth with his back to the wall. Cantrell watched him approach, had seen the minor confrontation with Frank.

"Well, well. The vampire walks among us," Cantrell said.

"How you doing, Harry?"

"Bloodsucker."

"Can we talk or you gonna jerk my chain?" Rane said.

Cantrell opened his hand. "Sit."

Rane sat.

"You walk in this joint I take it as serious. 'Bout three

quarters of these guys hate your guts. The rest give you the benefit of the doubt. So what's up, kid?"

"Mississippi, you been there?"

Cantrell laughed. "I went through, a little while ago on the way home. It ain't there no more."

"Say again?"

"You read *Huck Finn*? The part where Huck takes off to escape the Widow Douglas's efforts to 'sivilize' him?"

Rane shook his head. "It's been a while."

Cantrell grinned. "That's Mississippi. It's been 'sivilized.' Wal-Mart, Burger King. Kids growing up listening to homogenized anchor talk on TV. It ain't there no more."

Rane fingered the business card out of his pocket and handed it to Cantrell, who read it, looked up at Rane, and raised an eyebrow. "Corinth, huh?"

"I need a favor," Rane said.

"So you said."

"Need you to fax a letter of introduction to this copper. Tell him I'm cool, as photographers go. Know my way around law enforcement, that I wasn't hatched in a ferny Starbucks in Minneapolis. Like that."

"Lie," Cantrell said.

"Be creative."

"You got a good reason, I suppose?" Cantrell asked.

"You know anything about Civil War reenactors?" Rane said.

"Some."

"That guy from Stillwater who got killed at a battle in Mississippi, couple days ago?"

"Saw it on the news," Cantrell said.

Rane pointed to the business card. "That cop is investigating it."

"The report on CNN said it was an accident," Cantrell said slowly, the drawling banter leaving his voice. His eyes sharpened in the neon-tinted half-light.

"Off the record, I got a tip that cop thinks they might have an active sniper; a guy who likes to shoot people at Civil War battles. There's this thing on the Shiloh battlefield next week. The local cops are going to stake it out and provide security in case this shooter shows up. I'm hoping to get an in with this Beeman and get on the field."

"Oh-kay . . . and how much you want me to include in this letter of introduction? Like you want me to tell him how you fucked up during your pretend-cop blue period?" Cantrell narrowed his eyes. "Fucked up in a way very similar to the stunt you pulled last week?"

Rane gnawed his lower lip. "Nah, maybe skim over that."

"Look into my eyes, Johnny Rane," Cantrell said.

"Hey, it's a hell of a story," Rane protested.

"Sure it is, and perfect for you, huh?" Harry tapped his finger on the card. "You want me to lie to a brother officer you'll have to give me more."

"Not lie, just leave a few things out." Rane attempted to stare down Cantrell's agate-brown eyes. Lookit him, still combing his hair in a ducktail, affecting T-shirts and jeans and a leather jacket. Hanging onto sobriety by his finger-nails. Old-time lawman: screw the backup, kick in the door.

"So what's got you so excited about this story?" Cantrell persisted.

"Okay, okay." Rane dropped his eyes first. "Remember the woman?"

"*The Woman* you were crazy in love with," Cantrell emphasized. "The Woman you got pregnant . . ."

"Yeah."

"And wouldn't marry . . ."

"Yeah."

"Who you left hanging out there to have the kid on her own while you ran off to hide inside a camera," Cantrell said succinctly.

"Jenny," Rane said. "Jenny Edin. That's her married name. The guy who got killed down there was her husband."

"Well," Cantrell leaned back and scratched his chin. "For starters, looks like you got a big fucking conflict of interest, don't it?"

"I gotta do this. If they get this guy I want to be there. I need your help," Rane said simply.

"Why, Johnny? It's fuckin' morbid. Leave it Down South."

"I can't leave this one," Rane said.

Cantrell mulled it. "You're putting me on the spot here." He studied Rane for several seconds, weighing it, before removing a small notebook and a pen from his jacket pocket. Squinting, he swiftly jotted some information from the card Rane handed to him. Then he gave the card back.

"Thanks, Harry," Rane said.

"Go on, get out of here before I think about this too much and change my mind," Cantrell said. As Rane stood up and turned to walk away, Cantrell called to him: "One thing, Johnny. A little military goes a long way down there. Wouldn't hurt to drop a hint you did some time on the sand." Then Cantrell got up, drew close, and said, "Mississippi can get tricky. They're brought up to be real polite to strangers and all. But there's a line you shouldn't cross. Problem is, you don't always know where that line is."

BACK IN THE JEEP, RANE PUNCHED PERRY MACNEIL'S home number into his cell. Yes. Perry picked up on the third ring. "Perry, who on the staff has covered Civil War reenactments? Not local stuff. I mean battles."

"I think Borck was out to Gettysburg once," Perry answered quickly. Rane could tell Perry sensed he was on to something.

"Thanks." Rane ended the call, thumbed into his directory, and punched Borck's pager number. By the time he was pulling into his driveway, the cell rang.

"This is Craig."

"Craig, it's Rane . . ."

"Enjoying your vacation?"

"Right. Lookit, Perry said you shot a battle at Gettysburg with reenactors."

"Yeah?"

"What's it like access-wise? Getting on the field?"

"Depends if it's mainstream or authentic. Mainstream's kinda anything goes, campers and lawn chairs at the edge of the field. The authentic guys are real uptight about period-correct dress and gear. No modern stuff allowed. Usually no spectators, either. I had to borrow a uniform and hide my camera in this food bag they carry, called a haversack, and stay down low and find cover to shoot from, or sneak it from the hip."

"What'll fit in one of those bags?"

"Basic load. Camera body, wide angle, an 80–200 maybe . . ."

"Thanks." Rane ended the call and made two trips, carrying in the gear he'd taken from Jenny's house.

Then he put water on to boil, went in the bathroom, and turned on the shower. Waiting for the shower to warm he went back to the kitchen, grabbed an energy bar from the cupboard, and gobbled it. A few minutes later he emerged refreshed by the needles of hot water. He dried off, pulled on a worn pair of sweats, poured boiling water into a cup, dropped in a bag of black Earl Grey, and confronted Paul Edin's gear strewn across his couch.

Slowly, he began to unpack the clothes Paul had been wearing when he died. Dalton's remark—"we didn't get a chance to clean Paul's things"—prepared him for the blood. One whole side of a brown flannel shirt was cardboard-stiff. A paste of dried blood fouled with adobe-colored soil, bits of brush, and burrs had soaked the collar, shoulder, and front of the blue wool jacket. The clothing was intact, which meant that Paul had died before EMT got to him, otherwise they would have cut off the garments to check for more wounds.

He picked up the blue wool jacket, walked to the bathroom, and started running water in the sink. Fingering through the heavy fabric, he felt a stiff wad inside the lapel. He probed and found an inner pocket, from which he extracted a crumpled, folded manila card spattered with dried blood. Smoothing out the card, he could read a fragment of spidery pen work—*Pvt. Amos*—and beneath it, fairly legible in pencil, was a signature:

Paul Edin.

The rest was blotted out except a fragment: *Co. C.*

He turned off the water in the sink, draped the coat over the side of the tub, took the card to the kitchen, and placed it on the table. He went in the bedroom and dug the sheet of notepaper from his pants pocket, picked up his phone, and called the number Tom Dalton had jotted on the bottom.

A woman answered. Rane asked for Dalton. She said he was kind of tired. Rane said it was important.

"Dalton, this is John Rane, we just met at Jenny's," Rane said when Dalton picked up.

"Sure."

"We were going through Paul's stuff; I found this card in the coat pocket with old-fashioned writing on it? It's hard to make out because, well, it's all smeared with blood."

"Ouch. Definitely not cool. I should have gone through his effects."

"Why not cool?"

"It's called a fate card. They hand them out at some well-researched hardcore events. The name on the card represents the identity of a soldier who fought in the real battle. Idea is you open it when the shooting starts and find out if you're dead, wounded, or a survivor."

"Fate card," Rane said.

"Yeah."

"Thanks, Dalton. Get some sleep." Rane ended the call and toyed with the gummy edges of the folded card. If he tried to wash the blood off, he'd ruin it. He looked back toward the bathroom. What about the wool coat?

He picked up the phone again and punched in the Wisconsin number. Aunt Karen answered on the third ring. "Why, John," she said with amused resignation, "I must really be getting old. Have I missed a holiday. The only time we see you anymore is deer season . . ."

"C'mon, I call on birthdays, too. And the fact is, I called Mike a couple hours ago. How you doing?"

"If you're looking for Mike, he's in town at the Legion, drinking 7-Up. What is it you want?"

"Uh, bloodstains . . ."

"Are you bleeding? Nothing fatal I hope," she said tartly.

"I need to get bloodstains out of a cotton shirt and a wool jacket."

"Fresh or old bloodstains?"

"Three days old."

"Pour hydrogen peroxide directly on them. Blot it out. Then you can wash in cold water with soap. Do not use hot water. Hot water will set blood."

"Thanks."

"Need something else?"

"Remind Mike I'm coming out in the morning." Then he said good-night and hung up the phone.

Rane spent the next hour over the bathroom sink with peroxide, soap, cold water, and a 3M scrub, working the bloodstains from the shirt and coat. Satisfied he'd purged the worst of it, he held up the jacket and checked the tag. A size 42. Like he'd figured, they were about the same size. Tentatively, he tried on the jacket and buttoned it. He raised his arms and felt the wet wool press his throat, chest, and shoulder. Good, he could move freely. After he hung the coat on the shower rail, he scrubbed the residual red smears from his hands and the sink.

As he watched it swirl down the drain, he told himself the blood didn't bother him; just a piece of the jigsaw puzzle of the story.

He stripped off the damp sweatshirt, pulled on a dry t-shirt, and went back in the living room, hefted the heavy cased rifle and set it aside. He'd already decided the bulky muzzleloader was not making the trip. Then he laid out the leather gear, discarded the bayonet, opened the cartridge box, and took out the cluster of brown-paper cartridges snugged in two tin holders. They weren't making the trip either.

He kept the waist belt with the smaller leather pouch that contained brass percussion caps. The flat, round burlap-covered canteen was partially full. He carried it to the kitchen sink and raised the flask as a thirsty catch ached in his throat. He took a drink of the stale, rusty water, swallowed it, and dumped the rest down the drain.

Next he held up the haversack Borck had referred to and set it aside on his light table.

Then he tried on the dirty sky-blue wool trousers, pulled on the suspenders, slipped his feet into the muddy black-leather square-toed shoes, and laced them up. He squatted, walked around, and listened to the gritty hobnails clatter on his oak floor. The shoes were slightly loose, but thick socks would solve that.

He searched through the duffel, found soiled flannel underwear and two pairs of heavy gray wool socks. He tossed the underwear back in the bag, kept the socks, and retrieved the flannel shirt from the bathroom. Plucking burrs from the socks, he took them along with the shirt to the basement, ran cold water and detergent in the washer, and tossed in the clothing.

Back upstairs he brought his camera bag from his closet and removed a D200 Nikon camera body, a 17–55 mm lens and the 80–200 for backup, two digital gig cards, and a light meter. Emptying the haversack, he found a glasses case that contained tiny tortoiseshell frames smeared with mud, small cotton food bags, a fork, knife, and spoon, and the rumpled blue army cap that completed the uniform. Last, he lifted out a brown leather-bound journal, which he opened to a tablet of lined paper.

His eyes scanned the cursive penmanship on the first

page; it was right-leaning, like the signature on the card, written in the same black pencil.

Dearest Molly and Jenny,

We are encamped on boggy ground near Kirby Creek, Mississippi. It's raining and a little bit cold. The tops of the trees disappear in this white mist and sitting here I can almost imagine faces haunting the twisted branches.

For me History has always come down to a single human face by which all American faces are measured. If you want to know what History looks like, then look at the last photograph taken of Abraham Lincoln toward the end of the war. It's all there in his eyes, as if he had to take a sip from every dead soldier on both sides. Sorry, don't mean to sound corny.

What's happening here is the officers tell us the Rebs have occupied an entrenched position beyond the woods on the far side of a swamp. In the morning we will form company and deploy for the flank assault through the swamp to take them in the rear.

Get this. They gave me this identity card. I'm inhabiting the persona of a real soldier who fought in the battle. Won't know how he came out till I open the thing.

I figure 140 years ago he would have been thinking of his wife and daughter right now. And if he had a daughter named Molly she would probably be sitting in an uncomfortable desk in a chilly one-room schoolhouse, and after school she'd have to walk a long way home to a farm. No Walkman, no TV, no dance lessons; probably you'd have to do smelly chores in a barn. Yuck, right?

I'm sure once you got used to it, you'd do just fine.

*Just as I hope I will measure up on this march that's
coming, which is billed as pretty rough.*

    *I've tried hard never to give you or Mom any
reason to be displeased with me. But I don't feel I've
ever done anything to make you really proud. Maybe
this is my . . .*

The writing stopped in mid-sentence. The empty lines at
the bottom of the page were smudged with ferrous red dirt, a
splotched watermark, and a partial thumbprint. Rane rocked
back, closed the journal, and visualized the red-tinged water
sluicing down the bathroom drain. Paul's blood was on his
hands and it did bother him, as did the compulsion to wear
the man's clothing and taste the water from his canteen.

Inhabiting the persona . . .

Rane left the journal, walked into the kitchen, and sat
down at the table. The handwritten entry echoed, ". . . don't
mean to sound corny . . ."

He studied the glued edges of the manila card he'd taken
from the blue sack coat. What were the chances of reopening
a fate sealed in blood?

Never believed in corny shit like second chances.

But he had promises to keep.

He pushed the card back and forth across the table until it
came to rest next to his key ring, touching the quarter with a
hole blasted through it.

Cross my heart.

And hope to die.

24 RANE GRABBED A FAST OIL CHANGE
and tune-up at Jiffy Lube, inserted a quarter
to gauge his tire tread, and hoped they'd do.
By nine a.m. he was driving down a country
road east of Hudson, Wisconsin, on his way to Mike's place
on Mail Lake. Where he grew up. Back then the asphalt road
he was driving had been gravel.

Rane passed through cookie-cutter white-trimmed faux
Cape Cod condos that now lined the paved road. "Too many
rats in the cage," Uncle Mike would say.

He glanced up at an ambiguous gray sky that could rain
or clear off. A faint stir of northwest wind nudged the pines
crowns. Almost warm, close to fifty-five degrees.

He remembered fields and woods; an abrupt transition for
a boy nannied and tutored in the Summit Hill district of St.
Paul. Marcus and Julia Rane had been flying to a perfor-
mance in Milwaukee when their small plane hit shear winds
and went down.

Uncle Mike had been Rane's guide through the abrupt
switch from studying piano at the MacPhail Center for the
Performing Arts to splitting oak rounds with a heavy steel
maul. Mike introduced him to fishing, hunting, and the
white-chip fury of a bucking chainsaw.

He turned at the red fire number sign. A stand of pines
screened the access road curling down to the split-level ce-
dar house built into the bluff overlooking the lake.

Rane parked the Jeep, got out, and went inside to a living

room that was a picture gallery dedicated to his cousins Janet and Mark and their kids. Like always, he wondered if the blank spot on the wall begged the question of Molly's picture. A gaunt, rheumy-eyed golden retriever sidled up to him and nuzzled his hand. The dog and Mike were aging apace.

"So where's he at, Danny? Out in back?"

His father's ebony grand piano still occupied a corner of the living room with the top folded down. Wiped free of dust, the portrait of his parents perched on the waxed surface. He had his father's urbane smile when he wanted, his long fingers, and his mother's springy dark hair and gray-green eyes.

He looked away from the photograph and paused at the doorway to Mike's paneled den, where two picture frames hung over the desk. One glittered with the seven rows of ribbons and medals and badges Mike had earned in Vietnam. The other displayed pictures of the seven cars and trucks he'd totaled when he mustered out of the army—before he went straight and married Karen. The discipline of the keyboard and the lure of the den had been a tug of war.

Uncle Mike had won in the end.

"I'm round in front," Rane heard his uncle yell.

Rane went back out the front door and found Mike standing in the driveway, leaning on the Jeep with a pair of Nikon binoculars hanging around his neck. "Karen's at work." He grinned. "We can fart, swear, smoke . . . and maybe shoot. So what's up, Johnny?"

Rane said, "Road trip."

"What the hell for? You writing another book?" Mike raised his eyebrows, which emphasized the gray cast to his right eye. A durable husk of a man, who set off airport metal detectors, he'd been mostly used up in service to his country. Mike had given up on people and now preferred the company of reliable things; mainly old rifles, which he'd built and repaired and endlessly tinkered with in his popular gun shop in Hudson before he retired.

"I'm thinking about doing a story about the North-South Skirmish Association," Rane ad-libbed. "Don't they have a chapter in Wisconsin?"

Mike scratched his cheek. "I did some shooting with those guys years back. Gotta wear Civil War uniforms. Shoot at hanging flowerpots, offhand at a hundred yards mostly. Team competition kind of thing. I don't think they're active local anymore."

Rane nodded, regurgitating the information he'd stripped off the Internet last night. "I read the whole Civil War reen-actor scene started with the North-South Skirmish back in the fifties. Thought I'd take a look at them, maybe get back into a little shooting. See if there's an angle . . ."

Mike pondered. "Don't see many Sharps with the Skir-mish. It was one of the first cartridge rifles. Most of those guys are into muzzleloaders. Maybe exclusively. I'd have to check but you may be wasting your time with the Sharps."

Rane shrugged. "Guess I'll find out. You gonna help me or give me a lecture? Where's the rifle?"

"*Aw*right, I guess. You bought the damn thing after all."

"Mike, it was a present."

"Now you're taking it back," he grumbled. "Indian giver." Then he inclined his head toward the large Morton building next to the house, where he had his shop. "C'mon, I got it right over there."

They walked over to the big tin shed, where a rifle with a leather sling leaned against the doorjamb. Mike picked it up and weighed it in his palm. The Sharps was wickedly slim and balanced to the eye; a lever-action breechloader with an upright rectangular steel bulge to the breech and distinctive curl to the hammer. Mike cocked the lever open, dropping the block, and opened the chamber. He raised an eyebrow. "This was *the* most deadly piece of iron ever seen on a Civil War battlefield. This rifle could tell some stories about the men it killed."

Rane nodded. "An 1859 single-trigger Sharps military

rifle; original lock and hammer and barrel and wood. And what a rusty piece of shit it was when I spotted it in that antique junk shop outside of Lincoln, Nebraska," Rane said.

"You always had the good eyes, Johnny," Mike said.

"Yeah, well, you're the one fixed it up," Rane said. Then he waited patiently, seeing that Mike, the methodical gunsmith and former competitive shooter, was lapsing into lecture mode. Mike removed a flat plastic box from his jacket pocket, opened it, revealing white cloth tubes tucked in an orderly row with sharp lead points. He selected one.

"Fires a .52-caliber bullet in a linen cartridge. The round is within one-half thousandth of the diameter of the barrel. There's a wad behind the round to further cut down on gas leakage. Cast and loaded these myself."

He flipped up the rear ramp sight. "Sights are true from a hundred to eight hundred yards. I left the tick marks you put on that time." He indicated three thin hash marks, drawn in luminous white paint on the side of the flip-up sight. He inserted one of the cartridges in the open breech. Then he wracked the lever shut. The mechanism sealed the breech and sliced off the end of the linen cartridge.

"You still doing your rosary every day? Dry-firing that old Remington?" Mike asked as he handed over the rifle.

Rane slung the rifle over his shoulder. "Yeah . . ."

"Well, let's see if it worked. C'mon, we gotta take a little hike."

Mike led him up a path over the wooded slope into a long, overgrown field that butted up against a ridge. The side of the far hill had been dug away with a Bobcat and a frame of six-by-sixes sunk into the ground. A series of earth berms were thrown across the ground at two-hundred-yard intervals.

As they walked, Rane casually bounced an assumption off Mike's expertise. "You catch that story about the Minnesota reenactor who got killed in Mississippi?"

"Uh-huh. Saw it on TV."

"You think it was an accident, like they say?"

"Probably some dumb shit brought a loaded rifle. Never took the time to clean it from shooting live. Those are play guns; the Springfields and Enfields the reenactor crowd uses," Mike said. "Italian manufacture, strictly for the reenactor market to shoot blanks. Precision in the rifling isn't important. Use the same cheap cutter over and over to groove the barrels. Accuracy is not an issue."

Rane thought out loud, "So it couldn't have been an aimed shot?"

"Not unless the shooter swapped out the Italian barrel and put in a custom barrel and sights, like Badger makes in Bristol, Wisconsin. Down there he could get one from Whitacre or Dixie Gun Works I suppose. That's what the boys in the Skirmish competitions do, put decent barrels in those rifles."

Rane let the topic die as they stopped at a sturdy plywood table and a bench, next to a railroad tie half buried in the weeds. Squinting, Rane saw several tiny metal circles dangling from the frame on chains. At two hundred yards, the suspended targets were smaller than baby aspirins.

Mike removed the lid on a box built into the side of the bench, removed sandbags, and stacked them on the table. Then he took a small canister from his pocket and opened it. Percussion caps.

"Prime it," Mike said.

Rane plucked up one of the small winged caps, pulled the hammer to half-cock, fitted the cap on the cone beneath the hammer, and crimped down the wings to hold it tight.

Mike plunked the box of cartridges down on the bench and appraised his nephew. "The ultimate accuracy challenge, Johnny. Cast lead and black powder. That powder is extremely sensitive to temperature, humidity, and barometrics. Low-velocity round traveling eight hundred feet a second is way more susceptible to wind than smokeless powder firing a metal jacket . . ." He raised the binoculars hanging around his neck and squinted with his left eye. "The targets are fresh cast so I can mark the fall of the rounds. Range two hundred yards." Then he added, "She shoots a little low when it's damp."

"I'll take the one on the left," Rane said, easing down on the bench and adjusting the rifle on the pile of sandbags. He flipped up the rear sight, set the crossbar at 200, and squinted a couple times getting used to the front blade. Then he pulled the hammer to full-cock.

Mike laughed.

"What?" Rane said.

Mike nodded at Rane's right hand, the way he instinctively placed his middle finger on the trigger, laid his index finger along the side of the breech, under the hammer. "Point-shooter. Just like the first time you picked up a .22 when you were twelve."

Rane settled in, getting the feel of the wooden stock against his shoulder as he studied the tiny disc through the notched crossbar. A tickle of breeze kissed his left cheek, maybe three miles an hour. Hold a schoosh to the left.

His finger teased the trigger. The presence that had been hibernating in his blood roused.

Easy. It's been a while. It'll take some practice time to snap in. After some sighting rounds he'd stand and fire offhand.

An exercise in composition.

His heartbeat throbbed in the pad of his finger. When it faded, he squeezed the trigger.

25 **A THOUSAND MILES DUE SOUTH OF** Mail Lake, Wisconsin, Mitch sat cross-legged at the extension of his chain, scooped up a handful of red sediment, and let it trickle through his fingers.

"I'll tell you about the truth," he said.

About twenty feet away, in the narrow part of the cave, LaSalle sat on a pile of cement sacks, casually knocking the old mortar off a brick with a hand pick.

"Truth is I worked my ass off in that bank and never got a break. I hustled up that monument for old Hiram and he went and had a heart attack. Seven years I busted my hump tryin' to inject some life into that woman's dead nookie." Mitch shook his head. "The truth is I needed some relief."

Tap, tap, tap, went the pick.

Mitch pushed up on his feet, dragged his chain to the chamber pot, undid his trousers, and urinated. He recognized the pot now, an heirloom from the house; memorable because of the decal of Ulysses S. Grant's face stuck in the bottom.

Mitch did up his scratchy, dirty pants, went back, and sat down.

Tap. Tap. Tap.

"What's that suppose to do, wear me down?" he asked.

LaSalle held up a brick, sighted down its length, and said, "S'pose to get the rock so you can use them again." Then he placed the brick with a hollow click on the neat stack at his side.

"She'd never do that, what she said," Mitch said.

"Nope, probably have me to do it," LaSalle said matter-of-fact.

"Shit, man. That'd be premeditated killing."

LaSalle set down the pick, lounged back, and perused Mitch. "Depends how you look at it. I heard this guy on the radio, from that Southern Poverty bunch in Birmingham. He said that when Gabriel blows his horn gonna be hundreds, maybe thousands, of black men rise up from the rivers of Mississippi where you all dumped them with logging chains around their necks." LaSalle flicked dust from his jeans. "Walling off one murdering white boy won't hardly make a ripple in all that. Besides, you ain't even here. Says in the paper you went missing in Memphis."

Mitch shook his shackled leg. "Well here I am in chains with you lording it over me." He narrowed his eyes. "Feels on my end like you get off on it . . . like you got this black-white payback thing going."

LaSalle smiled slowly. "Nah. If it's just between you and me it's more a green-yellow thing, huh?"

"The guard; me not going." Mitch lowered his eyes.

"Don't take it so hard. You just did what most people did. We went driving the roads in Iraq and you stayed home and went shopping, like the president told you," LaSalle said with quiet, total contempt.

Mitch gritted his teeth and had a bad moment as the walls started to close in. "Goddamn, what's she want from me?"

"Between you and her. I learned a long time ago not to mess around in a domestic. I just patch up the casualties," LaSalle said in that breezy tone he had, like cold, blowing smoke. He got up and walked over to Mitch. "Okay, legs out straight and put your right hand under your butt. I'm going to look at that cut."

Mitch's hands were free but he couldn't see going after LaSalle. Besides, his leg was shackled and who knew where they kept the key?

So he assumed the position. LaSalle removed disinfectant and gauze from his first-aid bag. As he cleaned and re-bandaged Mitch's left hand, he said casually: "I see you watching me like I'm gonna slip up. And I heard all that you said about me being all blowed up and turned to mush. It ain't like that, Mitch. I'm not disabled. I'm healing, you hear." He pressed Mitch's reddened palm and asked, standing up, "When'd you have your last tetanus shot?"

"You got me chained up in the dirt and you're worried about a tetanus shot?"

When LaSalle grinned, the scars on his face pulled tight, like tribal tattoos. "That could get infected. Miss Kirby don't want you suffering needlessly."

Then LaSalle gathered up the cardboard leavings of a microwaved meal, retreated down the passage, canted his broad shoulders sideways to fit through the choke point, and disappeared into the gloom.

"Bullshit," Mitch said when he was alone. If LaSalle was "healing," he'd be driving the ambulance. More like he was the neighborhood retard; only one dumb enough to go along with Ellie's backyard kids' play. Edgar Allan Poe, she said. "The Cask of Amontillado."

Give me a break.

Okay, keep it simple, like they say in AA. Don't waste time wondering why you missed Beeman. Or worry what's going on out there. Here and now, Mitch.

She'd caught him doing something and she wasn't sure exactly what. Her not calling in the law was the key. She's the one fucked up. A man was dead and she wanted some kind of apology?

So just hang tight, face her down, and eventually she'd get over being pissed and realize he was too hot to handle. Wouldn't do to have the Kirby name mixed up in this scene. She'd have to let him go.

And then what? He had resources: Dwayne and Billie Watts. They'd figure out something. It could still work. Except next time he'd use a scoped deer gun on Beeman. Back off on that. You'll just spiral out.

Thing now is stay positive. Wait her out and maybe you can get free of this tar ball.

Mitch rubbed the growth on his chin and tried to estimate the time by the progress of his beard. Not sure how long he'd been in here. The utility light was a constant glare; no dawn, no sunset to go by.

LaSalle had brought him an inflatable air mattress, two blankets, and a roll of toilet paper when he delivered the first microwaved meal. Since then he'd had four meals, each accompanied by two plastic bottles of water. He'd slept twice and used the pot twice. Between his third and fourth feeding LaSalle had removed the chamber pot, hosed the crap off Grant's face, and returned it. So somewhere in day three.

Just LaSalle in and out. No Ellie.

He picked the crumpled Pall Malls off the blankets and counted the hoarded cigarettes left in the pack. Five. LaSalle took the lighter away and gave him a pack of book matches. ABE'S GRILL, OLDEST DINER ON ROUTE 72, said the front.

Could go for some of Abe's biscuits about now.

He walked toward the back of the chamber, away from the overhead light. When he lit a cigarette, the flare of the match cast a flickering shadow on the limestone walls. Damn place curled around him like the folds of a stone intestine. A broad seep of water blackened one corner. Smell of mineral salts. Cave formation.

Holding the match up like a tiny torch, he shuffled into the recess. Rusty wink of more chains curled in the corner. Talk about the fuckin' blues. Imagine what went through their tripping African minds crossing the big water to wind up in here? Mitch winced when the match burned his fingers. In the sudden blackness, he realized what happened. "Hang time," he said aloud.

Wet damned day. Low-velocity round. Beeman musta

moved before it got there. Not a perfect plan after all. Then he pictured Dwayne and Darl and Billie scrambling, wondering where he was. And Marcy, probably having a private laugh. Told you so.

Shit, man, creepy back in here. Mitch hugged himself and shuffled from the dark, back to the bright artificial light.

26 ON THE WAY BACK INTO ST. PAUL, Perry MacNeil called on the cell. When Perry offered to buy him lunch, Rane figured he smelled something after handing him off to Borck about the reenactors. He needed Perry to back him on the phone if his credentials were questioned Down South, and he needed Perry's contacts.

"Meet me at my place in an hour," Rane said.

Back home he carried the cased rifle inside, along with a much-thumbed technical manual he'd borrowed from Mike's shop: *Shooting Civil War Rifles*. Then he set out a gun-cleaning kit, some twine, a wad of gauze, and a roll of duct tape. He wrapped the gauze around the twine, secured it with narrow strips of tape, and soaked it in the gun oil. Then he inserted the plug two inches down the muzzle of the Sharps, which he had scrupulously cleaned until it passed Mike's inspection. The string would allow him to pull it out. Okay. Then he smeared the rifle's moving parts with a liberal dose of graphite lubricant. Last, he pressed a clumsy swatch of duct tape over the flip-up elevation sights to hide the white tick marks on the side of the rectangular aperture.

Satisfied he'd protected the breech, lever, and trigger mechanisms, he filled a wash bucket with water, carried the rifle outside, tucked it in the weeds of a flower bed, doused it with the water, turned it over, repeated the process, and flipped the rifle several times in the mud.

He left the Sharps in the dirt, went back inside, and had a pot of coffee going by the time Perry knocked on the door.

Perry accepted a cup of coffee, made a face when Rane lit a cigarette, and sat down at the kitchen table, where Rane had spread open an AAA road atlas to the two-page map of the U.S. interstate system. Perry sipped his coffee and looked up at Rane.

They trusted each other. Perry would put his job on the line, if the story was good enough.

Rane picked up a yellow Magic Marker and traced a bright chrome route east from St. Paul to Madison, then the line turned south and ran down the length of Illinois to Cairo, jumped the Mississippi River, followed the river's west bank through Missouri and Arkansas, and then veered east through Memphis, dropped into Mississippi, and stopped at the intersection of state highways 72 and 45.

"Corinth," Rane said, paging forward through the atlas to the Mississippi state map.

Perry connected the dots and their eyes met.

"The Stillwater guy who got killed . . ." he said slowly.

Rane nodded. "Paul Edin. It could be like they say, a freak accident. They never found a bullet. But, off the record, there's a cop down there who thinks they might have a sniper."

"No shit?" The cigarette smoke no longer bothered Perry; he leaned forward, staring at the map.

"I say again, it's off the record, they're playing it down. Because next weekend they're going to throw a lot of security into a Civil War event here." Rane circled the Shiloh National Park in yellow with the marker, just above Corinth. "They think the guy might hit again."

"Jesus," Perry perked up, "how'd you get . . ."

Rane narrowed his eyes. "You gotta keep this one to yourself."

Perry cupped his chin, thought about it. "Maybe we should bring in a reporter?"

"Reporter, bullshit," Rane said.

Perry held up his hands in a mollifying gesture. He and Rane had been over this topic before. Rane considered himself immune to the newsie gene; that congenital lust for secrets he equated with blabbing teenage girls in a high school cafeteria. Plus he'd already published three photo books heavy on narrative and was arguably the best writer on the staff.

"I mean it," Rane said, stabbing a warning finger. "I'm working on getting an intro to the cop investigating Edin's death. I don't know if he'll talk to me at all. I'm double-screwed going in: (a) I work for a paper; (b) I'm a Yankee interloper on his turf. If the sniper angle starts percolating he'll sure as hell freeze me out."

"What do you want from me?" Perry asked.

"I need an inside contact down there. Could you snoop out somebody who's worked for a paper in the area?"

"I'll see what I can do."

Rane watched the thought process in Perry's consummate deskman's eyes as he bobbed his head to one side, then the other, sussing out the potential blowback from management, the union, the staff—all of whom disapproved of Rane's style of leaving the paper for extended periods and "becoming the story." "You're already suspended. You could get fired again," he said simply. After a moment, he added: "The question is, could *I* get fired?"

Rane grinned. "Fuck 'em if they can't take a joke, huh Perry."

"How're you going to approach it?" Perry asked.

Rane jerked his head toward his truck outside. "Blend in with the reenactors. I have a Civil War uniform and all the trimmings." He left the kitchen briefly, came back with the haversack, and opened it, showing Perry the Nikon and lenses. "I should be able to carry this stuff without drawing attention."

Perry smiled expectantly, raised his eyebrows.

Rane reassured him: "And my laptop to transmit to you if I get anything."

Perry rose and carried his coffee cup to the sink. "So when are you leaving?"

"Couple hours."

"Why not fly, rent a car?"

"With a big-ass rifle? A cartridge box full of black powder?"

"Phew, you really went for this one," Perry said.

Rane ignored the remark as he walked Perry to the door. "I'll be in touch," he said as he shook Perry's hand and ushered him out.

An hour later, Rane carried one of his twenty-four-packs of bottled water to the Jeep and took an inventory. Paul's uniform and accessories were packed into the Jeep along with a thermos of coffee for the road. The Springfield was leaning in the back of the bedroom closet. The canvas rifle case lay flat on the living room couch to accommodate the Sharps marinating in the flower bed. The cap box on Paul's belt was full of percussion caps. Twenty rounds of live ammo were tucked in the bottom of his travel bag.

And he'd clipped Paul's fate card to the sun visor over the steering wheel, like the sword of Damocles.

He checked his voice mail and replayed a message from Harry Cantrell confirming that Harry had faxed a letter about Rane's credentials to the Southern cop, as instructed. Then he cleaned Hajji's cat box and filled it with a huge dump of litter. He was pouring dry cat food and water into oversized stainless bowls when he admitted to himself why he was delaying his departure.

He stood at his light table and studied the brown leather journal he'd discovered in Paul's haversack. Jenny and Molly should have the journal.

And there was something else Jenny should have. He grimaced. Have to think about *that*. But the journal definitely had to be returned. Could he drop it off? He had to go right past Stillwater on his way to Wisconsin. But he didn't really want to go back into that house . . .

C'mon, Rane. It's a duty call. Do it.

He had entered her cell number in his directory, so he thumbed down the key. After one last moment's hesitation he selected "Jenny."

One ring, two . . .

"Yes?" she answered in a tired voice.

"It's me, John," he said.

"I know who it is."

Rane waited out one of their awkward silences then asked, "Where are you?"

"Home. But I could use a break," she said frankly.

Just say it. "Look, Jenny, there's a journal I found in Paul's things. You and Molly should have it. Could I meet you . . . ?"

After several seconds, she asked, "Are you at the house?"

"Yes."

"I'll be there in thirty minutes," she said, ending the call.

27

JENNY DID NEED A BREAK.

She had been standing at the stove in the kitchen, watching the edges of a scrambled egg sizzle in the black, Pam-coated frying pan, when Molly walked in from the den where she had been staring at the computer all morning. "Mom, hold out your hand," she said.

Jenny extended her hand and Molly dropped four quarters into her open palm.

"What's this?" Jenny asked.

"Four quarters weigh about twenty-one grams," Molly said, knitting her brows.

"Yes?"

"Twenty-one grams is what a life weighs. It's been measured when you die. Twenty-one grams leaves the body, what religious people call the soul," Molly said, all serious eyes.

Jenny shifted the coins in her hand. "And you know this how?"

Molly cocked her head. "Dad and I figured it out."

"Really?"

"Uh-huh," Molly said solemnly.

"Tell me about it," Jenny said, turning the burner off under Molly's lunch with her free hand.

Molly exhaled, blew a puff of breath at a tangle of hair hanging close to her eyes, and said, "We were talking about it when I was eight. After Grandpa died. So I asked Dad what happens when we die."

Jenny smiled tightly and thought it might be a good idea to sit down at the table. She kept her hand with the coins held in front of her chest.

Molly continued to stand, slowly massaging her hands together in a meditative, washing gesture. "And Dad said, 'That's a good question. Let's go find out.' So we went on the computer and Googled it."

Jenny took a deep breath. Let it out. "Okaay . . ." Google was Paul's combination modern Sphinx and Sibyl. "And what did Google tell you?" Jenny asked.

"Well, there was a lot of sites to look at. We found this big one on Wikipedia with all these people arguing science. And Dad tried to explain it; how some said religion was just ghost stories. Then other guys said science was the real ghost story. It's like . . ." Molly frowned, took a step forward, and tapped her knuckle on the table. "It's like . . . the table's hard, right? Except it's really made out of millions of bits of tiny stuff . . ."

"Atoms," Jenny said, feeling a conjoining of sadness and encouragement at the way her child's mind was determined to work methodically through Death like a tough comprehension assignment.

"Right. Atoms, neutrons." Molly made a spinning motion with her finger. "Except, the atoms aren't really stuff either. They're this energy. Dad called it 'dark energy.' And nobody knows where it comes from or where it goes. But it holds everything together and makes our brains work. And that's what weighs the twenty-one grams when we die. The dark energy leaving. They said it weighs the same as four quarters."

"I see," Jenny said, staring at the shiny quarter on top the stack in her hand.

Molly nodded. "These four quarters leaving, kind of floating up like bubbles with George Washington on them. Except you can't really see them." She bit her lower lip and held it between her teeth. "Dad and I had this one idea: we're like cocoons and our job is to grow the energy until it's ready to leave."

"Leave to where?" Jenny's cheek twitched slightly.

"To whatever comes next. Like the next level in a game. Dad said nothing ever stops or goes away. It just . . . changes to something else." Molly abruptly looked at the pan on the stove and asked, "Is that for me?"

Jenny carefully set the stack of quarters on the table, got up, crossed the kitchen to the stove, flipped the burner back on, and put two slices of whole wheat in the toaster. A few moments later she'd prepared an egg sandwich and a glass of milk, which she took back to the table. Then she sat back down in front of the stack of quarters and watched Molly chew a mouthful of scrambled egg.

"Does it help, thinking about the twenty-one grams and the dark energy and the quarters?" Jenny asked.

Molly swept a yellow particle of egg from the corner of her lip with her tongue, chewed, swallowed, then said, "What helps most is playing the piano. The last time John was here with me on the piano he said music started when the first man listened to the rhythm of his heart beating. Or something like that."

Molly took another bite of scrambled egg and continued, "It's better than being mad at God I suppose. When Johnny Barns's mother died of cancer he blamed God, saying God had stolen his mother. So it helps more than thinking Dad got ripped off."

"And this is what you've been reading, glued to the computer all morning?"

Molly shook her head. "Uh-uh. I've been looking up burial ceremonies. I heard you and Gram talking about it last night . . ."

"When you were supposed to be in bed?"

"Uh, yeah. I learned so far there's three kinds. There's earth burial and then there's sky burial. That's when they leave bodies out for the birds to eat. It said in Tibet they used to cut up the bodies and feed the best parts to the dogs. And then there's fire burial."

"Cremation," Jenny said.

"Uh-huh, so you get ashes," Molly said. "I guess I like that better than the others. That way we could take the ashes up to the Quetico and scatter them in Poobah . . ."

Jenny nodded. Poobah had been Paul's favorite lake in the Quetico Provincial Park in Ontario.

Lois and Vicky came home from Cub with grocery bags, so Jenny helped unload the car, then retreated to her bedroom and sifted through the irony of Molly being better equipped to deal with Paul's death than she was. Maybe she'd been wrong about her daughter. Perhaps she was a swimmer after all; a deep-water swimmer.

Paul had just moved on to a higher level in the game.

Should call Patti about this. Maybe about a lot of things. The psychologist, another refugee from the inner-city trenches, had paid some dues and was the one trusted friend she'd acquired since moving to the valley. Call any time, Patti had said. And Jenny had said, I might take you up on that.

But how much do you tell her?

Jenny turned and eyed the broad walk-in clothes closet. Paul's body would be arriving on Thursday, and Jenny had been informed that he—it—would show up outfitted from a Mississippi Wal-Mart in white boxer shorts, a white T-shirt, and white cotton socks. She stared at the long line of Paul's clothes on hangers. As she faced the practical next step of dressing Paul's remains for the fire, her mind executed a dark pirouette and she considered the old East Indian custom of *suttee*.

Widow burning.

She pictured herself putting on her best dress, doing up her hair, applying lipstick, mascara, and eye shadow, and then lying down next to Paul's body in the furnace.

Ghost stories. Tables that aren't tables. Quarters.

In the Indian scenario, the dead man's eldest son lit the fire under Mom.

Takes a man to design that kind of ritual. Well, fuck that. She and Mom and Molly would decide how Paul was buried. No men allowed. That's what she was thinking when Rane called. Talk about dark energy. She agreed. Paul's journal belonged with Molly.

She definitely needed a break and there was something she needed to tell Rane face-to-face.

28

RANE SET THE PHONE ASIDE, THEN stooped and started to open the bottom drawer of his file cabinet. His hand paused. Not yet. Not like this. He stood up, reached for the pack of cigarettes, and again stayed his hand.

No crutches today, Rane. Straight ahead. Tick by tick he pushed the minute hand on the clock with his eyes. Watched the pot. He positioned himself at his front window and stared out into the street and finally exhaled when he saw the Subaru pull to the curb and saw her get out.

Jenny walked up the pavement to his front door, stepping to avoid the tufts of dead grass poking through the cracks. She wore faded jeans, a white T-shirt, scuffed sneakers, and a jean jacket. No purse. Car keys jingled in her left hand, marking each step. When she drew abreast of the Jeep in the drive next to the walk, she paused, noted the bags stacked in the cargo space, and slapped the keys against her thigh.

No makeup, clear-eyed; her widow's burden an ongoing icy shower that firmed her face. He opened the door and they met without speaking and she walked past him into the living room.

"So you're going down there," she said matter-of-factly.

"We agreed, last night," Rane said.

She nodded. "This isn't going to turn into another of your method-acting adventures, is it? Go use Paul's stuff to help you sneak around, then turn his death into a story with your name on it?"

The edge in her voice sharpened the tension set off by their bodies in proximity. He was leaving town. She was preparing for a funeral. It would be sacrilege to admit that their entombed past had been resurrected by Paul's death and now loomed over them.

"I don't know what it's going to turn into," he said.

Jenny cocked her head and slapped the keys against her denim thigh.

"Before you go there's something you should know. The day Paul left we talked about when to tell Molly about you. I came over here to propose a sit-down, you, me, and Paul, to discuss it," she said frankly. "But the way things are now . . ."

"Your call now. Whatever you decide, I'll back you," Rane said in a level voice, too quickly. And he felt the new idea of having a daughter suddenly dance away.

Then, seeing she was on the verge of saying more, Rane changed the subject. He turned and picked up the journal off the coffee table and handed it to her like a reminder of the dead man between them. "He wrote in there, to you and Molly."

Jenny accepted the bound leather book and held it in her upturned hand. "Did you read it?" she asked.

Rane nodded. "I get the feeling this Mississippi thing was a challenge he'd set for himself . . ."

"He was a serious guy, Rane," Jenny said. "Not exciting maybe, but steady and reliable. He never ran away."

The words slapped his face and he lowered his eyes.

Her voice working, she continued, "He was trying to figure out how to live the rest of his life. The way the world is now, he'd say, you practically have to be Bill Gates to make a difference. That's what attracted him to the reenactors; the idea there was a time when ordinary men took a stand and changed history. He helped Molly write an essay about what the First Minnesota did at Gettysburg. You should read it some time. And you know what? I think he pulled it off. I see it in Molly, the way he built tools in her that are helping her get through this . . . time."

Rane drew back from her steady gaze and said, "Look, I'm going down there after more than a story."

She studied his face, then lowered her eyes to the brown leather journal and tucked it in an inside jacket pocket. She loosened her shoulders and her hands fell to her sides, tense, fingers cupped, almost fists. Holding a lot in.

"How's Molly?" he asked quickly.

"She has these work sheets they use in the grief groups. My friend, Patti, talked to her briefly and told me Molly might have an advantage over some of the kids because she wasn't an 'over-feeler.' Where'd she get that I wonder—from Paul or you or from me?" Jenny said.

"Will the group help?"

Jenny shrugged and lowered her eyes. "I think time is what helps." Then she raised her eyes to his and said, "Given enough time people can get over anything."

Came out like a question. Eyes measuring him.

Rane made a quick decision to let this moment of truth pass. He turned, crossed to the light table. "Look," he said, banter coming into his voice. "There's something you could do for me." He picked a key from the table and held it up. "To the front door. I don't know how long I'll be gone. Maybe you could stop by and check on Hajji. He gets pissed off when he's alone and tips over the food bowl. Now that he's old, he's fussy and won't eat off the floor."

"Your cat?" Her voice verged on incredulity. But his eyes were far from frivolous; he wanted her to have the key for a reason. "Okay," she said simply, plucking the key from his hand.

Rane pointed to the kitchen, muttered about the food and water bowl; the broom closet where he kept the food bag. The cat box in the bathroom was, ah, optional, he explained. And suddenly Jenny realized they were through here. It was time for her to leave. She walked to the door, turned, and faced him. Impulse brought her hand out, hovering between them. He was going off into possible danger to look into who killed Paul. After more than a story, he'd said. In a way, she was sending him. The words instinctively formed on her lips. Take care.

But he simply shook his head and her farewell stayed unsaid. She had a last look at John Rane's face; his expression so like the mysterious, moving music he had played for Molly. Now Molly was toiling to master the piece in tandem with her piano teacher, so it seemed that Rane's melancholy presence had come to live in their house.

Jenny Edin turned and walked through the door, went down the steps, got in her car, and drove away.

After the engine sound faded down the street, Rane exhaled, sagged to the couch, and reached for that cigarette. He lit it and pictured Paul and Molly writing an essay about Civil War soldiers making a difference.

Rane blew a stream of smoke. He knew about the First Minnesota. He liked to think there was a time when schoolboys in the Upper Midwest learned their story as well as Southern boys knew their Pickett's Charge.

He pushed himself up off the couch, went outside, and lifted the now orange-speckled rifle from the flower bed. As he turned it in his hands, he visualized Rufus Zugbaum's oil painting that hung in the state capitol and portrayed the First Minnesota regiment's suicidal charge across Plum Run into Cadmus Wilcox's Alabama Brigade. Even when you subtracted all the romantic eyewash and nostalgia, the fact remained: on the second day at Gettysburg, two hundred sixty-four Minnesota boys stopped sixteen hundred Alabamians in their tracks for ten crucial minutes that helped save the battle and perhaps the war. Forty-seven of them came back.

Rane let the rifle hang loose in one hand, took a last drag on the cigarette, flipped it away, and bit his lip. Setting the bar kind of high, ain'tcha Paul?

Then, satisfied that he had an advanced case of rust eating

at the rifle's exposed metal, he carried it in the house, slid it in the canvas sleeve, and took it to the Jeep. He pulled a blanket over the case.

Back inside, he knelt, opened the bottom drawer of the file cabinet, reached in, and withdrew a black portfolio. He tore a Post-it from the pad on his desk, fastened it to the cover, picked up a pen, and jotted *jenny* on the note. Then he placed the portfolio on the coffee table in front of the couch. Hajji padded into the room and arched against his shin with that prescience cats have about impending events: earthquakes, floods, or the setting straight of a life.

He stooped, patted the cat once, and then walked out the front door.

29 DERANGE.

Jenny considered the word as if she'd assigned it to her fifth-graders on a vocabulary list:

To throw into disorder. To disturb the condition, action, function of . . .

To make *INSANE.*

Christ. She'd almost spilled it out; the times she'd driven past his house, the way she'd thought of him. She jerked the wheel, slewed across two lanes of traffic, and pulled into the parking lot of the Alcove Lounge, which was located just off University, about a mile from Rane's house . . .

. . . that she had left half an hour ago.

*Now children, use the word in a sentence for context.
Example. Mrs. Edin is deranged. She has been driving in circles. Now she's walking into a medium-seedy joint, amazed that it's still here. Walking in alone and sitting down at the bar and taking out a pack of cigarettes.*

The black bartender studied her and moved his lips in an amiable smile. "Don't listen to Joe Soucheray on KSTP do you?"

"Pardon?"

"He's got this riff about Minnesota being the state where nothing is allowed. They outlawed smoking in St. Paul bars."

"Oops." Jenny put the unlit cigarette in her pocket.

"What'll you have?" the bartender asked.

"Scotch on the rocks, pick a brand," Jenny said, looking around. Just the bar, a pool table in the back, booths along the side, and the all-important shuttered gray light that filtered out the cares of the day.

"We used to call this place the Alcove Knife and Gun Club," she said.

"Times change. We been pretty much gentrified."

"There used to be a piano," Jenny said.

The bartender shrugged. "Before my time." He turned to the serving counter. When her drink arrived, she paid for it and then reached into her jacket pocket, felt past the smooth shape of Paul's journal. Not now. She took out her cell phone, opened it, and hit the power button.

Disconnecting.

You see, children, Mrs. Edin has become disordered in her life. Her husband has been killed in an accident but now they tell her he could have been shot deliberately.

She returned the phone to her pocket and sipped the scotch, which curled, smoky, on her tongue and burned deeper going down her throat. A flush of sweat reddened her palms and dotted her temples.

Disordered goes with deranged. It means she's doing things the opposite of how she should be doing them. Right now she should be at home making final funeral preparations, sorting through her husband's closet, deciding what to save, what to throw away and what to put in the box for Goodwill. But she isn't at home. She's sitting in a bar she hasn't been in for—Molly was eleven, add nine months—for more than eleven and a half years.

*She was Miss Hatton then. Going on twenty-four.
And not bad-looking, with just a touch of gypsy flair:
loose, swinging cotton dresses, a headscarf. And she'd
come to this bar with a man who had this air of mysterious energy and who was a little bit scary. A St.
Paul cop who played the piano. She'd been substitute-
teaching when he came into her class to talk about the
D.A.R.E. Program.*

*The one time in her life she had felt the tug of
chemistry; the divining-rod impulse emerging green
and limber and runny with sap, and making her bold.*

She'd asked him out for coffee.

*She woke up the next morning in his bed. She left
Paul. They started dating and during that weight-
less first do-si-do he'd taken her to Wisconsin for
one magic afternoon, to meet his aunt and uncle.
He got in trouble then and she stayed with him as he
went through leaving the police department. He was
drinking a lot, which, it turned out, made him more
charming and open than he really was. They'd come
here with his cop pals, one of whom she remembered
clearly: an older guy who drank too much and who
was really scary, with a fifties' hairdo and a Southern
accent, who looked and talked like Elvis.*

*Exciting company for the young Miss Hatton.
They'd drink and the young cop would play the piano—we ain't talking "Chopsticks" here—and then
they'd drink some more and the cops would tell out-
rageous stories meant to impress her, and then the
other cops would leave and then Miss Hatton and the
young cop, whose name was John Rane, would go to
his house and they'd . . .*

Another new one for you, class.

Screw.

*Now this will all get clearer in a couple years,
when you girls develop breasts and get your periods*

and you boys become immersed in rampaging testos-
terone so all the blood in your mad little bodies rushes
into your dicks . . .

Jenny looked up and saw the bartender standing in front
of her, drying his hands on a towel. "You all right, here?" he
asked. Jenny realized she was trembling.

She knit her nerves into a tight girdle and controlled the
worst of it. "Fine, just a little tired."

"I hear you," the bartender said. "It's going around. Everybody's too busy. Too much going on."

"Exactly," Jenny said. The tremor passed and she sat up
straighter. The bartender nodded, moved off down the counter, and joined two older men in conversation. Refocusing,
Jenny eavesdropped on their banter.

First man, who was black, said to the bartender, jerking
his thumb at his larger companion: "Been telling Curly here
he looks like he's growing tits."

Second man, who was white, hunched over like a corpu-
lent toad pooled around a thimble of a shot glass. "Fuckin'
doc got it wrong. Damn testosterone injections. You take 'em
without the Arimidex it elevates the estrogen. Whatyacal-
lit—enhances feminine attributes . . ."

Jenny almost laughed, and the odd counterpoint snapped
her out of her funk. Methodically, she backtracked over every
moment of her recent conversation with John Rane. She pushed
the scotch away and stood up. He called her at home. The journal, of course. But there was more, he'd had a purpose.

Slowly, she lowered her hand in the jacket pocket and
closed her fingers on the key.

Rane didn't come out and say things. His style was visual:
to demonstrate, to act. Like playing the piano for Molly. It hit
her so suddenly it blew away all the obscuring clutter. Was it
that simple? He gave her a key.

A key to unlock what?
Him.

Five minutes later she was parked in front of Rane's house, staring at the empty driveway. Okay. He's gone. She got out of the car.

Holding the key in her outstretched hand, she walked up the cracked pavement, inserted the key in the lock, turned it, and then pushed open the door.

Hajji, the cat, poked his whiskers around the kitchen doorjamb, inspecting her, then withdrew. Immediately she saw the portfolio sitting on the coffee table in front of the couch. She advanced a step and read the name printed on the yellow Post-it.

JENNY.

She flipped open the cover and held her breath when she saw the crisp black-and-white photo on top of the pile. A picture of her with a full-term belly bulging over the elastic band of the loose blue calico skirt she'd worn the last week of her pregnancy . . .

In the picture she held a spray of flowers in the crook of her left arm and carried a pair of snips in her right hand. She was stooping slightly, cutting the wild flowers that grew in the garden. The old tilted cement birdbath in the background told her that had all been taken in the backyard of the starter house where she and Paul had lived next to Lake Como in St. Paul.

Jenny put out a hand to break her fall as she wobbled down and sat on the floor. Before the surge of emotion defeated her thinking and flooded her vision with tears, she had one moment of clarity. The chubby, radiant twenty-five-year-old Jenny Edin in the picture was not aware that she was being photographed.

When she turned to the next page, she had to palm away the tears. He'd captured a perfect moment in time. Jenny parked in a wheelchair, holding a bundled newborn Molly in her arms, at the door of St. Mary's Hospital. Waiting for Paul to bring the car around. Captured in an exact instant when no one else was in the frame.

Not even their shadows.

She couldn't put a name to the euphoric nausea. Not thoughts, not even images. She was overwhelmed by her own private album of sensations. The exact moment she conceived. Depression at his abandonment. Paul's sheltering arms. Then being buoyed up by goddess wonder as she created the salt sea in her womb where life stirred. Birth.

It shuddered in her now, below her navel. What she had wryly come to reference in her secret mind as the "angry living equipment." She saw it diagramed like components to be assembled in a booklet: instructions in English, Spanish, and French; Vagina, Uterus, Ovaries. To make baby, insert Tab A in Slot B. Called it "angry" because it had been in there doing push-ups for ten years, wanting to do it again.

Fingers flying, she paged through the few remaining photos. Jenny running the park trails at Como, propelling Molly in a sports stroller. Molly mastering her first steps. Molly riding her trike. Jenny in the driveway of the Croix Ridge house, lean and practical now, jaw set; settling into her medium-beige period.

The last picture was a coda to the rest. No Jenny. Paul jogging behind Molly as she pedaled her two-wheeler. Really a very good picture.

Like acceptance.

Jenny sagged and thought back. The last picture was taken about the time he called her and made an effort to get involved and she'd pushed him away.

Not stalking them, her practical mind asserted. Rane's stealth was innate; a trait marker. She recalled a phrase her father had used, before he died, to describe Molly's habit of stealing through a room: moccasin-quiet.

A dad curious about his kid from a distance.

Jenny rocked back and forth, and for the first time she really sobbed, keening, lamenting Paul who had stepped in.

And now Rane was the one stepping in.

Except you knew everything about Paul an hour after you met him, but she knew virtually nothing about Rane.

Jenny stood up. She didn't have time for this right now. She had to argue long-distance with Paul's parents in Kyoto, who were opposed to her decision to cremate Paul's remains.

She'd figure this out later.

So she wiped away the tears, closed the portfolio, and tucked it under her arm. At the door, she turned and looked back into the empty house.

Goddamn you, Rane; what's your problem?

30 ON THE AFTERNOON THE POLICE arrived at the big house on Grotto in St. Paul to deliver the news that twelve-year-old John Rane's parents had been killed, his Russian piano teacher was explaining that the polyphonic arrangement of a Bach fugue was like a good marriage. The right hand and the left hand play independent parts but the music fit together perfectly, like a puzzle.

The two cops, the housekeeper, and the piano teacher stood in the next room, whispering.

John, precocious, imaginative, and with excellent hearing, overheard the housekeeper insist that the police call in the family attorney to break the news. It took almost an hour for the lawyer to arrive. In the interim, the cops departed and the piano teacher thought it best to keep John busy, so he extended the grueling lesson.

John had overheard enough of the furtive procrastination going on just beyond the doorway to gather that he would never see his parents again.

Finally the attorney arrived, in gray pinstripe, exuding a scent of luncheon martinis. John absorbed the news sitting expressionless at the piano. He stared straight ahead at the dense notes arranged in a powerful complex order on the music sheet. The hesitant human voices attempting to comfort him were feeble by comparison. So he turned back to the keys and wrapped himself in Bach's strict rules.

It was the first of many exercises in which he surrounded himself with a flourish of talent to avoid feeling pain.

Of all the emotions that wracked him on that day, the one that persisted was anger at people who withhold the truth. So, at an early age, he found common cause with his uncle Mike, who preferred things to people. At first he found honesty in the mathematical structure of music; then he discovered photography. Unlike people, cameras never lied.

Interstate 94 going east cut through rolling Wisconsin fields with patches of dirty snow still coiled in the shadows of the tree lines.

More than geography rolled under his wheels. All his life he'd cultivated a talent for being invisible. He'd walk into a room, on assignment, raise a camera, and the verbal tic would fall from his lips: "Pretend I'm not here."

The Invisible Man was making his move driving simultaneously into past and future.

He drank a bottle of spring water and listened to the news until they delivered the butcher's bill from Baghdad and he switched the station. Past Eau Claire the rectitude of Minnesota Public Radio began to break up. He searched the airwaves. Find the right clear channel out of Chicago and you could ride it all night.

He left 94 behind at Madison. Stopped in a Borders at a mall and bought a book about the battle of Shiloh and a CD. Then he steered south. At Jaynesville, he stopped to pump three-dollar gas. Across the highway, massed on a ridge, giant, white, madly turning wind turbines revved the storm charge in the air. Down the road towering clouds filled with ink.

Back on the road, he turned to a new page in the atlas. Illinois; land of Paul's brooding Lincoln in the misty trees. South 39 turned deserted past Rochelle and the first fat raindrops splashed on the windshield. He jogged east on 74 and saw the lights of Bloomington glow orange, domed, in the twilight.

Found his station. "American Pie." Good old boys. Whiskey and rye. He stepped on the gas, heading for Mississippi, land of moonlight and magnolias, where the Civil War could still kill you.

As he turned south again on U.S. 57, he removed the blood-crumpled manila card from the visor, placed it on the dash, over the speedometer, and traced Paul's signature with his finger.

Driving straight down the middle of Illinois under a grumbling sky, he rolled down the window to listen for the distant thunder. He felt a warm tickle in the wind-driven rain. A crooked trident of lightning stabbed down and a few seconds later he heard the loud crash of thunder.

When he was a kid, his dad told him the thunder was caused by the giants playing tenpins in Valhalla. Father German, mother Norwegian; the flimsy layer of Sunday-school Lutheran lace could not disguise their pagan joy in violent weather that only the piano had the range to reproduce.

Rane slowed the Cherokee and flipped the windshield wipers on high to beat a tunnel through the lashing rain. Withdrawn into his shell of metal and glass, he eased open the CD and slipped the Beethoven sonata he'd played for Molly into the player.

The first movement began slowly, picking a magical calm path through melancholy. Then, having led you inside, the music accelerated until the tempo outran the beating of the wiper blades and surged with an intensity that challenged the power of the storm. Rane drove steadily through the downpour, playing the CD over and over. He lost track of time and slowed, entering the city limits of Effingham, and continued on, almost alone on the deserted highway, and then—the sudden eye-popping sizzle of a thunderbolt revealed a giant white cross looming over him, off the road to his left. The colossus vanished as the lightning flash trembled out.

Did you see that? Whoa! What? Wow! BIG mother. Special-effects big. Had to be almost twenty stories tall. Big enough to crucify King Kong.

That's it. Time out. Starting to hallucinate. He turned onto the next exit and backtracked, found a motel, took a room, and barely got his clothes off before he collapsed on the bed.

In the morning he showered, shaved, and ate a fast breakfast of fruit and oatmeal from a sideboard dominated by biscuits and gravy. The sky had cleared and, informed by a Cross at the Crossroads pamphlet he plucked from a donation box on the motel lobby desk, he sipped weak motel coffee and drove slowly past the scene of last night's apparition.

Seen in the rain-washed morning light, the cross's riveted panels soared a hundred ninety-eight feet skyward with an arm span of a hundred thirteen feet. With its heavy-duty industrial canopy, it could have been a launch gantry at Cape Canaveral. Rane didn't miss the monumental symbolism. A line from Shelley. Ozymandias' vast and trunkless legs of stone planted in the desert. This was a totem marking territory and proclaiming to passing travelers: Listen up, y'all— Jesus taken seriously from this point on.

He was entering the Bible Belt.

Soon he received other signals that he'd left the North country behind. Bugs started going splat on his windshield, clumps of magenta bushes bloomed by the roadside, green foliage sighed in the trees, and an iridescent haze of purple flax hovered in the fields. Starting to sweat, he pulled over at a rest stop and changed from his long-sleeved fleece pullover into a T-shirt.

Back on the road, less subtle markers popped up in the form of signs set, Burma-Shave fashion, along the shoulder:

> ON UNARMED FOLKS
> THUGS DO PREY
> ILLINOIS LAW
> KEEPS IT THAT WAY
> GUNSSAVELIVES.COM

Okay. Time to start loading up the voice mail cues. He palmed his cell and called Perry at the *Pioneer Press. Leave a message after the beep.* He recorded a query about a possible Southern contact. After calling Perry, Rane punched in the number on Deputy Beeman's card and again was talking to a machine. He identified himself as a photographer following up on Paul Edin's death and referred to the introductory fax from Lieutenant Cantrell at St. Paul PD. He was en route to Corinth and would be in town tonight. Would it be possible to meet tomorrow? After he gave his cell number, he set the phone aside and wondered if the whole revolving maze of voice-mail messaging was being controlled by a high school student sitting in a basement in New Delhi.

He took an exit, drove into a small town, and stopped for gas. He was leaning against the Jeep, eating a fast sandwich and watching a heavyset bare-chested guy driving a riding mower on a lawn next to the station, when Perry called.

"How's it going?" Perry asked.

"I'm in southern Illinois. Hear that? It's a guy cutting grass," Rane said. "You come up with anything yet?"

"Working on it. I called Chris in Atlanta. He's the only contact I got who really knows his way around down there. He's checking."

"Thanks. I figure I'll hit Corinth tonight. Be nice to have a guide."

Rane said good-bye, got back in the Jeep, and crossed the Mississippi. A few hours later, he swept south on U.S. 55 through Arkansas in a stampede of semitrailers. As he was coming up on his turn east toward Memphis, just a little while after his odometer turned a thousand miles from St. Paul, the cell rang.

"John? Kenny Beeman, Alcorn County, returning your call, sir."

"Thanks for getting back . . ." Rane took notice of the casual-slash-formal combination of his first name and "sir."

"Tell you what," the Southern cop said. "Right after you get into town—soon's you cross State 45—you'll see a Holiday Inn on your left. Decent accommodations if it suits your budget. Once you settle in, give me a call in the morning and we'll take it from there."

"Thanks, see you then," Rane said.

"Bye." Beeman ended the call.

One call down. C'mon Perry. Then he had to pay attention because Memphis was on him; a fast transition from the truck-crazy open road to snarled afternoon metro traffic. He found his way out of the city south on Highway 72. He thumbed the atlas to the map of Mississippi. Corinth was virtually the only town 72 passed through, almost four-fifths across the narrow neck of the state.

Out of sheer Midwestern stubbornness, he resisted switching on the AC in early April. He cranked the windows open and, rank with sweat, searched the radio dial and caught a weather report on the strongest station. The heat outside was pushing seventy-two degrees. The country going by floated in a green rural haze and he was closing on Corinth, listening to Patsy Cline singing "Country Legends," when Perry finally called.

"Okay," Perry said. "Got somebody for you. But they ain't in the business. Chris found her through the friend of a relative. Her name's Anne Payton. 'Anne' with an 'e.' He said her family's been in Corinth since before the kids' zoo . . ."

"Kudzu," Rane corrected. "Yankee plot to devour the state."

"What?"

"Nothing. Give me a number," Rane said, left hand on the wheel. Hunching the small cell phone between his shoulder and his ear, he reached for a pen with his right hand and jotted the number on the Mississippi map; read it back to confirm.

"You got it. Good luck," Perry said.

Rane immediately called the number and, to his surprise,

a woman answered in a voice that launched the word "hello" with a soft frontal glide.

"Anne Payton?"

"Yes . . ."

"This is John Rane. You don't know me, I received your number . . ."

". . . From Chris in Atlanta through my cousin Wilma in Jackson who knows a friend of his family. You're a photographer from St. Paul doing a follow-up on that Minnesota boy who got shot out at Kirby Creek. I have been informed, John."

"Ah, yes . . ." Rane paused, then added, ". . . ma'am."

"Now where are you, hon?"

"West of town on 72."

"Our better motels are in a clump just past Highway 45. I suggest the Holiday. I would avoid the Crossroads Inn unless your taste runs to bedding just got used by a trucker and a stripper."

"Thanks for the tip," Rane said.

"Well, you get situated and give me a call in the morning and we'll make time to talk," Anne said.

"Yes ma'am," Rane said.

"Welcome to Corinth, John," Anne said by way of farewell.

A few minutes later he passed two tall white Corinthian columns joined by an arch, on the right side of the four-lane, CORINTH spelled out on the sign post's brick base.

31

THEIR SIDE BLINKED FIRST.

After the seventh microwaved Hungry Man dinner of roast beef, peas, and mashed potatoes, LaSalle told Mitch to peel off his dirty shell jacket and cotton shirt. Then he handcuffed Mitch's hands behind his back, blindfolded him, removed the leg shackle, and helped him out of his trousers, socks, and underwear. Barefoot and bare-assed, Mitch was walked from the cave, through the old shed, and smelled fresh air for the first time in days.

LaSalle had him stand knee-deep in the lake, scrubbed him top to bottom with a soapy brush, like a horse, threw a few buckets of water over him, toweled him off, and took him back inside. Then LaSalle helped him into clean undershorts and the same nasty wool pants. The shackle clicked back on his ankle. The handcuffs came off, then the blindfold. LaSalle tossed him a clean undershirt and socks. As Mitch pulled on the T-shirt, he saw a backpack on the dirt floor. Opening it, he found his thermos, two packs of Marlboros, a gallon of water, a plastic cup, a toothbrush, and a tube of Colgate.

Mitch sat down, opened the thermos, poured a cup of steaming coffee, and took a sip. Strong with brown sugar, the way he liked it. There was this magnet plunk-on dealy stuck to the refrigerator door at the Corinth house. This Turkish saying: black as hell, strong as death, sweet as love.

Ellie's coffee.

Taking his time, Mitch opened a pack of Marlboros, lit one, and blew a stream of smoke at the harsh overhead light. Then his eyes settled on LaSalle.

"You're lucky," LaSalle said reluctantly, arms folded, leaning against a cave wall. "They didn't find a bullet. They're calling it an accident."

Mitch sipped coffee and smiled. "See. Could have been anybody. Your basic Civil War reenactor foul-up." He placed the thermos cup on the floor and said, "So—Ellie having second thoughts?"

"Could be you got a point. We're in sorta uncharted waters here." LaSalle gnawed his lower lip.

"Don't have to be," Mitch said, all reasonable. "I'll overlook you attacking me in the woods, jumping to conclusions about people getting shot, and this kidnap business."

"Kidnap? Hell," LaSalle said, a little defensive, "you're recuperating at your wife's house under medically qualified supervision."

When Mitch was a youth, Hiram Kirby had taught him one great secret of his success, which was to get people talking about themselves and listen carefully. So Mitch decided the diplomatic move was to change the subject. He heaved his shoulders, exhaled, and let his eyes travel the limestone walls, which were looking less grim; now an exotic setting maybe for a story down the line.

For a moment he relished the possibilities of dragging Ellie in here and bricking her ass up with a candle and a collection of Poe. But that wouldn't meet the threshold of an accident.

His eyes settled back on LaSalle. "I always wondered, what was it like over there, in Iraq?" Mitch asked.

"Hot," LaSalle grunted. "Sand and flies in everything. Got these camel spiders in the desert big as squirrels like to cozy up to you at night to get warm."

Mitch tried to imagine a spider big as a squirrel.

"I mean personally, for you?" he asked.

LaSalle, wary, shook off the question and turned to leave. Then he stopped and swung around. "Why you ask?"

Mitch stared at the dirt floor. "Don't know for sure. Maybe because I cheated my way out of going."

LaSalle shrugged. "Robert Kirby said you just showed your true colors . . ."

"That's bullshit, LaSalle. The way he run over me at the bank—how do you suppose it'd been in a combat zone him having all the more authority over me," Mitch protested.

"He might have surprised you," LaSalle said softly, "he surprised a lot of us when it came right down to it."

Mitch looked away. "I didn't mean about that, I mean what was it like for you before . . . ?"

"Actually?"

"Sure."

The big medic folded his arms across his chest. "The truth is I loved it. I picked up more about emergency medicine in three months than most doctors learn in their whole life."

Mitch cocked his head. "Why's that?"

LaSalle said, "Nobody's looking over their shoulder worried about getting sued in a combat zone. You jump right in and take chances to save people."

"Must be a bitch, huh?" Mitch asked tentatively. "Learning all that and not getting your job back?"

LaSalle fixed his serious brown eyes on a point in the middle distance between them, and Mitch imagined him meditating on a crowded foreign landscape of palm crowns and closed brown faces and red dust and minarets and the call to prayer suddenly exploding. After a moment, LaSalle said softly, "I was luckier than most."

"I can only guess." Mitch inspected the cigarette in his hand.

"Lot of guys I saw at Walter Reed would forget how to dress themselves, how to flush a toilet. Got so I was taking care of them full-time instead of therapy," LaSalle said.

"Not so lucky as you, huh?"

"Yeah, they were moderate to severe. I just caught a mild concussion. Takes a while to heal up is all." Then LaSalle grimaced like this wasn't his favorite subject, walked down the passage, and disappeared.

Mitch settled back and poured another cup of coffee.

Okay. Looking better. He wished he could see an article in the paper about them not recovering the bullet. They're coming around, figuring out they'd have some answering to do about why they kept him chained in a hole for days.

Mitch took a last drag and doused the cigarette in the dirt. Then he took a long time brushing his teeth.

Antsy, wanting to keep the forward momentum going, he got to studying the cement plug in the limestone wall, into which his leg chain was anchored. Could be two hundred years old, that cement. Hoping the old mortar had deteriorated, he searched the dirt floor patiently. Yes. Found him a bent rusty nail so old it could have come from John Brown's gallows. Using the brown bubbled iron, he began gouging at the cement plug around the chain anchor.

The light flickered, a shadow moved over the stone walls, and LaSalle was back, grinning at him. "A for effort, Mitch, but give it up. That chain was designed to hold somebody my size, huh? Not some skinny pissant like you." Then LaSalle extended his hand, palm open. "Gimme," he said, shaking his head.

Mitch threw the nail forward. LaSalle snatched it up and said, "What a dumb shit, don't know to quit when you're ahead."

32 RANE TOOK THE LOCAL ADVICE, checked into the Holiday Inn, and grabbed a handful of tourist brochures and a street map on his way through the lobby. Over a dinner salad at the restaurant next to the motel, he perused the brochures.

A highlighted block of type informed him that, not unlike his own St. Paul, the Corinth area had been a roost for hoodlums in the old days. In fact, this was Buford Pusser territory, of *Walking Tall* movie fame. According to the tourist handout, the Tennessee sheriff had battled "the state-line mob" in the sixties. The rest was mostly Civil War stuff about Shiloh and the Siege and Battle of Corinth. Rane concentrated mainly on the street maps.

Back in his room he checked out his camera and lenses, then plugged in his cell phone and laptop. Looking up, he caught his murky reflection in the blank TV screen and suddenly he was alone with the memory of Jenny Edin standing in his living room.

She was smart and would have figured out why he gave her the key. By now she'd have seen the pictures. A gesture to let her know he hadn't totally forgotten he had a daughter.

Rane abruptly went outside to the parking lot, opened the Jeep, and pawed through the glove compartment for the pack of Spirits. All through the thousand-mile drive he'd resisted them. Even during the storm. Now thinking about Jenny had him reaching for the cancer sticks.

He paced the parking lot with the unlit cigarette in his lips and breathed night air that carried a sultry reek of auto exhaust punctuated by the squeal of tires racing on hot asphalt. A tingle on his forearm brought him back. He swatted the mosquito, flipped the cigarette away, and went back in the motel, rubbing a dot of blood off his skin. He took a fast shower, lay down on the bed, and removed the two books from his travel bag. First he thumbed through the gun manual he'd borrowed from Mike, then he settled down with *The Battle of Shiloh.*

At nine a.m., rested, dressed in clean jeans and T-shirt, his camera bag packed, Rane ate a fast breakfast from the buffet in the lobby and called Anne Payton. She answered promptly and told him to meet her in half an hour at KC's Espresso on the corner of Waldron and Fillmore in the historic district.

As he mapped a route to the coffee shop on a Corinth street map, he called the office number on Beeman's card. The dispatcher at the sheriff's office handed him off to Beeman's voice mail. After the beep, he left a message identifying himself, confirming that he was in town, and left his cell phone number.

Mindful of Cantrell's suggestion that a little military goes a long way in the South, Rane dug out a worn army soft cap with faded camouflage badges stitched across the crown, weighed it in his palm, and decided to wait on that. Then he removed the pierced quarter from his key ring and stuck it in his wallet.

To look the part, he slung a camera body with the 17–55 mm lens over his shoulder, then tucked the cap, his cell, a pen, and a spiral notebook in the black haversack along with Mike's antique gun manual.

He walked to his Jeep in delicious morning cool. Soft air. A glaze of dew sparkled on his windshield.

Corinth's old town was located north of the newer commercial strip along State 72. Rane turned left off the highway at the first light east of the motel, passed through a section of old brick factory buildings, warehouses, and railroad tracks and entered the historic downtown. He located the coffee shop and drove a circuit of the streets, taking mental snapshots; people nodded to him as he stopped at intersections; old-fashioned diagonal parking made for narrow passage. The clean storefronts set in old brick buildings projected a prosperous feel, along with newer cars and trucks. He noted a die-hard Kerry-Edwards bumper sticker on a battered pickup. Then he passed a crew of street sweepers, black men in bright orange vests and striped green prisoner trousers, pushing brooms. Behind the work crew, a gust of wind unfurled the flag flying on the courthouse pole behind a Civil War statue. Rane saw the blue, star-studded St. Andrew's Cross in its red background flutter in the corner of the Mississippi state flag.

Now there was a "gotcha" snapshot.

He worked his way back to the coffee shop, parked, picked the fate card off his dashboard, and put it in the glove compartment. Then, camera and bag swinging, he went inside to tables, easy chairs, a mural-covered wall, a computer station, and the aromatic gurgle of an espresso machine. Ordering coffee, Rane sensed that his movements and his voice cut corners a bit too sharply in this languid space of easy smiles. Relax, he told himself. He took a seat facing the door and perused the morning soccer-mom crowd in shorts revealing tanned tennis legs.

Anne was ten minutes late.

Short, pretty once and now energetically plump, she was in her mid-fifties, with her blond hair styled in a pageboy. She came through the door, wearing slacks, blouse, and sandals, and walked straight to his table.

"Hello John," she said with an amused smile.

Rane smiled back. "That easy to spot, huh?"

She nodded. "Could be how you vibrate in this pale jagged kinda way."

They shook hands and she motioned for him to join her at the counter. "First off, not real sure if I can be of assistance." She batted her eyes. "I'm just a poor little housewife buzzing around the country club, church charities, and the garden club picking up gossip."

"I appreciate you taking the time to talk," Rane said.

Her smile remained the same but her blue eyes tightened. "Of course, Chris wouldn't point you at a dummy, now would he?"

At the counter, she suggested, "Why don't you refresh your coffee, let me get my latte and we'll go outside. Less ears."

After they had their coffee, she led him out the back door. "You're getting here a little after the fact. All the big stations in the state came last weekend. We even had CNN," she said.

Rane nodded. "This is more of a background piece; the area, reenactors. I'll tie it up at the Shiloh event."

"Uh-huh," she responded, clearly unconvinced.

They walked down the block, crossed a street, and entered a compact landscaped park with a shaded gazebo. Tourist stations with maps and factoids about the Battle of Corinth lined a wrought-iron fence overlooking railroad tracks. Rane glanced at a painting on one of the displays, in which blue and gray soldiers fought over the railroad depot.

"Watch your step, honey," Anne said. "We're drippin' in history." They sat down on a shaded bench. "Okay," she said, "so we understand each other: I talked to Chris last night. He used to be your boss?"

Rane nodded. "Before he went to Atlanta."

"He said I should give you everything you need to get started . . ." She pursed her lips. "Actually what he said was, point you toward a minefield and watch to see if something useful blows up."

Rane shrugged. "Chris always had a subtle touch."

Anne sipped her coffee. "He also said you have a habit

of working alone, ditching reporters and pushing the edge."
She raised an eyebrow. "I'd be careful of the pushing-the-
edge part down here, in this."

"In this," Rane repeated.

"Uh-huh. The Minnesota boy's death has been ruled an
accident. No weapon, no bullet, no suspect. Case closed."

Rane smiled as his eyes took in the quaint clean streets,
the state flags hanging on the storefronts, and the amiable
pedestrians. "Rumor has it you got a sniper who gets off
shooting people at Civil War reenactments," he said.

Anne smiled back and said slowly, "My my. So that's why
you're here."

Rane shrugged. "Worth checking out."

"Well," Anne said, "if they could print gossip in this town
you'd have a newspaper thick as the Memphis phonebook.
You are not going to get anyone to say 'sniper' on the record. Good Lord, John, this is a tourist trap for buses full of
Yankees."

"Off the record, then?"

"Well," she sniffed. "I *suppose* I could give you what the
gals in my lunch bunch think."

Rane leaned closer. "Anything would help. Later today
I'm meeting up with a cop named Kenny Beeman. He was
standing right next to Paul Edin when Edin was shot. What's
he like?"

"What he's like is—off the record—I'd say right now nobody is real keen on standing next to Kenny Beeman." She
cocked her head and studied him thoughtfully.

"And . . . ?"

The busy-bee coyness vanished from her face. "And I
mean, in all due respect to that unfortunate Edin boy, this
ain't about Minnesota, honey; this is about Mississippi. And
you're a long way from home."

"Okaay," Rane said slowly, "what I heard is, some of the
locals think somebody took a shot at Beeman during the reenactment and hit Edin by mistake."

Anne lowered her eyes and studied the spots on the back of her hand. "I didn't say that. You did." Then she raised her eyes and said, "But what you've just described does meet the criterion of an accident according to a certain logic."

"Who's got it in for Beeman?" Rane asked.

Anne sipped her coffee. "Well," she said, "a number of people in town, who watch such things, think Beeman is running for sheriff. He was chief deputy but didn't like the desk work, liked investigations. Given the meager county budget, anyone wanting to be sheriff has to figure out a way to keep costs down. So he's zeroed in on one family that uses a disproportionate share of our police calls, court time, and limited jail space. His solution is to run them out of the county, back up into Tennessee. Some of them insist on staying and stealing cars and selling drugs and shooting at people. So in the last year he's sent two of these boys down to the state prison. Like, let the folks in Jackson pay for their room and board. In fact, he shot one of them in the knee after a car chase." She paused. "Bee is big on car chases. Well this boy he shot was a state champion hurdler at Selmer High and his remaining kin, the ones Bee hasn't sent to the penitentiary yet, are fairly pissed off and word is Dwayne Leets, who's big in the Memphis drug trade, took out a contract."

"Leets," Rane said.

"Uh-huh." Anne paused. "There's a couple dozen Leetses spread around but it's the bunch out of Selmer in particular that's got it in for Bee. There was four brothers to start. There's Dwayne and Darl and Dumb and Dumber. Dumber is Danny, who tried to drive a big cat off a construction site and then ran over a city police car before Bee climbed up and brained him with a flashlight. Then there's Dumb, that's Donny, who shot a customer at a gas station checkout over in Iuka. Shot him dead. He's the one Bee run off the road and blew out his knee.

"That leaves Dwayne and Darl, who have airtight alibis

for last Saturday. So the gossip favors Mitchell Lee Nickels as the person of interest. He's a cousin to the main Leets nest. Mitch turned out almost normal except for a case of the social bends and an occasional drinking problem. He married into a prominent Corinth family and now he has mysteriously vanished. They found his travel bag at a motel in West Memphis, along with a sizable check he had just collected for his local charity project. No sign of him since."

"So why him?"

"Well," Anne said, "Mitchell Lee and Beeman are not the best of acquaintances owing to the widely held but unproven theory that Beeman's father killed Mitchell's father." She paused to sip her coffee. Then she trailed one hand idly in the air. "And Mitchell Lee likes to shoot old Civil War rifles in competition. In fact he got drunk and shot at Bee with one of them last year. But most folks say that was just showing off."

"Is this more gossip?" Rane said.

"Nope. There's a police record. Mitchell Lee went on a rampage, beat up the girlfriend he had on the side, then took this rifle and a bottle of Jack Daniels to the National Cemetery at dawn and was having target practice with those star-shaped GAR grave ornaments on the Yankee graves. Bee came to collect him and Mitchell Lee shot the side-view mirror off Bee's cruiser." Anne held up her hand, thumb and finger about four inches apart. "Missed Bee about yea much and they say he was a hundred fifty yards away. Bee was sitting in the car at the time."

Rane raised his eyebrows and whistled softly. "I guess."

Anne nodded. "There's also the fact Beeman sent his wife and two boys out of town to stay with relatives last Sunday morning after somebody shot out his picture window."

With that Anne stood up, walked to a nearby trash container, and deposited her cardboard cup. "I should think that's enough minefields to keep you occupied before lunch."

Rane got to his feet. "Well, thank you, ma'am, for being so . . . direct."

"Do enjoy your visit to our little town, John. You have my cell?"

Rane nodded.

"If you trip across anything interesting that explodes in your face, you will call?" Anne said with a warm smile.

33 RANE WAS WATCHING ANNE WALK away, thinking how most times you take a flyer and drive a thousand miles to run out a rumor you come up busted, when his cell rang and Deputy Beeman said, "Where you at, John?"

What is it with everybody calling me by my first name? "Ah, downtown, by KC's coffee shop."

"I had to stop over on the city side. Meet you in five at the police station lobby in the basement of city hall on Childs. You're three blocks away."

Rane went back into the coffee shop, asked directions, and was told to walk two blocks north and take a left. As he was walking the first two blocks, three people smiled and said hello. Entering a shaded residential block, he saw a tall church steeple up the street and green GENERALS SLEPT HERE signs by the curb in front of several old houses.

City hall was on the edge of the business district; a tall, modern concrete structure at odds with the older and lower surrounding architecture. Rane stopped for a moment and looked across the street at what he thought might be magnolia trees in a walled yard. Then he found the basement entrance to the Corinth Police Department, entered the lobby, and stepped up to a dispatch window to the left just inside the door. "I'm supposed to meet Deputy Beeman here. My name's John Rane," he said to a burly cop in a tight blue uniform and a brush cut.

The cop at the desk keyed on his voice and scanned the

worn black haversack hanging from one shoulder and the digital Nikon with the wide lens on the other. "Reporter?" he asked.

Rane shook his head. "Photographer."

"Where you from?"

"Minnesota."

"Oh, *that* damn thing," the cop said with a catch of genuine discomfort in his voice. Then he nodded, picked up a phone, talked briefly, put it down, and said to Rane: "Beeman's upstairs talking to Captain Shipman. Have a seat, he'll be down directly."

The chairs in the lobby lined the wall across from the dispatcher and were taken up by a weary heavyset black woman and three anxious-looking children. She was having a conversation with an equally tired-looking white officer with forearms the size of Easter hams. Rane couldn't avoid hearing their back-and-forth. Her son was in jail and there was a problem with paperwork. They looked like they'd been having the same exhausting conversation for about a hundred years.

Rane left them to their patient, dead-end dialogue and paced the lobby, shifting the straps on his shoulders. The elevator across the lobby opened and two men stepped out. One was a hefty bullet-headed officer in blue, who gave Rane a fast once-over. A catlike smile lit his face and he darted a look at the other man, raised his eyebrows in a "better you than me" expression, and strode off down the hall. The other man crossed the lobby toward Rane.

Beeman.

So this was the guy he'd spoken to on the cell phone last Saturday afternoon; Jenny going into shock, Paul's body not yet cold.

Beeman wore casual dark chino trousers, an ash gray short-sleeved golf shirt, black ankle boots, a holstered pistol, and a five-pointed badge on a leather cuff clipped to his belt. He was lean and tanned, about five eleven and change, with slow brown eyes and shaggy dark brown hair overdue for a trim. What Rane noticed was his effortless bemused smile, like he'd spent his life being privileged to methodically peel back the layers of an endless joke.

"John," he said, extending his hand, "Kenny Beeman. I got Lieutenant Cantrell's fax from St. Paul. He said you ain't the most likable picture-taker but I just might wind up respecting you."

Thank you, Cantrell. Rane had to grin slightly as they shook hands. "I just hit town and everybody calls me by my first name."

"First time down this way?" .

Rane shrugged. "I covered the Olympics in Atlanta. Was in the army."

Beeman's eyes twinkled. "Well then," he said with a slight self-deprecating twist to his smile, "you been exposed to our hospitality."

A response formed in Rane's mind. The army training cadre had tended to be Southern and they did call him by his first name. Which, at the time, they determined to be Shithead. But he held his tongue and looked at Beeman as if to imply all this chitchat was fine and all that, but he was here because a man was dead.

"I get it," Beeman said slowly, sliding gracefully over the speed bump. "Small talk's not your strong suit. Okay then, before I drive you out to Kirby Creek and show you around where Paul Edin was killed I'm gonna give you the short local tour." He jerked his thumb toward the other end of the lobby. "See that elevator over there?"

"Yeah."

"Well, before they fixed it up there used to be this big nick in the back end. March, 1973, the police chief walks in the lobby here, maybe had a few drinks. These two cops were getting on the elevator. The chief was pissed, you see, 'cause these cops had arrested a friend of his. So he says to them, 'I want you to let him go,' or some such.

"They say words to the effect 'Hell no, we got him good.'

"The chief pulls out his weapon and points it at the cops and repeats his demand. Bullshit, say the cops.

"Bang, the chief lets off a round, misses, hits the door-jamb, and skims the back of the elevator. One of the cops draws, fires, and shoots the chief deader'n shit right here in the lobby, about where you're standing right now. True story."

Beeman's patient smile did not alter one tiny muscle. "Welcome to Corinth, Mississippi, John."

34 BEEMAN SHOWED RANE THE WAY TO his black Crown Vic parked on the street. They got in and Beeman leaned back, relaxed, as he drove through the residential section. The big houses thinned out, then the smaller houses thinned out, and he turned right on an access ramp.

"We're going north on new 45 to the Kirby estate, where the reenactment was held," Beeman said.

Rane nodded and made a gut decision to test Beeman's tolerance for Northern newsies. So he started right in, "You got a new side-view mirror, huh?"

"How's that?" Beeman said, not taking his eyes from the road.

"To replace the one Mitchell Lee Nickels shot out," Rane said.

Beeman slouched back behind the wheel, still smiling, and asked softly, "You like newspaper work?"

"Like being on my own, out of an office," Rane said carefully, confirming his impression that Beeman was a tricky slow dance in deep water.

"Usually photographers come with reporters who ask the questions," Beeman said.

Rane turned and looked right at Beeman. "I met with Manning and Dalton, the two Minnesota guys who came down here with Edin. You spent some time with them after he died."

Beeman nodded. "Yes sir, I did. Helped expedite the remains from the autopsy lab in Jackson . . ."

"I got the feeling it was more than that. I heard you confided in them that you argued with the coroner's cause of death," Rane said.

Beeman's smile tightened a bit. "I thought you'd come to take a few pictures. Damn if you ain't starting to sound like a reporter." He slowed the car, and Rane thought, Uh-oh, I've crossed one of those bright lines. This is where I get dumped off. But Beeman was slowing to make a left turn across the four-lane onto a gravel road. A sign announced: PRIVATE PROPERTY. KEEP OUT.

Beeman said, "This is the back way into the Kirby land. Right up here a ways, not long before the reenactment, Old Man Kirby had a massive stroke driving this road. They got him in Magnolia Regional on life support and he ain't expected to live."

They drove through an archway of shadowy branches smothered in a gray mesh of vines. Perry's kids' zoo.

"Don't look like the road crew's been through here lately," Rane said as a branch scraped the top of the car.

"How Banker Kirby likes it, pretty much growing wild. Except for the battlefield," Beeman said. "He puts crews on it, light-sentence inmates from county. Has them trim back the fuckin' kudzu. Ran a mess of goats in here for a while to eat the stuff. That's a losing battle."

They drove out of the trees and the land opened. Sunlight dappled a swampy stretch of flooded cypress and, up ahead, the land rose in a long low ridge. Rane heard a rush of water, and a moment later they crossed a narrow bridge over a creek running out of the swamp. The road forked: one branch went up the ridge, the other descended into a broad amphitheater of fields surrounded by thick woods.

Beeman took the ridge road, and when they reached the top he stopped the car. The heights overlooked a long lake to the left. Halfway down the ridge he saw a white one-story house at the crest of the slope, with a gleaming monument in the front yard, next to what looked like four Civil War cannons.

"Those cannons?" Rane asked.

"Yep. Boys'll be by eventually, load them up and truck them to Shiloh. Let's get out. Give you the overall lay of the land. Then we'll go down where it happened."

They got out of the car and Beeman explained. "The main battle started down the ridge opposite the house. Some of the Yankees come up through that swamp we passed. I worked security on the swamp walk part . . ." Beeman turned and casually closed the distance so he stood a fraction closer to Rane than was comfortable for civil conversation. " . . . That's when I got to know Paul Edin."

"Know him," Rane said.

"Well, slogging side by side for hours, you get to talking. He was new at this stuff, so I kept an eye on him."

Rane asked, "What was he like, Edin?"

"Well sir, he was . . . ah . . ." Beeman looked down, "he had a wife and a daughter." His eyes swept down the slope, came back at Rane constricted to pinpoints. "I had to tell the woman, talked to her a couple times. It was . . . hard . . ,"

Rane waited for Beeman to continue as the cop's right hand slid casually to the butt of his holstered pistol and he edged a fraction closer. "Hard," Beeman repeated. "See, thing is, if Paul wouldn'ta moved when he did and threw off the shot and took that *accidental* bullet, it woulda hit me right about here." The cop's left hand came up in a fist, knuckles protruding, and thumped Rane on the sternum with the perfect amount of force. Just hard enough to be menacing.

Rane smiled and did not flinch.

Beeman dropped his hand and narrowed his eyes.

After a moment Rane said, "Okay, let's cut the shit."

Beeman reached in his back pocket, withdrew a sheet of folded printer paper, and handed it to Rane, who unfolded it and saw it was a printout from the *Pioneer Press* Web site—the story about his suspension.

"Internet's a wonderful thing," Beeman said.

"So?"

"So I read up on you. You write books, you been on TV, you was even a cop for a while, and you have a reputation for being big-time trouble. You got a habit of getting out in front of people. Like policemen. That can create problems. So you gonna tell me exactly why you're here? Take your time answering 'cause what you say's gonna determine whether you sleep in Alcorn County tonight," Beeman said.

Rane went for it. "For starters I don't believe a hunk of broken ramrod killed Edin, or some guy came here with a loaded junky Italian repro and didn't know it," Rane said.

"Okay," Beeman said slowly.

"Looks to me like you got a sniper," Rane said. "And people say it's personal, he's only interested in shooting one person. You. I figure if I stay close to you I'll be there if this Nickels guy tries again. Like at Shiloh."

Beeman laughed. "Mitchell Lee? Hell, man, that's just barroom gossip."

"Bullshit," Rane said. "Why'd he disappear all of a sudden?"

Beeman mugged his lips, looked away, and said more seriously, "Done some homework, huh. Well? Stay close to me? You'll be the only one, considering what happened down there."

"You're in the middle of a story," Rane said. "It started when Edin got shot and it'll end when you get the shooter or he gets you."

"Let me get this straight," Beeman said. "You want to follow me around and wait for a nut to take another shot at me?"

Rane shrugged.

"My own personal picture-taker," Beeman said, mulling it.

Rane watched Beeman's face and tried to clock the Southern cop on the ego meter. Many policemen dreamed of having their stories told. But to tell their story they had to overcome a toxic aversion to journalists. It was a ticklish balancing point.

"Be right there with me, huh? So you can write one of your books about it?"

Rane smiled. "Gravity's a myth; self-interest makes the world go round."

"Well," Beeman said, hitching up his belt and scanning the surrounding trees with a spooky cop stare, "ain't like I got a lot of folks in a clamor to hang out with me right now . . ."

"Is that a yes?"

Beeman rubbed his chin. "We gotta work out some ground rules."

"You let me in, I keep my mouth shut till it's over and the chips fall where they may," Rane said.

"It ain't ever that simple, John," Beeman said.

"Why don't we find out," Rane said.

35

BEEMAN CLEARED HIS THROAT AND changed the subject. "Okay then. Now look down the slope to where the trees curve around. That's where we come out of the woods. Paul and I were on the extreme left of the Union line . . ."

"So you were close to wood line on the right?" Rane said.

"Varies, between a hundred and two hundred yards give or take. He was hit after we fired the first volley. C'mon. Let's go down there."

As they walked to the car, Rane said, "Edin took a bullet, you said. I thought you didn't recover a round?"

"We're keeping it quiet for now. This Ohio reenactor, one of the guys standing behind us, found a spent round he says penetrated his pack. He gave it to Dayton Homicide. They forwarded it to the sheriff's office. State crime lab's got it now."

Rane nodded. "What kind of round?"

"Lead cast minié round, looks to be a .577, kind an Enfield fires. Which don't help much. We got the registration lists for the Confederate reenactors and there was more than four hundred Enfields on the field last Saturday. Smart, huh? Make it look just like an accident." Beeman nodded at the field below. "You can imagine what the crime scene looked like, all trampled to shit."

They got back in the car; Beeman turned around and

took the other gravel road down into the clearing at the base of the slope. Rane removed the gun manual from his haversack and consulted the section on Enfield rifles. Beeman craned his neck and glanced at the thumbed pages illustrated with ballistic charts and notations crowded in the margins.

Rane returned the book to his bag as they parked. They left the car and walked into the field through knee-deep brush toward yellow bands of crime-scene tape that rippled in a soft breeze, threaded through the tall grass, anchored to tiny saplings. The tape formed a rough square about thirty yards across. They stepped over the tape and stood in muddy, trampled weeds.

"Near as I can recollect I was standing right here. Paul . . ." Beeman took Rane's arm and tugged him into position to his immediate left, ". . . he was right next to me; elbows touching." He extended his fingers, making a knife-edge palm, and sliced the air to the front. "Reb infantry was about ninety yards in front of us on slightly higher ground."

"Who decides where you come out of the woods, before you get out in the open?" Rane asked.

"The Union troops come out the same place every year they do this thing." Beeman pointed. "There's a trail comes through the woods leading up to the edge of the trees."

Rane's eyes tracked across the field, up the slope into the trees. The yellow tape rustled against the grass in a gust of rising wind, and grasshoppers darted at his feet. He turned to locate the scamper of a squirrel, then he walked a few paces and sat down on a fallen tree. He reached down, dug his fingers through the grass, and brought up a clump of damp red earth, kneaded it between his thumb and first two fingers, raised it, smelled it.

"What was the weather like?" he asked.

"Stormed the day before, rained off and on all night," Beeman said.

"Wind?"

"Dead still the day of the event, real thick ground fog all morning."

"Humid, lot of moisture in the air," Rane said, thinking out loud as he got up and studied the ground between where Beeman stood in the crime-scene square and the edge of the trees. The area was dotted with tall brush and saplings.

"Our best guess, from the angle of the wound, was a shot from that copse of trees up yonder, on that knoll," Beeman pointed to the tree line on the left.

"That's under a hundred yards," Rane said.

"Ninety-four yards, we measured it," Beeman said slowly, narrowing his eyes with interest.

"And you think the round you recovered is from an Enfield?"

"Yep."

"You recall reading in Civil War history how the officers were always telling the troops to fire low, aim at their feet?" Rane asked.

Beeman squinted at him. "So? Large-caliber rifles in the hands of rookies tended to climb."

"There's another reason," Rane said. "The baseline sight on a three-band Enfield was service-set for a hundred fifty yards at the factory in England."

"Huh," Beeman said.

"Off the record, you think it was Nickels, right?"

"Go on," Beeman said slowly.

"He any good?"

"Shot competition with the Forrest Rifles. People who know say he once put three out of five shots in a can of Skoal, offhand at two hundred yards," Beeman said.

"Iron sights or with a scope?"

"Original sights on an original Enfield with a re-rifled barrel by some fancy gunsmith up North. No expense spared. His father-in-law's gun."

"If that gun was here he didn't shoot from ninety yards,"

Rane mused. "The round would still be in trajectory at that range. He'd have to hold low for a serious chest shot. That's leaving too much to chance. You'd want your sights dead on target."

Beeman thought about it as Rane left him and walked back to the edge of the trees, where Beeman said the reenactors had emerged from the woods. Trying to reconstruct what happened, he spent twenty minutes picking along the tree line, then he took another ten minutes walking slowly toward, then past Beeman, moving serpentinely through the clumps of brush. Every few steps he looked past the copse of trees deeper into the woods at a low saddle of ground.

He stopped about fifty yards past where Beeman stood in the rectangle of tape. "Hey Beeman, come over here."

Beeman joined him and Rane pointed to the branch of a frail scrub oak, no more than six feet tall. Beeman extended his hand and fingered a long wisp of frayed brown yarn wrapped by rain and wind around the slender branch. Virtually invisible.

"Like from a scarf, got snagged when somebody walked through? It was cold that morning when we got up. Some guys were wearing knit scarves," Beeman speculated.

"Uh-huh," Rane said. "Same guy walked through about fifty yards over there." He pointed back toward the woods. "C'mon."

Rane led Beeman through the field to another thicket, bent down, picked up a twig, and used it to lift a barely intact length of yarn fouled on a bush. A wad of dead leaves was loosely tied on the end.

"How the hell you think to look for shit in the bushes?" Beeman asked, now giving Rane his full attention.

Rane shrugged. "Ninety-eight percent of what I do is watching. About two percent involves pushing the button on a camera. I've covered black-powder shooting competitions where they hang pieces of cardboard from their spotting scopes on string so they can judge the wind."

"Wind dangles," Beeman said slowly. "Sonofabitch." He raised his eyes to the copse on the knoll. And Rane, looking across the field, up the slope, was thinking he was looking at the last view Paul had seen. He turned away from Beeman, calling over his shoulder, "I'm going to have a look up in those woods."

"I was all through that knoll with a half a dozen deputies and city cops . . ." Beeman said. Then he nodded. "Might as well . . ." Beeman's cell phone rang; Rane heard him say, "You go ahead, I'll be along directly," as he flipped it open.

Rane continued to walk toward the trees, absorbing Paul's death at every step. He saw Jenny's eyes go wide with shock, saw Molly uncomprehending at first, then that first intimation of the vacancy, of something torn out at the root and gone forever.

Rane did the tricks, bore down, rinsed his eyes clear of distraction, and focused on the trees ahead, on the idea of the man who had crouched up there with his smug plan and confidence in his skills with his rifle. The man who took away Molly's father.

As he walked, he instinctively figured angles, distances, and the roll of the ground. Didn't want to shoot downhill. And you thought the wind would be a problem, so you came in here, set up your kill zone, strung the dangles. Figured you could monitor them with a spotting scope or a good pair of binoculars. The copse would put you in under a hundred yards but you're good and you trust your sights. So you were deeper in the trees, more cover there, and you'd have a flatter shot. Wanted the round to fall exactly where your sights were placed.

He looked over his shoulder to confirm his direction and distance to the square of rippling yellow tape where Beeman leaned his head back, stretching his spine, still talking on the cell. He turned and snagged the toe of his Nikes on a root. Off-balance, he stopped, blinked, and looked at his sweaty hands. Christ, he was shaking.

And then, almost mechanically, by a process of elimination, he arrived at the possibility that feelings don't emerge one at a time. The whole messy gob tumbles out. John Rane had lived his life through his eyes, instincts, and reflexes. So what's this? Thawing out?

The tremor passed and he carefully approached a low saddle of ground secluded in the trees.

Five minutes later, Beeman joined him as he squatted above a leaf-matted depression behind a thick fallen oak. The hollow was screened by trees to the left and right, but they opened in front to give a view of the portion of the field with the yellow tape.

Carefully, he probed the decayed leaves with a stick and turned over a soggy cigarette butt. "You know anybody who smokes Pall Malls?"

Beeman studied the butt and said, "Fucking Darl Leets. But Darl was located down the field from me. Got witnesses . . . still," he thought out loud.

Rane raised the stick and extended his arm, directing Beeman's attention to frail wisps of fuzzy material snagged on a branch; bare remnants of the same yarn thread. Real fast, they'd reached a point where they were communicating pretty much with their eyes.

"I make the range at two hundred yards, maybe a little more," Rane said, thinking out loud, hunkered down, forearms on knees, looking out at the field. "Game it out. He was shooting a low-velocity ball traveling maybe eight hundred feet a second at a little over two hundred yards. There's a lot of moisture in the air and that could slow it down more. Do the math. The round takes almost a second to get there. That's enough time for Paul to turn in front of you." Rane stood up, dusted off his jeans, and then gently placed his fingertip on Beeman's chest. "If he's as good as you say, he didn't miss."

Beeman cocked his head. "Go on?"

"Things don't jump in front of your target on the

range, Beeman. And soon as he shot he was blind with the smoke."

Beeman squinted. "You get that out of your book?"

Rane smiled blandly and shrugged. "You make certain assumptions you come up with a hypothesis."

"Hy-poth-e-sis, huh?" Beeman said, enunciating carefully.

Rane leaned back, hoping he was coming across to the Southern cop as Just Plain Rane, a news guy long on bookish technique and short on experience.

"Sonofabitch," Beeman breathed. "We didn't look back here inside the trees that much, figured he'd be up on that knoll. Leave this. Don't touch anything. I'll get somebody out here with an evidence kit and take some pictures." He pulled a blue bandanna from his back pocket and tied it to a branch to identify the site. "C'mon," he said. "I gotta get back to the sheriff's office."

They walked to the car without speaking. When they got there, Beeman casually pointed into the passenger seat. "Left your camera. Taking pictures was the last thing on your mind, huh John." It was not a question.

Rane did not respond. Make a note: beneath his good old boy routine, Beeman's a lot smarter than he looks.

36

THEY DROVE BACK TO TOWN NOT saying much until Rane got out of the police car and Beeman admonished, "Don't go 'way. Stay on your cell and we'll hook up a little later." After the cop drove off, Rane got in his Jeep, wiped sweat from his eyes, reached for a bottle of water, and drank half of it in one long gulp. Then, seeing a slight prickle of red on his forearms, he dug a tube of sunscreen from the glove compartment and massaged it into his arms, neck, and face. So far so good. Or was it? He didn't quite trust how he and Beeman went from zero to sixty so fast.

In the meantime, he wanted to have a look at this Leets bunch. So he flipped open his cell and called Anne Payton, who answered on the third ring; apparently the last living American without voice mail.

"Anne, this is John Rane. Where can I find Darl Leets?"

"Wow," Anne said, taking a deep breath. "That's not *exactly* my neck of the woods. I believe you'll have to go out old 45 into Tennessee. Right over the line on the left you'll see the ruins of the old Shamrock Motel, where Buford Pusser shot Louise Hathcock, which is the same place, incidentally, where Louise shot her ex-husband, Jack. Or, by the alternative version, where Towhead White, Louise's boyfriend, shot Jack. A little ways up the road from there on the right side you'll see a sign for the XTC Lounge. The letters are a play on words, like 'ecstasy.' That's Darl's beer joint. Long as you're out that way you might as well take a drive up New Hope Road. That's where they ambushed Buford and killed his wife, Pauline."

"Thanks," Rane said, rolling his eyes at the information overload and jotting notes on his pad.

"And John . . ." Anne said.

"Yeah?"

"It can still get kind of wild and woolly up that way. I highly suggest you don't go out there alone."

"I hear you, thanks," Rane said, ending the call. Then he drove to a station up on the highway and gassed the Jeep, went in, and asked directions. A cashier with frosted hair and tanning-booth skin produced a county map and marked it for him. "Hon," she advised, "you picked the one place that is definitely not on the Civil War tour." She nodded at the Jeep pulled up right next to the door. "I'd lose the Minnesota plates. And maybe get a voice implant."

Rane thanked her, paid, got back in his Jeep, and headed north out of town. After one wrong turn, he found a sign that marked old 45, and took it across State Line Road into Tennessee.

Like Anne said, right over the state line he passed a pad of cracked asphalt on the left. He met a tan-and-white police car coming in the other lane, checked the rearview, and watched the cop car swing in a U-turn and fall in behind him. Moments later he spied a burned-out neon sign, from which most of the lights had been replaced by hand-lettered plywood: XTC.

The cop car continued on up the road as Rane turned right up a gravel access and found the one-story building tucked in brush next to a rusted chain-link fence in which caged, cannibalized auto chassis sprouted weeds. Three trucks were parked in the gravel lot. One of them, a muddy metallic gray Ram Charger, sported vanity plates that caught Rane's eye: OJDIDIT. Another "gotcha" picture.

He got out, debating which set of reflexes to wear into this place. Take his camera bag and talk the story? Or play the wandering tourist soaking up the local color?

The camera won. He tucked it in the haversack, slung it over his shoulder, and walked into the bar that smelled of sawdust and smoke and beer. The interior was one long dark room with a glow of jukebox red and green in the back. Another light hung over the bright green felt of a pool table. A cue tapped a ball, the ball clicked on another ball. The second ball dropped in a pocket with a muted leather thump. The two men at the table chalked their cues and did not look up from their game. A third man sat behind the bar, reading a newspaper. He had a cup of coffee in front of him and a cigarette burning in an ashtray.

The fourth man in the room sat on a barstool, bent over a glass of beer, thickset and whiskered, in field-dirty flannel and denim. To the right of the bar, an office door was ajar, and from inside the room Rane heard the quiet static and squelch of a police-band radio. A trinity of framed Civil War paintings decorated the brown imitation-pine-paneled walls: Lee, Jackson, and Stuart.

He walked toward the bartender, keying on the red pack of Pall Mall cigarettes lying next to his ashtray. Maybe here was a chance to gall Beeman with another amateur-detective gambit?

As Rane sat down, the guy reading the newspaper looked up. He had a long torso sheathed in a tight blue T-shirt on which white letters read: *get-r-done*. If this was Leets and that was his truck outside, he had a flair for punchy abbreviations. He had smallish vigorous hands and stubby muscular arms covered in bristly black hair. More of the coarse hair was combed straight back on his head. The porcine quality softened on the boyish features of his face. His dark brown eyes, however, were hard and alert.

"What can I get you?" he asked amiably, putting aside a copy of the *Daily Corinthian*.

Rane said offhand, "Whatever the locals prefer." His

voice and choice of language produced a barely perceptible waver in the smoky air as the three other men in the room shifted their eyes. One of the pool shooters casually exited the front door, returned a moment later, and whispered to the other guy at the pool table.

Minnesota plates.

The raggedy guy down the bar gave a phlegmy snort without raising his eyes from his glass. "Fetch'm a map, Darl, I think he missed his turn to Chicago." A working odor of sweat, alcohol, and manure wafted off him.

The bartender ignored the comment. He said, "We got weak-ass Baptist Mississippi beer and we got Tennessee beer. Brands don't count. The Tennessee beer's got more alcohol by percent."

"Bud. Tennessee," Rane said, unslinging his bag and setting it on the countertop. The heavy Nikon and lens made a dense, expensive clunk next to the ashtray.

As the bartender bent to a cooler behind the bar, Rane shifted his bag away from the ashtray, plucking up a cigarette butt and dropping the hand to his lap. When the bartender brought up an opened bottle and a glass, Rane took the chilled brown bottle, held up his other hand, refusing the glass. Then he picked up the napkin the bartender set down next to the glass, palmed the cigarette butt into it, and slipped it in his jeans pocket. One smooth motion.

As he hoisted the beer to his lips, he noticed that the big guy had moved silently down the bar and now leaned, too close. "See you got a haversack there," he said.

Rane sipped his beer, nodded.

"Haversack's for food," the guy said, knitting his brow.

"Camera," Rane said, flipping open the flap and showing part of the Nikon.

"How much it worth?" the guy said, appraising the complex nomenclature with a grin from which two of the front teeth were missing.

"Back off, Sweet; give the man some air," the bartender

said, quietly in charge. The big guy leered, moving his face to within inches of Rane's, then slowly retreated down the bar. "That ain't no tourist camera, is it?" the bartender inquired with a smile.

Rane leaned forward, resting his forearms on the bar. "I'm a news photographer. I work for a paper in St. Paul, Minnesota."

"Photographer, huh? You ever take any pictures for the *National Geographic* magazine?"

Rane smiled and shook his head. "Nope, never have."

The bartender swiped at a smear on the bar counter with a flourish of his bar rag. "What would you say if I told you that every *National Geographic* magazine published in the world from the sixties on was printed right down the road in Corinth, Mississippi?"

"No kidding," Rane said.

"True fact, up until about a year and a half ago when they sold World Color. So what brings you down here?"

"The Minnesota guy who got killed at Kirby Creek. Figured I'd look around, take a few pictures. Ask a few questions."

"What do people say?" the bartender asked, curious.

Rane shrugged. "Depends. Officially they tell me it was a freak accident. One theory is a piece of ramrod broke off. Another is somebody had a loaded musket and didn't know it. They never found a bullet, so I don't know . . ." He became aware of someone standing next to him; he turned his head and saw a lean, fox-faced man in a flowing Hawaiian shirt, one of the pool shooters.

"Go on the Internet, to AuthenticCampaigner.com. That's a Web site for hardcore reenactors. There's a big-ass debate going on about safety after Kirby Creek." The guy bobbed his head.

Now the big guy down the bar chimed in, "Shouldn't let these hardcore assholes spring rammers. Mainstream ain't allowed. My cousin was at Perryville couple years back and this Yankee dickweed actually blasted a rammer across the field . . ."

"Oh yeah? What was that like?" the bartender asked.

The guy called Sweet giggled. "Well, I guess it wobbled about thirty yards and stuck in the ground."

"Not exactly a lethal weapon," the bartender said.

"Bullshit." Now the other pool shooter had joined the discussion. "I read where at Petersburg the two sides got bored in the siege works and were shooting rammers back and forth at each other."

"Bullshit is right," said the bartender with a droll scowl. "I think what you got is a shooter."

Rane lowered his beer bottle and studied the man behind the bar, who, he was pretty sure now, was Darl Leets.

"Yeah," the bartender said. "Some crazy fuck stirring the pot. Wouldn't put it past some of those League of the South boys . . ."

"Or some mental militant coon ass," Sweet said, stroking his chin.

The bartender nodded. "Hell yes, you got all this red-state-blue-state pressure building up; thousands of guys eye-to-eye only a few minié balls away from the whole thing starting up again, huh?" He grinned.

"You're putting me on, right?" Rane asked.

The bartender stared him down briefly, then his face split into a slow grin. "Yeah."

Sweet cackled, "Darl had this fantasy about starting a Civil War paintball game, get all these guys lined up . . ."

The bartender leaned forward, planting one elbow on the bar in a conversational posture, fingers trickling open. "Fact is, you get thousands of guys out there with black powder it's like deer season. Miracle more people don't get themselves killed."

Rane's lips turned down in a Gallic shrug. "Good comparison."

"Don't get me wrong. It was a stone bummer. I was there," the bartender said sincerely. "Was with the Fifty-second Tennessee dressed in blue last Saturday and I was standing no more'n two hundred yards away when that dude got hit."

Rane shifted on the stool and observed something close to remorse flicker in the bartender's eyes.

"Did you see it happen?" Rane asked.

"Nah, just all the confusion. I was way down the line," the bartender said as his hand came up and his fingers stroked his nose.

Rane had followed a professional poker player once and learned that this mannerism was a tell: a nervous tick that covered a lie. He considered raising the question of the missing Mitchell Lee and rejected it.

But the bartender, no slouch in the people-watching game himself, had noticed the sudden intensity in Rane's eyes and asked, "Kirby Creek's on the other side of State 45 below the line. How'd you wind up here?"

Rane shrugged. "I read in this tourist brochure about the old state-line days. Figured I'd take a look. Was this where they filmed those *Walking Tall* movies?"

Wrong thing to say.

"Fuck no," Sweet erupted. "We run 'em into another county to tell their fuckin' lies." He advanced and menaced a finger at Rane. "I growed up here all my life 'cept when I went away for that machine-gun thing. My daddy knowed the evil sonofabitch, Pusser. Biggest shakedown crook in the region. Killed his own wife out on New Hope Road and made it look like some local boys did it . . . put that in your fuckin' newspaper up North." Sweet's rigid finger jabbed Rane's chest hard.

In a joint like this, showing weakness can take you down quick. Rane had trained six hard months for the book on cage fighting, working off a karate foundation he'd kept up since high school. The old reflexes from two years as a street cop bristled. His hands reacted ahead of his mind.

"Back off," he said, flat and cold, as he slammed his left palm up under Sweet's elbow. The instant the arm straightened, he clamped his right hand down on Sweet's wrist and cranked. Using the trapped wrist as a lever, he twirled the bigger man and smashed him hard into the bar counter in an efficient motion.

Sweet careened off the bar and stumbled back, caught his balance, and grabbed a bottle by the neck and raised it club-fashion, beer slopping down his arm. "Why you little pissant . . ."

The bartender vaulted the bar counter, stood between them, hands outspread, and scrutinized Rane. "Where's a photographer learn to move like that I wonder?"

"Whattayou thinking, Darl? Is he dumb or just plain crazy?" Sweet said, agitated, shifting from foot to foot.

"Not sure," Darl said carefully.

"Maybe he's an undercover they run in on us," Sweet grinned broadly, moving around Darl and smashing the bottle on the bar. He thrust the jagged edge up to the light as shards of glass skittered across the floor. He bared his gapped teeth. "I think what we got here is a case of suicide by redneck."

Rane snatched up his camera bag, slung it quickly over his shoulder onto his back so it wouldn't interfere with his hands, and eyed the distance to the door. The two pool shooters were coming forward, cues lightly balanced in their hands.

"I ain't done anything to rate a cop so he must be crazy," Darl said thoughtfully.

As Rane danced back, the two pool shooters moved to block the exit, so he swept the balls off the table with both hands, gathered several in the crook of his left elbow, and cocked one in his right hand. The pool shooters surged forward, swinging, and Rane fired the pool ball into the stomach of the nearest one. As he went to his knees, the other guy caught Rane a glancing blow across the forehead with the cue.

Rane staggered, the pool balls clattered on the floor, and the guy skipped to avoid them. Rane darted in, stripped the cue from his hand, reversed it, and butt-stroked him hard in the throat with the handle. The guy gasped and went down, raising a hand to his neck. Rane stabbed the cue tip down into the table's corner pocket and was about to snap it off, turning it into a lethal spear. Paused.

No one moved on him?

They'd stopped. Sweet had dropped his bottle and discreetly kicked it away. Darl Leets leaned back on the bar counter, shaking his head. Then. Oh shit. A pair of powerful hands seized Rane firmly by the elbows from behind. He dropped the cue, craned his neck, and saw two clean-cut, solid men in tan on darker tan. The guy holding him smelled of aftershave, his uniform shirt was freshly pressed, a loaded leather duty belt strapped his waist, and the patch on his shoulder read, MCNAIRY COUNTY SHERIFF'S DEPARTMENT.

"Everybody just take it easy, now," a third man in plainclothes said, stepping forward. He glanced at Rane. "Sir, you're bleeding."

"Nothing," Rane mumbled. "Little argument."

"Leets," the speaker said, "what's going on?"

Darl shrugged. "Like he says. He come in here and proceeded to lecture us on local history and it became heated."

"Anybody hurt? Anything broken?" the speaker asked.

Leets and Sweet shook their heads; the one pool shooter was catching his breath, massaging his throat.

"Okay then. I'm going to escort this fella on down the road. To ensure he ain't followed, Deputy Mason's gonna sit outside for a while. We clear?"

With that, the three Tennessee cops escorted Rane outside. One of them took a first-aid kit from the trunk of his cruiser, wiped blood away from the bump on Rane's forehead with a compress, and applied a Band-Aid.

As the cop treated him, Rane listened to the plainclothes man talk on his cell phone.

"Bee? Yeah, Sam Terell, over McNairy. Your Yankee pilgrim you asked people to keep an eye on? Red Jeep. Minnesota plates? Well, I got him over at the XTC on old 45 and he ain't bleeding too bad . . ."

37 THEY WAITED FOR KENNY BEEMAN, parked off the side of the road just inside the Tennessee line, next to the cracked foundation of the Shamrock Motel with the ghosts of Louise and Jack Hathcock. Sergeant Terell, an investigator for McNairy County, had driven Rane's Jeep to give Rane's head some time to clear. A county cruiser trailed them to give Terell a lift back to his car and was parked behind the Jeep. Now they were out of the Jeep and Terell was satisfied that Rane was walking and talking normally.

"Just a formality, you understand," Terell explained, his eyes now unavailable behind sunglasses. He asked for Rane's driver's license after he looked at his photo ID from the *Pioneer Press*. Then he walked to the cruiser and called the license in to Selmer dispatch to run the NCIC check.

"Figure where you're from the cops all got the mobile video terminals. We're still in radio cars," Terell said. When Rane cleared the check, Terell returned his license and then asked casually, "You ain't packing any guns or drugs in your vehicle are you, Mr. Rane?"

"There's reenactor gear and an old rifle I borrowed, in the back," Rane said. "I was planning on going to Shiloh on Saturday."

"Mind if we have a look?"

Rane said, "Sure."

As Terell and the other cop poked through the gear, Rane tested the swelling over his forehead. Dumb. Then he checked through his haversack to make sure his camera was still working. No damage he could see. He set the bag on the hood as Beeman pulled up in his black car and got out.

Beeman stood with his hands behind his back, flexing slightly on the balls of his feet. Terell walked up to Rane, holding the cased rifle in one hand and the black leather cartridge box in the other. He grinned at Beeman, leaned the rifle against the side of the Jeep, and opened the flap to the leather case. "Usually they have tins in here to hold paper cartridges. You have, let's see, a reporter notebook, a pen, a pack of, ah, baby wipes, a pair of wool socks and what's this?"

Terell held up a compact plastic rectangle.

"Light meter," Rane said.

Terell tucked the meter back into the case and snapped the slotted flap over the brass-button latch. He looped the strap over his shoulder, picked up the rifle case, undid the tie, and slowly pulled out the slender weapon. "Fuuack," Terell grimaced as he rubbed a finger along the scum of rust and dried mud that streaked the barrel, the hammer, and the lock.

Rane gave his best weak-ass smile as Beeman widened his eyes and rocked on his heels.

"Mr. Rane," Sergeant Terell inquired in a pained voice, "you know what you got here?"

"Ah, this old gun my uncle had back in his closet. It weighs less than those bigger ones the reenactors use . . ."

"And this tape you got here over the rear sight?"

"To keep them from flopping around?"

Terell exhaled and gritted his teeth, turning the rifle in his hands. "Mr. Rane, this is an original, single-trigger, Model 1859 Sharps military rifle. They only made a couple thousand of these."

Rane shrugged and smiled helpfully.

Terell drew himself up, raised one hand, and tipped his sunglasses down on the bridge of his nose, revealing a glare of hazel eyes. "I got a mind to run your ass in for abuse." He glanced over at Beeman, who was stifling a hopeless laugh. "Whattaya think, Bee. Can I hold him twenty-four hours till I get a legal opinion?"

The third cop had left the squad and joined them. "Yankee city boy," he muttered softly.

"Is anything wrong, officer?" Rane asked Terell nervously. The three cops grumbled and walked off a few paces and huddled briefly. Beeman poked through the uniform and gear in the back of the Jeep, then joined the other two, and they proceeded to bray over the Sharps and the contents of the cartridge box. Terell elaborately cased the leprous rifle and placed it in the back of the Jeep along with the leather bag. Then the two Tennessee cops shook their heads.

"Good luck, Bee," Terell said philosophically as he got in the cruiser. Beeman and Rane stood on the side of the road and watched the Tennessee car head back up north. It was quiet on the highway, just a whisper of breeze, the tick of insects, and, far off, the sound of a tractor.

Beeman turned to Rane with a pained expression. "Baby wipes?"

"To keep my hands clean in the field."

Beeman scratched his hair. "What happened to the ground rules, John? Look around. Think where you're at." Still smiling patiently, he said, "Okay. It's like this. Ever since we hooked up this morning there's something been bugging me about you. Something I can't figure out. You say you're a photographer and you been in town for hours and you don't take any pictures. You analyze a shooting scene in half an hour flat. *Then* you go off on your own into a redneck joint that most local cops wouldn't venture in without backup."

He took a step closer. "Terell says you hit a guy in there with a pool cue. The guy's name is Jimmy Beal, Dwayne Leets's driver. He's Dixie mafia."

Beeman shook his head, turned, and picked the haversack off the hood. After a brief look inside, he handed it to Rane.

Rane slung the bag over his shoulder, reached in his pocket, pulled out the folded napkin, and handed it to Beeman.

"What's this?" Beeman asked, opening the tissue and staring at the cigarette butt.

"I picked it out of Darl Leets's ashtray. The crime lab in Jackson can run it against the one at the scene for a DNA match," Rane said hopefully.

Beeman smiled manfully and let the butt drop to the ground. He patted sweat on his forehead, then bit his lower lip in a patent grimace, and said, "You keep this detective shit up I'm gonna start calling you Virgil. But you gotta understand—this ain't Sparta, Mississippi, in the sixties and I ain't Rod Steiger with a busted air-conditioner." He squinted. "Now how the hell did you get onto Darl?"

Rane said, "I didn't want to hit a strange town without a guide. So my photo editor checked with a former boss of mine in Atlanta and got onto a local lady named Anne Payton who . . ."

". . . talks a lot," Beeman said, his smile broadening.

"You know Anne?"

"Know *of her*. We're not exactly close."

"When we found the cigarette butt you said his name. So after you dropped me off I called her up and got directions to his bar."

Beeman sighed and clucked his tongue. "Tell you what, John," he said. "I suggest you drive back to the Holiday Inn and check out."

"I thought we had a deal?" Rane protested.

"Yeah. Be nice if you stay alive to keep your end of it. So how about I invite you out to my place for a couple days," Beeman said slowly, like he might be regretting it.

Rane pointed to Beeman's wedding ring. "Don't want to impose."

Beeman nodded. "Wife and two boys, six and eleven. They're at Marge's folks' in Tupelo, went down with a police escort Sunday; right after we came home from church

and found the picture window shot out. Or did Anne Payton
leave that part out?"

"I guess she did mention it," Rane said.

"And after I got this." Beeman took out his cell phone. He
thumbed into a directory and showed Rane the text message
on the screen:

MISSED YOU @ KIRBY CREEK. CATCH YOU @ SHILOH
IF YOU GOT THE NUTS. I'M CALLIN YOU OUT BITCH.

"Could be bullshit," Beeman speculated. "Like a crank
call. Things are heating up and the assholes are coming out
of the woodwork. Monday night somebody put a pipe bomb
in my mailbox. Then," he glowered, "last night they dumped
some kinda poison in my catfish pond."

"Leets?" Rane asked.

"Punks, kids, probably come in from West Alcorn be my
guess, where the Leets family has allies." Then he held up
the cell phone. "But this is more serious; these messages
were sent from a phone account listed to Mitchell Lee Nickels."

"There's more than one?"

"Oh yeah," Beeman sighed, selecting another message.

HEY BEE, UR WIFE KNOW U R STILL FUCKEN THAT
NIGGER NURSE?

This time, Rane decided it best not to comment. After a
moment, Beeman said, "Officially we're still carrying Paul's
death as an accident but the sheriffs are having a meeting,
Jimmy's on his way to Savannah, Tennessee, to get with his
Hardin County counterpart. Gonna discuss how to handle
Shiloh . . ."

"Meaning?" Rane asked.

"Meaning how to use me as bait."

Rane chewed his lip. "Okay. So where do you live?"

"Just go back to town, check out of the motel, and wait in the lot. No side trips, you hear?"

"No side trips," Rane said.

"Okay. I'll be right behind you soon's I make a call. Now go. Git."

Rane picked up his haversack, got in the Jeep, turned the key, pulled onto the road, and headed for Corinth. Looking in the rearview mirror, he saw Beeman standing beside the road, tapping numbers in his cell phone.

38

PAUL'S BODY ARRIVED IN THE morning.

At one p.m., Jenny wheeled the Forester into the lot of the Bradley Circle of Life Center off Highway 36 at the western edge of Stillwater, parked, and turned off the key. She heaved her shoulders and exhaled as she watched traffic stream along the highway.

Other people doing normal things.

After what she hoped would be her last long-distance showdown with her mother-in-law, it was time to sign the papers giving the center permission to cremate Paul's remains. Paul's family did insist on minimal due diligence; that someone view the cadaver to make sure Jenny was consigning the right body to the fire.

Jenny was unfazed. Her mind was made up. And she had Paul's will to buttress her decision. Molly's last memories of her dad would be of him alive. She would not see him pumped full of chemical preservatives and tarted up with cosmetics in a casket.

Dutifully, she got out of the car, hauled from the backseat the biggest suitcase they owned, and carried it toward the discreet one-story building.

Molly viewed the cremation as more than a practical matter and had insisted that she be allowed to participate in the funeral discussions. After half an hour of discussion she did not back off on her stubborn desire to pick the last clothes her dad "would wear." Then she expressed a desire to pack a farewell bag.

Jenny, Vicky, and Mom saw it as a step toward acceptance, and agreed.

So now Jenny carried a suitcase that contained Paul's bulky green terry-cloth robe, his Acorn slippers, and the frayed Minnesota Twins cap he'd always worn on canoe trips. A smaller wooden latch box Molly had purchased with her own allowance at Michaels craft store was tucked in the folds of the robe. She'd selected a favorite handmade Father's Day card to pack in the case.

To Dad. Happy Father's Day.

Molly, age five, struggling with her first cursive penmanship. She had drawn a red cardinal with mismatched wings in pastel.

She'd also included Paul's favorite coffee cup, a package of Pecan Sandies, and a box of green tea. The final item she'd added was the much-handled copy of *The Red Badge of Courage*, the last book she had seen him reading.

Jenny hefted the suitcase and opened the door, like a traveler heading for baggage check-in at the airport. She cleared the door, walked through the quiet lobby to the reception desk, and told the woman behind the desk, "I have a private viewing for Paul Edin."

The receptionist nodded, picked up her phone, spoke for a moment, and then said, "Mr. Bradley will be right with you."

Donald Bradley, director at the center, appeared in less than a minute. He was a tall, white-haired man with deep blue Himalayan eyes, a reliable Sherpa who would guide Jenny through the foreign terrain of the Dead Zone.

"I have some things," Jenny said, nodding to the suitcase.

"Of course," Bradley said, leaning forward, offering to carry the case. Jenny smiled tightly and held on to the suitcase. She would carry it herself.

"This way," Bradley said. He led her down a corridor to a large elevator, like a freight elevator; big enough to accommodate a wheeled gurney.

Going down evoked a bevy of odd thoughts. Shrouding. Sally Fields in a movie, dutifully washing her dead husband's body and sewing a winding sheet from bedsheets.

Women's work.

She didn't know what to expect. She and Paul had given up on *Six Feet Under* after one season.

The basement level was a clean, quiet corridor. Bradley's staff were apparently all ninjas, who walked without making a sound.

"In here," Bradley said, opening a door to a carpeted room.

Jenny stepped into the room and held her breath. Not Paul. A manifestation of Paul lay on a table draped in an off-white sheet. His eyelids were shut. According to Molly's relentless Google research, the eyes were closed with tiny curved plastic discs called "eye caps," inserted under the eyelid. The cap was perforated to hold the lid in place. Bradley had explained they didn't use the caps. Stitches.

Jenny exhaled.

The manifestation of Paul wore a braced waxen expression, the head resting on a dark rubber block with a sheet pulled up to the chin. A livid bruise marred the forehead and the neck wound had been closed and tidied. Bradley indicated a portable table on casters and helped Jenny hoist the suitcase and open the latches. Two metallic clicks dissolved in the huge silence.

"As you requested, we've removed the travel garments. You understand, when I lift the sheet, you will see the autopsy sutures," Bradley said.

"I understand," Jenny said. Staring at the antiseptic mangle in the neck brought back phrases from the coroner's description on the death certificate:

Projectile clipped the carotid artery left side, penetrated the windpipe, causing massive hemorrhage . . . missed the vertebrae column . . . exited through soft tissue . . .

Jenny took a deep breath as the sheet was removed and she saw the puckered pattern in the pale skin. No actual stitches were visible.

New word: *Autopsy.*

She removed the bathrobe, which, on Bradley's instructions, had not been divided down the center of the back to facilitate draping. In keeping with the center's natural approach, dressing a body meant dressing without costume gimmicks.

> *They cut the body open and take the insides out and inspect them to help determine the cause of death. They start by making a Y-shaped incision from each shoulder, which meets over the breastbone. Then they cut down to the pubic bone. After they peel back the skin, the chest cavity is opened by cutting the bones away with an electric saw . . .*

With Bradley's assistance, Jenny lifted the body slightly. When she inserted one arm in the sleeve, the joints of the elbow and shoulder resisted moderately and some effort was required to thread the sleeve. They lifted the chest and head and tugged and tucked with their free hands. The empty sleeve was scooted underneath the raised back to the other side.

Scheduling this visit, Jenny had asked Bradley a specific question. She'd wanted to know just how much of her husband had been returned, embalmed, from Mississippi, following the forensic procedure conducted at the state lab in Jackson.

Jenny's eyes riveted on the Y-shaped line of puckered

skin, diagonal across the chest to the stomach and down to the pubic bone. She tried to imagine the bright steel electric saw. What it sounded like.

The director had assured her that all the organs had been returned after the examination; although they might not be in their proper places.

Did he know that for certain?

No.

Jenny's doubting mother was not convinced. She'd read stories about pathology labs lifting organs for dissection and display purposes after autopsies. Paul's cadaver, according to Lois, could be packed with sawdust.

Now Jenny and Bradley moved to the other side of the table and repeated the procedure of fitting the sleeve and lifting and tugging. After the difficulty of managing the sleeves, the rest of the robe easily draped around the torso and legs. Finally, the stitches were covered.

Sometimes the saw makes so much dust cutting through the bones that they use big shears instead. They cut through the ribs on each side so they can lift the ribs and sternum out in one piece. This piece is called the chest plate.

So they can get at the stuff inside.

They also cut around the circumference of the skull, leaving a flap intact in the front so they can tip it forward and remove the brain.

People wearing white coats, masks, and vinyl gloves had used shiny steel saws, big shears, and scalpels to eviscerate Paul's body. Briefly, she wondered if there were flirtations around the autopsy table? Did they wash their hands a lot?

The point was, when they were finished, they put it all back, replaced the chest plate, sewed the chest up, and fitted the top of skull back on, like one of those eggs silly putty comes in. Except what if Mom was right? What if the egg was empty? And the chest. After the examination, what if they'd carted Paul's insides off to an incinerator and burned them? Or pickled them in jars?

Jenny's chest ached and her stomach heaved. It was a new sensation that she now thought of as advanced crying. No tears came anymore. The sadness had become a deep, regular vibration that echoed her breathing and her heartbeat and glowed in her bones. She wondered if it was going to be permanent.

Jenny reminded herself that Paul had been an unsentimental man with slightly Buddhist leanings and he would have approved of her frank reactions to the leftovers of a life. Such were her thoughts as her hands touched the cool, stiff skin of the man she'd lived with for eleven years. Carefully, she adjusted and tied the robe, put the slippers on the white feet, fitted the hat, and positioned Molly's briefcase on the chest.

My gentle, decent man.

She looked at the smooth, wax-museum face for the last time, laid her palms alongside the cold cheeks just once, then stepped back and nodded to Bradley.

Bradley escorted her upstairs to his office and held out a chair at a small table. Jenny sat, declined a cup of coffee, but took his advice and drank the small cup of water he held out. Then he placed the form for the cremation authorization in front of her.

"You've had a chance to thoroughly look this authorization over?" Bradley asked as he placed a pen next to the form.

"Yes," Jenny said as her eyes flicked at the document's upper right corner, where she noted the blank line identified as "cremation number."

I authorize and request . . . cremate the body of . . . (hereafter Decedent) who died . . .

I assume legal responsibility for the disposition of the Decedent . . .

Jenny's eyes bounced over the small type descending through the subparagraphs at random . . .

> *to the best of my knowledge the body of the Decedent does not contain any implanted or attached mechanical, electrical, or radioactive device that may create a hazard when placed in a cremation chamber . . .*
>
> *. . . the cremated remains of the Decedent will be mechanically reduced to granular appearance and placed in an appropriate container . . .*
>
> *. . . even with the exercise of reasonable care it is not possible to recover all the particles of the cremated remains of the Decedent and that some particles may inadvertently become commingled with . . . other particles of cremated remains . . .*

Routine setting in. The wheels keep turning. She picked up the pen and signed the form in all the appropriate places.

Next Bradley opened the price list for cremation caskets and alternative containers. "Have you made a decision as to a cremation container?"

Jenny smiled briefly. "Do many people choose the velvet-lined mahogany casket for over three thousand?"

"No."

"It was my mother-in-law's first choice in lieu of an earth burial," Jenny said. "Fortunately Paul left a will. He wanted a simple ceremony and then an unadorned temporary urn. We've decided to scatter his ashes in Quetico. So we're going with the standard alternative container . . ."

Jenny stopped in mid-sentence when her cell phone rang inside her purse. She retrieved it, checked the display, and saw the 662 area code.

Mississippi.

"Excuse me," she said as her heartbeat doubled. With a steely finger, she connected to the call. "Hello?"

"Mrs. Edin? This is Deputy Beeman, from Alcorn County, Mississippi."

Her chest relaxed visibly. "Yes, ah . . . could we talk later, I'm in a funeral home and . . ."

"Mrs. Edin, I'm sorry to bother you but I think we gotta talk now," the cop said forcefully.

The quiet decor of the office swam in her vision and she began to sweat. Her eyes settled on a framed Dr. Seuss cartoon on the wall over the desk. An odd Seuss-type character reclined in a coffin, talking on a phone. It was too far away to read the caption. "Just a moment," she said to Beeman. Then she turned to Bradley. "I'm sorry, but I have to deal with this."

"Of course," said Bradley.

"I'll just be a few minutes. Could I take this outside?" Jenny asked, rising from the chair. Courtly and low-key, Bradley escorted her out of the office, across the hall, through the room with casket and urn displays, and through a door into a patio area. She walked to a wooden bench in front of a block wall, sat down, and raised the phone. "Deputy?"

"Are you familiar with a news photographer with the St. Paul paper, named John Rane?" Beeman said without preamble.

Familiar, Jenny thought. It was an imprecise term.

"Mrs. Edin?"

A siren whelped on Highway 36 and her eyes caught the green, white-trimmed ambulance racing through traffic. Closer in, she noticed the grounds beside the walking path were planted in prairie grasses emerging from winter sedge.

"Yes," Jenny said. "I am." She was staring at the wall in front of her, which she realized was a repository for cremated remains. There were names and dates on some of the panels.

"I know this is . . . hard, ma'am. We never really met and I'm a thousand miles away but I got a situation here and I need to know more about this man," Beeman said.

"So do I," Jenny said.

Now it was Beeman's turn to pause on the connection. After a moment, he started again. "Thing is, he's carrying his camera in Paul's—your husband's—haversack. And he's got his uniform in his car. I read his name in the bag and on some of the clothing. He's been in town all day and he ain' . . . isn't taking any pictures . . ."

"I guess we have to trust each other," Jenny said.

"Ma'am?"

"You were next to Paul when he died. Davey Manning said you tried real hard to save his life, so I guess we have to trust each other." She was trying to fit the man to the voice, but it was hard to read him through the filter of his Southern accent.

"He ain't like any newspaper guy I ever met," Beeman said.

"In your line of work I'm sure you know all the usual reasons people get in trouble. Well, John Rane is the kind of man who gets in trouble because he's very, very good at everything, except getting close to people."

"That may well be," Beeman said patiently, "but what I'm after is something more specific, like exactly what's he doing here with Paul's bag and clothes?"

Beeman's voice had this gentle sway, almost like music. "Of course," she said, more attentive, "I see. When I met Rane almost twelve years ago he wasn't a photographer . . . he was a St. Paul cop."

"I know," Beeman said. "I read up on him online. He's been a lot of things. And now I got him in my county."

Jenny became stuck. She stood up, advanced a step, and placed her open palm on one of the blank panels. The day was cloudy and threatening to bluster. The stone was cold to her touch.

"Mrs. Edin? You still there?" Beeman said, trying to keep the conversation going.

"The thing you should know, Deputy Beeman . . ."

"Yes?"

"The day you called, last Saturday afternoon. When you told me, I collapsed. A man picked up the phone and spoke to you. That was John Rane."

"Damn," Beeman muttered. "I knew there was something about him. It was his voice. I heard it before."

Jenny looked over the names on the panels and wondered how many of these people died violently; abruptly scissored out of the family picture. She tried to visualize the size of the shears they used to cut through a cadaver's chest.

"Mrs. Edin?"

"I'm here," Jenny said. "The reason he's got Paul's things is my fault. Rane was at the house when Davey Manning and Tom Dalton came over to return them. That's when he heard Davey and Tom discuss what happened, how they'd talked to you and how you expressed the opinion Paul's death wasn't an accident. I let him take Paul's things. And your card." She paused. "So, on the surface, yes, he works for a newspaper and he's there to investigate a story. But I don't think that's why he went."

"Why's he here, then?"

"Ah, I think he's trying to figure out how to be a father."

"Say again?"

Jenny watched a large crow strut stiff-legged among the desiccated tufts of prairie grass. The bird was close enough for her to distinctly see the stern flash of the remorseless, alert eye against the swept black feathers. Beeman could be like that. Single-minded, suspicious. Cops spent their lives tidying up human roadkill, didn't they?

"Mrs. Edin?"

Jenny debated. Rane was playing with fire again and she'd had a part in it. People could get hurt. She had intended to confide this to Patti but now she was telling it to a stranger.

"Deputy Beeman. Paul and I had—have—a daughter named Molly. But Rane is the biological father. I was pregnant by him when I married Paul. I had not spoken to him since before Molly was born except once on the phone when she was starting kindergarten. He's been absolutely scrupulous about not intruding in Molly's life." Jenny paused and considered the photos and decided not to mention it. "Molly had—has—no idea who her biological father is . . ." Jenny paused again. "I know how scattered this must sound . . . how . . . bad . . ."

"Ma'am, I ain't exactly. . . . a good-and-bad kind of person."

Something in the deeply felt way his voice wrestled through that statement prompted her to say, "You're struggling with this too . . ."

"Mrs. Edin . . ."

"Jenny."

"All right, Jenny. The way it's starting to look down here is somebody came to Kirby Creek with a plan to shoot me and hit your husband instead."

She was looking at a wall full of ashes, talking to a man she'd never met, and it was turning into a surreal communication. Strangers linked by a cell phone, like a passenger on one of the doomed hijacked planes thrust in sudden intimacy with a 911 dispatcher.

"Deputy Beeman," she blurted, her voice shaking. "I got a feeling you better catch the guy who shot Paul and lock him up quick. Last Saturday John Rane spoke to his daughter for the first time and had to tell her that her father was dead. The man has an almost suicidal habit of charging into dangerous situations. I think all this has turned his life upside down. And this conversation is starting to have the same effect on me. *Right this minute I'm standing outside the undertakers!* We have to stop this for now . . ."

"Damn right, ma'am. Hell, I mean . . . you have my number?"

"Yes." Calmer now. "It's written down half a dozen places at home. It's on my cell."

"Can we talk again?"

"I just need some time to think," Jenny said. Then her tone relaxed and she asked, "Where are you?"

"Ma'am?"

"I mean where are you physically right now, what's it like?"

"Ah, well, I'm standing on this back road, kinda, out here all alone. It's a clear day, almost hot . . ."

"I gotta go," Jenny said. She ended the call, stood up, and swiped a damp spot on the seat of her slacks. Something on the bench. Absently, she thought it might stain. Then she started walking back toward the building where Paul's empty shell lay held together with Frankenstein stitches. With the bizarre echo of Beeman's call still ringing in her mind, she realized that she'd never know if Mom was right about Paul leaving his heart in Mississippi.

39 BEEMAN LIVED DOWN A GRAVEL ROAD north of town, in a large split-level rambler set in a wooded lot with a crater, edged in crime-scene tape, where the mailbox had been. More tape picketed the lawn in front of a picture window blinded by a sheet of fresh plywood.

"You been redecorating in yellow," Rane said when they parked side by side in back of the house.

Beeman made a face. "Go on in, John. Door's always open. There's a spare bedroom and bath in the basement. I'll be back directly and we'll take a drive. You want to go to Shiloh with me you'll stay put. Hear?"

Then Beeman put the Crown Vic in gear, turned around, went back up the drive, and left Rane alone.

Rane got out of the Jeep and spotted another long sag of the yellow tape surrounding a pond in the back acres. White floaters caught the sun.

He thought about it.

Okay. What's happening is he's holding you close; behind his folksy shit, *he's checking you out.* Not like the Tennessee cops, who routinely ran him in the computer to see if he had any outstanding warrants. Rane got the impression Beeman became a cop because he had to; the kind of guy called to make a difference in people's lives. *Paul's kind of guy*, who had to walk the walk in cadence with Tex Ritter's mournful lyrics.

Strap on the iron and do what a man's gotta do . . .

Corny.

Except he steps in and catches you up as you're about to spin out of control.

I wasn't out of control.

Yes you were. They would've stomped you good in that bar if Beeman hadn't been on the lookout.

Rane picked up his travel bag, climbed the deck steps, and pulled open the sliding door. He paused on the threshold. Door's always open. First-name hospitality. Trusts me in his house?

He went in through the kitchen. The upstairs was conventional cozy. A clean, pressed county deputy's uniform shirt hung on a hanger hooked to a chair. Magnets held a gallery of family pictures on the refrigerator door. Beeman's wife was a wiry, dark-haired woman with large serious eyes and a smiling mouth. One of his sons looked to be seven or eight, shown hugging a black Lab. The other boy was older, perhaps twelve, with a stoic jock face to match his football jersey misshapen with shoulder pads. There was no sign of the Lab, so Beeman must have sent the dog away with his wife and kids. From the pictures on the walls it looked like he'd married early and stayed married.

Rane spied a diamond ring lying in the middle of the kitchen table, on a flyer advertising a barbecue at a Baptist church. File that away.

A panorama of Civil War paintings lined the walls of the living room and dining room; variations of Lee and Jackson on horseback. A large framed photograph showed a younger Beeman in a gray uniform, wearing full kit and shouldering a rifle, standing next to his wife, who wore a hoop skirt and bonnet and held an infant in her arms. A bivouac of white tents dotted the background. Finally, Rane's eyes were drawn to the portrait of Nathan Bedford Forrest, who peered from the wall over the desk in the living room with the iconic ferocity of a defiant Christ.

He carried his bag downstairs and found the guest room.

Most of the lower level was taken up by a den with walls papered in a solid collage of law enforcement pictures mixed in with badges and shoulder patches from Mississippi, Tennessee, and Alabama sheriff departments. It had the look of Alary's South. All he needed was a car door hanging from the ceiling. Antique guns, pistols, and swords filled a display rack.

One corner was hemmed in by bookshelves full of crime fiction, which surrounded a comfortable easy chair and an ottoman. A lamp sat on a side table next to an ashtray and a corncob pipe. Something caught his eye on a shelf lined with nonfiction. Among the volumes of Civil War history, a single book stood upside down. Rane craned his neck and read the title: *The Mind of the South* by Wilbur J. Cash.

Four generations of men stared from framed photos over the fireplace mantel. Rane presumed that a sturdy man in a police uniform, in the newest picture, was Beeman's father. The formally posed, whiskered elder would be a grandfather. Finally, a yellowed, acid-splashed tintype under glass showed a wisp-bearded young man in a Confederate uniform. The Rebel ancestor held a revolver across his chest and his dark eyes were fixed on the camera with the intensity peculiar to the 1860s, which one does not see in the eyes of modern Americans—the one picture he had taken in his life.

Another picture was familiar: Beeman in chocolate-chip camo and E-6 chevrons, standing with a black M2 rifle in one hand and plastic liter bottle of water in the other. The barren blend of sand and sky felt like Kuwait.

Rane checked the bump on his forehead in the bathroom mirror. He didn't replace the Band-Aid. A car came down the drive. As he pulled the faded army cap from his bag and slipped it on, Beeman walked down the stairs.

"Let's go," he said, noticing but not reacting to the cap.

"Where to?" Rane asked.

"How about we try an' figure out why Mitchell Lee Nickels went off his nut and wants to kill me," Beeman said.

They eased out of the afternoon traffic coursing down Highway 72 and slowed in the left-turn lane. The light changed and Beeman turned south. "Tate Street, old Highway 45," Beeman said, chewing on the stem of the unlit corncob pipe he had retrieved from his den. "We got two kinds of history, John: we have the Civil War for the tourists and we got the state-line mob days . . ." Beeman looked at Rane and smiled. "We don't usually lay that on visitors too heavy up front; especially after we had to live down the Hollywood's version of Buford Pusser."

As they cruised past a strip mall into more open country, Beeman said, "But there was a hell of a criminal operation here in the fifties and sixties. Started up when they closed the cathouses and casinos in Phenix City, Alabama, and run the assholes out. They settled on this road across the state line north of town and here, just past the city limits." They drove by a pasture, some car body shops, and a machine shop, then pulled over to a deserted patch of cracked asphalt stitched with weeds.

"They called this stretch Drewry Holler. Had your gin joints, hookers, gambling, and the El Ray Motel where Towhead White was killed. Not much left now.

"Around midnight, August 10, 1972, Tommy Lee Nickels, Mitchell Lee's pa, was shot DRT—dead right there—on that slab of blacktop. Shot four times in the chest with a .38. According to the legend that's how all this started. Everyone says my dad did it. Story was he put Tommy Lee down like a mad dog."

"Did he?" Rane asked.

"Don't honestly know. Daddy never would talk about it; died letting everybody still wonder. But Daddy did favor a .38."

"He have a reason?" Rane asked.

Beeman sucked the empty pipe. "Didn't take much in

those days. Look at somebody wrong'd get you killed along
this strip. Let me put it like this—I live in a lot of house for
a deputy's salary. My daddy built that house and I suspect
illegal moonshine had a hand in it. My momma never liked
that house and when the old man died she moved home to
Rankin County with her family." Then he waited for traffic
to clear, executed a U-turn, drove back to 72, turned west,
and in a few moments they were on new 45 heading north
toward Tennessee.

"So there *is* bad blood between you and Mitchell Lee,"
Rane said after a while.

Beeman laughed soundlessly. "You could say that. But up
till now all we ever had was a few fistfights in high school."

"What about the scene in the cemetery that time he shot
at you?" Rane asked.

"That was for show. Him and his scummy lawyer cooked
up that deal so he went to alcohol treatment and got out of
shipping to Iraq with the guard. That's what I mean, see,
he *plans* things, schemes. Everybody knew he was going
to marry Miss Ellender Kirby far back as high school and
it took him twelve years but damned if he didn't." Beeman
shook his head. "So why's he making his move now all of
a sudden? And in such a dumb-ass way, sending text messages?"

Beeman let the thought hang as he took a left turn,
crossed the four-lane, and drove down a winding blacktop
road with close-in foliage. Then he pulled to the shoulder,
put the Crown Vic in park, got out, and popped the trunk lid.
A moment later he returned with a Vietnam-era M16 rifle,
the fully automatic military version with a forward assist on
the side. He jammed a magazine into the rifle, pulled the
operating rod to load a round, set the safety, and leaned the
weapon in the front seat between them.

"Don't mean to get too dramatic, John, but we're headed
out to Guys and this is prime Leets territory." Beeman looked
around. "I'm outta my jurisdiction and I ain't real popular

hereabouts. So keep them famous eyes of yours open." He put the car in gear and drove slowly down the twisting road.

"Where are we heading?" Rane asked.

Beeman smiled. "Going to swing by Fiona Leets's house, see if we can get a look at King Shit Dwayne himself. When he comes to visit he usually hangs out at his ma's. He's in from Memphis, has been all week."

"The drug kingpin who put a contract on you for shooting his brother?"

"Word is."

Rane scanned the surrounding tree lines and brush. "Can this Dwayne make a contract stick?"

"Oh yeah, big-time. He got rich selling drugs and now he's invested it in pizza joints, dry cleaners, car lots. There's a rumor he's putting together a construction company. He's got the connections to bring in a pro if he wanted."

"Okay, I give. So why ain't you dead?"

Beeman shrugged. "Almost was, last Saturday. In fact Dwayne was seen up by the Kirby house during the reenactment with a pair of binoculars, scanning the field."

"Ouch," Rane said.

"He wasn't exactly out of place, 'cause he bought two of them cannons for the artillery boys. But when you think of it, him on one side, Darl on the other and Mitchell Lee maybe somewhere in the middle with a rifle?" Beeman raised his eyebrows.

"So bring Dwayne in?"

"No probable cause. They decided to carry Paul's death as an accident. Woulda been me, they mighta ruled that an accident too."

"Cleaner than a hit," Rane said.

"Yep. Except it bounced funny."

"Beeman," Rane said, "we been driving around for a while and," he pointed to the radio handset clipped to the dash, "that radio's been awful quiet."

"You noticed that," Beeman said. "Well, it's like this.

Paul's death is officially closed to keep 'em happy at city and county. But the sheriff knows something's going on, especially with Mitchell Lee missing and me getting weird threats, so he's taken me off everything else and's letting me poke around on my own." He grinned. "That way, the shit hits the fan he don't get hit with too much splatter. Like I said, folks on the west side of Alcorn tend to favor the Lee-tses in this alleged feud. And they vote, even the ones who can't read."

Beeman slowed and pulled to the side of the road in front of a broad, well-tended lawn with a large bronze water sculpture set in front of a newer, sprawling ranch-type house.

"Fiona Leets's place. Dwayne built it for her. Now look in back of the main house, see that one-room hillbilly shack with the sagging gray plank siding?"

"Yeah," Rane said, scanning the house, the lawn, the surrounding tree line for a glint of sunlight on metal. Like a rifle barrel.

"Well, Fiona's got this brand-new house with all the latest gadgets. I heard there a plasma TV in there the size of my garage door. But she likes to stay out in that one-room cabin with nothing but an old bed, a rocking chair, and a wood cook stove. She's probably in there now, rocking, maybe with a pinch of snuff she keeps in this old silver Rooster Snuff tin. Then she'll take a twig from a black gum tree, gnaw it down to fiber and make her an old-time toothbrush to tidy up her remaining teeth."

Beeman sighed and leaned back. "Don't see Dwayne's Caddy. Guess he ain't around." Then he pointed to the lawn. "That's what I really brought you out to see."

"A fountain," Rane said.

"Take a closer look and tell me what you make of that?" Beeman asked.

Rane scrutinized the stylized bronze tiers of tanks and tubes. Sunlight hitting the falling veils of water cast a trembling rainbow. "Some kind of metal sculpture?"

"Dwayne brought in the artist special from Nashville. Got heating elements built in so it never freezes and runs all year."

"Yeah?"

Beeman leaned forward. "John, man, you *are* a city boy," he said patiently, "that's a sculpture of a fuckin' moonshine still."

40 AS THEY APPROACHED THE MAIN highway, Beeman stopped, unloaded the rifle, and secured it back in his trunk. Then they drove back to Corinth and entered the residential streets north of city hall. Beeman pulled to the curb in front of a white frame house with one of the GENERAL SLEPT HERE signs in front.

"The Kirby Cottage," Beeman said. "This is where Mitchell Lee lives with Ellender Kirby; a whole world away from Drewry Holler and Guys."

"So?" Rane asked.

"So he had a way of getting noticed and Hiram Kirby picked him up when he was sixteen and sponsored him and he meets the banker's daughter, huh? Mitch figured out a good thing when he saw it and kept a discreet distance from his outlaw cousins. After school let out, instead of playing sports or raising hell, he'd worked as a janitor, sweeping up in the bank. When he graduated he started as a teller, driving to business classes at Northeast Mississippi Community College. He finished up over at the University of North Alabama in Florence.

"Miss Kirby went to Ole Miss, split town after college, spent some time as a flight attendant with Delta to look over the pilots, then tried advertising up in Nashville. When her mother became ill with cancer she came back to help her father and brother get through it.

"After her mother's funeral she rediscovered Mitch, who

had worked his way up to loan officer. They sent the gossip mill into orbit when they ran off and got married."

Rane thought he detected a hint of envy creeping into Beeman's tone and filed it away with the lonely wedding ring on his kitchen table. "What's she like, the wife?"

"Well, she runs all the local charity efforts. Since her brother died in Iraq, the word is, she's getting interested in doing something with wounded vets."

"Where this headed?" Rane asked.

"C'mon, John," Beeman said, "you were a cop for a while . . ."

Rane guffawed. "Two years after the academy."

"That's long enough to grasp Street Sociology 101. Most people who go bad have poor impulse control. After a few drinks on Saturday night they start wearing the shitty cards life dealt them on their sleeve. One of the things I remember about Mitchell Lee in high school—besides fighting with him in the parking lot—is he was in the chess club. That boy always plans two moves in advance. Anything he does is for a reason."

"So he was wrapped too tight and flipped out?" Rane speculated.

"Yeah, right. People say he's been fighting this outlaw gene all his life. But I don't buy it. This is a guy so smooth he could hustle Bill Clinton out of his last dick rubber. That stunt at the cemetery was family politics. See, his brother-in-law, Robert, ran the bank after the old man retired and stuck it to him every chance he got. Mitchell Lee worked it so he stayed back when Robert deployed with the guard. Once Robert was out of the way, he resigned from the bank, started this radio talk show, and set up a battlefield preservation charity. And Old Man Kirby really liked that idea. You remember the statue out at the Kirby estate?"

Rane nodded.

"Mitch had that built; he raised all the money on his radio show. I didn't help any," Beeman sighed. "I figured he was up to something so I got an admin subpoena and went through the charity bank records. All that did was make me look bad and him look better."

"So the feud goes both ways," Rane said.

Beeman scratched his cheek and admitted: "Yeah, I guess it does get a little tense when we get in the same room."

"So if he didn't flip out, how's he go from building statues to shooting at you at Kirby Creek?" Rane asked.

"Paul Edin," Beeman said.

"What?"

"I mean, why are you having this conversation with a cop sitting in a car in Corinth, Mississippi?"

Rane stared back. Beeman's quiet brown eyes were doing his slow, tricky roping routine. "It's a story . . ."

"That's right, John. About *Paul*," Beeman said. "What if Paul wouldn'ta stepped out and caught that bullet? What if it had killed me deader'n shit, huh? What would have been the next step? Just me ain't worth Mitchell Lee going off the deep end. Once I'm dead, then what? That's what I'm trying to figure out."

"Not sure I . . . " Rane said.

"Think, man—Paul *changed* things," Beeman said, slowly scanning Rane's face. "Maybe his dying had a way of changing people's plans, and their lives . . ."

Rane shrugged, said nothing, and broke eye contact. The moment passed.

"Anyrate," Beeman said briskly. "Mitchell Lee has this one reliable flaw and that's our next stop."

"Drinking," Rane said. "The scene in the cemetery shooting at your car."

"Other women. He always catted around. You see, the night before he started shooting at Yankee grave ornaments he roughed up his girlfriend. T'ween you and me, I think that was part of the scenario. When she showed up at Emergency—that's what got us out looking for him."

Beeman turned the car around, drove into the business district, and parked down Fillmore from the coffee shop. They got out, ambled along the storefronts, and stopped in front of a plate-glass window full of ferns. An arch of delicate cursive script over the door spelled out MARCY'S SHOP.

"You met Darl Leets this morning, right?" Beeman asked.

Rane nodded. "And, you know, I got the impression he's a reluctant sort of bad guy."

"Well, his wife did haul him out of the Memphis drug scene and away from Dwayne. Got him so he spends more time coaching Little League than he does in that beer joint. Darl was a bad boy once but now he's what you call a house husband. When you get a look at his wife you'll see why," Beeman said as he leaned to the window and peered inside. "Yep, Marcy is in the building."

"Wait a minute," Rane said. "The girlfriend?"

"Uh-huh."

"Mitch and Darl are cousins? And . . ." Rane pointed at the salon.

Beeman said, "Yep. Her and Mitch been having a side thing going for a year at least. It's a mystery why she stays with Darl. I asked her straight out once." Beeman grinned. "And Marcy says, 'Darl's a married man. He comes home at night.'"

"Hot?" Rane wondered.

Beeman waffled his hand. "Depends. What I hear is you take your chances. Sometimes you get the fire. Sometimes you get the undertow. And fast. Three digits on the radar gun." He opened the door and an overhead bell jingled.

Marcy Leets stood at the shop's one chair snipping at a customer's hair. When she heard the bell she looked up. Coming through the door, Rane detected an earthy underscent of patchouli oil, an aroma that California cops refer to contemptuously as "hippie piss" but that he had always found boldly sensual.

In this case, the bold sensuality was on a tight leash, wearing a short, clingy blue nylon dress. If onomatopoeia is the formation of a word that imitates the sound of its referent, then Marcy Leets was the frank physical equivalent.

Marcy lowered her heavy-lidded blue eyes, tossed her tawny, shoulder-length blond hair, and continued chatting with her customer. The shop was small; mirrors, more plants, a hair dryer, a sink, and the one barber chair. Several chairs lined a waiting area to the left of the entrance and a counter past the chairs. The work area was separated by two bookshelves that contained magazines and plastic bottles of hair products. Beeman and Rane sat down in two of the chairs by the door and waited.

After a few more snips, Marcy set the scissors aside and picked up a blow dryer. The whir of the dryer combined with a musical twitter of their conversation.

Then Marcy put the dryer away, removed the sheet from around the customer's shoulders, and shook it to the floor. She and the customer walked to the front of the shop. Beeman rose and nodded to the customer, who regarded him with a polite, slightly stiff smile, noting his gun and badge intruding on her haircut.

Marcy made change from the cash drawer, exchanged pleasant farewells, and the lady hurried from the shop. Beeman followed her to the door and, as soon as she exited, he twisted the lock and flipped the OPEN sign to CLOSED.

When he turned, Marcy leaned against the counter with one hand cocked on a hip.

"Why Kenny Beeman," she batted her eyes, "the only man in north Mississippi to look a gift blow job in the mouth." Her voice was bored, husky.

"What'd I tell you," Beeman said to Rane, who was sitting upright, thinking that looking at Marcy was like having a bright light in your face.

"Who's he?" she asked.

"My personal picture-taker only he don't take no pictures," Beeman said. Then he craned his neck and looked around. "Don't suppose you got Mitchell Lee hiding in your back storeroom? He's gone missing."

"You ain't missing till you're gone two weeks. It's not even one week yet. He's probably shacked up in Tunica with some little gal blackjack dealer with a big chest, tryin' to forget that uptight titless mouse wife of his," Marcy said.

"So you haven't seen him?"

Marcy shook her head with feigned boredom. "Heard all the talk, though. Folks say you and him are gonna do a sequel to Buford Pusser and Towhead White."

Beeman withdrew a card and a pen from his chest pocket, leaned on the counter, and wrote on the back of the card. "Here's my cell, Marcy. I appreciate your situation and all, but if anything starts to worry you, you give me a call . . ."

Marcy ignored the card. "Bee, honey, what genuinely worries me about Mitchell Lee is that babyless bitch makes him screw her standing on her head, you know, to try and get the thingies to run down to the proper place. Now that worries me."

Not a bright light, Rane decided. More like a fire-breathing Circe.

Beeman flipped a farewell finger to his brow and nodded. "You take care, Marcy." He turned and Rane followed him out onto the sidewalk.

"Phew," Rane breathed as he glanced back into the shop.

Beeman grinned. "Tomorrow, first thing, we'll go out to Kirby Creek and meet the titless mouse, Miss Kirby herself."

41

MITCH, UNSHACKLED, STOOD IN THE doorway of the potting shed, holding a cigarette in his cuffed hands, and watched sunset streak Cross State Lake. He shifted his feet, making room in the clutter of orange terra-cotta pots strewn on the floor. The back end of the shed had a table, two chairs, bunk beds, a small icebox, and a microwave for the summer help. LaSalle had pried a rear partition loose to gain access to the cave.

Meals had improved. The coffee kept coming.

Mitch could tell by the way LaSalle avoided his eyes: pretty soon they'd be letting him go. He relished the inevitable talk with Ellie, to nail down the terms of that particular arrangement.

LaSalle's dusty blue Chevy pickup was parked near the shed. Mitch eyed the big medic—sleeves rolled up, showing off his Shaka Zulu biceps—who knelt over his medical bag next to the steps.

As the shadows lengthened, Mitch cocked his head as a night bird called from the woods. The whip-poor-will, it was said, could snatch your soul in flight, the way it picked off bugs in the dark.

Then a sharp report shattered the twilight.

"There it is again." Mitch jerked his head and darted his eyes.

"Car backfire," LaSalle said, unconcerned.

"Bullshit. That's a muzzleloader, I can tell from the

blast. Sounds like it's just down the lake, hear the echo?"

"Out in the woods maybe?" LaSalle said. "Poachers." He took out a pair of white rubber gloves, laid them aside, and held up a slim syringe with a little cap on the end.

"Miss Kirby says I got to give you this tetanus shot before you come down with lockjaw," he said.

"How do I know it's not poison?" Mitch asked, half-serious.

LaSalle removed the cap from the needle. "C'mon. This goes in your butt. Turn around."

Mitch tossed the smoke away, unfastened the top two buttons on his pants to loosen them, then turned, and La-Salle peeled down the waistband in the back. Mitch smelled a pinch of alcohol in the evening air. Then he felt the cool, damp cotton swab over the skin high on his right buttock; a marvelous, clean sensation.

Then the nip of the needlepoint. Before half the shot was in, Mitch's eyelids fluttered and he collapsed forward, his face smashing into a pile of terra-cotta pots. But he didn't feel it, because he was lifted by a feathery euphoria. Maybe he heard the whip-poor-will again as he entered a vast marble silence . . .

LaSalle was loading Mitch into the foot well on the passenger side of his truck when Ellie jogged up. She wore a sweatshirt, shorts, and running shoes. A sooty smear dabbed her lips and chin on the right side of her mouth.

"What'd you give him?" she asked.

"Versed. Three mils. I'll give him another shot when I get there."

"I should go with you," she said.

"You'd be noticed. I won't," LaSalle said matter-of-factly, covering Mitch's sedated body with a blanket. Then he tossed his bag in the truck.

"Okay," Ellie said, wiping the back of her hand across the smear on her chin, "let's do it."

LaSalle nodded, got in his truck, and drove away.

* * *

TRICKY GETTING INTO TOWN, LOTS OF PEOPLE ON
the streets walking to the concert at the courthouse. The
sound of the pickers tuning up guttered on the wind. La-
Salle eased the Chevy up the darkened alley, turned off the
engine, and slipped on the vinyl gloves with an elastic snap.
He leaned over and monitored Mitch's breathing, which
was deep and regular. He measured out another injection
and put it in Mitch's arm. Then removed some gauze pads
and a roll of tape from his bag and stuck them in his hip
pocket. After checking the breathing again, he waited a
few moments to make sure no foot traffic came this way.

Do it now. Quick out of the truck, around to the passenger side, he hoisted Mitch's limp body on his shoulder and
carried him to a doorway in the shadows.

The door opened and Marcy Leets said, "Hurry, get in."
She looked up and down the alley as LaSalle shouldered
past.

"Where?" he asked.

"Right here, inside the door," she said.

He lowered Mitch to the floor, then stood up and looked
around. Cardboard boxes on shelves lined the walls. Light
eked into the storeroom from the ajar door to the front of the
shop. Marcy bent and studied Mitch's somnolent face. "His
eyes are open?"

"Just a flutter, he's stoned; ain't seein' or hearing nothing."

"Will he feel . . . ?"

"Not that either," LaSalle said.

Marcy straightened up, squared her shoulders, exhaled.
"Okay, we gotta make this look real."

LaSalle nodded, preparing himself. "You ready?"

She nodded. He reached out and seized her bare arms.

"Harder." Marcy bared her teeth, broke his grip, and
swung her open hand at his face. At the goading slap,

LaSalle grabbed her shoulder, spun her, and wrapped his powerful fingers around her neck. She fought back and they struggled, their breath coming in sobs between clenched teeth. He lashed his other hand around and clawed her shoulder, then wrenched down, shredding bra straps and dress to the elastic of her panties. He released her and she staggered, turning.

They faced each other, panting. Hair askew, the blue dress hanging in tatters, she glanced down at her heaving bare breasts and torso where the striped bruises started to pimple with blood.

"What're you waiting for?" she said.

LaSalle took a measured breath, towering over her; he could smell the fear and anger mingled in her sweat, some perfume she wore. "I'm gonna try not to . . ."

"Hit me, goddamn it!"

LaSalle swung his left fist in a short arc that caught her jaw and knocked her sideways into the shelves. Marcy stumbled, kept her feet, flailed at the shelf, and pulled it over. As the shelf clattered down on her, she kicked the boxes aside, pushed away the tangle of metal, and faced him again, her eyes astonished with pain.

"You gonna have to do better than that, sport," she hissed through bloody lips.

"Shit," LaSalle muttered. Then he set his feet and threw a serious straight right hand that mashed into her eye and cheek. She grunted, folded up, and went down flat on her back. Slowly, shaking her head, she rolled over, pushed up on all fours, and crawled to where Mitch lay against the doorway.

She reached out her trembling left hand and took a grip on his dark, curly hair to steady his head, heaved up on her knees, and cocked her right hand back, tendons raised under the skin like rods, the fingers spread and arched. With a sob, she clawed her nails into his left cheek, put her weight into it, and ripped down.

"There." She swooned, falling back on the floor.

Immediately, LaSalle lifted Mitch with an arm under his shoulders. With his other hand he manipulated one of Mitch's cuffed hands, brought it up, and pressed it to the bleeding cheek. Then he turned Mitch and mashed the bloody hand on the doorjamb, taking care to leave a distinct thumbprint.

"Marcy . . . ?" LaSalle said.

"I'm good," she groaned, attempting a game smile through her split, puffed lip. "Thank you for a wonderful evening."

"Christ," muttered LaSalle. Then he quickly bandaged the torn cheek to stanch the bleeding, opened the door, and checked outside. A grumble of thunder overlaid the concert music. Without looking back, he hauled Mitch to the truck.

MITCH WOKE UP IN THE DIRT UNDER THE UTILITY lamp, wearing the shackle. He floated his hand to his cheek. All numb with pain there. Saw LaSalle hovering, concern on his face. "Just take it easy, Mitch."

Huh? He started to explore his throbbing cheek.

LaSalle trapped the hand and eased it down. "Don't be doing that. I just put a bandage on."

"Bandage? Wha?"

"You had a reaction to the shot. My fault. You collapsed and lacerated your face on those damn flower pots." LaSalle nodded his head. "Here, take this for the pain."

Mitch squinted at a pill in LaSalle's palm.

"C'mon, it's Demerol, some good shit. Make you feel better."

Mitch let LaSalle funnel the pill into his mouth and accepted a bottle of water to wash it down. Still gliding from the first shot, he had to remind himself to swallow.

42 "PUBIC BONE TO TAIL BONE, BELLY button to spine, rib cage, sternum, head . . . it's an articulation, every vertebrae should move individually into your curl . . ."

Intermediate Pilates at the River Valley Athletic Club.

Jenny, in running shorts and a sports bra, tucked in her chin, extended her arms, and lowered her back ever so slowly to the gym mat. The isometric torture anchored on her butt and her bare feet planted hip-width apart, in line with her bent knees. With her torso curved like a strung bow, she hovered six inches off the floor, five inches, trembling at four.

"Slower, lower," the instructor commanded.

Jenny was a regular in this class. The other women knew, of course, and placed their red exercise mats at a respectful distance.

After her phone conversation with Deputy Beeman, she had left the center and returned home, where she'd spent two hours with Molly and her mom, sorting through family photos for the slide show the center would prepare, all the while thinking about the folder of Rane's pictures she'd tucked out of sight on the top shelf of her closet.

Following the picture selection and the memory-sharing it involved, Molly sat down at the kitchen table with the grief group worksheets Patti had left. Jenny watched her study one, in particular, that prompted: *This is what my grief looks like*—over a gingerbread man silhouette. *Where*

do I feel in my body? And then instructions to color-code a
list of feelings: sad, scared, happy, angry, jealous, loving,
and the one that jumped out at Jenny—GUILTY. Molly
brought a box of colored pencils to the table and assigned
happy and loving her favorite color, yellow. She drew a yellow heart on the outline's chest and filled it in. Sad, scared,
and angry became a chunky red square in the pit of the
stomach. She did not ascribe a color or a location to jealous
or guilty.

Jenny did, though, in her imagination; they would be
gray, located below the yellow heart and the red square knot
in the belly. Dirty gray, down there.

Then she gave Molly the leather-bound journal. At that
point she'd decided she needed some sheer physical pain that
had no emotional origin.

A fine speckle of sweat moistened her upper lip and her
forehead as her stomach muscles curved in, threatening
to crack. Less than a week into Paul's death her body had
taken on the lifeless density of vinyl. It was time to fight
back.

"Dig; your abs should be totally engaged," the instructor
chanted as she padded among her prone students. "DIG."

Jenny dug, first into her straining muscles, then into the
past; anything but the present.

"If you're doing it right you'll feel the burn."

Am I doing it right?

She imagined Paul's body being trundled into an oven
like a clay pot into a kiln. After the firing, the shards of
unburned blackened bone would be compacted into particles. Maybe the burning and the crushing was taking
place at exactly this moment. Gas jets, steel jaws, a belch
of smoke.

"Roll up," the instructor commanded.

But Jenny didn't hear; she had muddled through ordinary
deranged into the clarity of fire.

Molly seemed to take comfort from the idea that Paul

would be reduced to dust and placed inside a container called a scatter urn, that it would come home with them and they'd have to pick a place in the house to situate it until the journey to Poobah.

Jenny could almost see her daughter's young mind working: it's like having a shrine. So now we've skipped right over Sunday school all the way back to ancestor worship?

Dad.

Her father had soldiered as an adviser to the South Vietnamese Army. He'd told her one story from the war, when she was twelve, not much older than Molly. Waiting in groups for the helicopter lift, the ARVN troopers would write prayers on slips of paper in the predawn gloom and then they'd burn the slips of paper.

"Why, Dad?"

"Because their dead ancestors could only read smoke."

Jenny lay on her back and imagined the stoic helmeted faces her father had seen in the Asian darkness, flat of nose, wide of cheek. Indian-like faces flickering in the tiny blooms of flame.

What would Dad say about all this?

Cut the bullshit. Don't kid yourself. Pass the potatoes.

She was losing track of the class now, lying flat on the floor, staring at the ceiling, arms loose at her sides in a yoga pose called Corpse.

The pixie-cut instructor appeared above her like a buff Tinker Bell, concern softening her strong features. A Stonebridge mom; they were acquainted.

"Jenny, are you okay?"

"Fine. Just need to rest a minute."

The instructor stooped, squeezed her shoulder, and nodded. As she walked away, Jenny studied the sinuous tattoo that curled over the hem of her low cut tights up the small of her back and disappearing under her abbreviated T-shirt.

"Deep cleansing breath. I want to hear the exhale. Now for our favorite exercise. Teaser."

Jenny, no tattoos, continued staring at the ceiling and remembering. Sometimes she'd catch her dad looking at her with this curious piercing expression; hope, pain, and wonder in his eyes. A look that said "I don't deserve this beautifully formed, innocent child." She had to travel to this last margin of herself, one foot in pain, the other in crazy, to make the connection.

She had caught Rane looking at her the same way. And then he disappeared.

Paul's mother thought it was a mistake for Molly not to see her father one last time. Jenny couldn't tell them the real reason for not allowing Molly to attend the private viewing.

There are no rules for this . . .

How can I agree to show Molly the corpse of her father when her father is in Mississippi doing God knows what for reasons I don't fully understand?

The memory was, if anything, magnified by a wall of grief.

For a few days Rane had been warm, spontaneous, acceptably intoxicated on pure romance, and had driven Jenny to a cabin on a lake in Wisconsin. Jenny had no idea where they went. All she remembered was sequined sunlight flashing in the passing trees and the clean scent of the hollow of his neck. He'd introduced her to an older man, a man about her father's age, with hair already going gray—an uncle named Mike—and his wife, who'd raised him after his parents died.

Jenny remembered a long autumn afternoon of turning maples and long silences.

This woman is special, the silence whispered. Let me show her to you. This only happens once. The rest is echo. Shadow. Smoke for the dead.

The memory scattered. Jenny frowned, serious now.

Maybe in Wisconsin she could find the aunt and uncle

who could fill in the background on John Rane. She was mindful of the concern in Beeman's voice on the phone. But if, as she now suspected, there was something scary in Rane, she was damn well going to protect Molly from it.

With sweats pulled on over her workout clothes, she sat in the Forester in the club parking lot. She arranged a notepad on her purse, stared at her cell phone, rolled a Sharpie between her thumb and forefinger.

Grab a straw.

She punched in 411. What city? St. Paul, Minnesota. What listing? The St. Paul Police Department. An operator, then a machine voice read the general information number.

Jenny punched the select option to connect to the number.

"St. Paul Police, how may I direct your call?"

"I need to contact an officer I met over ten years ago. I think he was a sergeant . . ."

"Do you have a name, ma'am; an assignment, a division?"

"I can't recall the name but he had a Southern accent and his hair, well, he looked and talked like Elvis Presley . . ."

The operator chuckled. "I think you want Lieutenant Harry Cantrell in Homicide. He's gone for the day but I'll connect you to his voice mail."

"Thank you."

A moment later she heard Cantrell's Midwesternized drawl on a machine. "This is Lieutenant Cantrell, St. Paul Homicide. Leave a message after the beep."

"Lieutenant Cantrell, this is Jenny Edin. We met a long time ago at the Alcove Lounge in St. Paul. I was Jenny Hatton then. We met through a rookie cop named John Rane. You and he seemed to be close so I'm hoping you've kept in touch. Rane had an aunt and uncle I met briefly somewhere east of Hudson, Wisconsin. I need to reach them but I can't remember their name. This is urgent so any help would be greatly appreciated. Thank you."

Jenny left her home and cell numbers, ended the call, and stared at the phone. She'd been putting off the next call but it was time for a reality check. She thumbed in the number.

"Patti? It's Jenny. I know it's short notice but could you get away for a little while to talk?"

43

THEY WOUND UP AT MARTHA'S MENU, a downtown restaurant where Beeman insisted on buying Rane the chicken-fried steak with red-eyed gravy and biscuits.

"Home cooking," Rane said.

"Yep," Beeman said with a slow grin. "This building? Used to be a whorehouse."

Rane shook his head, looked out the restaurant window at a flag hanging over a storefront across the street. "Down home Mississippi. Still got the Rebel battle colors on your state flag."

"Slow down, John. Technically, the thirteen stars on that Southern Cross stand for the original thirteen colonies, not the Confederate States. And the bars are red, white, and blue—the national colors."

"Right," Rane said.

Beeman frowned. "Whole state voted to keep that flag, two-to-one. Not just people look like me." Beeman leaned back. "April 17, 2001. My daddy remembered where he was when Kennedy got shot. I remember where I was when the vote came in, on patrol between 72 and Kossuth."

"Man," Rane said, "I'm a long way from home."

Driving back to his house, Beeman got around to asking, "So why the hat with the military badges?"

"I was told some military trimmings would help out down here so I dug it out of the closet," Rane said.

"Goddamn, I guess," Beeman grinned. "Thing is, I read

you were a photographer in the army. How do you rate a combat rifle badge?"

"After I graduated out of photo school I talked them into letting me research whole blocks of training and then I'd go back and shoot it for *Army Times*."

"Kinda like those books you wrote," Beeman said.

"Yeah, the army's where I started with that approach. So I picked up a list of MOS . . ."

"Uh-huh. So how many different MOS you go through?"

"Well, I did infantry AIT. Then airborne. The ranger school. Survival school. The mountain course at Fort Drum. By the time we went into Kuwait, I was attached to the 101st. Some artillery rounds fell a couple hundred yards from the battalion CP." Rane tapped the black-and-green camo badge on his cap, above the jump wings. "And the colonel put everybody with an infantry MOS in for a combat infantry badge. I saw the pictures on your wall downstairs. You were on the sand, Beeman . . ."

"With the guard; they reconfigured us as MPs down in Hattiesburg at Camp Shelby."

"So you know there was a lot of medal inflation in the Gulf War."

"Yep. We had it easy, compared to those poor fuckers running over bombs and slogging street-to-street," Beeman said as he drove up his driveway. They got out and climbed the deck stairs.

"Beer sound good?" Beeman offered. When Rane nodded, Beeman opened the sliding door to the kitchen. "Get comfortable. I'll be right back after I unload this gun belt."

A few minutes later Beeman returned. He'd changed into jeans, a loose flannel shirt, and worn moccasins. He carried two opened bottles of Dixie beer, handed one to Rane, and they sat on two facing wooden deck chairs. Beeman took a swallow of his beer, set the bottle down, and removed the corncob pipe and a packet of tobacco from his shirt pocket. Slowly, he filled the pipe, then struck a Blue Tip match with his thumbnail. He puffed and blew a meditative stream of cherry-scented smoke into the twilight.

Rane swigged his beer and watched the spreading evening quiet and Beeman watching him, puffing on his pipe; the glow of the bowl highlighting the faint, bemused smile on his face.

Rane reached into his haversack, pulled out the pack of Spirits and the Bic, and lit up.

"Surprised you smoke; thought they outlawed it up North," Beeman said.

Rane lifted the bottle. "It's the beer; old pattern."

"Uh-huh. You got any more surprises? Anything you want to tell me, John?" Beeman asked casually.

Rane glanced around and said, "If I had an expert shooter hunting me with a rifle I wouldn't sit out on this deck with the kitchen light on my back."

Beeman pointed his pipe at Rane and said, "You're changing the subject."

"What do you mean?" Rane said, his voice steady and his face blank.

"I mean," Beeman said slowly, "you didn't come down here to take pictures, did you?"

Rane started to shrug it off but there was enough light left to see the edge of Beeman's smile fade. Absent the smile, his face at home in the closing darkness. Rane said nothing.

"Won't beat around with you, John. I called Jenny Edin," Beeman said.

Rane stared at Beeman, expressionless, a little off-balance. Like he'd just lost one leg of the chair he was sitting on.

"I called her," Beeman continued, "'cause I saw you were carrying your camera in Paul's haversack. His name's right inside the flap. You got his uniform in your car. Most, but not all, the bloodstains scrubbed out."

"What'd Jenny say?" Rane asked quietly.

"She said you're down here trying to figure out how to be a father."

Rane stared beyond Beeman into the twilight fuzzing the tree branches together across the broad lawn. Someone had been here and cleaned the dead catfish out of the pond.

Beeman circled a finger next to his ear. "She explained what's been bugging me about you. How it was you I talked to on the phone last Saturday. When I met you I had your voice going round in the back of my head and couldn't pin it down."

"She told you about Molly," Rane said.

"Uh-huh. It seems you didn't have any problem with getting *started* on the father part; the screwing-the-woman part. Now, you going to tell how wearing a dead man's clothes is gonna help you figure out the rest?" Beeman asked.

"Maybe I need to learn what he went through down here," Rane said quietly.

"What? Researching getting shot?"

Rane shrugged. "I don't know for sure."

"I believe that. From what I've seen so far, you've got all these snappy skills and you're lost, ain't you John? You don't know where you're at." Beeman shook his head. "You got this veil between you and life, like a widow."

Rane drained his beer, dropped his cigarette into the empty bottle, and stood up. "Okay, so now what?" he asked.

"Finish what we started. Go to Shiloh. Be worth getting shot at to see if you'll actually take a picture," Beeman said.

"You're a tricky guy," Rane said.

"Takes one to know one, huh?" Beeman said.

After an interval of silence, Rane said, "You've seen *High Noon* one too many times, Beeman. You want to fight a duel with this Nickels."

"And what about you?" Beeman asked.

Rane ignored the question. "Look, I'm beat. All the driving. Getting thumped on today. I'm going to turn in." He left

Beeman sitting on his deck, smoking his pipe, and staring into the gathering dark, patiently dissecting the motives of Mitchell Lee Nickels. And John Rane.

He walked through the kitchen, noting that the ring was still twinkling on the kitchen table, went down the stairs, padded across the den under the gaze of Beeman's ancestors, carried his travel kit to the bath, brushed his teeth, and got ready for bed.

Moments later, lights out, lying between clean sheets on the single mattress, he raised a hand and explored the darkness. A veil, he thought. Then, exhausted, he fell asleep to a faint rumble of thunder.

44 RANE NEVER DREAMED. THE INSISTENT hand rousing him from sleep was real. Blinking, he squinted at a shadow bending over him, backlit by the basement light coming in the doorway.

"Wake up," said the shadow and materialized into Kenny Beeman, whose breath smelled like beer and cherry pipe tobacco.

"Huh?" Rane pushed up on his elbows.

"C'mon and get dressed," Beeman said more urgently. "It's déjà vu all over again."

Rain turned the black asphalt of Fulton Drive into a glitter of reflected lights.

"Marcy Leets got beat up," Beeman said, weaving in and out of traffic. "They just brought her into Emergency. Some people were coming back when the concert at the courthouse got rained out. Found her staggering from the alley behind her shop. Called 911."

Beeman banged his horn, blew through a four-way stop, turned up Tate, and floored it toward 72. He slapped a red flasher on the dash, threaded through another light, turned west on the highway, and gunned the gas. The thirsty Interceptor engine surged.

"Joe Timms, sergeant with the city, responded, took her in. Called me en route."

"How bad is she?" Rane asked.

Beeman heaved his shoulders. "Don't know." Then he

retreated into his fierce driving. "Hold on," he warned as
he drifted into a turn; toe to brake to gas, straightened
out. Tiers of lights loomed ahead in the rain, a sign. MAG-
NOLIA REGIONAL HEALTH CENTER. They shot through a
parking lot full of cars, toward an ambulance parked under a portico.

Rane cleared his thoughts. When your heart is beating
fast, the word EMERGENCY, stamped in red neon, looks like a
frozen shriek in the night.

Beeman clucked his tongue, reflected, "Margie don't like
it when I go to Emergency on Thursday nights."

Then he drifted in a four-wheel skid, slewed at an angle
behind the ambulance, and jumped out. Rane followed
Beeman, who was moving fast, his bare ankles showing
above the worn moccasins. The cop had just tucked in the
flannel shirt and buckled on his gun belt. He was no longer
smiling; striding, his body coiled, hands and arms held in
close.

A tall, handsome tanned man with styled blond hair stood
by the door, smoking a cigarette, wearing a Memphis Marathon T-shirt, stone-washed jeans, and soft, orange, ostrich-
quill cowboy boots. Beeman walked up to him and got right
in his face, nose to nose.

"You got anything to do with this, you piece of shit?"
Beeman said in a low growl.

"Not me," the guy said, not giving an inch and flicking
ash from his smoke. Some of the ash dribbled down Beeman's chest. "I was out at my mom's when Darl called, playing Monopoly with her, as a matter of fact. You can check,"
he said casually.

Rane heard a car door open across the lot and saw a
lean, fox-faced man heave up from behind the wheel of a
sleek cream-colored Cadillac SRX, step into the rain, and
smooth his flowing Hawaiian shirt a certain way. The pool
shooter from the bar, the one Rane had clubbed in the throat
with the pool cue. The guy in the ostrich boots dismissed

Fox Face with a subtle wag of his cigarette, never taking his eyes off Beeman.

"Wanna push it, Dwayne?" Beeman asked softly, hands swinging loose.

"Not me, officer," Dwayne Leets said in a level voice. "I'm here 'cause my sister-in-law's been roughed up. Strictly family."

"Uh-huh," Beeman said, shouldering past Dwayne. Rane quickstepped to keep up as they went through the door, past an overweight security guard in gray and brown, who stepped back to let Beeman pass. More doors; Rane stepped over a bloody dressing on the floor. Figures in lime green scrubs moved through curtained bays filled with Stryker gurneys and muted plastic machines and the acute concentration of medics.

A willowy black nurse with wide, elegant Ethiopian cheekbones stepped in Beeman's path. She raised a white, vinyl-sheathed hand.

"Whoa there, Peaches," she challenged.

Peaches?

"Let me by, Sheba," Beeman said. Rane noted that the nurse Beeman called Sheba wore on her scrubs a name tag that said NOLA.

Whatever her name was, Beeman firmly put his hands on her arms and moved her aside. Half a dozen hospital personnel in the immediate area paused a beat, and Rane concluded that when Beeman was in motion people made room.

"Where is she?" Beeman asked. Then, looking past the nurse, Beeman spied Darl Leets standing by the nurses' station. Two scrubbed children stood quietly big-eyed next to Leets; the younger one held a stuffed kitty. The older one had an Atlanta Braves cap sideways on his head.

Beeman slowed and the smile was back. "How you boys doing," he said, instinctively stooping to get on eye level with the younger boy.

"We're fine, sir. It's Ma got hurt," the young boy said. Rane figured he was six; the taller one maybe eight or nine.

"But she's going to be fine, right?" Beeman shot a look at Darl.

Rane watched Darl Leets's face shift from pissed to concerned back to pissed. "That's right, she just got banged up a little," he said. He had a hand on each kid's shoulder and he pulled them in closer to him.

Beeman stood up and before he could address Darl, a cop in a blue city uniform, sergeant's chevrons on his sleeve, stepped from a curtained alcove down the hall.

"Bee, leave him. Was somebody else," the cop said. Rane floated, trying to be invisible, staying next to Beeman as Darl bent and said, "Boys, I want you to stand over there by the wall. Keep out of people's way but stay where I can see you. I got to talk to the policeman. You hear?"

The two boys nodded solemnly and crossed the hall. Darl turned and looked Beeman directly in the eye. "Listen to Timms, Bee. Weren't me . . ." But Darl had enough situational awareness to fix on Rane's face. "You," he said simply.

Beeman squinted at Timms, who held up a cellophane baggie that contained a plastic vial. Timms said, "She clawed the fuck out of his face. I got skin parings from under her nails."

"What happened?" Beeman asked Darl.

"Swear to God, I don't know," Darl said. "I was home with the kids when they called."

"What's Dwayne doing standing outside?" Beeman demanded.

"Shit, Bee. I don't tell him where to fuckin' stand."

Rane studied Darl's face. No longer the laid-back, confident man he'd met in the state-line barroom, Darl was now keeping his anger in check with meat hooks of control.

Beeman turned to the city cop. "She say . . . ?"

Timms shook his head and took Beeman by the arm.

"Excuse us, Darl," he said, walking Beeman down the hall, where he bristled when Rane followed. Beeman cooled him with a curt head shake. "He's okay, he's with me."

"Was dark. She said this guy jumped her from behind, at her shop; in the storeroom in back. She resisted, he hit her, then she clawed his face and he ran," Timms said.

"You been over there yet?" Beeman asked, looking up and down the hall.

"Got a team processing. They just called. Get this. They say there's a bloody thumbprint on the door, bigger than shit." Timms dropped his eyes, then looked up. "All the talk, boys are speculating we got a Mitchell Lee situation," he said.

Beeman grunted, then asked, "How bad is she, Joe?"

Timms flexed his jaw, conjured his eyes back and forth. "Ain't pretty. Took a bad one alongside her eye, 'nother on her chin; face all cut up, got some loose teeth. Tore her dress damn near off. Got bruises on her neck and shoulder and down her front. Could be a lot worse, I guess. But she caught him a deep one on the face. Got wads of tissue in this baggie."

Beeman set off again, down the hall, with Rane keeping pace. The doorkeeper nurse was back, beside them. She put a restraining gloved hand on Rane's elbow.

"He can't . . ."

Beeman took Rane's other arm and yanked him forward. "How is she?"

The nurse shrugged. "We're cleaning her up, checked her vitals. She has multiple abrasions, contusions, and the bruises. We have some concern she might have lost consciousness. So the doctor might order an X-ray, possibly a CAT scan . . ."

The three of them stepped into the curtained cubicle where Marcy Leets sat on a raised gurney with the shreds of her dress hanging down her waist. A coppery-red residue of blood and Betadine disinfectant trickled from her swollen left eye and dribbled down her smooth neck and breasts and pooled in the crease of her stomach. A nurse was blotting a tiara of caked blood from the widow's peak above her forehead with a disinfectant wipe. Heavy purple stripes of blood bruising raked her chest.

One of the blackest men in Corinth, Mississippi, looked up and furrowed his thick brows when he saw Beeman and Rane. "You will leave, please," Doctor Durga Prasad ordered in precise, clipped English. Late of Calcutta, he was a vigorous stump of a man with a shiny bald head.

The nurse named Nola, addressed as Sheba, pursed her lips and turned to Prasad. "Doctor, you're new here but we've seen this before. We need police on this, to talk to her. This is Deputy Beeman with the Sheriff's Department."

"Is my face damaged?" Marcy asked in a too-calm voice.

The other nurse was removing a blood-pressure cuff from Marcy's arm as Prasad looked Beeman up and down, then raised a pencil flashlight and shined it in Marcy's eyes.

"Doctor," Marcy enunciated doggedly, "when the swelling goes down on my cheek, will my face be damaged?"

"Please. Can you open your mouth?" Dr. Prasad asked.

Marcy opened her mouth with some difficulty. Prasad peered, probed gently with the pencil light and a wooden tongue depressor. His gloved finger and thumb quickly tested around her teeth, tongue, and the roof of her mouth. "You have a few loose teeth, cuts inside the cheek, and we'll want X-rays," he said to the nurse. "Run an IV, one milligram of Ativan."

"No drugs, please," Marcy mumbled.

"Just to take the edge off, honey; get you calmed down," the nurse said, her fingers busy with a bright needle and plastic tubing.

"I guess," Marcy said, her eyes gliding, sitting up straighter as the nurse screwed a syringe in the IV, pressed the plunger. "What I mean is," Marcy said, "will I need stitches for my cheek? Will I be . . . disfigured?"

Prasad's exact eyes studied the swollen, liverish cheek. "No, this is abrasion, some quite deep, and swelling. You'll have a . . . black eye," he said, knitting his prominent eyebrows.

"Doctor, I am very concerned about my face," Marcy said.

"We will see X-rays," Prasad said. Then he nodded to the other nurse at the table. Deftly, the nurse stripped the torn blue dress down around Marcy's hips. Sheba stepped forward to assist. The two nurses gently lifted and turned Marcy so Prasad could examine her back.

"You two out. This woman deserves privacy," Prasad insisted as Marcy was disrobed.

Beeman and Rane stepped back as the curtain was pulled in their faces.

"What do you think?" Rane asked Beeman.

"Don't know. Don't like it Dwayne's here."

The curtain swept open. Now Marcy wore a shapeless purple gown with a faded floral design. Little daisies.

She looked up and seemed to recognize Beeman for the first time. She plucked the loose material of the smock with her thumb and forefinger, let it fall, and attempted to smile, showing red-rimmed teeth in swollen lips. "They musta washed it with purple . . ."

Beeman stared at her, then turned to Dr. Prasad. "Can I talk to her alone for a minute?"

Prasad diplomatically looked to Sheba, who nodded.

"One minute. She must go to X-ray," the doctor said.

As the doctor and the nurses left the cubicle, Beeman put a hand on Rane's arm, signaling him to stay. Then he drew the curtain. When they were alone, Marcy experimentally explored her teeth and puffy lips with her tongue. Carefully, she spit bloody saliva into an antiseptic wipe, used a clean corner to blot her lips. Then, wincing, she motioned with her head for Beeman to come closer. As he leaned forward, she whispered through tiny bubbles of blood, "Watch yourself, Bee, he ain't acting this time. He's really crazy out there."

"I need something, Marcy; anything?" Beeman asked.

Marcy shut her eyes, shivered, fought a rush of tears, and then nodded imperceptibly. In a barely audible voice, she whispered, "Billie Watts."

"What about Billie?"

"He's got his dumb ass mixed up with Dwayne and Mitchell Lee. Now he's scared shit, hiding out at Pickwick in his condo . . ." Her eyes pleaded: no more.

Beeman nodded and said gently, "Okay. You got my cell. You call, hear."

Marcy shut her eyes and nodded.

"That's all," Dr. Prasad said with finality, stepping back in, "you go out of my ER. Now."

Beeman and Rane sidestepped a wheelchair and retreated down the corridor toward the admitting desk. Darl Leets, standing with Sergeant Timms and the two kids, narrowed his eyes at Beeman and Beeman returned the look; a fast negotiation Rane could not track.

They kept walking, and Sheba appeared beside them. Beeman took her aside by the arm. "Take good care of her."

They looked at each other. Sheba moved in close and said quietly, "We can take care of her. We've done it before. Somebody should take of *him*." She was muttering, squeezing her gloved hands so tight the rubber squeaked.

Rane watched them continue to stare at each other. Then the nurse said, "We gotta talk. Outside. I'll just be a minute."

Rane braced himself going back through the door, expecting Dwayne Leets and his driver to be waiting. But the Caddy was nowhere in sight. So he stood under the portico, listening to the rain beat down. An after-scent of blood and Betadine clung to him in the humid air. The pain, fear, and adrenaline rickets he'd felt coming off Marcy Leets did not have a specific smell. A soundtrack, maybe, of gentle Southern voices smoothing over violence. Then Rane realized he was hearing faint snatches of music from a car radio drifting across the parking lot through the rain; they sounded like "Tupelo Honey."

Sheba came through the door, peeling off her gloves. Watching her approach he considered a professional question. Did black pigment hold passion tighter to the features?

"Who's he?" Sheba asked as she slipped a pack of Newports from under her blouse, put one in her lips, and flicked a lighter.

"He's okay," Beeman said.

Sheba tossed her head, blew a stream of smoke. "State cop, in from Jackson?"

"It don't matter, go ahead. You can talk," Beeman said.

Sheba briefly bit her lower lip, thinking. "This is all looking like some crazy damn soap opera the white folks got going, huh, Peaches? You and Mitchell Lee . . ."

"People like a show that fits their . . . prejudices on a thing," Beeman said slowly.

Rane watched the careful, almost decorous, way they held themselves in each other's presence.

Sheba said, "You can just feel it in the air. I hear the dumb-ass yahoos are laying bets in the beer joints. Word's out you and Mitchell Lee going shoot it out cowboy-fashion at Shiloh this weekend."

"Who the odds favor?" Beeman started to smile.

Sheba screwed her lips around her cigarette. "Well, one thing people say about Mitchell Lee is that boy can shoot."

"That what you wanted to tell me to cheer me up?" Beeman asked.

"No. There's something else. You know LaSalle's back?"

"So?"

"So, he's staying out at Kirby Creek. Miss Kirby's put him to work around the place. They won't take him back on the ambu yet."

Beeman shrugged. "Don't surprise me. It's the kind of gesture you'd expect after what happened with Miss Kirby's brother . . ."

"I don't think it's like that. I get the feeling she *reached out* to him," Sheba said. "Had him out to change the locks on the house first thing."

Beeman paid more attention. "Got him out at the estate . . . huh?"

"Thing is," Sheba said, "he comes around here and visits the old crew. And he goes down and hangs around the OR with the anesthetists. He was going to nursing school before he deployed with the guard, had a plan to work his way into nurse anesthetist. Well, Alma I work with, she's not real sure but maybe he slipped the key to the room where they keep all the surgery carts." She raised her eyebrows.

"Just what do they keep in those carts?" Beeman asked.

"Serious class IV narcotics."

"You think ole LaSalle is self-medicating?"

"I worry his head's all fucked up in ways we don't fully understand from a medical viewpoint. TBI. Traumatic brain injury. Asymptomatic in-head wounds that don't show, from concussion. It's going be the Agent Orange of Iraq."

Beeman pondered briefly, then nodded. "Okay, thanks."

"There's another thing," Sheba said. "Alma said LaSalle's going strapped."

"Really? I never known LaSalle to carry since . . ." Beeman's eyes were working now.

". . . His bad days on the block in Combs Court," Sheba said as she stubbed out her smoke in a planter next to the door. "I gotta get back in." Her regal face softened as she extended her hand and squeezed Beeman's forearm. "You watch your skinny white ass, hear?"

Back in the car, they sat staring at the rain drumming on the windshield. Rane had questions but clearly Beeman wasn't in a mood to talk. Then, finally, the cop broke the silence.

"You catch the drift, John, how it's shaping up with Mitchell Lee?"

"People expect you and him to have it out," Rane said.

"More'n that. People made a decision." Beeman exhaled, put the car in gear, and spoke straight ahead, to the rain. "We got a saying. The man needs killing."

Then he drove home without saying another word.

45 **PATTI HALVORSEN PARKED HER ACCORD** across from the historic Washington County courthouse on Stillwater's south hill. Floodlights and slowly rippling flags circled the steel-ribbed steeple of a Veterans' Memorial next to the parking lot. Across the street, the red brick building sported an arched balcony and an Italianate cupola, plus a Civil War statue on the lawn. Jenny sat on the courthouse steps wearing a sweat suit.

She stood up and greeted her pal. "Thanks for coming. I need a gut check."

"You pick this place for a reason?" Patti asked. Five years older than Jenny, she was a solid, durable blonde.

"Connections," Jenny said, pointing to the statue of the Union soldier. "Paul took his first step to Mississippi here. We were out for a walk and he started chatting with this guy about the statue. Then the guy mentioned there's a house just up the street that was originally built by a veteran of the First Minnesota Regiment. Paul walked up the street, looked at the house, and discovered the Civil War. All the books started showing up. Next thing he went out to Fort Snelling."

"Are these good memories?" Patti asked, inclining her head.

"Patti, the service is Sunday. I know this is bad timing," Jenny said frankly. "But Molly isn't Paul's."

She explained it all in succinct detail, including the in-

criminating irony of being in Rane's living room when the
call came. How Rane drove her home and wound up being
the one to tell Molly. Taking Paul's uniform. Where he was
now. Beeman on the phone. Her call to locate Rane's relatives.

"I always wondered what you were holding in," Patti said
simply.

"At first I encouraged him to go. I wanted to know what
happened to Paul. It's, like, his job," Jenny said in a rush.
"Now I'm worried this is more than compensating for being
an absent father." She hugged herself. "When I met him I
thought he was exciting."

Patti gave a wry smile. "And now?"

"With hindsight I think I confused exciting with scary."
Jenny hugged herself tighter and pursed her lips. "What if
the same thing that drove him away in the first place is still
driving him down in Mississippi?"

"We can discuss your personal drama later when you
have made some decisions, like whether to tell Molly who
he is, how much access he gets to her." Patti was blunt. "You
got a bigger problem, girl. You worked with street kids. You
know the rules. Could Rane harm himself or others?"

Jenny unclamped her arms, opened her hands. "Patti, I
talked to a *cop*."

"That's right. And cops don't care about your love life
coming back on you. They deal in motive and probable cause.
If you've led this Mississippi cop to believe Rane could be a
public danger then you better follow through and talk to the
aunt and uncle."

Jenny bit her lip. Patti said it first: "Even staring a funeral
in the face."

Jenny turned and looked at the shadowy Union soldier
advancing with a fixed bayonet on the courthouse lawn.

"Right," she said.

46 BREAKFAST WAS FAST, WITH LITTLE talk; toast and ink-black coffee. A few minutes later, Rane was sitting in the passenger seat of the Crown Vic as Beeman drove north on new 45, and he figured enough time had passed, so he said it.

"Peaches?"

"What's she like? Jenny Edin?" Beeman asked right back in a slightly surly drawl.

"Little defensive this morning?" Rane asked.

"C'mon, what's she like?" Beeman persisted.

"I think going out with me was the only impulsive move she ever made."

"Different from you, huh?" Beeman gave Rane a sidelong glance. "Charging into stuff . . . infiltrating that police cordon to get close to a barricaded shooter. That was some picture, him pointing a twelve-gauge at you just before he stuck it in his mouth."

"Where'd you get that?"

"On the fuckin' Internet. You got your picture . . ."

Rane smiled faintly, looked out the side window into the evaporating ground fog.

"You always get your picture, huh?" Beeman said with slow amusement. "Gives a guy the shakes, like having a ghoul perched on my shoulder."

"Peaches," Rane repeated.

"Aw *Gawd damn . . .*"

Rane shrugged. "Maybe I get it. Slow night. Two a.m. Cops, nurses, EMTs. Only place to get a cup of coffee is the emergency room . . ."

"Wasn't like that. She was in the guard, went over together to Saudi. There was this ruckus outside the base. We had these sand berms set up and a water point, where we'd wash down our vehicles. And Spec Four Nola Johnson was out there washing a Humvee when this Mercedes full of religious police roared up and these guys get out and start swinging camel whips." Beeman turned and smiled. "She was stripped down to Skivvies and a halter, see, and they didn't like that.

"Well I was on patrol and there was a report of shots fired so I drove out there and found her backing off these raghead assholes with her M16. *That's* how we actually met."

Beeman smiled. "Then I was manning a checkpoint and one of them shamal winds blew up and socked me in. Nola took cover with me in the bunker for the night. So there we were down to one pack of Kools, two liters of bottled water, and my last can of peaches."

"Where'd the nickname Sheba come from?" Rane asked.

Beeman sighed. "Seemed to fit, being stuck out there in the neighborhood of the Rivers of Babylon . . ."

"And when you came back?"

"Well, things have changed. We had us a black mayor for a while and all. But they ain't changed *that* much. What happens in Saudi stays in Saudi. She married black and I married white. Gotta face facts . . ." Beeman said.

". . . If you want to run for sheriff?" Rane probed.

"Oh, I don't know," Beeman mused, leaning forward, punching on the radio, pressing the tuning key through several country stations until he hit on Jim Morrison singing "Riders on the Storm." "Sheriff can get away with having some black pussy on the side. Ole Buford did. That ain't what doomed me," Beeman grinned.

"Really?"

"Yep. I was out one night in a two-man squad and made the mistake of saying a lot of country music sounded like a cow pissin' in an empty bucket." Beeman winked. "Was a preference for classic rock that done in my career . . ."

"Isn't my business but you seem to be on pretty good terms with all the women we've been meeting," Rane said with a sidelong grin.

Beeman grumbled, turned off the radio, and started singing an impromptu version of Johnny Cash's "I Walk the Line," keeping time with his toe on the gas pedal and bouncing Rane around on the front seat.

Rane gazed out the window after they turned off 45. "You're taking a different road than yesterday."

"Good memory. Yep, this is the front-door road to Kirby Creek."

The trees thinned and the house appeared in a white flicker of columns through breaks in the foliage. As they drew closer, Rane spied a silver Lexus and a blue Chevy truck parked in front of the house. A minute later, Rane could make out the chiseled detail on the monument that rose in front of the house. There was enough fog clinging to the hill to give the statue a sentinel aspect.

"Looks brand-new," he said.

"Put up last week. Mitchell Lee's butterfly kiss to the old man. 'Course now old Hiram's expected to pass any minute. Story of Mitchell Lee's life."

Beeman parked next to the Lexus. They got out and hadn't taken two steps when a pneumatic clatter started around the side of the house. Beeman motioned to Rane to follow him toward the source of the racket. They turned the corner and discovered the noise came from a seventy-five-pound Bosch electric demolition hammer cradled in the powerful arms of a black man wearing a respirator. He was coated in brick dust, his body shuddering with the banging hammer, busting out concrete steps at the base of a side door. Seeing them approach, he switched off the jackhammer, set it down, and pulled the mask down around his neck.

"Hey LaSalle, what you doin', man?" Beeman said. "I thought you're on the sick list."

As they shook hands, Rane noted the casual homeboy thumb clench and dap; a more than passing familiarity. Despite the dust coating the black man's face and arms, he saw fresh scarring. Another thing, his grimy T-shirt bulged behind his right hip in a way to suggest a handgun.

"This here's John Rane. He's a photographer from up North. My latest Yankee pilgrim I'm trying to keep out of trouble," Beeman said.

"LaSalle Ector, pleased to meet you, John," said the black guy, shaking Rane's hand. "Bee givin' you the tour, huh? He tell you how Corinth's big on Yankee tourists?" LaSalle's grin was careful, smoky-cool. "How the first couple thousand liked it so much they stayed."

Beeman grumbled. "Fuckin' with me, as usual. He means the National Cemetery on the south side where the Union dead are buried."

"Yeah," LaSalle said, "the good citizens of Corinth went out of their way to honor them Yankee boys by building our black slum around the cemetery. Ain't that right, Bee?"

Beeman smiled. "LaSalle has this forlorn hope I got a social conscience."

"Redneck with a heart and a brain is a man in constant turmoil," LaSalle said.

Beeman looked away. "Yeah, well . . ." Turning back to LaSalle, "What's with you riding a buster? What're you doin' here?"

LaSalle heaved his shoulders. "Miss Kirby wants to replace these old steps and redo them like they were on the original. She found this old photo."

Beeman said, "LaSalle was our ace EMT drive-like-a-raped-ape ambulance driver. Then he deployed to Iraq with the guard last year and got banged up." He nodded to Rane. "John was over there the first time. Army picture-taker."

"Oh yeah, whereabouts?" LaSalle asked.

"I tagged along with the 101st when they leapfrogged into Kuwait. You?" Rane asked.

"Shit, man, third month I was there the airport road—fuckin' Route Irish—blew up in my face. Got to see a lot of Walter Reed, though."

"What do the docs say?" Beeman asked in a more serious tone.

"Residual issues from concussion. More tests. They won't take me back at Magnolia till it clears up. So Miss Kirby's put me to work for the duration," LaSalle said.

"LaSalle," Beeman lowered his voice slightly and took a step closer. "You hear her say anything about Mitchell Lee?"

The big man cocked his head. "Like he went goofy and took a shot at you Saturday and killed that boy? And maybe he beat up Marcy Leets last night? Phone's been ringing all morning. There's lots of gossip goin' round."

Beeman hitched up his belt. "Well, if it *was* him, no telling what he might do next."

LaSalle frowned. "Maybe why I'm here, huh? She's not staying in Corinth till this blows over. I drive her back and forth to the hospital to see the old man." He jerked his head at the house. "He don't have a key to this place 'cause I changed the locks. And she quit running on the roads. He shows his face here he'll have to get past me. Fuck him. Hope he does show. Hope he's drunk and drowning in a ditch. He runs off and leaves her with her daddy dying. After all Hiram Kirby did for him."

"Well, I gotta go talk to her about it," Beeman said, screwing up his lips.

"Is it like they say, Bee?" LaSalle asked. "You and Mitchell Lee?"

"People love to talk," Beeman grunted, then he cuffed

LaSalle on a dusty shoulder and motioned Rane toward the front of the house.

"Nice meeting you," Rane said.

"Likewise. And don't let Bee distort your thinking," La-Salle said amiably.

As they walked away, Rane said, "Strapped."

"Definitely." Beeman didn't act overly concerned.

"No love lost between LaSalle and Mitchell Lee," Rane said.

Beeman shrugged. "Mitchell Lee was in the guard with LaSalle and Miss Kirby's brother, Robert." Beeman stopped, turned back toward the sound of the jackhammer, and said, "Miss Kirby's brother died pulling LaSalle out of that ambush where he got messed up. You was LaSalle how'd you feel about Mitchell Lee?"

"So what are we doing here?" Rane asked.

"Ask a few questions. Then you're going to chat with Miss Kirby while I nose around. I want to get a look at the gun rack, see what's missing. Mitchell Lee didn't have any muzzleloaders of his own; always used the old man's."

They rounded the house and met a lean, freckled redhead who would have been pretty except you looked twice at her jaw. She waited on the veranda by the front door. Ellender Kirby wore a white halter, short green shorts, and flip-flops. She had a marathoner's legs.

"Bee," she said with a weary smile. "I wondered when I'd be seeing you?"

"Miss Kirby, I'm real sorry about your daddy."

"Thank you, Bee. It's getting down to the hard part. DNR orders. No special measures," she said.

"That's a tough one," Beeman said.

She dropped her eyes. When she raised them, she said, "But I don't think you drove out here to inquire about my father?"

"No ma'am. Fact is, I'm trying to get a line on Mitchell Lee."

"I figured." Then she brightened. "First things first. Who's this you have with you?"

Beeman nodded. "This is John Rane. He's a photographer down from Minnesota. I'm showing him around."

They shook hands and Rane felt the steely undercurrent in her slim fingers. "Welcome to Kirby Creek, John. I take it your visit to Corinth is not a pleasure trip."

"No ma'am. I'm following up on the Minnesota reenactor who was killed . . ."

"Right down there, last Saturday." Ellie Kirby pointed down the slope toward the edge of the woods. She smiled tightly. "They still have the yellow tape. Never thought we'd have a crime scene on the place." She turned to Beeman. "Nobody really believes that shooting was an accident, do they Bee? I heard what people are saying . . ."

Beeman lowered his eyes, looked up. "Ain't no easy way to put it."

Ellender pursed her lips. "Well, before the killing starts why don't y'all come on in. All I have is soda in a cooler. I'm sorry but we have the kitchen and the back rooms sealed off because of the dust."

"How's he doing, LaSalle? Should he be doing bull work?"

Ellie smiled tightly. "So many of the boys are coming back with these concussion problems because the roadside bombs are so powerful. He has dizzy spells but he can feel them coming on. With his medical training, I trust his judgment. As for the work, you know LaSalle . . ." She fluttered her eyes. "Once he gets started I just stay out of the way."

"Miss Kirby, he's carrying a gun," Beeman said.

"Knows how to use it, too. Which Mitchell Lee will become very aware of if he shows his face," she said emphatically.

They walked into the house, with Ellie throwing comments over her shoulder to Rane in gaps from the banging hammer. "The scars on the columns and walls are left over from the battle in 1862. House was built in 1857 and is an example of the Greek Revival style popular at the time. Really the design is quite simple: a central passage. That's the drawing room on the left, then the dining room. Library and bedroom are on the right." As she talked, Rane caught glimpses of floor-to-ceiling mirrors and intricate molding beyond the tall doorways.

The back end of the central hall was masked with plastic sheeting fastened to the doorways with duct tape. Blankets covered what appeared to be a piano along the left side of the hall. Beeman stepped away into the library as Ellie opened a cooler next to the piano and took out three cans of Classic Coke.

She handed one to Rane and said, "One-story layout, John; no grand *Gone With the Wind* staircase. To find those you must travel south and east; northern Mississippi wasn't plantation country. In fact, before The War, when this was all Tishomingo County, the people voted to stay in the Union. Of course, after Fort Sumter, the politicians in Jackson stampeded them into the fight." She smiled tightly. "Farther south you go in Mississippi the more gray they bleed."

Beeman returned; Ellie gave him a Coke, led them back down the hall and out the front door, saying, "I can't talk over that racket." They followed her across the lawn to the base of the monument. She stepped to the crest of the hill and stood between two of the cannons, one hand on a tidy hip, the other raising her soda. A gust of breeze ruffled her short copper hair, and when she turned, she looked to Rane like an angry Liberty leading the mob.

Her eyes blazed at Beeman. "I ain't seen him, Bee. I ain't heard a peep. And you don't have to slink around. Daddy's match Enfield is missing from the gun cabinet. Not saying he took it. But it's definitely wandered off."

She held up her left hand, solemn as an oath-taker; the narrow white ring of untanned skin showed naked on the third finger. "I threw it away, Bee. I can't stand any more of his bullshit on top of what Daddy's going through," she said as she swung her head and glared at the new monument. "And now I'll have to look at this thing every day for the rest of my life and think of him, which was not the original intention."

Beeman toed the grass with his boot. "Hadda check in. It's my job, Miss Kirby."

A ripple of disgust crossed her face. "The last night I saw him, the night before he left for Memphis, he came in after midnight and I could smell her on him clear down the stairs, that summer barnyard stink men love." She wrinkled her nose. "I swear, someone should shovel Marcy Leets *out*."

"Guess you didn't hear," Beeman said.

"Of course *I heard*." She rolled her eyes and her freckles reddened. "Three of my friends already called this morning. Are you surprised? Family she married into. That beauty shop is just for show . . ."

She drew back her hand and flung the pop can at the base of the monument. It spiraled off, leaving a frothy brown stain on the clean granite. Then she stalked back toward the house. Halfway to the steps she turned and yelled over the bang of the hammer:

"You looking for Mitchell Lee, I'd start with his goddamn whore!"

They set their unfinished Cokes down at the base of the monument, walked back to the cruiser, and remained silent until the house was out of sight. They slowed, meeting four pickups with lowboys in tow. "They're coming to pick up the cannons for Shiloh," Beeman said, waving to the drivers going past. Then he pulled back on the road.

When they cleared the property, Rane turned to Beeman and said, "You defer to her."

Beeman exhaled. "It's a game we play. You hear her: 'I *ain't* seen him.' 'Y'all.' She don't talk like that to her friends. That's what they do, talk down with the help."

"You check out the gun case?"

"Yep; like she said. The Enfield's missing."

"Well, she isn't covering for him," Rane said.

"Nope."

"And she don't care much for Marcy Leets."

"Yeah, pretty vocal about it too. Same as Marcy was about her. What's that line in Shakespeare? About women protesting too much . . ."

Beeman didn't pursue the thought. When they pulled onto the highway, Rane noticed a dusty brown Mustang parked on the shoulder near the Kirby road. The windows were an opaque grime, impossible to see the driver. As they turned south on 45, the Mustang fell in several cars behind them.

"Now what?" Rane asked.

"Track down Billie Watts."

"Like Marcy Leets said."

"Yep."

"What's Marcy Leets's part in this?" Rane wondered.

Beeman grinned. "Now that's a serious spiritual question. Marcy's enough to turn a Southern Baptist into a fuckin' Buddhist . . ."

"Say again?"

"Deeper I get into this mess I'm starting to think Marcy Leets is the reincarnation of Louise Hathcock."

47 THE MORNING MIST BURNED OFF, THE air sweated gray, and the roadside gravel gleamed moist adobe-red. They pulled off the highway at Shiloh Road on the outskirts of Corinth and Beeman got out to make some calls. Rane watched the funky Mustang pass them, slow down, and pull off farther down the road in the shade of some trees.

Rane got out and waited while Beeman talked.

"Now Morg, think on it, man. You don't cooperate certain things are gonna come out. Now you check and see if he's there 'cause he's been out of the office all week. Call me back at this number."

Beeman ended the call, stretched, and hitched up his gun belt.

"See that Mustang up ahead," Rane asked.

"Yep."

"He's been following us," Rane said.

"No shit. Yesterday it was a blue Xterra. When I said the sheriff's keeping an arm's length from me and Mitchell Lee I didn't mean he's gonna hang us out here all alone. Jimmy's had a deputy shadowing me since they shot out the picture window. Was a car parked outside of the house last night."

"So you weren't kidding about being bait."

Beeman crinkled his eyes. "*We're* bait. You still in?"

Rane shrugged. "Who're you talking to?"

"First I called his daddy's law office. Billie Watts didn't come in today or any day all week. So I figured he's repaired to his hideaway condo on the Tennessee River. The guy I just talked to is a security guard works out there. I snatched him up a while ago with a trunk full of bonded whiskey he sells with his brother out of a garage in Hatchie. Alcorn's a dry county outside six-percent beer and wine in the Corinth city limits. I let him go to have a handle on him for just such an occasion as this."

The sky to the north made a dragging sound, like a match before it strikes. They both looked up at the fitful clouds. "Gonna rain all weekend, just watch," Beeman predicted.

Back in the car, Beeman whipped a U-turn. The Mustang swung around in a similar maneuver and fell in behind. They were cruising the edge of town when Beeman's cell phone rang.

"Okay, good," Beeman said. "Now you're gonna meet us at the side gate. Then you're gonna walk us up to the room and help us get in.

"Never mind who. Less you know the better. And don't let his accent throw you. Let me remind you the federal district we're in don't stop at the state line. We cool? Okay. Give me an hour."

Beeman turned off the phone. "John, might help if you act kind of aloof and federal-almighty," then he smiled and added, "shouldn't be too hard, with that permanent case of Minnesota hemorrhoids you got."

When he pulled up to 72, Beeman leaned over, opened the glove compartment, dug around, and withdrew a hockey puck–size canister, oxblood-colored, with a gold top. As he removed the lid, he said, "Copenhagen Long Cut is a filthy habit. What my daddy did when I was a kid, he had me emptying the damn spit cans he kept all over the house. I wouldn't even have it in the car if Margie was in town." He offered the tin. "You want a taste?"

Rane violently shook his head.

Beeman carefully inserted a pinch of chew in his lower lip and then searched under the seat for an empty pop can, which he placed between his thighs. Then he adjusted the wad in his lower lip, floored the gas, and left rubber as he fishtailed through traffic onto Highway 72.

"When my daddy was young he ran with Buford," Beeman said, eyes lidded, leaning forward, raising the pop can, and spitting. "Old Clarence would say: 'There comes a point when you just gotta kick in a few doors . . .'"

EAST ON STATE 72, GOING BY TRAFFIC LIKE IT WAS standing still, they streaked past the Iuka turnoff. As they turned north on an exit, Beeman thumbed his cell.

"Dell? Yeah, Bee. Tell you what. Why don't you hang back for a while. Don't think you want this detour on your trip ticket."

They lost the Mustang and worked the bigger roads down to smaller roads until they were on a wooded two-lane that meandered down toward the river. About halfway down, Beeman braked suddenly and swerved to miss a bobbling animal that looked like an ambling seashell crossing the center line.

"What the hell was that?" Rane asked, craning his neck for a second look.

"Why'd the chicken cross the road?" Beeman chuckled.

"What?"

"To teach the armadillo how to. They been moving into the area from the west."

"I guess," Rane said. "Up north we have possums getting squashed on the road to Duluth."

"Must be global warming, huh."

Laughing, they came around a bend, the trees cleared, and two white towers rose next to a wide marina. Rane counted seven stories of balconies and cupolas atop little green roofs.

"In Xanadu did Kubla Khan a stately pleasure-dome decree," Beeman recited. Then he sighed as they turned into the rear service entrance, "I been itching to get inside this place for years. They got their own private security force, don't like cops coming around. This here's where the gentry hangs, to recreate in ways they couldn't get away with in places like Corinth. This is gonna be *fun*."

"Just what exactly are you going to do that's fun?" Rane asked.

"Well, technically this comes under cultivating a snitch. Except he's a smart-ass, rich-kid lawyer from a family that goes way back. So we gotta be creative." Beeman gazed ruefully down the river. "So we get him out of his element and fuck with his buttons. Just follow my lead."

Beeman drove toward a tall man running to flab, who waited next to a gate in the chain-link fence. As they pulled up, he worked the sliding gate open. He wore a tractor hat, jeans, a Darryl Worley T-shirt, and a sheet of nervous sweat on his face.

"I don't know, Bee," the guy said, fingering a badge clipped to his belt as Beeman eased through the gate. "I ain't working today. Came in special for this. Don't have my uniform. I could get in a lot of trouble."

"Correction, Morg," Beeman said. "You're already in a lot of trouble and this little assist is gonna make a piece of it go away. Now is he still here?"

Morg bobbed his head. "And he's starting early. He buzzed in a female visitor under an hour ago." Morg swallowed. "Boys at the desk say she was on the young side."

"How young?" Beeman asked.

"Like call-the-truant-officer young," Morg winced. Then he pointed to the building. "Park under that overhang next to the door, in the shadows," he said, eyeing Rane, who glowered back with an expression he hoped looked like infallible contempt.

They parked the car and got out fast as Morg shook out a

ring full of keys, opened the door, and they stepped into the building's lower level. "Service elevator's this way," Morg said. "He's on six."

Beeman said, "Now Morg, once we collect him, we need you to scout ahead. Be nice to get him out with nobody seein'."

Morg bobbled his head, not unlike the armadillo. "Long as we go out the way we come in."

Beeman turned to Rane. "I got no problem with that. How about you Agent Rane?"

Rane grunted in the affirmative. They walked down a corridor, stopped at an elevator, and Morg pushed the button. As they waited for the lift, Morg ground his teeth. "So how do I get him to open the door?"

"Tell him something's wrong with the air-conditioning or heat or the sprinkler system. You gotta check all the rooms," Beeman suggested.

The elevator arrived, the door slid open, and they got on. Beeman pushed 6. Morg's slack face worked and he muttered under his breath, "air-conditioning, sprinklers and heaters . . ."

Rane thought of Dorothy in *The Wizard of Oz* leading the Cowardly Lion, the Tin Man, and the Scarecrow along the Yellow Brick Road. He stifled a smile. *Lions and tigers and bears . . .*

The elevator stopped, they got out, and Beeman asked Morg, "Does one of those keys fix this elevator to run straight to the basement and skip all the floors?"

"Uh-huh." Morg stepped in, selected a key, and monkeyed around with the control panel. He stepped back out. "All set. It'll stay here open and shoot straight down when we get back."

"Good. Soon's we get in you scoot back here and make sure for us." Morg nodded and they padded on thick carpet, following him to an anonymous door in a beige corridor full of doors.

Beeman nodded to Morg, stepped back, tensed, bent his knees slightly, and unsnapped the strap on his holster. Morg swallowed audibly at the sound of the strap breaking free. Beeman did not draw the SIG.

Morg knocked on the door, three hard raps. Then he raised his badge to the peephole.

"What?" A muted annoyed question beyond the door.

Beeman prodded Morg in the kidney with a rigid finger. "Security," Morg yelped. "We gotta check all the air-conditioners on six."

The voice was closer now to the door. "The what?"

"Air-conditioners, wiring's acting up. Fire danger. Gotta check all the rooms . . ."

"Aw shit, okay . . ."

The deadbolt clicked, then the lock over the keyhole. As the door cracked a fraction, Beeman shoved Morg down the hall, cocked his knee back to his chest, uncoiled, and smashed the sole of his boot just above the doorknob.

Flying open, the door connected with flesh and bone. Rane heard garbled profanity and a cry of pain as Beeman, one hand on the butt of his pistol, lunged into the apartment. Rane rushed right behind him.

Low black-leather couches. A man in a paisley silk robe sprawled against the back of the nearest couch. His chest and splayed legs were deeply tanned. His naked buttocks and groin were pale, hairy dough. As Beeman stood over the prone man, Rane moved through the apartment; kitchenette off the living room, bathroom down a short hall leading to a closed door. The bedroom. He stopped at an oval glass table between the leather couches, saw sprinkles of white powder trickled out from the edge of a glossy magazine, the cover read *VIP* something, showed smiling people raising wine glasses.

He lifted the magazine and saw three lines of disturbed white powder next to a rolled hundred-dollar bill. A bank of windows with a sliding door opened on a balcony and the river six stories below. An ebony set of samurai swords perched on a display wall rack. The plants were fabric.

And then a girl with straight brown hair opened the bedroom door and stood in the doorway. She wore a matching paisley robe open down the front. Rane sympathized with her, straining so hard to be invisible and not having a clue how to do it.

Rane and Beeman stared at the girl and Rane intuited Beeman's thoughts: was she sixteen going on forty or a deer in the headlights?

Beeman stepped over dazed Billie Watts and moved closer to the girl. "Don't move, Billie," he said firmly, then he faced the girl. "You skippin' school, honey?"

"Oh shit," the girl said, staring at the badge and gun on Beeman's belt. Her chin began to tremble and she shook her head violently. "Teachers' meeting."

Encouraged, Beeman said in a calm, reasonable voice, "I'd like to see some ID, young lady."

"Hey, wait a fuckin' minute," Billie Watts protested, lurching up on his elbows. "Renee, you don't say a word."

"Do up your robe, Renee," Beeman said calmly. "Better yet, go on and get dressed."

As she darted back into the bedroom, Beeman turned on Billie Watts.

"Show me a warrant," Billie snarled, sitting up and working with his skewed robe.

"A warrant? Way the roads corkscrew in here, I ain't even sure which state this fuckin' place is in," Beeman said as he leaned over and unloaded his cud of tobacco into the fake moss at the bottom of a planter.

The girl came hopping through the doorway in unzipped jeans and a blouse, pulling on a shoe, stuffing her socks and underpants into her purse. "I never done this before, sir, honest," she pleaded to Beeman.

"I believe you, I do. Just calm down and sit there on the

couch." The girl sat, primly drawing her knees together. "Now how'd you get here?" Beeman asked.

"Drove."

"Sure you can drive? You're a bit shook up. How long you been driving?"

"Six months, a little more. I never had a ticket."

"Aw shit," Billie Watts muttered.

Beeman ignored him. "Uh-huh. Better show me the keys, I want to make sure you got a way home."

Her face working, she dug in her purse and held up a jangle of keys. Beeman palmed the key ring quickly and studied a round plastic coin pouch, the kind with a slit in the middle, from a car dealership.

"Buick? That's a good car," he said amiably.

Renee nodded, ashen-faced. "Buick LaCrosse, 3.6 liter V6. Daddy's partial to Buicks . . ."

"And he buys them at this dealership down 72 in Muscle Shoals, huh?" Beeman asked, turning to Billie. Then he handed the keys back to Renee. "Now I'm letting you go with a warning, you understand?"

She bobbed her head vigorously.

"Okay, now. Go on, git. And you drive carefully, back to Alabama, hear?"

"Yes sir," Renee blurted, then she gathered her purse, launched off the couch, and hurried from the room.

When they were alone, Billie demanded, "What the hell's going on here, Beeman? Am I under arrest?"

"Not even close, Billie. Far as I'm concerned this never happened. I just want to have a little chat with no minors present is all," Beeman said judiciously.

"So talk," Billie said suspiciously.

"I don't want to talk here. Get up," Beeman said.

"Who's he?" Billie said, looking at Rane.

"I don't want to talk here, either," Rane said in a flat Upper Midwestern twang that attracted Billie Watts's attention.

"I need to get dressed," Billie said, getting awkwardly to his feet.

"I don't want you to get dressed," Beeman said, clamping a hand on Billie's arm. Rane moved in and gripped his other arm. Keying on Beeman's lead, Rane helped propel Billie, barefoot and clothed only in the flimsy silk robe, through the door into the hall.

48 WITH MORG SCOUTING THE CORRIDORS ahead, they spirited Billie down in the elevator, out the back door, and stuffed him in the caged backseat of Beeman's car. Rane last saw Morg in the rearview mirror, nervously locking the gate as they drove back up the wooded road. Beeman and Rane stared straight ahead, ignoring Billie's increasingly anxious questions. Then Beeman spun the steering wheel at an opening in the trees. The Crown Vic crashed to a halt as the trail petered out in thick brush.

"Everybody out," Beeman ordered.

The heat draped down like a wet gray slurry and Rane had the feeling a fast move could start the air to dripping.

"Ow, shit," Billie cringed, stepping barefoot gingerly on rocks and deadfall as Beeman pushed him down the slope. Off to the right, through the trees, they could see the white seven-storied condominiums on the sluggish river.

Despite the dishrag heat, Billie was hugging the thin robe tight to his chest.

By the time they reached the shore, Billie had tripped and fallen twice; his hands, forearms, and feet were bleeding from minor cuts. Beeman continued to ignore him, looking up and down the river's edge at the patches of sand, fallen trees, and thick, yellow clumps of grass.

"I ain't going to lay a hand on you, Billie," Beeman said absently.

"You're flirting with kidnapping, you dumb redneck," Billie fumed.

"Yep. And when'd you start tutoring high school girls on pharmaceuticals and the birds and the bees? And bringing her across state lines to do it? I know where she lives and I got a witness," Beeman said reasonably, still scanning the shore. Then he turned and faced Billie. Rane hung back, all eyes and ears cranked wide open.

"I suspect you got an idea what this is about. I need some answers about Mitchell Lee; like did he rip on Marcy Leets last night?" Beeman asked patiently.

"Privileged relationship. He's my client. You know that," Billie said sullenly.

"Uh-huh. Walk with me," Beeman said, taking Billie by the arm, slowly leading him through the deadfall and dense grass as Rane fell in behind. "Billie, let's you and me get outside the legal game and deal some cards. For the sake of conversation let's put aside the Mississippi Criminal Code. How about I trade you the conspiracy statute for that privileged relationship . . ."

"Fuck you, Beeman. You're gonna do jail time on this," Billie snarled.

They were ambling toward the marina; easy going for Beeman and Rane, agony for Billie and his tender bare feet. Through breaks in the budding foliage Rane could see the hazy sunlight tickle the white hulls of moored power-boats.

"Here's my question for you, Billie. If I'd been accidentally shot dead last Saturday what would have happened next?" Beeman asked.

Billie Watts stared at Beeman with more contempt than fear. He was recovering from the shock of having his door kicked in. His comfortable world was only four hundred yards away along the riverbank. Billie Watts smirked.

Rane had studied fear on human faces his whole adult life. He was on less sure ground with the nuances of chemical addiction. He suspected the twitchy discomfort on Billie's florid, tanned face had more to do with irritation at being separated from his drugs and his teenage playmate than fear for his safety.

Beeman clearly understood this and was casting around for a method of dropping the conversation down to a more primal level.

"Walk," Beeman said, giving Billie's shoulder a shove, and they continued along the shoreline. Billie hugged his robe around him and picked his steps, grimacing every time his feet sunk into the matted grass.

They had traveled perhaps fifty yards when Beeman stopped and reflexively raised his hand like a point man signaling a halt. Slowly, he smiled.

Rane detected a persistent rustle, close by in the grass. He checked the trees. No wind. Billie merely blinked, probably hearing more noise inside his head than outside.

"They don't run," Beeman said absently. "Sometimes they'll actually chase after you." He looked around and selected a sturdy dead branch and snapped it off. He turned it in his hands, evaluating it: curved at the end, about five feet long. He took a cautious step into the grass. "I've heard stories about them dropping from a tree into a boat to attack you."

Instinctively, Billie shied back and bumped into Rane, who nudged him forward. Now Beeman was moving in a fluid crouch through the knee-deep grass, the stick extended in one hand. Rane thought of the stance and careful footwork of a saber fencer.

"Uh-huh," Beeman said. "Caught him moving. Usually they hang out on limbs or rocks near the water. Come here Billie. Take a look."

Rane shoved Billie forward and they both lurched back, out of reflex, when they saw the snake that was ominously thick along its black middle, tapering at the tail and head. It was coiled in the grass next to a log. The triangular head

cocked back, swaying, testing the air. It had intense, ellipti-
cal cat's eyes and the wide-open mouth showing stark white
against the sleek black coils.

"How's the story go," Beeman mused, figuring angles and
distances with his stick. "Eve had questions and the snake
give her the scoop on the knowledge of good and evil."

With deceptive speed, Beeman caught the snake in mid-
weave and mashed the stick down. The snake writhed in the
grass, pinioned by the heavy stick just behind its head.

Billie had surged back against Rane, who gripped his
arms from behind. Rane willed himself calm and hoped to
hell Beeman knew what he was doing. That was a cotton-
mouth water moccasin he was getting into. A big one, almost
four feet long, thick as Rane's forearm around the middle.

"Trick is," Beeman said slowly, stooping, keeping the
pressure on his stick with his left hand, reaching with his
right, "getting a hold on them . . ." His fingers probed right
behind the fulcrum, where the stick held the snake's head
immobile. ". . . Just so." The black body writhed under Beeman's extended arm. Each time the thick coils lashed the
grass, Billie Watts spasmed back against Rane's chest. He
rose on tiptoe as if to compress his bare feet and make them
a smaller target.

Deftly, Beeman dropped the stick and raised his right
hand, in which he now held the snake pinched below the
base of the head between his thumb and index finger. He
gripped the twitching black body firmly in his left.

He rose, turned, and held the squirming snake up with
an appraising smile. "Whatcha think? Bet he goes close to
fifteen pounds."

Rane couldn't see Billie's face but he could feel the visceral revulsion pulse in Billie's arms and smell it in the gum-
drops of sweat that popped on the back of his neck.

"Jesus, Bee . . ." Billie groaned, pressing back against
Rane.

Beeman took a step forward and turned the snake's head

slowly back and forth. A foot of air separated Billie Watts's face from the straining white maw, the curved, glistening fangs. The venom. Beeman extended his arms. Six inches.

Rane, taller than Billie, could clearly see the snake's moist, white-padded mouth. The fear he felt was controlled optical fascination, like switching to a more powerful lens setting. He tightened his grip on Billie Watts, whose breath was coming in deep, shuddering sobs.

Beeman had not shaved this morning, so the shadow of beard added an edge to his spare, tanned face. The easy humor had vacated his brown eyes. He seemed totally at ease with the poisonous snake in his hands.

Rane was getting a palpable sense there were a few open manholes in Kenny Beeman.

"Now, Billie, this is the way I see it," Beeman said. "I was just doing my job, trying to figure out where the hell Mitchell Lee Nickels disappeared to. So I went out and talked to his wife, who is pissed off at him and so no help there. Marcy's all beat up and not real talkative. So I decide to check with his lawyer. And I walk in and find you with a nose full of coke and this pink sixteen-year-old pussy that don't have no skid marks on it at all. Well, you coming from a big powerful Corinth family—and me being just a hired-hand cop and all—naturally I remember my place and back off.

"Then it seems you became distraught and wandered away in your bathrobe, a little addled maybe, from shame about the girl, and maybe guilt about what you're mixed up in with Dwayne Leets and Mitchell Lee. Or could be you just had too much cocaine for lunch. You got these cuts on your feet and hands and forearms from thrashing through the brush . . ."

Beeman paused and squeezed the snake harder, causing it to rage in its confinement.

". . . and you musta tripped and fell down and that's when you met Mr. No Shoulders here, who struck you three-four times in the face."

Rane was hard put to decide who had more hostility in his eyes, Beeman or the snake.

"Oh God," Billie gasped, going loosey-goosey against Rane. Beeman had moved the snake close enough for Billie to feel its probing reptile breath.

"Probably you make it back to the condos and they get you to medical help, but that could take half an hour," Beeman continued. "On the other hand, the face is close to the heart and lungs and this hemotoxic venom is some ugly shit . . ."

The snake's tongue flicked against Billie's cheek.

"I'll get to the bottom of this," Beeman said. "Just take me longer with you dead in the woods."

"Okay," Billie gasped. "Please . . ."

Beeman moved the snake back a few inches and waited.

Billie sagged, catching his breath. When he raised his eyes, the snake was right there, three-four inches away.

"You talk I'll take a step back," Beeman said.

"You got to promise to immunize me," Billie started.

"Shit, boy, you ain't hearing me," Beeman said as he released the snake with his left hand so its body thrashed free. Then he stooped, seized Billie's bare foot with his left hand, and thrust the snake against it.

Billie screamed and twisted in Rane's grip.

"You don't need to be immunized. What you need is to get inoculated. And pretty damn quick," Beeman said, coming back up and collecting the writhing snake in his left hand.

"Oh Christ, oh Christ," Billie panted.

"Calm down, Billie, more excited you get the faster that shit pumps through your blood. Now, that's just your little toe. Want to try for your pecker?" Beeman said in an even voice.

"I don't know . . ." Rane ground his teeth, blinking sweat.

"*I* know," Beeman said hotly. "I know Paul Edin's dead and all these fuckers are walking around laughing about it. He better start talking . . ."

"All I know is Dwayne wanted you gone for laming Donnie and Mitch wanted a favor in return," Billie whined as his eyes darted in a flood of sweat. "If something was to happen to Ellie Kirby . . ."

Beeman smiled. "Now we're getting somewhere. Go on."

Billie panted, "My dad's law firm represents the family, so I hear things. After Robert Kirby died the old man got religion or something and decided it was a sin to die rich. He planned to draft a new will. Gift all of Kirby Creek and the battlefield to a public charity like the Sons of Confederate Veterans with a proviso they leave it untouched; all but a parcel by the lake where the estate would bankroll a research clinic."

"Research clinic," Beeman repeated.

"Yeah, for Iraq veterans, name it after Robert. I don't know, Christ, Bee," Billie pleaded, "get me out of here."

The snake was trying to wrap its coils around Beeman's left hand. Beeman stretched it out and eyed Billie. "C'mon."

"Okay, okay," Billie muttered. "What happened was Hiram tore up his old will and . . ." Billie paused, straining against Rane's hands, staring down at the red spot on his little toe.

"Clock's running," Beeman said, holding the snake almost absently now.

"Except the old man had a stroke before he drafted the new will. Get it? Now he's incapacitated and isn't expected to live. He'll die intestate. In the absence of a will specifying a different requirement it all goes to Ellie as the sole surviving heir . . ."

"And you told that to your buddy, Mitchell Lee?" Beeman asked.

Billie nodded his head vigorously up and down, his breath coming in hyperventilating gasps. "I was just showing off some inside information. Mitch didn't know . . . about the will being torn up. At that point probably . . . Ellie didn't either. My dad is hoping the old man will rally. At least enough to bob his head so Ellie could have power of attorney. That way they could follow through on Hiram's desire to gift the land and reduce the estate prior to death to ease the tax burden."

Beeman narrowed his eyes. "Absent that outcome, if the old man dies, then if Ellie dies sudden-like?"

Billie licked his lips. His whole body was drenched in slippery sweat and Rane could barely hold on to him. Billie swallowed, panted, then said, "The inheritance flows through Ellie's estate to her surviving heir . . ."

"And Mitchell Lee gets it all," Beeman said as he rolled his eyes contemptuously. "See, John. This isn't about me or what my daddy did back when. This is New South Money bullshit." He glared at Billie. "And you heard them talk this out? Mitchell and Dwayne Leets?"

"Bee, for the love of God, man. Take me to the hospital," Billie pleaded.

"Answer the fuckin' question. Or get bit again," Beeman warned.

"Okay, okay. No, I never heard them actually say it; they don't talk specifics around me about stuff like that. Just connect the dots. Don't matter now," Billie panted.

"Why's that?" Beeman asked.

Billie's eyes bulged. "Because part of Ellie's decision to take her dad off life support was drafting a new will of her own basically giving it all away like he wanted; the battlefield, the clinic, the works. Mitch wouldn't get shit now if she died." Billie gritted his teeth. "When he missed you it all came apart and he musta flipped out. Don't you see, what if Mitch thinks I tipped her? And now he's out there, nuts, going after folks, like why'd he beat up Marcy last night? Dwayne called and told me. He's shook, Bee. He don't know what's going on either. That's why I'm out here where Mitchell Lee can't get to me," Billie blubbered.

"Let him go," Beeman said. Rane released his death grip

on Billie's arms, stepped back, and stared at his bloodless, cramped hands.

"The hospital," Billie said.

"Relax, Billie, you ain't been bit," Beeman said with a slow smile. "All I did was bring him in close and pinch you hard between my fingernails . . ."

"You sonofabitch," Billie trembled.

"Whoa, hey—shit!" Beeman fumbled and lost his grip on the snake with his left hand. "Goddamn, he's getting away from me." His hand flailed. "Billie, man, grab him in the middle so I can get a better hold."

On pure defensive reflex, Billie grabbed at the thrashing black body and squeezed it desperately in both hands.

"Hold on," Beeman said, "that's it, good." Now Beeman's left hand circled the snake below Billie's hands and shoved them up the snake's length until he pushed them hard against his thumb and forefinger.

Rane had taken a respectful step back and watched the tense choreography of two men and a thrashing snake.

"You got him?" Beeman asked urgently.

"I got him," Billie gasped, wide-eyed, squirting sweat.

Beeman released his fingers and stepped back. Billie's fists, knuckles white with effort, formed a tense socket that clamped the snake just below its head. Beeman grinned. "Damn, Billie, look at you. You got one real pissed off water moccasin all to yourself. Been nice talking to you."

"Ah, ah, ah," Billie panted as the snake twisted and wrapped its thick coils around his rigid, trembling forearms. "Bee. Bee. What do I do?" Billie pleaded.

"First, keep your mouth shut about what we been talking about. Then, I suggest you keep a good grip on him with one hand and unwrap him with the other."

Billie experimentally loosened his lower hand, the black coils instantly tightened on his arm, and he quickly returned to the two-handed grip.

"Plan B is you walk real careful back to the condos and

see if there's a country boy at the guard desk who'll help you un-ass that rather large snake," Beeman said.

Then he motioned to Rane. "C'mon, John, we're finished here."

As they turned and started up the slope toward the car, they watched Billie begin his journey. Choosing a route in the shallow water along the shore, he took one cautious step at a time, holding his squirming black burden at arm's length. "Thank you, Jesus, thank you, Jesus," Billie implored. "Oh God, oh God, oh God . . ."

Beeman turned to Rane and shook his head. "That's town for you," he said. "Grew up here his whole life and he ain't got a clue in the woods."

49 **JENNY AGREED TO BRING IN AN** Episcopalian minister to conduct an ecumenical service as a concession to Paul's family, who would watch the service live online from Japan. Jenny met him at the center at noon on Friday to go over the ceremony, after which guests would adjourn to a large common room for coffee, cake, and what the minister referred to as "fellowship."

Paul's ashes were at the center, contained in a simple rectangular maple scatter urn roughly the size of a Webster's desk dictionary. They weighed approximately six and a half pounds.

The service was scheduled for eleven a.m. on Sunday morning.

Then Jenny sat with one of Bradley's assistants and clicked through a dry run of the slide show. For the first time Molly set foot in the funeral home, with her piano teacher, to rehearse the "Moonlight Sonata" she would play to begin the service.

After the meeting at the center, Jenny drove Molly back home. Originally, she had planned to take Molly shopping this afternoon to get something new to wear on Sunday. Molly had torpedoed the shopping expedition with one of Paul's favorite maxims from Henry David Thoreau: "Beware of all enterprises that require new clothes." Molly would wear the black dress she'd worn to her last piano recital.

Jenny parked the car, entered the house, and saw the message light blinking on the cordless phone in the kitchen. She pushed caller ID and watched RESTRICTED NUMBER surface in the gray viewing panel. Had to be Cantrell. They would apparently communicate without ever speaking directly. This struck Jenny as apt, given that the subject was John Rane.

She took a deep breath and retrieved the message:

Jenny, this is Harry Cantrell returning your call. Of course I remember you. The party you want to contact is Mike Morse. He's a retired gunsmith who works mainly out of a shop at his lake home east of Hudson, Wisconsin, on Mail Lake Road. I don't have a house address but I can give you his home number.

Sorry to hear of the circumstances of your husband's death in Mississippi. Anything else you need, don't hesitate to call . . .

Jenny copied the Wisconsin number, sat down at the kitchen table, and took a moment to compose herself. Cantrell knew about Paul. So he had been in contact with Rane. She tapped her pen on the blank notepad under the number she'd just jotted down. Looking around, she realized that she always sat in the same chair, as did Molly. She wondered how long the chair across from her, Paul's chair, would remain unoccupied. She continued to sleep on the right side of the bed, with Molly occupying Paul's place on the left.

Habits of a marriage, she thought. If she picked up the phone and made the connection with Rane's relatives, she could be tampering with Paul's place in Molly's life. There would be consequences. But she had to know.

So she punched in the Wisconsin number. One ring, two, three, four, and to the machine.

You have reached Mike and Karen Morse. We can't

come to the phone right now. Please leave a message.

Christ, what if they were on vacation?
Beep.

Mike and Karen, this is Jenny Edin. You probably don't remember me but we met, once, briefly, over eleven years ago. Your nephew, John Rane, brought me out to your lake place. I have some questions about John and they're kind of urgent. Would you be willing to speak to me tomorrow?

Jenny left her numbers, ended the call, and consigned it all to the vagaries of voice mail.

At four thirty in the afternoon, Jenny was sitting in the den with Paul's partner, Bill, going over Paul's insurance policies. Molly was practicing the piano. Lois and Vicky were in the kitchen, baking brownies for the after-service coffee hour.

The phone rang.

Jenny picked up. "Hello?"

"Jenny?" asked an older woman's voice; confident, but curious.

"Yes."

"This is Karen Morse. Mike's not here right now."

"Karen, thank you for returning my call. I know this is sudden but would it be possible to meet with you and your husband?"

"About . . : John?"

"Yes."

"When?"

"Tomorrow?" Jenny controlled her voice, not wanting to sound desperate or pushy.

Karen paused on the line, then said: "Would you like to come out to the house tomorrow early afternoon, say one or so?"

"That would be fine."

After another long pause, Karen asked, "Will you be coming . . . alone?"

The silence on the connection was suddenly freighted with implications.

"Yes, alone."

"Okay, let me give you directions."

Jenny filled a page with detailed directions, thanked Karen, and hung up the phone. Then she turned back to Bill, who picked up where he left off: explaining an insurance policy that paid double in the event of accidental death.

50

THEY PICKED UP THEIR MUSTANG TAIL and headed west on 72 toward Corinth. Beeman drove the speed limit and slouched behind the wheel, almost pensive.

"You look disappointed," Rane ventured.

"Yeah, would have been nice if Dwayne was there with Billie, huh?" He tapped his teeth together. "Might have finished some of this on the spot."

"You're going to put a watch on the Kirby woman, right?"

"You know, John, I don't think so."

"But you should warn her," Rane said.

"Think somebody already did," Beeman said slowly. "You seen LaSalle out at the house. Most people'd think twice about trying to get past him. Know I would."

"Hey, Beeman," Rane protested. "We just heard a plan to commit premeditated murder."

"Yesterday's plan," Beeman said softly, rubbing his cheek. "What's today's plan, I wonder?"

"Well, Mitch makes sense now," Rane said. "The wheels come off his get-rich scheme and he loses it."

"Sure looks that way, don't it."

Rane shook his head. "I don't get you, man."

Beeman leaned back behind the wheel, his face all calm and composed. He probed inside his lip, made a face, extracted a remnant of the chewing tobacco and flicked it away. "You see," he said, "when we hooked up you said let the chips fall where they may. Maybe it works that way where you're from, where people zip around and don't talk to each other. Down here it just isn't that simple. Everybody knows everybody from way back. I'm getting a feeling that this time the chips are gonna fall where they've been carefully placed."

"Meaning?"

"Meaning we wait for the next breadcrumb, or chip, that leads us deeper into the woods." Beeman grinned. "You having fun yet, John?"

"Billie said . . ."

Beeman cut him off. "Billie'd say anything with Mr. No Shoulders looking him in the face; what you call 'hearsay extracted under duress.' What a smart defense attorney calls 'torture' and ain't admissible in court. But I believe the part about the will. And that's what we simple country boys call a motive. But now Ellie took the motive away. So what's left?"

"Fucking vengeance, that's what," Rane said.

"You got that right," Beeman said. "But why would Mitchell Lee telegraph when and where the next round's going to happen? I think Sheba's got a point; it's starting to look like some damn soap opera. Somebody's setting the stage, is what."

"Who?"

Beeman screwed up his lips and laughed softly. "Who keeps soap operas in business?"

"Oh, that's good. Riddles?" Rane shook his head. "So what are you going to do?"

Beeman craned his neck. "Show up at Shiloh like it says in the script. Up till then, not much, judging by the look of those clouds up ahead."

Rane flopped back on the seat, exasperated. "You got a guy out there running around who's supposed to be this dead shot?"

"Uh-huh."

"Marcy at the hospital; Mitchell Lee beat her up," Rane said.

"Sure looks that way, don't it; right in character, just like he did last time he got strange," Beeman said, staring into the burgeoning storm cloud.

They drove into a wide, gray rain curtain that burst into a solid downpour. A few minutes after the windshield wipers started slapping, Rane jumped when the radio came alive in a squawk of static.

"A-six, dispatch."

Beeman picked up and keyed the mike. "A-six."

"You got a meeting."

"Ten-four." Beeman replaced the mike and slouched deeper behind the steering wheel. "Gotta go in and talk to the boss."

Coming back into Corinth, Beeman stopped at a light, and a rough-cut man in a pickup in the next lane smiled at him through the rain, slowly extended his hand, index finger pointed, and dropped his thumb like a hammer.

"One of your fans, huh," Rane said.

Beeman paid no attention. He drove on into town on Fillmore and pulled over next to Jarnagin Outfitters, where the caravan of four trucks they'd passed at Kirby Creek was parked. Now the cannons and limbers were lashed on lowboys and the rain thrashed on the barrels like bronze fire. Beeman rolled down the window and called to one of the men hunkered, drinking coffee, under an overhang on a loading dock. "Hey Loren, when you guys going out to Shiloh?"

A man jerked his thumb upward. "Got me. This mess isn't suppose to let up till tomorrow afternoon."

Beeman nodded, rolled up the window, and worked the rainy streets, turning up Fulton and pulling into the parking lot next to a sprawling one-story building in tired-or-ange brick, with ALCORN COUNTY SHERIFF'S DEPARTMENT spelled in dull silver letters on the front. They parked, jumped out, jogged through the rain, and went in the front door.

A queue of people with paperwork crowded a doorway to the left under a sign that read DRIVER'S LICENSE EXAMINATION ROOM. "Wanted" posters papered a bulletin board. The dank interior of the building was cluttered with boxes and equipment and the walls were the color of fatigue and old nicotine. A wiry, bearded cop with military sidewalls above his ears and a shoulder holster showing through a blue track-suit jacket stood at a counter next to the dispatch station just to the right of the door. "Go on in. He's waiting for you," the cop said to Beeman, who was fluffing the rain from his hair.

"This way," Beeman motioned. Rane followed him past the counter as a tall, mustachioed, ruddy man in a Western shirt and belt leaned out of an office ahead on the left. "Hmmm," the sheriff said noncommittally, seeing Rane. He raised a hand and gave his modest Wyatt Earp mustache a twirl.

Beeman pointed to a chair along the wall. "I won't be long." As Beeman disappeared into the office, Rane noticed something suspended over the desk. Then the door closed. Rane took a seat.

The cop in the track suit ambled by, paused, and looked him over.

"What?" Rane said.

"You the one from Minnesota who's following Bee around?"

"Yeah."

"The photographer who doesn't take pictures?"

Rane did not respond. After a moment he cocked his head. "Got a question for you."

"Shoot."

"What's that hanging in the office over the sheriff's desk?"

"Splinter of the True Cross. That's a Buford Pusser Ax

Handle Sheriff of the Year award. Western Tennessee down into northern Mississippi, we're forested with 'em."

"Thank you," Rane said.

"Any time." The cop lowered his eyes, then raised them and said, "And you watch yourself. Minnesota and Bee ain't exactly been a winning combination lately."

In five minutes, Beeman exited the office, holding some sheets of paper in his hand. Not looking real happy, he walked past Rane with a curt wave of his hand. Rane got up and followed him down a corridor into the heat of a crowded kitchen, where they squeezed past two prisoners in baggy green-striped jail clothes, who toiled over a large pan of macaroni on a greasy, industrial-size gas stove.

"So what happened? You tell him about Billie?" Rane asked.

Beeman ignored Rane's question and muttered, "The sheriff of Hardin County, Tennessee, happened, that's what."

Investigations was located past Narcotics at the end of the cluttered hall. Going in, Rane perused an office that looked like an equipment dump.

"We need a new jail; space is cramped," Beeman grumbled. "Got the jail and the sheriff's office lumped together." He plopped into his chair and stated in a mincing, "in quotes" tone: " 'We can't let the five-year-olds run the day care can we?' Shit."

Then Beeman handed one of the papers in his hand to Rane. A color-printer picture of a handsome man with dark, curly hair and a salesman's smile. "That's him."

"So this is Mitchell Lee," Rane said, holding up the picture. "Nice smile." He covered one side of the face with his hand, then the other.

"What's that for?"

"Sometimes lets you see something. Eyes don't lie like a smile. Like, the left half-face is normal. But . . ." he covered the left side again, "the right kind of snarls, see? How the eye glitters?"

"Parlor games, John? I told you. He's not crazy," Beeman said.

"You sure about that after what Marcy and Billie said?"

"No, I ain't," Beeman said.

Rane put the picture aside and perused four diplomas on the wall; three from law enforcement courses and a bachelor of arts from the University of Mississippi. Rane pointed at it. "What'd you major in?"

"History and English; two guaranteed nonstarters. Four years on scholarship right out of high school," Beeman said in a dismissive tone.

"Athletic?"

"Academic." Beeman sat down at his computer, clicked the mouse, and, after a moment, read from the screen. "Latest e-mail: 'Beeman you skunc now your goin to get yers.' Dummy spelled skunk 's-k-u-n-c.'"

"What about the Tennessee sheriff?" Rane asked.

"Shiloh's in Hardin County and their sheriff is running security at the event, providing extra deputies and a SWAT team on site. Oh, he takes the threats seriously—up to a point. So he still wants me to play staked goat and all. But now he's decided that I won't carry any weapons on the battlefield. He doesn't want to do anything to encourage the popular excitement that Mitchell Lee and I are going to fight some damn duel."

"So?" Rane asked.

"So I been disarmed," Beeman glowered. "All I carry is a radio and a play Enfield. Saturday I hang out at the Confederate camp at Hurlbut Field. Sunday morning I'm with the Union guys over by the History Center at the river landing." Beeman sagged back in his chair.

"What about me? Can I bring my reenactor gear and camera?" Rane asked.

"Don't see why not. We gotta dress the part." Beeman abruptly stood up and looked out his office window. "Well shit. Gonna rain all night and most of tomorrow so we might as well kick back tonight and take it easy."

Beeman's cell phone rang.

He answered and said, "Hey, Danny. Yeah . . ." drawing it out as he looked up at Rane and raised an eyebrow. "Got him standing right here in my office."

Rane looked up, his face instantly questioning. Beeman warned him off with an upraised hand, intent on listening to his conversation. Rane twisted in limbo for almost two minutes.

"Thank you Danny very much, I owe you one," Beeman said, ending the call. He got up and perused Rane. "Gets curiouser and curiouser. That was Danny Landry, investigator at the State Crime Bureau in Jackson . . ."

"And?" Rane asked.

"Tell you a little later," Beeman said. "Right now we got some shopping to do. Don't know about you but I sure could use a drink. Whattaya say?"

51

"EVERCLEAR GRAIN ALCOHOL?"
Rane wondered. "That shit's illegal in Minnesota."

They'd stopped at a grocery, a hardware, and a pizza place, and then proceeded to Beeman's house. The Mustang tailing them peeled off at the driveway. Outside it was raining like hell. Inside, Beeman was munching on a wedge of sausage-and-cheese pizza and opening cans of lemonade and pouring them into a wide-mouthed Igloo water jug on his kitchen counter. So far he'd dumped in a generous slug of the Everclear, a bottle of vodka, and three oranges—carefully hand-torn and squeezed, peels and all.

"Avert your eyes," Beeman admonished with mock severity. "This is a closely guarded secret recipe that evolved in my uncle Hutch's hunting camp up the Tenn Tom Waterway." He dumped in some ice cubes, tipped the container under the tap, and ran in some water.

"But Everclear?" Rane repeated, staring at the bottle on the counter. "My uncle used that stuff to soak his pipes to remove tobacco tar?"

"Negative," Beeman said, picking up the bottle and sloshing in another slug. "Tonight it's gonna serve as hundred-ninety proof *broomstick* remover. It's time we extracted that uptight Minnesota broomstick out from your ass, don't you think, John?"

Beeman placed the bottle back on the counter and pointed

to the jug's open neck. "Now put your hand in there and stir it around, redneck-style."

Rane tucked in his thumb, reached in his hand, and swished the cold concoction around. Then he withdrew his hand and licked his fingertips. "Smooth," he said.

Beeman winked. "Deceptively smooth. Ain't what it seems. Kinda like you, huh?" Then he screwed on the top and carried the bucket and two glasses out to the screened, covered porch at the end of the deck. They pulled up two lounge chairs, Beeman situated the jug on a low table between them, and depressed the spigot, then filled two glasses and handed one to Rane.

Rain misted in through the screens. A crooked trident of lightning illuminated Beeman's back acreage enough to reveal that several more dead catfish had floated belly-up in his poisoned fish pond. Rane took a strong pull on his glass and found it fruity and ominously easy on the throat. He pictured it going down like a depth charge, saw himself strapped to it, plummeting deeper into Beeman's world.

"Truth," Beeman said, raising his glass. "How the hell are you and me going to find the truth in all this, John?"

Rane shrugged. "You mean about Mitchell Lee? That's not my department. I leave the truth to my Nikon. Whatever else goes down, bottom line, the camera doesn't lie."

"Bullshit, that's a cop-out. Camera's just a machine feeds back what you point it at," Beeman said. "And I ain't talking about Mitchell Lee. I suspect that's going to work out in a way I'll never fully understand 'cause I ain't privy to the counsels of the people who run this town." Beeman pointed his corncob pipe. "What I'm getting at is you."

Rane blinked as a flush of sweat swelled his eyes. One-ninety proof on top of vodka. Jesus. He took another drink.

Beeman stuffed his pipe. Rane lit a Spirit. They refilled their glasses.

"Thing about you, Beeman," Rane said with a rambunctious edge as the Everclear stripped off the veneer of his control, "is you don't come right out and say a thing. Everything curves around indirect. Reminds me of Go, the Japanese . . ."

". . . Board game." Beeman nodded. "Ran into it in college. A game of encirclement, all these black and white stones wrapped tight all mixed up in a stranglehold around each other." He chuckled. "Bears a certain resemblance to the South . . ."

"I mean, you got something to say to me, goddamn it, say it," Rane challenged.

Beeman stroked his chin, sipped from his glass, and leaned back in his chair. "Thing that struck me weird about the game of Go is—something I read, in Mailer I think it was *The Naked and the Dead*. How the Japs invent this subtle strategy game at the same time they come up with the banzai charge . . ."

"Jesus, there you go," Rane muttered.

Beeman sat down his glass and scrubbed his knuckles into his frazzled hair. "See, my job, when they let me do it— which ain't often—is to solve what happened. So Paul gets killed and you show up . . .

"Then turns out when I called the new widow I wound up talking to you. Next I find out Edin raised your daughter. And you show up with his clothes and gear. So I got a press guy with a personal agenda. I ask Jenny Edin and she says you're all fucked up and are trying to be a father. Okay. Seeing's how you got hiding behind a camera somehow confused with real life, I think . . . this guy's turning this tragedy into a personal coming-out party . . ."

Beeman had turned out the kitchen lights, and the pockets of twilight rain shadow slowly spread out from his eyes.

"Get to it, Beeman," Rane said, leaning over and refilling his glass.

"When the Tennessee coppers ran you on NCIC you came up clean. But now we got your license and social security in the system. So I gave them to Landry in Jack-

son, asked him to call up North and ask around about you
with his sister agency, the Minnesota Bureau of Criminal
Apprehension." Beeman pitched forward in his chair and
wagged his finger. "He hears back that the FBI visited you
in 2002, during the DC sniper shootings. They were combing through military records checking on sniper-qualified
personnel who had anything unusual flagged in their records . . ."

"Oh give me a break . . ." Rane mumbled, his voice
weary.

Beeman inclined his head. "When you were listing all
those schools you went to you left one out. Appears the army
sent you to the Marine Scout Sniper School and you completed the course."

"C'mon, Beeman, it was just another school I covered.
Doing background. I went back and shot a photo spread.
I explained to the Feds that a couple of instructors at the
school resented me taking up valuable training time on a
photo lark and entered their opinions in my records. Check
that with your guy in Jackson. It ended there."

"I doubt it," Beeman said.

Rane thought of the pierced quarter, his graduation key
fob from the police sniper school at Camp Ripley, sitting in
his wallet between the credit cards. Probably only a matter
of time before Beeman ferreted out the reason he'd quit the
St. Paul cops.

But then Beeman lurched in his chair when a monkish
shadow in a rain poncho crossed the patio. He'd pulled out
the SIG as the figure stamped up the deck steps. "Who's
that?" Beeman called out.

"Jesus, Bee, sounds like you're half in the bag," said the
hooded man, opening the screen door and throwing back
his rain hood. Rane recognized the bearded, sidewalled cop
from the sheriff's office. "We got Marcy Leets out front, and
she ain't driving that white Caddy. Got this old rattle-trap
Honda. She wants to talk to you."

Beeman rolled his eyes and laughed. "What the hell, long as she ain't armed." He didn't try to hide the slur in his drawl.

The cop grunted and batted his eyes. "I'll strip-search her if you like. Expect all I'll find is fifty caliber tits, slightly banged up, and a depleted-uranium jelly roll."

"Send her in," Beeman said as he returned his pistol to his holster with difficulty, missing the first time.

Rane tipped his glass and took another drink; rolling with it, loose as dice, on a rainy night in Mississippi.

MARCY LEETS DROVE UP THE DRIVEWAY AND GOT out of a battered Honda Civic, wearing a well-cut raincoat. She trudged stiffly up the steps, came onto the porch, and tipped her head carefully to shake raindrops from her hair. A square of taped gauze covered her puffy cheek.

"I hate this fuckin' thing," she said by way of hello.

Beeman held up his glass. "We're drinking tonight. You want some?"

"I took a Percocet," Marcy said. "I shouldn't even be driving."

"Where's the Escalade?" Beeman asked.

"It attracts the eye, so I got one of Darl's junkers," she said, craning her neck toward the kitchen sliding door, trying to look into the darkened house. "So this is where you live, huh?" Then she turned and felt her pockets. "I'll take a smoke if you have one. Left mine in the car."

Rane shook out a Spirit, which Marcy accepted, along with a light.

"He's still here?" she said, waving the cigarette at Rane.

"Can't be helped. Don't trust him out of my sight," Beeman said.

"Well, he makes me nervous. Gotta be the quietest man I ever seen . . ."

Beeman shrugged. "We're joined at the hip for the duration."

"I can dig it." She raised a hand and tentatively touched her bandaged cheek. "Me? I got a crazy fucker calling me up."

"Really," Beeman said, "all I get is text messages."

"He apologized," Marcy said.

"That was sweet," Beeman said.

"Pretty-boy asshole never could handle his liquor," Marcy said with an edge of fatal boredom. Rane watched rain shadows mate with the dark bruises on her throat as she puffed nervously on the cigarette. "He's sorry and wants me to run off with him. Then he's enraged and he swears he's going to kill you if you show your face at Shiloh, like he's getting off on all the talk . . . out in the woods playing Rambo or some damn thing. He's not stable, Bee."

"Call you on your cell phone?" Beeman asked. She nodded. "Let me see," he said.

She dug the phone out of her pocket and handed it over. Beeman took out his cell and thumbed them side by side, the panel lights playing on his face. He glanced at Rane. "Numbers match." Then he turned to Marcy. "Don't suppose you got him on voice mail?"

She shook her head.

Beeman handed the phone back and said, "I talked to Billie Watts."

"We all heard," she said, eyes darting at the rain. "You ain't wearing a recording device, are you?"

Her comment struck Beeman as hilarious and he laughed out loud.

"It's not funny. Dwayne especially is not happy. He came right in the hospital this morning when they let me out and asked me how to arrange a meet with Mitchell Lee, afraid he's going to run his mouth in the fucked-up state he's in. Wants to talk him down out of his tree and tuck him away. Maybe permanently." She shuddered convincingly. "I'm caught in the middle and this shit's getting too crazy. I want a deal, Bee."

She was good. The scared was real. Rane couldn't tell if she was lying or not.

"Why don't you sit down, Marcy," Beeman said softly, pointing his glass at the third chair on the porch. Marcy sighed and nodded, then lowered herself to the chair.

Beeman opened his hands in a "whattaya got?" gesture.

"Let's say I heard some things," she said cautiously. "Pillow-talk things . . ." Her eyes tipped up with a plea. "Hearing a thing and wanting a thing ain't the same. The law understands that, right, Bee?"

"You cooperate, and it pans out, you'll be a protected confidential informant. You got my word," Beeman said.

"Darl got dragged into the margins of this thing and I want him clear if I cooperate. Agreed?" She shot Beeman a hard, bargaining look.

Beeman nodded.

"Okay," Marcy said. "You heard how Dwayne is putting together a construction outfit? And you know that big developer bunch in Nashville who paid for the monument? Well, that statue Mitchell Lee built for Hiram Kirby is a Trojan Horse full of condominiums . . ."

"Hmmm," Beeman mulled, sitting up straighter now, setting his glass aside.

"He's got this plan to develop Kirby Creek, after old Hiram dies. They got it on paper. They done studies. Civil War–themed condos on the lake, named after generals. Put in tennis courts and little jogging paths through the battlefield and such." She paused, stared at the smoke curling up from her cigarette.

Beeman flopped back in his chair and exhaled, "The battlefield . . ."

"Billie told you about the will business I suppose?" Marcy asked.

Beeman blinked and leaned forward. "Get down to it, Marcy."

"Tried to talk them out of it," Marcy said frankly. "They wouldn't listen to me."

"Less wallpaper, Marcy, more cooperation. I can run you downtown as a material witness and you'll be wearing striped pajamas in county," Beeman prompted.

"Well, his scrawny wife wouldn't hear of it, anything to do with coming in and disturbing that ground, what with the unmarked graves and all . . . so Dwayne and Mitchell Lee were going to get rid of her when Hiram dies; run her down on the road when she's out training for her marathon."

"Another accident. Like me getting shot at Kirby Creek," Beeman said. Rane could almost hear his eyes clicking in the dark.

"Too many players. Too many moving parts. I told them it wouldn't work. And it didn't," Marcy said in a cool, practical voice.

"Goddamn it, stop beating around," Beeman demanded.

Marcy raised her wide, blue eyes and they glistened through the bruises and bandages. "I can give you Mitchell Lee," she said.

"How?"

"Tell you where and when he's going to hook up with Dwayne. They're using me as the go-between."

"How about telling me where he is now?" Beeman asked.

"I won't know that until it happens. And don't go putting a tail on me. Just be extra work to lose them."

"Shit," Beeman said.

"Look, I got a feeling he's camping out at Shiloh. But I ain't sure. And I can't promise he won't still be gunning for you. So, you going to be out there tomorrow?"

Beeman nodded. "I'll be at the Confederate camp at Hurlbut Field tomorrow afternoon and spend the night. On Sunday morning you can find me with the blue-suiters, over by the History Center."

"We got a deal, Bee?"

"We got a deal," Beeman said.

"Okay. Keep your cell phone charged," Marcy said, standing up. "I'll be in touch."

"YOU BELIEVE HER?" RANE ASKED AFTER MARCY left.

"Nope," Beeman said, head inclined, studying the bottom of his glass. "Don't believe you either with your camera you never use."

"Sounds like a trap," Rane said.

"Definitely a trap," Beeman pondered. "Question is, for who?" He set his glass aside, stood up, crossed the deck, looked out through the screens, and said softly, "How do I explain to my sons the kind of mind that poisons fish?"

"You going to tell the Tennessee cops about talking with Marcy?" Rane asked.

"Not sure yet."

Rane gave a soundless laugh. "Afraid they'll rob you of your moment?"

"That was uncharitable, John," Beeman said heavily as he returned to his chair, flopped down, and signaled for Rane's glass. After he filled it and topped off his own, he raised his glass in a toast: "To all the invisible shit."

They clinked glasses and took a drink.

Beeman shook his head and waved his glass at the darkness. "What I got in front of me is all this invisible shit. You look out there all you see is rain and dark. Me? I see these ruins, like arches of Roman aqueducts marching across the countryside. Spend your whole life looking at the ruins and trying to make 'em come out right. Well, it wouldn't be a complete set of ruins without catacombs. And that's where we are, John; down in the catacombs of Corinth. The living and the dead are all present."

Rane expelled a breath. "You lost me. 'Course I'm at

a disadvantage. I didn't learn English and history at Ole Miss."

Beeman blinked and cleared his throat. "It continues to amaze me how a shallow Yankee puke like yourself picks up on all the details."

"Like, ah, the wedding ring right in there on the kitchen table?"

Beeman looked away, so Rane stayed silent for a moment. Then he said, "We've come up short on details to go on. All you have is fragments, from a freaked cokehead lawyer and a scared cheating wife."

"And a couple text messages, a blown mailbox, a picture window, and some dead catfish," Beeman mumbled. *"Now,"* he said with more energy, "if I was one of those detectives in the books down in the den I'd have this figured out. Guess I just ain't haunted enough." He giggled, raised a hand, and fiddled at thin air. "They see the sunlight strike the fuckin' trees a certain way and they start free-associating about their drinking demons, flashbacks to some heavy shit in Korea or Vietnam and dozens of gorgeous women they screwed. But it ain't like that." Beeman slowly shook his head back and forth. "Half the time I think we see about one-tenth of what's in front of us. And most times, when we scrutinize the tenth we do see, we smear it up with our fingerprints . . ."

Rane laughed out loud. "I've taken pictures of some of the guys who write those books. The scariest thing most of them ever survived is a tense faculty meeting in a college English department."

Beeman leaned over and slapped Rane on the knee. "Damn, you just laughed for the first time. That's progress." He stayed pitched forward, masked in shadow. "The quietest man I ever seen," he said under his breath. "What about you? You got any demons stirring around in all that quiet?"

Rane gently reached over, removed the glass from Beeman's hand, and set it on the table. "You're shut off, partner. You're working tomorrow."

"C'mon," Beeman persisted, "any demons explain why you're down here, with me, in the fuckin' dark?"

"No demons, some pictures I've taken, maybe," Rane said, feeling light with alcohol, "a veil . . ."

Beeman pushed up to his feet. "So what'd ya see through your veil? You're the professional peeper."

Rane floated a hand loosely through the air. "Could be you're right, somebody's manipulating you toward an outcome."

"Redneck's birthright is to be manipulated," Beeman said with deliberation. "It's getting trickier. Used to be simple. They'd get us to look down on the niggers to divert our attention from the shit wages they pay us." He raised a hand apologetically and spoke to the darkness, "Sorry, Paul, I know, shouldn't say that." He turned to Rane, perplexed, "but they was 'niggers' for three hundred years, only been 'black' since . . ."

Beeman hitched up his belt, fingered his deputy's badge, and peered back into the night. "I don't mean it like my daddy did."

"Only comes out one way," Rane said.

Beeman shook his head. "Daddy's generation of lawmen meant hang 'em, burn 'em, blow up their kids in church . . ."

Rane let it go, exhaled, and sagged in his chair. "We're going to be a fine pair tomorrow . . . hungover and looking for an iceberg that's nine-tenths submerged."

Beeman turned, smiled, and asked: "Where your people come from?"

Rane shrugged. "Father was German, mother Norwegian."

Beeman grinned. "That's your Norwegian ancestors talking, John. Iceberg's a winter image. Submerged? Repression ain't our style. We tend to be outgoing, to include acting out violently. It's the hot climate and all the Celtic hooha about honor, chivalry, and blood debts. All that shit's still twitching . . ."

"To poisonous snakes that hold their ground," Rane said, raising his glass.

"Amen. And chase you out of pure meanness," Beeman said.

52

KEEP BUSY.

Jenny's house resembled a beehive hung in black crepe. Neighbors and acquaintances buzzed in, bringing pies, brownies, and cakes, which stacked the kitchen counters for the visitation after tomorrow's service. An aura of cloistered intimacy swirled around them. Damp-eyed, they hugged her and kissed her and squeezed her arm. Jenny thought of a power failure, when people huddle with candles, except behind her visitors' sincerity she detected a discreet assurance that, for them, the power hadn't really gone out.

Patti Halvorsen called to verify Jenny was on track. Jenny assured her she was.

Bluff Vicky had assumed the function of Il Duce, making sure the funeral trains ran on schedule. Mom took a supporting role, overseeing questions pertaining to food and dress.

Miss Vanni, Molly's piano teacher, whom Paul had helped, two years previously, with a tangled insurance dilemma involving her house, donated her time to help Molly master the bridging of the "Moonlight Sonata." She would sit beside Molly tomorrow at the service and carry her through the difficult piece. They were in the alcove now, practicing.

At a quarter to one, Jenny approached Vicky, who sat at the kitchen table, going over a detailed checklist on a legal pad. She had charted out the family activities up to the service at eleven a.m. tomorrow morning. Midway down the list, she'd entered a scheduled item: *Jenny, three hours personal time—1:30 p.m. to 4:30 p.m.*

Jenny pulled on her coat, picked up her car keys, and signed out with her sister. As Jenny went out the door, Vicky bore down with her pen.

Check.

She drove east on Highway 36 to the Bayport turnoff, where she curved around the brick-and-chain-link baffles of the sprawling state prison. Then she turned onto 95 and slowed to thirty-five miles an hour as she entered Bayport and passed Andersen Windows and the winking tower of the King Stack. She continued south along the river to the entrance ramp for eastbound I-94. Past Hudson, she checked her directions on the seat next to her. The Mail Lake turnoff was fourteen miles ahead.

She wore a tidy white cotton blouse and clean jeans with the creases showing on her thighs. No lipstick, no mascara, no jewelry. Her face was set in a practical mask.

To get to sleep last night she'd struggled past an image from Ridley Scott's opulent movie *Kingdom of Heaven*, which she had seen with Paul. The king of Jerusalem wore a fixed silver mask to conceal his leprosy-ravaged face. What would happen if the mask dropped and Molly learned the deception in which Jenny, Paul, and Rane were complicit?

She had fallen off to sleep huddled against Molly, counting her shallow breaths.

Jenny blinked and realized cars were whipping around her. One driver threw her a stare as he went by. She had let her speed slip to forty-five and everyone was going damn near seventy.

Her eyes slits of concentration, she turned off on the designated exit, negotiated the turns until she crept along an unpaved road looking for a red fire number sign. She found it, stopped, backed up, and turned down a winding gravel driveway. She passed a tree with a yellow sign posted: NO HUNTING. NO TRESPASSING.

Karen Morse stood on the porch, trim and iron-gray, in comfortable denim and a green flannel shirt. The balanced strength and wit in her eyes reminded Jenny of Patti. As the red Forester crunched to a halt, she came down the steps with her hands extended.

"It's been a long time," Karen said. Jenny didn't think either of them had planned to hug, but they did. "This way," Karen said with moist eyes, "Mike's on the back deck."

As they started through the house, Jenny paused and said, "I remember the piano and the photograph of Rane's parents."

Karen smiled. "I believe John still plays."

Then Jenny followed Karen out a sliding patio door to the back deck, and a man of medium height, with all his gray hair, stood up slowly, favoring his knees. Still broad-shouldered, he had an aspect of ruggedness collapsing inward. He extended a leathery hand.

"Jenny, I'm Mike. It's been a while." They shook hands. He opened one creased palm and indicated a chair. "Please sit down."

"Can I get you coffee?" Karen asked as Jenny sat down.

"Yes, please. Black," Jenny said. As Karen went back in the house, Jenny turned to Mike. "I don't have a lot of time, so I have to be blunt."

Mike cleared his throat, and his lined face remained calm, but his clouded gray eyes tightened. He raised one hand and opened the fingers expectantly.

"Until last Saturday afternoon I hadn't spoken to John face-to-face for eleven years."

There were blind spots in the gray eyes that explored her face. "We only know a little about one side of that. Go on," he said.

"What has he told you about me?"

"Not much. That you had a daughter and you got married." He shrugged but his occluded eyes stayed tight on her face and felt cold on her skin.

Jenny drew herself up and turned her head slightly as the flare in her eyes got away from her. "And about *my husband*?"

"Johnny was tight-lipped about it. Don't even know his name. Your married name, I mean," Mike said deliberately, still meaning to be polite, helpful.

Karen appeared, holding a ceramic mug. Seeing her husband's expression, she asked, "Is anything wrong?"

Mike's hand sliced up, a crisp gesture to silence his wife.

"My husband's name was Paul Edin," Jenny said. "He was killed in Mississippi, at a Civil War reenactment battle last Saturday. His funeral is tomorrow morning."

"Shit," Mike muttered, pitching forward in the chair.

From the corner of her eye, Jenny saw Karen react to her husband's abrupt movement. Her hand shook, she spilled steaming coffee on her wrist, sagged, and carefully placed the cup on the porch rail.

"Karen," Mike said immediately, calmly, forcefully, "kindly bring me the phone and Johnny's cell number."

As Karen hurried back into the house, Mike scoured Jenny's face with the hard, cold spots in his eyes. "I guess we both have to be blunt. Do you know where he is?"

"He went to Mississippi. He took my husband's Civil War uniform. There's a cop down there, a Deputy Beeman, who thinks Paul was killed by a sniper who shot at him and hit Paul. He suspects the sniper might try again, this weekend at another Civil War event. Rane's hanging out with the cop. So it's a story . . ."

Karen returned with the phone and a slip of paper. Dots of sweat appeared on Mike's forehead as he pushed in the number then waited long enough that Jenny knew the signal had gone to voice mail.

"Johnny, this is Mike. Whatever you got in mind you stand down. You lied to me, Johnny. And you took my rifle. You better call me pretty damn quick."

When he lowered the cordless phone, Jenny noticed the

liver spots on the loose skin on the backs of his rugged hands, and that his hands were shaking ever so slightly. He let the phone drop into his lap and stared out into the middle distance over the placid lake.

"Mike, what is it," Karen's voice caught.

"I didn't just give him the damn Sharps, Karen. I gave him match-grade ammunition for it. I took him out to the range and let him snap in. Remember, years back, when I was in that North-South Skirmish Association? We shot at targets on teams? He told me he was researching the Skirmish for one of his projects . . . he didn't say anything about *this*."

He swung his head, and when Jenny saw his eyes, the cold fix had broken and now they were tense with concern. "You have a way of contacting that cop?" he asked.

Jenny nodded and realized she was hugging her arms to her chest.

"Then you better call him," Mike said.

"Why?"

"Because Johnny's natural talent for taking pictures makes him one of the best snap shots with a rifle I ever saw under three hundred yards, and I've seen them all," Mike said, leaning forward.

"What do you mean?"

"I mean this is not an academic question, Jenny. In Iraq, in ninety-one, he started out to take pictures and wound up in a fix. You might have noticed he's been on the remote side ever since."

Jenny's fingers cupped her throat. Felt the vulnerable pulse quicken. "What kind of fix?" she asked.

"The kind where he had to kill a bunch of people."

53 RANE WOKE UP FUZZY-MOUTHED, with a head that throbbed every time a raindrop splashed on the patio stones outside the basement door. The bedside digital clock read 10:30. They'd slept in. He stood up, jockeyed for balance, and inspected his trembling right hand.

A hot shower knocked the top hackles off the hangover. He wrapped a towel around his waist, climbed the stairs, and found Beeman, hair disheveled, wearing only undershorts, sorting through a pile of Confederate and Union wool uniforms on the living room couch.

Hydrate. Rane opened the refrigerator, found a bottle of spring water, and drank the whole thing. Then he poured a cup of coffee from the pot on the counter and saw the bottle next to the pot, so he tossed down two aspirin with his first swallow of black coffee.

"How's your head?" Beeman grumbled.

"It's been better. What are we doing?"

"We got to dress both ways: gray today, blue tomorrow."

Rane took a second pull on the coffee and studied the dull sparkle of the wedding ring, still on the kitchen table. He walked into the living room and pointed to the old scar that trailed over Beeman's ribs. "What happened there?" he asked.

"Fella with a knife in the Waffle House parking lot, up on 72; long time ago," Beeman said.

"And there?" Rane said, turning and pointing at the wedding ring on the table.

"You know, John," Beeman said evenly, "we got to get ready."

"And you know, *Kenny*," Rane said just as evenly, "we've been hanging out for two days and I haven't seen you on the phone to your wife and kids."

Obstinately, Beeman ignored the question and picked up three small drawstring cotton bags. "These go in your pack. Shake a leg, it's time to bring up your gear."

Rane backed off, for now; but as he descended the stairs he wondered why Marcy, Sheba, even the Kirby woman, all cranked a little extra torque into their conversation around Beeman. Maybe he was reading too much in; maybe Southern women just naturally showed more tail feathers.

More important things to do, John. He shut the bedroom door and unplugged his cell from the wall charger. He listened to make sure Beeman was still upstairs and then removed a sandwich-size Ziploc from the bottom of his duffel bag. The baggie contained ten rounds of live ammunition for the Sharps, wrapped in a paper packet. He opened the baggie, undid the packet so the rounds were loose and easier to get to. He removed the notebook, the light meter, and the spare wool socks from the leather ammunition bag and set them aside. Then he unsealed the pack of baby wipes, took most of them out, inserted the baggie, and stuffed the wipes back in on top. After he resealed the baby wipes, he put them back in the cartridge box and shoved the light meter and socks on top.

He pulled on the itchy blue trousers, the rumpled flannel shirt, and buttoned the suspenders. Then he put on the wool socks, slipped on the leather brogans, and laced them up. The hobnails skittered on the linoleum floor as he hoisted the duffel and walked to the stairs, where he paused to get centered.

Didn't work. Blinking, he held up his right hand and watched it tremble. The hangover had sandblasted the edge off his reflexes, blurred his vision, and ignited a parched thirst in his chest.

Okay, what did you expect? If you're going to walk a mile in Paul's shoes, you can't have it both ways. No protective gimmicks would accompany him to Shiloh.

He joined Beeman in the living room and dropped the duffel.

"Okay, this is not a battle we're going to. Gray and blue will be apart. No lining up and shooting at each other; they'll put on demonstrations in the separate camps. What you call a Living History."

Rane nodded. Like Dalton explained back home.

Beeman, on the surly side himself, sorted Rane's tangle of leather belts, straps, and pouches and put them on the couch. "Okay, blue pants and the shirt is fine and the shoes. Keep the sack coat and hat for tomorrow. Take off the belt buckle."

"What for?"

"Turn the U.S. insignia upside down, that way it's acceptable fashion in the Reb camp. Do the same with the badge on the cartridge box. Tomorrow you can switch them back."

When Rane had made the adjustments, Beeman handed him a gray sack coat and cap. Rane put on the jacket and flexed his arms to make sure he could move freely.

Breakfast was spring water and leftover pizza at the kitchen table with the wedding ring marooned, unmentioned, between them. Beeman talked on his cell to the Tennessee cops.

"I'll meet you on 22 where it crosses from McNairy into Hardin County. I'm leaving my cruiser at home. Look for a red Jeep with Minnesota plates. I'll just bring my personal weapon which I will hand over when we meet. So all I'll have is a radio. That suit you? Okay. Say about one?"

Rane had emptied his haversack and was checking out his camera and lens. He looked up.

"You got film in that thing?" Beeman asked.

"Digital."

"Right. Where's your rifle?"

"In the Jeep."

"We have some time. You want to clean it up?"

Rane flipped his hand in an "irrelevant" gesture. "What for? It's just going to get wet."

"Jesus," Beeman shook his head, "okay, fill your canteen and let's square away your pack, blanket, and poncho. You'll need the overcoat tonight."

They carried all the gear to the Jeep and as they loaded it, Beeman perused the big pack of water bottles in the back. "One thing for sure: we ain't gonna run out of water."

Tennessee Highway 22 cut a shiny black ribbon through curtains of rain. The fog hugged the budding thickets and it was a good day to stay indoors. Rane said, "This isn't working out the way you thought."

"Nope. I was planning on slinging that M16 under my greatcoat," Beeman said. "Now I'm going in naked. Fucker could be out there with a scoped deer gun."

Rane said, "My uncle Mike was in Vietnam. He used to say the map is not the terrain."

"Ain't that the truth. No plan survives first contact with the enemy," Beeman said. Then he turned, with a less-than-copacetic smile. "About the ring?"

"Yeah?"

"Last Sunday when all this started to look like a grudge bout between me and Mitchell Lee my wife gave me a choice: I go to Tupelo with her and the kids or else. I told her I had to see this through."

A couple miles went by in silence. Then Beeman ruminated, "They had rain, just like us. The roads were just tracks through the woods and soon they were churned to slop. Forty thousand men marched from Corinth. Albert Sidney Johnson figured he'd surprise Grant at Pittsburg Landing. Most of them were rookies; it took them three days strung out in the mud. We'll do it in half an hour."

Rane sat behind the wheel, staring straight ahead

through the slap of the windshield wipers, intent on the road.

"One thing I regret is I didn't get to talk to Paul more." Beeman sighed. "Feel kind of bad, actually; I threw him this verbal elbow to back him off. Figured he was going to start right in with the Slavery Lecture . . ."

"Sure, I can see that," Rane said, not taking his eyes off the road. "If I had to make it come out right I'd put that way down on my list."

"Wasn't that simple," Beeman frowned.

"Right, have it your way. How about the reason your Rebs were marching in the mud is you guys fired on the American flag." Rane looked out at the rain-swept woods. "They should have stayed home. All Shiloh accomplished was create Grant and Sherman as a team."

"Jesus," Beeman breathed. "I liked it better when you didn't talk."

"That them, your cops?" Rane nodded to a police cruiser parked beside the road ahead.

"That's them."

One cop actually. A Hardin County deputy, who was a little pissed off, called in to work his day off. After introductions, they sat in the Tennessee cruiser; Beeman in front, Rane in the back. As Beeman handed over his pistol, the cop said, "Not my idea, Beeman. You ask me, this whole thing is a damn snipe hunt. Bunch of gossip outta Mississippi."

"Hope you're right, I really do," Beeman said.

"Okay. Here's the setup. We printed up fifty of these pictures Alcorn forwarded." He held up the picture of Mitchell Lee that Rane had memorized. "They've gone out, with a description of his truck, to our guys, the park rangers, and key folks participating in the event.

"You put your radio on our frequency," the cop said. "SWAT is in a tan Chevy van, they want to keep you in line of sight at all times. Try and work with them. Four of our people are wearing plain clothes, mixed in with the spectators, they'll shadow you. Then there'll be uniformed officers and park rangers on normal patrol. Anything pops, you go to ground and let us handle it."

"Lousy assignment," Beeman said.

"You got it. Crummy weather and muskets and cannons going off. Civilians wandering all over the place. All we can do is keep our eyes open and react. Smart move would be to call it off but since the Kirby Creek incident was ruled an accident, the Park Service bent to pressure and let it go on as scheduled."

Then they got out of the Tennessee car, returned to the Jeep, and followed the deputy.

They entered the park and drove slowly through patches of woods and open fields studded with dark granite markers and black rows of cannons. Event monitors wearing orange aprons waved them toward a parking area roped off with yellow tape. They pulled in next to the Tennessee cop, who parked alongside a light brown van. Three men and a woman in jeans and parkas huddled in the light rain, talking to the van's driver. One of the plainclothes cops carried a long bag on a strap over his shoulder. The canvas bag, designed to carry a folding chair, probably contained a short automatic weapon.

Rane stood back while Beeman met with the cops and discussed radio procedure. His eyes automatically scanned the surrounding area, which was a security nightmare. If a muzzleloader were to discharge at this instant in the nearest tree line, the telltale smoke would be lost in the fog.

Then his eyes drifted to a tiered monument directly across the road, where three robed, blackened figures hung their heads in a stylized pantomime of grief. This, Rane understood, was the Confederate Memorial. Beyond the statues, people gathered by a bivouac of white pup tents. A double line of men in gray had formed. They lifted their muskets. An audience of spectators applauded when they fired a volley in the air.

As the echo rolled along the trees, Rane opened the Jeep's passenger door, reached in the glove compartment, took out the crumpled fate card, and slipped it in his trouser pocket.

Beeman left the group by the van and returned to the Jeep. "C'mon, time to suit up," he said. They opened the rear hatch and pulled out their gear. "Second time I done this in a week," Beeman muttered as he helped Rane sling the cartridge box over his left shoulder, then cinched the belt with the cap box over it. Then Rane shouldered the pack and slung the haversack containing his camera over his right shoulder along with the canteen. Finally, he pulled the rusty rifle from the canvas sleeve. Beeman yanked the shapeless gray forage cap down over Rane's eyes, grabbed his own rifle, and handed Rane a folded Shiloh brochure. The park map on the back was marked with dotted arrows in ballpoint.

Beeman traced the map with his finger. "We'll skirt the Sunken Road, cross this big field, then the Hamburg-Purdy Road, walk between a Confederate burial trench and the Shiloh Church and wind up here." He indicated a faint blue curling line marked "Shiloh Branch."

They set off, Rane carrying his rusty rifle squirrel-hunter fashion over his shoulder. As they breasted the monument, he paused to study the three mournful statues. Head downcast, the Grecian-robed woman in the middle relinquished a victor's laurel crown to the hooded, deathlike specter on her right. Another hooded figure hovered on her left.

"Our Lost Cause Madonna," Beeman said without irony. "Victory Defeated by Death and Night."

They walked past the monument toward a broad field, falling in step, shoulder to shoulder. Beeman's eyes softened as he gazed across the battlefield, and he said, "When I was a kid my dad would bring me here to go fishing and he'd have me drag my fingers in the dirt. Back then it wasn't hard to find what we called Civil War lead, minié balls. We'd tie 'em to our fishing line as sinkers."

Their hobnails crunched on pavement, then muted as they walked onto the wet grass. The van slowly paced them on the road. The four undercover cops split in twos and strolled wide to either side, mingling with sightseers, who trailed across the fields in bright red, yellow, and blue rain jackets. Here and there kids dashed ahead of their parents. From the corner of his eye, Rane caught a man pointing Beeman out to his wife. The couple followed them at a distance.

Rane shivered in the drizzle and looked into the trees. Shiloh brooded back at him in gray and black.

Like dripping acid on a Civil War wet plate.

So this is what it feels like being out in the open, unprepared. This time someone else could be gauging the distance, measuring the angles, and picking the time.

Instinctively, he brought the Sharps off his shoulder and carried it slanted across his chest. Should have loaded it back at the parking lot. No time, too many people watching. He was calculating the time and motion of digging into the cartridge box and opening the baby wipes when Beeman asked, "What're you thinking, John?"

"If he's out there, watching," Rane answered.

Beeman asked, "How would you do it? You been to that school?"

Rane's eyes scoured the trees. "Just common sense. If he's not dumb, he'll wait for the show to begin; when stuff starts going off, use the racket and smoke for cover to get away."

Beeman nodded. "That'll be in about an hour when they have a demonstration on Hurlbut Field. Problem is, what if he ain't concerned with getting away . . ."

"Then it gets more difficult," Rane said.

"Exactly," Beeman said with a stiff smile, reaching out and tugging Rane's sleeve. "So stay tight on my elbow. No disrespect to Paul, but this Mitchell Lee has a habit of missing me and hitting Minnesota."

Brushing elbows in a gesture of gallows humor, they con-

tinued across the damp open field. Then they crossed a road
and threaded through tree lines and monuments and thickets
until they passed a small Methodist church with a smaller,
restored log cabin located to the left. They stopped on a
thickly wooded slope overlooking a brush-choked gully.

"You know what happened here, the first day?" Beeman
asked.

"Some," Rane said. "This is where Sherman had his camp
on the Union right. The Rebels marched out of the woods
across the valley . . ."

"Yep. Right down there," Beeman said, pointing to the
tangle below. "When the Rebs attacked, most of Cleburne's
Brigade got mired up in the marsh farther down the ravine.
Two regiments, the Sixth Mississippi and the Twenty-third
Tennessee, skirted the swamp, crossed the creek and come
up through here. Sherman's troops rallied after the first
shock, hunkered down on this ridge and put up a fight. The
Tennessee boys broke and ran. The Sixth Mississippi re-
formed and hit them again."

Hearing the husky undertone come into Beeman's voice,
Rane might be tempted, in different circumstances, to reach
for his camera. "Well," Beeman said, "the Sixth Mississippi
got wiped out on this slope, three hundred out of four hundred twenty-five men killed and wounded. My great-great-
granddad, Matthew Beeman, was one of the lucky ones who
walked away . . ."

Rane was thinking of the fixed stare on the face of the
young man in the picture on Beeman's fireplace, when his
cell phone jingled in his trouser pocket. The electronic
chimes struck a jarring counterpoint to the vision of Beeman
against the black trees, paying homage to his ancestor.

Rane took out the phone and felt a twinge when he saw
the number of the incoming call pop on the display. Uncle
Mike? He let it ring, twice, three times, four, and go to voice
mail. When he looked up, Beeman was watching him delete
the call.

"What is it, John? You okay?" Beeman asked.

"Sure," Rane waved vaguely and said, "So, the Sixth Mississippi got stuck in that briar patch?"

"Yeah, and other brigades got mixed in and it turned into this real clusterfuck."

They walked along the ridge and Beeman pointed back toward the church. Tongue-in-cheek, he said, "We almost lost Sherman over there. Now that woulda been a shame . . . especially for the folks in Georgia."

Then Beeman's cell phone rang. Rane concentrated on the raindrops that trickled down the pumpkin-colored steel barrel of the Sharps rifle as Beeman hunched to the phone, face intent. Rane thinking . . . maybe it's Marcy Leets . . .

Then no. Because he saw Beeman's expression soften.

The undercover cops were fifty yards away on either side. The van was barely in sight, screened by trees. Rane stared down at the gully full of brambles, where the Sixth Mississippi perished.

"Yes, ma'am," he heard Beeman say. Then Beeman's eyes narrowed with that slow, "no shit" amusement. He advanced, holding the phone to his ear, and his polite, controlled voice sounded like reverberating thunder: "Just a moment, Mrs. Edin."

Beeman lowered the phone, stepped up to Rane, and said in a firm voice, "Okay, John; you just relax. You get any ideas I'll have them in on you real quick." He nodded toward the nearby undercover cops. Then he lifted the Sharps from Rane's hands and slung it on his shoulder.

John Rane expelled a lungful of air and fingered the fate card in his pocket. The long-range gamble was coming apart. Iraq. Jenny. Now this. Shit comes in threes.

Turning back to the phone, Beeman said, "Mrs. Edin, I got to move around a little, see if I can get better reception. Just bear with me . . ."

54 AS SHE WAITED FOR DEPUTY BEEMAN to relocate, Jenny stared across the lake. There was a small bay to the right, and at the end of it she saw a mound of debris she thought might be a beaver dam. For one moment, the wind held its breath and the surface of the lake popped tight as a silver platter filled with pumice-colored clouds.

Beeman said, "Can you hear me better now?"

"I can hear you fine," Jenny said.

"Okay, you can relax, I got the rifle. I'll get the ammunition next."

"His uncle stressed the fact that what he did in the war was a long time ago. He doesn't even know the whole story . . ." She turned and looked up the yard at Mike and Karen standing on the deck. Mike had one hand over his wife's shoulder. She turned back toward the lake and said, "His uncle feels kind of bad, like a squealer."

"You did the right thing, Mrs. Edin. Tell his uncle not to worry. I'll take it from here."

"Where will you take it from here, Deputy Beeman?"

"Well," Beeman said slowly. "He came down here to take a picture. I'm going to hold him to that."

Jenny blinked at his answer. Wincing slightly, she asked, "But about the gun and bullets?"

"Mrs. Edin, Jenny, there's hundreds of men walking around with rifles and black powder. Bound to be a few live rounds here and there."

Jenny frowned. "But . . . is he . . . in trouble?"

"I don't have a lot of law to work with in a case like this and I'm currently out of my jurisdiction, in Tennessee. I could try and read him the riot act. But John, well, my impression is he don't scare easy."

"This is serious, Beeman. God knows what he's trying to prove but, goddamn it, it sounds like he went down there to *shoot* somebody, *and he knows how to do it*," Jenny said, her voice rising.

"Yes ma'am, and I'll talk to him real hard about that," Beeman said in a reasonable voice.

Jenny's voice trembled. "I don't know what's going on. And I have other things to attend to. But one thing I know is that I certainly don't approve, and my husband would not have approved, of some . . . crazy, *macho, vigilante bull-shit* . . ."

"Yes ma'am. And I respect that. Don't you worry, you got enough to deal with," Beeman assured her. "We'll get this straightened out and send John home directly."

After thanking Jenny for the heads-up and tendering a polite expression of sympathy, Beeman ended the call. Jenny turned and raised her hands in a befuddled gesture.

Mike called out, "What'd he say?"

"He said he'd send Rane home. He sounded . . . relieved."

55

MITCH WAS HAVING A BAD MOMENT. He'd bolted awake, the lamp was off, and it was pitch-black. Panting, he realized he'd been trying to hold his breath in his sleep to avoid the smell from the chamber pot. Huddled against the damp stone wall, hugging the blanket around him, he shivered and pawed to fend off the buzz and tickle of the flies.

Could live with it in the light. Not in the dark.

Like this since he fell down and cut his face. Demerol vibrations. The pills eased the pain of his aching cheek but brought bad dreams. Flashes of his earliest memory in that country shack; clinging to his decomposing mother out of fear of the dark.

Gonna stop taking the damn pills.

Then the overhead light switched on.

"Sorry Mitch, came unplugged." Blinking, Mitch saw LaSalle come down the passage and step through the choke point. "Assume the position. We're going up front. Somebody wants to talk to you."

Finally. Darkest before the dawn. Ellie was facing up to the mess she'd made.

Mitch sat straight-legged and put out his hands. LaSalle put on the cuffs. Then he removed the lock from the shackle.

"Outside," LaSalle said.

Ellender Kirby wore running shoes and a damp gray sweat suit with a small Ole Miss logo on the left breast and dark sweat stains on the chest and under the arms. Strain raccooned her eyes and drew her freckled cheeks tight. Her shoes were scummy with mud and bits of leaves, like she'd been running the trails in the woods. Mitch recognized the expression on her face. Something was bugging her and she had to go run it off.

Well I guess. Standing in the doorway of the shack, he watched rain billow across the lake. Gray fuckin' day.

She took a deep, preparatory breath, then pulled a cell phone—his cell phone, looked like—from her sweatshirt kangaroo pouch, turned it on, and stabbed the buttons.

"Here," she said with a mortified look on her face. She leaned over and placed the phone on the shed steps and backed away. He bent forward, picked it up, and put it to his ear just as . . .

Marcy!

"That you, Sport?" Marcy said in that low, screw-your-brains-out, bored voice.

"Marcy?" Mitch grinned. Relief like anointing oil, like his brain dumped about a quart of serotonin.

"Look. I only got a minute. Hang tight. We're gonna get you out. Your weird wife approached me and I talked to Dwayne. We're working on it. She's following our instructions so listen to what she has to say."

"What's going on?" Mitch bounced on his feet.

"One for the books. *She's* paying *us* to let you go."

"That's all," Ellie hissed. LaSalle grabbed the phone from Mitch's hand, ended the call, and turned it off. "Back inside," he said.

Mitch kept grinning as he noticed that ole LaSalle was working manfully to keep his face straight. Ellie was walking back and forth in the rain, down by the lake, with her arms clamped across her chest. Lips moving.

Damn.

The shackle now a minor bother, Mitch sat erect, cross-legged, shaggy and dirty as a barbarian chieftain holding court in his cave.

He lit a Marlboro, poured a cup of thermos coffee, and savored the minutes until Ellie dragged her ass in here for an audience. *Always had her daddy, her brother, and me to protect her from her impulsive decisions.*

What we got here, Ellender Jane, is a little more serious than blowing your monthly allowance on furniture in Memphis.

He cocked his head. Scuff scuff went her running shoes on the rocks and rubble and dirt. Head lowered, arms stiff at her side, Ellie walked down the passage, stopped, and raised her eyes; the poor little rich girl discovering what her tantrums can cost out in the real world.

Mitch stood up so he could look down on her, smiled, and asked, "You think I could get a razor and some hot water? A mirror?"

"Shut up, goddamn it," Ellie said, her jaw pulsing red like it was going to sprout gills.

Mitch waited, couldn't help smiling.

She folded her arms across her chest. "This whole thing has become impossible. I need to get you out of here. But you have to understand, Mitchell Lee. This is the last one of your messes I clean up. Killing that poor boy . . . ?"

"Prove it. You can't, can you? And you realized that. You and your brain-dead zombie had your fun and now the bill comes due and you're looking for a way out."

She drew herself up, indignant. "While my daddy is dying I have spent the week dealing with the scum of the earth." Her lips curled in disgust. ". . . setting up this . . . arrangement."

"I'm all ears, sweetheart."

"I had to deal with your slut." She balled her fists and took a combative step forward; seething now but careful to keep her toes on the safe side of the line. "Now I'm mixed up with your crooked cousin, Dwayne," she cut him with a sharp look. "That gets out . . ." She shook her head. "You have no idea what I've been through."

Mitch curved his lips in feigned sympathy—*right, bitch,*

and I been sunning myself here by the pool—but, you know, just maybe Marcy and Dwayne could untangle it. Sonofa-bitch.

"What's the arrangement?" he asked.

"Tomorrow morning LaSalle will turn you over to Dwayne. And we'll . . . just make all this go away."

"Uh-huh."

She glowered and cut him off, "Don't say *anything*. Just listen. We clear so far?"

Mitch bit his lip and nodded.

"Then Dwayne will take you back to Memphis where they'll concoct an alibi. Something. I suspect Billie Watts will be involved. That's not my concern."

Mitch accepted her dirty look. This was starting to sound like it could work. "You think this up?" he asked.

"I'm paying for it, is what I'm doing," she said in a fraz-zled voice.

Mitch nodded again. "And the rifle?"

Ellie raised her chin and sniffed. "Kenny Beeman's al-ready been by and I told him the rifle disappeared from the gun rack. LaSalle passed it off to Dwayne. I suspect it will turn up in the trunk of an abandoned car, along with other stolen items. The Minnesota guy's death will stay as is, an accident."

"What about Beeman?" Mitch asked, tapping his teeth together.

"What about him? Marcy says you'll work something out with Memphis PD. Turn yourself in, like all the gossip had you spooked. I don't know."

Mitch mulled it. The plan, the dream, the land. Shit, if Dwayne had his hooks in her, it could still work. Even better with her on board. She'd have to go along and maybe get to keep her funny little life. He shrugged, "It could work."

"I never want to see you again," she blurted.

"Oh, I don't know. Now that you're getting to know my family?"

"Don't even!" Her eyes flashed.

Mitch exhaled and nodded. "Okay. So where do I meet them in the morning?"

"Not around here, that's for sure. Someplace over the line in Tennessee. We're working that out," Ellie said.

As she turned to leave, Mitch couldn't resist calling out. "Ellie? Why'd you do this in the first place?"

She just kept walking, shouting, furious, over her shoulder. "You were in trouble. I was trying to help you, you dumb shit."

After she disappeared down the corridor, LaSalle returned with the rinsed chamber pot. As he placed it on the floor, he gave Mitch one of his cold smoke looks. "You get all the twisted white-folks shit straightened out?" he asked. Then he placed a fifth of Jack Daniels next to the chamber pot. "Little going-away party for you tonight. And here's two more Demerol." He set a folded napkin next to the bottle. "You go with the Jack, lay off the pills. They don't mix." Then he withdrew down the passage.

Mitch studied the bottle of bourbon as he plucked up the napkin, dumped the pills into his palm, weighed them, and glanced back at the bottle.

Then he folded the pills back in the napkin, stuffed it in his pocket, dragged his chain to the empty pot, undid his filthy wool trousers, and splashed urine on General Grant's scruffy face. As he buttoned up his pants, he caught his reflection flicker in the bottom of the pot. First look he'd had of himself in a week. Wincing, he jockeyed around to get a better view and fingered his week-old growth of beard, his unkempt hair. The idea of a hot shower . . .

Then, slowly, he ran his fingers over the square of gauze taped to his cheek. Looking at it got him thinking how his cheek hurt a hell of a lot more than falling on a flowerpot. So he dragged the pot closer to the overhead bulb and gingerly loosened the dressing and let it hang. Shifting around to get the best angle on the light, he knelt, waiting for his image to settle down in the lapping circle of piss. Slowly, his face came into focus and the four deep slashes on his cheek didn't look anything like a laceration caused by falling down.

What the hell? Did the crazy bitch claw on him when he was out? What was in the tetanus shot anyway?

Mitch replaced the bandage and methodically peeled the cap off the bourbon. He took one drink, relishing the hot trickle down his throat and warming through his chest. Then he poured most of the bottle into the chamber pot, recorked it, and placed it aside. If he drank too much Jack on top of the drugs he'd been taking, he'd be easy as a baby to handle in the morning. Best wait on the party, think this through. He lit a cigarette, poured another cup of coffee from the thermos, and sat back against the wall.

Marcy's voice on the phone was real.

But.

Were they getting tricky on him?

56

"BULLETS," BEEMAN SAID, HOLDING out his hand.

"What'd she say?" Rane asked, hunched against a rising wind.

"Touched on a number of things. Bullets," Beeman repeated.

Rane realized that Beeman wasn't calling in the undercovers; that this was still between the two of them. So he rummaged in his cartridge box, pulled out the pack of baby wipes, extracted the sealed baggie, and gave it to Beeman, who opened the wrapping, studied the packet, and then slipped it in his cartridge box. "Now tell me about this rifle. Why's it all rusty?" Beeman asked as he slipped the Sharps off his shoulder and held it in both hands.

"I sprayed it with water and left it in my flower bed before I left St. Paul."

"Lord. Will it fire?"

"I plugged the barrel and I greased the breech and hammer and protected the cone."

"And the tape on the sights?"

"Go ahead, peel it off." After Beeman removed the tape, Rane said, "Trick of the trade. See the white marks along the right side of the flip-up sight? You place the top of the open aperture on a normal man's head. If the first line falls on line with his eyes, he's a hundred yards. If the second line is level with the bottom of his chin it's two hundred. Third line across the bottom of his neck even with his shoulders it's three hundred."

Beeman flipped up the sights and scanned across the field, nodded, lowered the rifle.

"Now slide the catch back to free the lever," Rane said.

When Beeman freed the catch and cranked the lever, the block dropped and the breech opened smoothly. He inserted a finger and withdrew it, rubbing a light coat of graphite lubricant between thumb and forefinger. Then he dug around and eased one of the linen-wrapped bullets from his bag, turned it in his fingers, and felt the sharp, conical lead tip. He inserted the bullet and closed the lever.

Rane said, "It takes a regular percussion cap." After a moment, he added: "My uncle built that gun. I put about thirty rounds through it before I left home. The ramp sights are true. Hundred yards up to eight hundred."

"Slick," Beeman said. "I see a rusty rifle and I think, this is a dumb-ass city boy from up North who doesn't know squat about guns, huh?"

Rane shrugged.

"What about the camera, you shining me down the road there too?" Beeman asked.

"Camera's legit," Rane said, shifting from foot to foot.

Beeman grunted. "Well, you had me fooled on the rifle." Then he said softly, "Play to your opponent's prejudices. Something Sheba taught me. A smart black dude'll play that one to perfection against a redneck. Have the range on him every time."

"Something like that," Rane said as he looked around. "Okay, Beeman, now what?"

Beeman grinned and they locked eyes. "Now I'm *armed* is what. And you're gonna help me get the sonofabitch if he shows his face. What you came for, am I right?"

"Something like that," Rane said.

A raw wind came off the Tennessee River and whipped through the trees with enough force to scatter dead leaves

They removed their packs and leathers, unrolled their sky-blue greatcoats, and put them on. As they restrung their gear, Beeman handed Rane his Enfield and his bayonet, then shouldered the Sharps. With the caped collars of their coats turned up against the wind, they started walking back toward the parking lot.

Like a tiny school of sharks following prey, the undercovers and the van conformed to their movements.

"Would you have gone after him, given the opportunity?" Beeman asked.

"You asking as a cop or man to man?" Rane asked back.

Beeman sighed. "C'mon, John, we're both bending the rules right about now, don't you think?"

Rane stopped, turned, and looked directly at Beeman. "Yeah. I would have gone after him. If I got a fix on him and the conditions were right."

"You mean if no one was watching?"

"I had an idea. Not a plan. If I really had a plan would I be talking to you about it?"

"You come all this way?" Beeman asked.

"He shot a good man. He ruined a little girl's life."

"C'mon, John. Gotta be more," Beeman said. "Wearing Paul's shit. This habit you got about stepping into a role before you do a story?"

Rane withdrew the fate card from his pocket and handed it to Beeman, who studied it a moment, then handed it back.

"Man, that's creepy, 'specially here. Ain't gonna bring him back," Beeman said with slow appraisal.

"Might bring me back," Rane said softly.

He put the card into his pocket and turned away. The fields were emptying, as spectators and reenactors hurried toward the shelter of their tents and cars. Only the monuments and the bleak rows of black cannons stood fast. "Everybody who writes about this place describes it as special," he said finally.

Beeman rubbed his knuckles across the stubble on his

cheek, then blew on his hands to warm them. "I been to Gettysburg several times and it's sacred ground but it's kinda this marble sacred ground. Shiloh's out here all alone in the woods. Pretty much the way it was. Only two of the Confederates buried here were ever identified. And just a third of the Union dead. You spend the night here camped on the ground and listen long enough you get beyond sacred pretty quick into haunted. It was fierce, what happened here, John, the first modern battle . . ."

"You ever been shot at, Beeman?" Rane asked abruptly.

Beeman studied Rane's face in the pale storm light. "The truth? Couple piddly contacts going into Kuwait. Small arms, some mortars. And years back, Wally Hunter took a pop at me with a .32 as he was going out the back door of his house over south. Missed me by four feet and drilled a hole in a picture of Bobby Kennedy his mom had over the kitchen table. I had a twelve-gauge pump so I put a load of birdshot in his large black ass to slow him down."

"Didn't try to kill him?"

"Why would I do that? I known him since we were little kids clipping tamales off Rat Ferguson's cart down by the depot. Shit, we played ball against each other when he was at Easom High. Plus his wife and four children were hiding in the parlor. 'Course the reason I was there is he was beating on his woman. Friday-night drunk, was all."

"What about the Leets kid, the one you put in prison?"

"Donnie? He emptied a nine at me during the car chase. After I run him off the road he reloaded and let a few more fly as he was running away. I was so amped when I jumped out of the car I damn near mashed handprints in the grip of my SIG. Won't lie. I tried to put him down. Wound up hitting him in the knee."

Rane looked past Beeman into the trees, where the mist churned like troubled breath. "What happened here must have been like fighting in your backyard," he said.

"More like fighting in your living room. There were brothers shooting at each other," Beeman said.

Rane reached for his canteen, pulled the cork, and took a drink. "You remember the desert?" he asked.

Beeman nodded, clearly intrigued that Rane was finally starting to talk. "I remember sand in everything and damn near forgetting what green looked like."

They were walking past a row of cannons lined up facing the Sunken Road. Rane slowed his pace and peered across Duncan Field into the oak thickets beyond a split-rail fence.

"I don't believe in ghosts, Beeman. Or demons," he said slowly. "But I do believe in consequences."

Beeman cocked his head, listening.

"It was just that one time," Rane said. "I put down seven Republican Guards in less than five minutes. They never got a round inside twenty yards of me." Then he stopped, extended his hand, and touched the slick, wet muzzle of a cannon. Turning to Beeman, he said, "I've never been shot at. Not really to my thinking. Not the way I shot at people."

They walked back to the Jeep in silence.

57 BEEMAN TALKED WITH THE TENNESSEE cops in the back of the Chevy van while Rane warmed himself in the Jeep. Warmed his outside. After Jenny's call, it felt like he had the whole cold, wet battlefield in his chest. Beeman left the van and climbed in with Rane, who was holding his cell phone.

"You going to call the Edin woman?" Beeman asked, dusting raindrops from his hair.

Rane shook his head, killed the power on the phone, leaned over, and put it in the glove compartment. Beeman plugged his charger into the cigarette lighter and hooked up his cell.

"So what does our security detail say?" Rane asked.

"They still think it's a snipe hunt," Beeman said as he shifted in the seat and checked the connection between the portable radio clipped to his belt and the mike fastened under the collar of his overcoat. "But they're pros. They'll see it through."

The drizzle and the wind moderated to a random drip by the time they'd put their gear back on and tramped across the Rebel encampment toward Hurlbut Field. A regiment of Tennessee infantry was forming up in front of their tents. Off to the right, twenty cavalrymen were mounting their horses along a tree line.

On the field ahead, behind a rope barrier fastened to engineer stakes, artillery crews stood to four cannons and their

limbers. On a wooden stage set up next to a triangular pile
of black cannonballs, a group of singers with banjos roused
the gathering crowd.

Beeman led Rane to the left until they were about two
hundred yards from the crowd of spectators and the mar-
shaling reenactors. A modest group detached from the crowd
and started to trail Beeman. A uniformed cop herded them
back.

"Vampires," Beeman muttered. Then he hunched over and
keyed the shoulder mike clipped inside his collar. "We're going to hold here, try'n keep clear of the crowd." On the other
end, they depressed the squelch key twice, as an affirmative
response. Beeman glanced warily at the surrounding tree
lines. The wind had died down and the fog was making a
comeback.

"Like father like son, huh," Rane quipped as he watched
Beeman take out the tin of Copenhagen and insert a pinch
in his lower lip.

"Can't hurt," Beeman said as he eased the hammer of
the Sharps to half-cock and worked a percussion cap out
of the small pouch on his belt. Casually, he placed the cap
on the cone under the hammer and bent the flanges down.
Then he reached in his trouser pocket and took out something that he began to knead between his thumb and fingers
like worry beads.

"What's that?" Rane asked.

Beeman opened his hand, revealing a shiny brown nut.
"Buckeye. My daddy gave it to me. Suppose to be good
luck."

"Shit," Rane hunched his shoulders, "now you're making
me nervous."

"The time to take a shot would be when those cannons
go off. Which is gonna happen pretty damn soon," Beeman
said, squinting at the far tree lines.

The spectators applauded when the cavalry trotted in
twos. Then the Tennessee regiment marched to the far end

of the field and formed in two long ranks. Rane tracked the SWAT guys as they parked their van down the road, and two of them got out wearing period, ankle-length slickers and Reb slouch hats and walked casually toward the trees. The undercovers had melted into the crowd of spectators.

Rane studied the two men who had left the van. "Guy on the right is carrying something under his coat; a slinged rifle, probably a 308, hanging down under his right armpit. The other one's also got something," Rane speculated. A moment later the SWAT duo disappeared into the trees.

"Got him a spotting scope and an M16," Beeman said.

The shoulder mike emitted a muted squawk: "Snipe, this is Bag Man. How do you hear?"

Beeman grimaced. "Sniper with a sense of humor." Then he keyed the mike. "Hear you five by."

"We're thinking you guys should stroll up and down, kind of stay in motion. Make it a little harder for somebody trying to put your lights out."

"Roger," Beeman said, showing the whites of his eyes.

As they started to slowly walk perpendicular to the field, they both ducked when all four cannons fired at once and a long, low cloud of smoke spread out.

"Oh boy," Beeman said with a thin smile. "Does kinda pucker you up." He was squeezing the buckeye in his right hand.

"Do me a favor and put that away," Rane said, half-serious, as he instinctively reached for the Nikon in his haversack. His hand, wanting the Sharps on Beeman's shoulder, was indifferent to the camera. Beeman pocketed the good-luck charm, changed direction, and angled back toward the field. Now the cavalry was riding forward, eighty hooves thudding on the wet ground. The horsemen wheeled into line, advanced, reigned in, and dismounted. Every fourth man remained in the saddle and led the horses to the rear. The dismounted troopers spread out, kneeled, and began firing their carbines into the woods.

"Jesus. That should make the SWAT boys feel real cozy," Beeman said, ejecting a stream of brown spit.

On the platform, an emcee with a microphone explained the demonstration to the crowd: "Now the cavalry has engaged a little more than they can handle in those woods so they're sending back for the infantry to come up." A mounted courier rode back and conferred with an infantry officer, who raised his sword and shouted orders.

Rane half-heard. He was intent on the far tree lines, across from the demonstration.

The emcee said, "Now the infantry is deploying in company front." Rane glanced back to the field, where the long double line of gray was segmenting and reforming forward in a series of double ranks, one behind the other. As a drum began to beat a hollow cadence, the ranks set off in step. Rane found himself briefly fascinated by the earnest pageant of infantry advancing with measured tread; the dull flash of hundreds of rifles and the red flag furled in fits of wind in the center of the second company. At the other end of the field the meager screen of dismounted cavalry fell back and moved to the side.

Beeman glanced over his shoulder and said, "Not bad for a bunch of fat boys, huh?" Then he jerked Rane's sleeve. "Better keep moving."

They walked slowly, watching as the lead company of advancing soldiers began to pass between the spectators and the artillery. The cannons fired in sequence, flooding the field white.

Rane squinted. For a fraction of a second, the soldiers became timeless shadows suspended in the vale of smoke. Absently, he thought, That's the money shot. Then the smoke tattered away and the columns fanned out into a double line across the field.

But now Rane had turned away and was watching the broad, grassy area leading to the parking lot and the woods beyond. He instinctively flinched when two hundred reenactors fired a loud volley behind him.

As the sound echoed away, he tasted the acrid black powder trinity of carbon, saltpeter, and sulfur lightly spiced with nitrates. That's when he caught the movement, felt it; a palpable sensation tiptoeing inside his chest. A man in gray lurched out of the trees next to the parking lot. He was carrying a rifle and he broke into a fast jog.

"Beeman! Ten o'clock, three hundred yards," Rane said in a loud, clear voice.

They both went turtle when the reenactors behind them triggered another volley.

Rane jerked at Beeman's arm with one hand. "See him?" Out of reflex, he dropped his other hand to the Nikon.

A second later, Beeman's radio erupted in urgent static. "Beeman, get down, man, we got somebody moving your way . . ." Rane recognized the trained, hyper-controlled, Chuck Yeager voice of a police sniper clicking off the safety.

Beeman, half-crouched, waved his hand to clear the film of smoke, and bared tobacco-stained teeth as he swung the Sharps off his shoulder by the sling. "Yeah," he said. "I see him."

The figure in the gray uniform and swinging gear jogged in a brisk, stiff-legged gait, straight toward Rane and Beeman. His rifle dangled low in both hands, his arms loose, at the ready. He was coming straight on, with purpose.

Rane quickly sorted details; two guys had jumped from the van. All four of the undercovers were running from the back of the crowd. In the distance, the flashers atop a Hardin County squad car started to rotate as it lurched forward.

"Get down, Beeman," the SWAT sniper said urgently in the radio.

Rane raised his hand. "Stand down. Tell them to wait."

"What?"

"It's the guy from the bar. Darl," Rane said.

"Darl?" Beeman craned his neck. "You sure?"

"I'm sure," Rane said.

"Back it off. This ain't the guy," Beeman said into the radio.

The man had slowed now, seeing the cops running toward him, plus two accelerating police cars swerving off the road, coming across the grass. Carefully, he leaned over and laid the rifle down. Hands half-raised, he continued walking toward Beeman and Rane until the approaching cops overtook him.

Beeman turned to Rane. "It *is* Darl. But how could you tell?"

"Saw his face."

"Way out there you saw his face?" Beeman wondered as they walked quickly to where the four cops surrounded a nervous Darl Leets. As they came closer, they heard snatches of Darl's breathless conversation. He was gesturing, trying to explain he'd arrived late. "I should be on the field there," he said, pointing, "with that Tennessee regiment."

Two of the cops, still kinked up with adrenaline, insisted on frisking Darl, checking his haversack and cartridge box. When they finished their search, they pushed him roughly aside.

"Jeez, Bee, what the hell," Darl gasped, wide-eyed, his baby face pale with sweat, "call off the dogs, man . . ."

Beeman's discussion with the pissed off security detail was drowned out by another musket volley, then a cheer from the crowd as the infantry fixed bayonets and double-timed forward, yipping and howling.

The disgusted cops trudged back to the parking lot to regroup. Beeman and Rane stood over Darl as he stuffed strewn items back in his pouches.

"That took some balls," Beeman said.

Darl shook his head, his eyes flitting. He gritted his teeth and said, "No, man. Not listening to Marcy, that would take balls." Then he angled his eyes away from Beeman's dour gaze, stood up with his repacked gear, and started back to where his rifle lay on the grass.

"Okay, let's have it," Beeman said.

As they walked, Darl said, "Marcy says you got to lose all the cops or it ain't gonna happen."

Rane laughed and rolled his eyes. "Shit, they just made your security."

"Is he here?" Beeman asked.

Darl ignored the question and said, "Where can I find you in the morning?"

"At the Union camp by the Visitors Center."

Darl bit his lip, looked back across the grassy area to the parking lot where one of the cops was gesturing in frustration and kicking the tires of the van. "Look for me around nine," he said. "But you gotta lose those guys or it won't happen," he repeated. Then he stared at the wet grass, bit his lip, and raised his tight brown eyes. "Won't bullshit you. Mitchell Lee is snakeshit. This is strictly touch-and-go . . ."

"And?" Beeman asked.

"And I'm saying I got nothing personal against you, Bee. Donnie was a fuckin' psycho deserved what he got. What I'm saying is you best watch yourself." Then Darl turned with a nervous shrug of his shoulders and left Beeman and Rane standing alone, watching him march off toward the rows of white tents where the Tennessee regiment was filing back into camp to the beat of a drum.

58 RANE SAT WITH HIS BACK AGAINST A tree in the grassy open space, midway between Hurlbut Field and the parking lot where Beeman stood conferring with the security detail. He sipped SWAT coffee from his tin cup and huddled deeper into Paul Edin's greatcoat. Wood smoke drifting from camp fires put an autumn bite in the April haze.

Fast and sharp had always been his style.

He could not imagine living when his eyes and his body gave out. Among the few things he'd learned in his thirty-seven years was that the majority of people get trapped in little personal hells. Most of us settle for less than we want was the gist of what Jenny had said that night on her back deck.

Kept his distance from the herd, rode the thermals. Where the bovine eyes saw a blur, he spied a mouse dart in the stubble and swooped.

Rane plucked a handful of wet grass and threw it in frustration.

And now here was Beeman in his life. He watched the Southern cop, who had no discernible bottom that Rane could fathom, leave the parking lot and walk heavily through the indigo early evening. Corny Beeman, steeped in primitive superstitions, who alluded to invisible shit in the air. Who took his family to church every Sunday. Coming at him in his Confederate cowboy suit and dragging his chain

of ancestors behind him across Shiloh's killing fields like
Marley's Ghost.

Rane stood up in a clatter of leather bags and buckles and
Beeman's bayonet and useless rifle. He dumped the dregs of
coffee from his cup, buckled it through his haver strap, and
shook his head.

Fuck a bunch of Tex Ritter bullshit. Man's gotta do what
a man's gotta do dah do dah . . .

"You tell them what Darl said?" Rane asked, knowing
it was a rhetorical question before the sound was out of his
mouth.

"Nope."

"So what are they going to do?"

"The Hardin County boys will give it till noon tomorrow."
Beeman squinted past Rane, over toward a campfire, where
the cavalry horses were picketed along the woods. Beeman
shrugged. "So we'll play it by ear. See if Darl shows in the
morning . . ."

"Big if?"

"Nah. He'll show. And more I think about it I might be
wrong about Marcy," Beeman said philosophically, purs-
ing his lips. "She probably ain't the reincarnation of Louise
Hatchcock. More like Bonnie fuckin' Parker," he added with
his slow smile.

"Riddles." Rane shook his head, then opened his hands,
"So?"

Beeman nodded toward the parking lot. "So maybe we'll
have to give those SWAT boys the slip . . ."

"Great," Rane popped his eyes. "Go after him alone,
into a fucking trap? With a rifle you've never shot? What if
Mitchell Lee, Marcy, Darl, and the whole family is waiting
out there?"

"Calm down, John," Beeman said mildly. "You was ready
to go it alone."

Rane stabbed a finger. "That's different. You know why?"

"No I don't. You gonna tell me?"

"Yeah. Because *I know* I'm fucked up and arrange my life accordingly," Rane blurted. "You *don't know* you're fucked up—you believe the local hype. Blood over brains. Chew tobacco and have a gunfight." Rane had to laugh. "Jesus. I suppose I deserve this?"

Beeman nodded. "Yep. For how you lived your life. What you call karma." Beeman narrowed his eyes in the failing light. "Good place for it, don'tcha think? Sun going down on the Shiloh battlefield?" Then Beeman started walking and said, "C'mon."

"What now?"

"Over in the parking lot I ran into a boy I know with the Tennessee Cavalry. They got a big pot of venison stew cooking. We been invited to spend the night."

The Tennessee troop camped along a tree line in a smog of wood smoke, damp hay bales, and wet horseflesh. As they approached, Rane detected an under-scent of sweet grains in burlap bags. The horses were tethered along a picket line and Rane noticed that saddles had been lashed to the trees in stacks of two and three and covered with waterproof ponchos.

A dozen men in rakish cavalry jackets and high leather boots bristled with pistols and sabers and huddled, shoulders hunched, around the fire. "Oh shit," one of them drawled, seeing Beeman and Rane walk in. "Here comes Beeman. Gonna bring fire down on our ass for sure."

"You got your Kevlar under that sack coat, Bee?"

One of the men held out a copy of the printout with Mitchell Lee's picture. "Could you autograph and date this? Might be worth something if you get yourself shot."

Beeman laughed, unhooked his tin cup from his haversack buckle, stooped, and poured coffee from the large pot next to the simmering cauldron of stew. He stood up and said, "Sorry about the fuss, boys. Probably nothing."

"No problem. Breaks the routine. This Living History can get monotonous after twenty years."

"Go easy on the bloodthirsty stuff," Beeman said. "This here's John Rane. He's a photographer for a paper up North. Got eyes like an eagle and ears like a bat. Even got a camera somewhere."

Rane endured a round of grumbling. Someone piped up, "Ain't bad enough you're drawing fire, Bee. Now we been infiltrated."

As Rane shifted from foot to foot, one of the men finally hoisted the coffee pot in a gesture of welcome. He had a trim black mustache and was the only trooper wearing gray top and bottom. "Manners, boys," he said amiably. Rane unclipped his tin cup from his haversack and accepted the coffee.

A general discussion ensued about the Kirby Creek incident—probably, Rane thought, for his edification—then spiraled into an account of accidents at Civil War reenactments. The consensus seemed to be a lapse in safety when it came to pistols. The famous casualty at Raymond was cited; the wound being consistent with a .36-caliber pistol ball.

"The problem with pistols," one of the troopers said as he hefted up a Colt Navy and handed it to Rane, "is you have six charges to check, each one with its own cap. Infantry just slap on one cap, point the rifle at the ground and go pop."

Another man offered: "What happens is, guys will bring one empty cylinder for the safety check and a pouch full of loaded ones. Gets hard to monitor."

A natty fellow with a groomed beard and a stylish vest protested. "Remember at Gettysburg, that big Yankee sonofabitch stuck his pistol right in my face when we went over the wall . . ."

"Well, now Kenny," a tempered voice came from the circle. "You *were* tryin' to grab the flag out of his hand now weren't you?"

"Was picking Cream of Wheat outta my face and eyes for a week."

"Cream of Wheat?" Rane wondered.

"Use it to plug the powder charges in each cylinder," said the man showing Rane the pistol, "otherwise the whole wheel can chain-fire when you pull the trigger. Blow up in your hand."

Rane asked, "And Kirby Creek, was that another accident?"

One of the troopers pointed toward the horses where Beeman had wandered over to talk to a tall figure in a long duster and slouch hat. "They seem to be taking it pretty serious, don't they?" he said.

The talk frittered away diplomatically as the stew was ladled out. The man in the long coat disappeared into the twilight, Beeman returned, and he and Rane took their plates a little back from the fire and sat on a log.

"Two of the SWAT boys will take turns staying up, watching us tonight. In the morning we change outfits and they'll trail us to the blue camp at the landing," Beeman said between mouthfuls. "We'll take the first picket watch. When it's quieted down, then you and me can talk."

Rane nodded, scraped his plate, and then went through the motions of making his bed with poncho and blanket on a pallet of hay next to a row of shelter half-tents. Beeman kept the Sharps slung on his shoulder as he spread his bedding next to Rane's. Then he left Rane alone and joined the circle at the campfire.

Rane lay on his back as night closed in, listening to the banjos and carousing drift from the fires at the infantry camp across the field. Slowly, the partying and the fires burned down and a vast, starless quiet descended, punctuated by the stamp and shift of tethered horses and snatches of talk from the cavalry campfire.

"You were on that Custer's Last Ride event up the Little Big Horn?"

"Yep, back in, jeez, was the early nineties when I still had a full head of hair."

Rane reached for a cigarette, decided against it, and instead stuffed his hand in his trouser pocket and closed his fingers around the manila card.

"That story true, what happened out there?"

"Uh-huh. See, we were playing Custer's troopers, skirmishing our way up the valley with these local Indian boys from the Crow Reservation.

"Those guys were seriously turned out and they could *ride.* I'd wrangled with some of them playing extra on a few pictures. So this one big dude trots up in all his feathers and he says, 'You guys look like the real thing, you could be the Seventh Cav.' "

Rane squeezed the crumpled card. *Talk*, Beeman said. He stared at the tremble of firelight, the way it played shadow peekaboo in the spidery canopy of branches, and tried to see it like Paul did. Father Abraham frowning down with black, tormented eyes.

"So the ride is supposed to stop at the Custer Battlefield Park boundary, right? Park Service don't want you burning powder at each other on their land. But this Indian says, 'Shit, you guys look almost good as us and, you know, this is *our* reservation. So fuck a bunch of park rangers. *Let's do it.*' "

Faces.

Rane had interred the seven faces in synaptic holes burned in his nerves.

"So we did it. Formed up in twos, rode onto the battlefield and spurred right down Medicine Tail Coulee, whooping and blazing away with Colts and these big ole .45-70 carbines . . .

"And the Indians came boiling across the Little Big Horn River and up that draw. Yipping and yelling, all feathers and dust, and us banging away. Lemme tell you, man," the speaker's voice dropped to a hush that brought Rane up on his elbows to barely hear. "Them coming bent over those ponies bareback, shooting these padded-tip arrows they had. Those arrows going *whoosh* by your head.

Talk about your period rush. I mean you *were right there* in the fuckin' moment."

The other storyteller laughed. "Those park rangers and tourists from New York and Chicago and such, they shit a brick and dropped their dentures."

Rane lowered himself and huddled in Paul's blanket.

Right there in the fuckin' moment.

And he shut his eyes and saw the seven swarthy Sunni faces in the order that they died; a slender strip of negatives curling across the darkroom of his mind.

59 RANE WAS DOZING ON PAUL'S PACK when Beeman roused him. The conversation and the fires had died down. Shiloh slept in the dark. Rane got up, pulled the greatcoat around him, picked his way through the sleeping troopers, and built up the campfire while Beeman checked the horses. Then Beeman returned, carefully set the Sharps beside him on a log, and squatted by the fire circle. He packed his pipe, put a twig in the coals, raised it to his pipe, puffed, and turned to Rane. "So tell me about the sniper part."

Rane scoffed, "A sniper's like a nature photographer. He'll lie up in a pile of rocks for days waiting for a bug to pop out of a hole. I was never a sniper. Shit, man, I don't even *like* guns."

"That may be, but back on Duncan Field you said seven kills," Beeman said.

Rane eased his wallet from his pocket, extracted the pierced quarter, and handed it to Beeman.

"What's this?" Beeman asked, turning it in the firelight.

"Souvenir for you. A 168-grain Sierra Boat tail out a Remington 700 Model 308 made that hole. Probably the same rifle those SWAT guys have. My 'diploma' from the police sniper school they have at Fort Ripley in Minnesota. They give you one round to carry during the course. Toward the end they put you out alone to see if you can make The Shot. Mine was a quarter at about a hundred forty yards in freezing rain, crawling through the mud and weeds with a dozen cadre trying to find me." Rane shrugged. "They saw my military records and offered me the course. I did it to fast-track access, you know, to get to know more people in the department."

"More research?"

"Yeah."

"And?"

"It blew up in my face about a month after I got through the probation period, the first time they put me on a SWAT perimeter. I was supposed to sit tight and observe on the radio net. We had a guy who should have been in a mental hospital except he was barricaded in his house with a deer rifle, freaking out the neighbors. That's when I realized I had a problem left over from Iraq."

"What happened?" Beeman asked.

"I abandoned my post and rushed the door. Surprised the shit out of me *and him*. He ran out the back into a tag team of cops. So I get suspended pending a psych eval, for violating protocol. I declined the evaluation and left the department. I was dating Jenny at the time."

"Hmmm, that sounds a lot like the standoff story in the St. Paul paper," Beeman said.

"Yes it does," Rane said, staring at the flames.

"John, you understand, I gotta draw the line at helping you commit suicide wearing Paul's clothes," Beeman said frankly.

Rane jerked alert when a drunken howl echoed deep in the trees.

Beeman explained: "Some of the boys get over-motivated and go off hunting haints every year."

Rane turned to Beeman and said just as frankly, "I'm not haunted, Kenny. I don't obsess about it. It's not *what* I did. It's *how* I did it."

"That's cutting a pretty fine distinction, don't you think?"

Rane shook his head. "Look, I've read the whole damn *DSM*, the *Diagnostic and Statistical Manual on Mental Disorders*. This isn't some stress-complex thing. Hell. I like stress. It's . . ." Rane put his hand out, feeling at the night. "You were close when you said a veil. But it's more like a transparent barrier. Like this lens between me and people. I keep charging it to break out."

The fire crackled and cast war-paint streaks across Beeman's face, and the ghost-seekers hallooed again in the distance and Rane lost his train of thought and wondered how many trees were still growing today that Lincoln had looked at?

Beeman brought him back. "What happened to you in the desert, John?"

"Okay, why not." Rane held up a hand and let it drop. "Like your guy in Jackson found out, I went through the marine school at Quantico. The sniper course was divided into three blocks of instruction: marksmanship, observation, and field craft. I always could shoot a rifle. My uncle Mike taught me and he thinks there's a natural connection between photography and shooting, that they use the same skill sets. He calls them kinetic instincts. But it's a perishable gift. You have to practice it; that's why I spent some time with the Sharps before I came down here."

Rane probed at the embers with a stick, stoking the fire.

"You could really identify Darl all the way across that field?" Beeman asked.

Rane nodded and jerked a thumb at his face. "Twenty-ten in both eyes. But there's more to it. I'd seen him that day in the bar; how he was built, how he moved."

"And you remembered that?"

"Observation. That's the part of the sniper course I really aced. We'd play this game. It's called the Kim's game. The name comes from the book *Kim* by Rudyard Kipling. Kim is this young guy being trained as a spy in India. They show him this tray full of various rocks and gems for one minute. Then they cover the tray and quiz him on the details of what he saw. We played a variation on the game every day for two months. Kinda like 'junk on a bunk': they lay out all these objects in the morning, then we'd train all day, and at night they'd have us write a detailed summary of what we'd seen in the morning. I think on my best day I identified forty different objects out of forty-five. There's a variation of the game you play in the field, identifying stuff through a sniper scope."

Rane paused, his face intent in the flicker of the fire. "And then?" Beeman asked.

"And then nothing. I go on to my next assignment." Rane tossed up his hands. "Saddam invades Kuwait. I ship over. When Desert Storm kicks off I wind up following the 101st around taking pictures." He leaned forward, elbows on knees, staring at the glowing embers. His face worked and he said, "Thirsty."

Beeman held up a canteen. Rane took a sip of rusty water, handed the canteen back, and said, "You remember when everybody was hunting Scuds?"

"I remember hearing them go over, seeing the Patriot light show," Beeman said.

"Well, there was a scout platoon attached to this battalion so I'd hang with their sniper and do some shooting to establish street cred."

"Showing off?"

"Maybe a little. So after a week burning rounds, I'm regularly punching bottle caps at two hundred yards with an M24. My new sniper buddy has this bright idea to take me on a reconnaissance. They had Intel on a Scud launch site way out in the desert. I get to fill in as a spotter plus I take my camera to document the strike if we confirm the target. The colonel likes the idea and gives us a go. Wasn't much else going on."

"A slow day in Bumfuck, Egypt," Beeman chuckled.

"You got it," Rane said. "It's supposed to be simple. I'd

seen it before. You go in with a sat phone and an IR light, a laser designator. There's an F-16 on call with a JDAM five-hundred-pound bomb, has a targeting pod calibrated to your target designator. You sneak in, verify the target, contact the jet, then paint the target with the laser, and bang. It's called lassoing the target."

"So was it simple?" Beeman asked.

"Shit." Rane gave his hollow laugh. "We jump off the Blackhawk before the sun comes up; two miles from the alleged target area. Except the pilot misjudges the distance to the deck and we hit hard. About an hour into the march we discover the sniper lost the laser designator in the jump.

"So he tells me to stay put, he'll retrace our steps in the sand to the DZ, find the gear, and be right back. About twenty minutes after he splits, the wind does that scary change and the sand starts to blow in, slow at first. It's getting light and there's a wadi up ahead with some overhang along the ridge, so I head for that.

"As I get close I go to ground when I hear a motor. The Iraqis had the same idea because they are pulling this rig with a big-ass Scud missile in tow into the ravine to take shelter. There's a truck with a security detachment of RGs. Counting the driver there's seven all told."

"Where's your sniper?" Beeman asked.

"He's the hard-ass ranger type so he's carrying the big ruck with the water, the M2 A1, the sat phone. I'm the pussy photographer so all I carry is the back bag with his sniper rifle, my camera, and one canteen. Total brownout. The war stops. I don't see him again for almost three days.

"My canteen didn't last long. Ever go forty-eight hours without water in the desert during a sandstorm? Hollows you out, does things to your head."

Beeman waited patiently as Rane stared into the dark trees when one of the horses shifted position. The fire popped a shower of sparks. A trapdoor opened briefly in the clouds and a crescent moon briefly limned the empty forest and was gone.

"I have the rifle out to use the scope. I can see them down there, through pauses in the storm. They're hunkered into this sand cave. They have water in plastic five-gallon jugs. Six of these big fat jugs. I study them, get to know their faces, rank them numerically according to age. Number Seven, the oldest, had the most interesting face. Kinda like Anthony Quinn in *Lawrence of Arabia*. I watch one, two, three of the jugs fly, empty, cast on the wind across the bottom of the ravine. I can hear the empty jugs bumping on the rocks. Christ. What are they doing, taking baths? They're drinking all the fuckin' water . . ."

Rane reached for the canteen, drank, handed it back, and spoke methodically, like he was reading from a page. He never allowed himself to go all the way back there, not even now.

"Before dawn on the third day the wind falls off. You know how you tell severe dehydration? You stop sweating. Your piss turns dark. You have these severe muscle cramps and your spit is white paste. My lips and fingers were cracked and bleeding. Parts of my reflexes were starting to fall off. I was afraid of going into coma.

"I had a rifle that I'd trained on, that I'd been shooting regularly back at the base camp, and twenty rounds of ammo. The sniper's cheat sheet with his scope settings was taped on the stock. You know how you figure the range with just a scope? You use the mil dot reticle on the scope like a slide rule to measure the height of a target . . ." Rane paused, shook his head, lapsing into technical jargon.

"Sure, I'd been to all the schools but I was just there to *watch*. I never thought I'd actually have to *do* any of that shit. And now they were rousing down there, getting ready to send people out. They had AKs and a light machine gun and I was too weak and cramped to get away. Then I felt the rising sun on the back of my neck and saw it was blinding them.

"No choice. I started at three hundred fifty yards, crawling down the elongating shadows. I caught most of them bottled up along the side of the ravine. They couldn't locate the source of the fire. I reloaded twice.

"Number Seven knew what he was doing. He figured my general position by the sound of the shots and rushed me with Number Four. Might have worked with more guys, except it was just the two of them and they had the sun in their eyes."

Rane heaved his shoulders; his voice hollow, matter-of-fact.

"The hardest part was crawling down to the water on my hands and knees. I was afraid I'd pass out before I got there. A couple of them still had light in their eyes when I took the first drink."

Beeman started to say something, then stopped.

"Don't get me wrong. I'm no pacifist," Rane said. "But it wasn't war. And it wasn't murder. It wasn't even the water." He gave a hollow laugh. "Shooters have a slang expression, 'F/8 and be there.' It means you set the aperture on your lens for enough depth of field to forget about focusing. You just point and shoot."

Rane stood up and addressed the silent forest.

"It was just too damn *easy*, Kenny. Pure instinct. I was *taking pictures*, except my viewfinder was a scope and the pictures killed people."

After a moment, Beeman slung the Sharps on his shoulder, rose to his feet, his face questioning in the firelight. "Then what happened?"

Rane shrugged. "I found their food. I ate their salt. Then I blew up the gas tank on the truck to make a signal fire. When the choppers came in I was drinking Iraqi tea and smoking Turkish cigarettes I'd found on one of the bodies." Again the hollow laugh. "The colonel wanted a picture with his trophy Scud, said he'd write me up for a decoration. I told him to shove his commendation up his ass. He never got his picture."

He turned to Beeman. "*What happened was* I had trouble getting involved with people, huh? Like the woman who was pregnant with my kid."

Beeman toed some coals, stared at the fire, and said, "And now you come down here to revise your fate card."

"Whatever," Rane said. Then he pointed at the Sharps. "But if we run into Mitchell Lee, and it gets real tomorrow, you best hand me that rifle."

Beeman shook his head. "I can't do that, John. All this I learned about you ain't gonna be some Hardin County prosecutor's business."

60

Mitch's eyes popped open. LaSalle stood over him, put the toe of his boot in his side. Looked down. The relief in his voice was forced. As was his smile. "Get up, let's get this over with so I can go home."

"Okay, okay," Mitch mumbled, looking up and shading his eyes. Something in the way LaSalle looked down at him? Yesterday's hope scattered like cockroaches under a bright panic. Cave closing in.

"C'mon. Time to meet your cousin Dwayne. Now sit up, get your shoes on and put out your hands."

As Mitch pushed to a sitting position, pulled on the battered leather shoes, and tied them, he noticed the black butt of an automatic pistol jammed in LaSalle's waistband. The handcuffs clamped on with a dull click. Then the iron ring shifted on his ankle as LaSalle fiddled with the lock. LaSalle's eyes settled on the almost-empty bourbon bottle lying on its side next to the air mattress. The sheen of sweat on his face sparkled, at odds with the masklike, calm smile on his lips. LaSalle couldn't quite disguise the ruthless deadbolt set of his brown eyes.

More than Ellie's paid help. He moved with the efficient purpose of a man discharging a mortal obligation.

Mitch wanted to plead, Hey, LaSalle, buddy, if I woulda been there in Baghdad I would have pulled you from the fire. Honest.

Except he wasn't there and now LaSalle had re-
turned from the fire with a twitch in his brain and
scars on his arms and face and today he was wearing
his tight black skin like an executioner's hood.
Everything Ellie said was more sedative.
Jesus, God—they were going to kill him.

Then he blinked and it was like he woke up for real and the paranoia receded like a last ripple from the Demerol vibrations. He exhaled and remembered Marcy's voice on the phone.

Okay. Better now. LaSalle's face had lost its sinister aspect.

"What's that for?" Mitch asked, nodding at the pistol.

"Shit man, maybe Miss Kirby trusts Dwayne Leets on the phone but she ain't going alone in the woods with him," La-Salle said and Mitch almost grinned, because that injected some healthy reality. Yes it did.

They walked down the narrow passage for the last time. Good-bye, cave. When they were in the shed, LaSalle pointed out the doorway to his truck.

"Sorry we don't have better transportation but you're going to have to lay in the passenger foot well. I'm gonna cover you with a tarp and tie your legs."

Mitch managed to get out one "Hey?" before LaSalle tied a rag over his eyes. The near panic returned when he heard the sound of tape tearing and then the sticky grip of adhesive slapped across his lips.

The air on his face changed from musty and moldy to a soft breeze, and he was outside. A stillness and a tickle of cool morning mist. His clumsy shoes slipped on wet grass, and then crunched on gravel. A car door opened.

Then he was lifted and pushed into a fetal position in the cramped space. Something looped and tightened around his ankles. Felt like a bungee cord. Stiff, rubbery folds descended over him. He heard LaSalle get in the truck, the engine start, and then the whir and rattle of road noise beneath him. Mitch pressed his manacled hands against the bandage on his cheek, using the stabs of pain to back off the panic. Listen to them, Marcy said. He concentrated on getting his breathing under control.

Maybe half an hour passed that way and then the truck went off road and bumped over muddy ruts and stopped. La-Salle got out and a moment later opened the passenger door. Mitch wasn't ready. He made his body into a tense pretzel, fighting the strong hands that were methodically prying him from his fragile sanctuary.

"C'mon now, we're almost there," LaSalle said patiently, like a man soothing a skittish dog. The reasonable tone of his voice untangled the sweaty slipknots of panic and Mitch relaxed to catch his breath. His feet were untied and he was helped from the truck. "See, that wasn't so bad, was it," La-Salle said.

Walking now, propelled forward by a steady grip on his elbow. A familiar mush of leaves squeegeed under his shoes, the damp snap of dead sticks and the swipe of branches. Mitch heard a mourning dove, the scamper of a squirrel. They were in the woods. This all started in the woods.

"Got to hand it to you, you're quite the ladies' man," La-Salle said in that voice, like a cold, slow burn. "You're the only guy in the world who could get Miss Kirby and Marcy Leets to sit down and put their heads together to sort out this mess you made."

A metallic pop, a flare of igniting gas and tobacco.

LaSalle said, "Now, I'll remove the gag and give you a smoke. You start making a ruckus I'll slap the tape back on. Nod your head if you want the smoke."

Mitch nodded his head and the tape was pulled gently from his mouth. LaSalle placed the cigarette in Mitch's lips and he puffed gratefully.

"Thing about women," LaSalle ruminated as they continued walking, "they make up the rules as they go along. We used to have this discussion over in the sandbox. You know, all the gals they got in the line of fire now. Like can they handle it? And this one doctor had a theory that the army was making a big mistake jumping over too many generations of culture and shit like that. Women don't have all the macho posturing that goes with sports and jive like fighting on the playground, huh? What they got is maternal instinct, you dig? When push comes to shove they'll just plain *obliterate* you."

"LaSalle," Mitch mumbled, "where we going?"

"It's cool. We're almost there. You just smoke your cigarette and listen. This ain't what you call a conversation."

Mitch nodded, stumbled, and was pulled back upright.

"See," LaSalle said, "the thing wrong with that doc's theory is women don't go for the fight first thing like a guy. They'll, what you call it? Ask for directions when they're lost, you follow me?"

"I guess," Mitch said. The nicotine, the delicious morning air on his cheeks, and LaSalle's conversational tone had a calming effect. It made sense, Ellie washing her hands and kicking him down the line to Dwayne. Then they stopped walking and LaSalle took him by both shoulders and shuffled him back against a tree.

"You know, it didn't have to be this way, Mitch," LaSalle said. "You think back over the last few weeks, since the old man went into decline, Miss Kirby kept inviting you to participate in the next step, huh? Like talk to the folks at the bank and the lawyers about plans for the estate? But you was too busy making your own plans, I guess?"

And Mitch heard a long, low roll of drums building in the distance, bouncing and echoing through the trees and the pitch of the ground. But not that far away. And the drumsticks felt like they were beating in his chest.

61 A LITTLE STIFF FROM SLEEPING ON the ground, Rane woke with surprising lightness to the smell of horses and the slap and jingle of McClellan Saddles being hoisted and girth straps being cinched. The rattle of sabers and carbines mixed with soothing soft drawls as the troopers talked the bridles over muzzles and set the bits into foamy yellow teeth. Clouds of steam jetted from flared nostrils. Rane looked into a sidelong equine eye.

Beeman handed him a cup of camp coffee and explained that the cavalry unit was mounting up for their traditional Sunday-morning canter around the battlefield. As the horsemen wheeled into line to be addressed by their commander, Beeman and Rane did up their packs, looped their leathers over their arms, picked up their rifles, and hiked, sipping coffee, toward the parking area across from the Confederate Memorial.

The sun was out, for a change. Delicate streaks of orange and purple layered the sky above the trees on the east side of Hurlbut Field. Rane started the Jeep so Beeman could charge his cell. He discarded the Reb clothes and then changed into his blue sack coat and cap. Beeman took his leathers aside and flipped the USA insignia upright. With Beeman momentarily distracted, Rane fiddled with his camera as he slipped his hand into his duffel, found the spare packet of rounds, loosened the wrapping, and tucked the ten bullets into his right trouser pocket. The percussion caps in his cap box would work on the Sharps.

As he tucked the Nikon back in his haversack, he spied the security team assembling by the road next to the brown van. They looked like they'd lost their edge this morning, after pulling shifts all night and the false alarm with Darl yesterday.

Then he watched Beeman, who stood staring at the blue coat and hat he'd brought. Slowly, Beeman shook his head. "Damned if I will," he said under his breath. "Ain't wearing blue going past those burial trenches. Not at Shiloh."

Rane withheld comment. Whatever it takes.

They left their packs and overcoats in the Jeep, to travel light, then, after Beeman slapped a fresh battery into his radio, they started walking up the Corinth-Pittsburg Landing Road toward the National Cemetery on the Tennessee River. The security van fell in behind and the undercovers tramped the field to the right.

Beeman pointed to the road on his Shiloh Park map and said, "You're in character this morning, dressed in blue. This is the direction the Yankees ran like hell the first day of the battle."

Rane slung the Enfield over his shoulder and declined to take the bait. Beeman deserved his drama and Rane felt no need to complicate the day by arguing the history. Let him massage his lucky buckeye as his eyes darted into the trees that, this morning, were exorcised by beams of slanting sunlight. Let Beeman have his moment, carrying a Yankee rifle, seeking the enemy of his blood on the battlefield of his ancestors.

But if shit starts going downrange I will get my hands on that rifle.

They veered off the blacktop down a leaf-strewn muddy trail lined with vehicles and horse trailers; license plates from Tennessee, Mississippi, and Alabama. Then the path branched, and they came to a small clearing where cannonballs outlined a rectangle of ground. Beeman removed his slouch hat and Rane likewise doffed his cap respectfully, thinking absently: this was one of four Confederate burial trenches on the north side of the battleground, which Sherman's division had helped fill up as they ran like hell.

Beeman screwed up his lips. "Just threw them in here and left 'em. Never had a proper burial or words said like the Yankees they moved to the bluff. Gotta get permission from the Park Service to lay flowers." He glanced at Rane. "Same government that burned down Japan and Germany and built 'em back up. Reagan over there at Normandy, put a fuckin' wreath on Nazi graves."

Like with the snake and the lawyer, the open manholes were back in Beeman's eyes. Well why not? Might need all the edge he had, pretty soon.

"Okay, here we go," Beeman said, putting his cap back on and giving it a determined tug down over his eyes, "lct's bushwhack through the woods and lose them in the thick stuff. Hook up with Darl before they spot us."

Rane shrugged, fell in step, and shook out his senses. A minute later the shoulder mike rasped. "Hey Beeman, we're losing you. Angle up toward the road where we can see you."

Beeman keyed the mike. "Roger that." Then he reached down to the radio clipped under his jacket and switched it off. "You up for a little cross-country?" he asked.

They set off at a trot, holding their rifles at port arms, equipment swinging and jangling, weaving through the trees and gullies. Then they slowed to climb the tangled slope of a broad ravine, recrossed the empty road, and plunged through more thickets until they worked up the side of a slope toward rows of black cannons.

"This is where Grant set up his last line," Beeman said, breathing heavily and wiping sweat from his forehead. Moments later they emerged from a path into a grassy area where twenty or so soldiers in blue stood around a campfire, sipping coffee next to a triangular canvas tent. One of them in particular raised a curious eye as they walked past; a mixcd couple in blue and gray. Rane presumed he was an officer, because he wore a sword. Then the man returned to discussing the battle with a group of early-morning spectators. Rane overheard him say something about a General Peabody deserving a Congressional Medal of Honor for pushing out the recon company that detected the Rebel advance.

"Bingo," Beeman said, nodding toward the brick park building across the road on the bluff of the Tennessee River, next to the cemetery. Darl Leets pushed off the shadowed west side of the building in a camo hunting jacket, a tractor hat, and jeans. Darl inclined his head to the west along the road, so Beeman and Rane turned left and slipped back into the trees. They'd traveled a hundred yards when Darl crossed the road and joined them.

Darl glanced back toward the small Union camp, satisfied they'd lost the security detail. "Okay," he said, taking out a park map. "You go due west through the thick stuff, cross Tilghman Branch, and come out here." His finger tapped a black triangle monument marker captioned OGLESBY/HARE. "Then you cross Highway 22 and head toward this picnic area." He tapped the map again. "This side of the parking lot there's a long field screened by trees with a cannon at the north end. If he's going to show he'll meet with Dwayne in the trees past the cannon on the west side of that field."

"You going to take us in?" Beeman asked, studying Darl's face.

Darl shook his head. "This is far as I go. Dwayne finds out I been talking to you . . ." He bit his lip and let his flitting downcast eyes fill in the rest. Then he looked at the rusty Sharps. "Jeez, Bee, hope you got more than that?"

"Why's that? He out there with a deer rifle?" Beeman asked softly.

"Don't know what he's out there with. You gotta take your chances, I guess," Darl said, his face blank.

"Okay. Fair enough," Beeman said, hitching up his leather belt, as his eyes turned to the thick western woods. Then Darl handed Beeman the park map, pursed his lips in a relieved expression, turned, and hurried back toward the road.

Beeman watched him go and then said, "Well, this is it. What's your fate card tell you, John?"

"We're walking into an ambush, eyes wide open," Rane said, slightly amazed at the calmness in his voice.

"Yep. For somebody. They could all be out there," Beeman said, gnawing on his lower lip. "Or maybe I been maneuvered in to clean up a done deal. Only one way to know for sure. You ready?"

More than ready. Rane floated into the tangled brush, his step light. He was almost oblivious to the heavy toy rifle in his hands, the strapped equipment, or his camera swinging in the sack at his left hip. This, finally, was what he came here for: to see if the lost roads of his life would converge ahead. He eyed the rusty Sharps swinging on Beeman's shoulder. Roll the dice. Be the man in the open this time.

They moved fast through a deep ravine choked with brush, jumped a creek, and stumped up the other side. Rane inhaled his woolly sweat, felt and heard the tickle and whisper of insects. They both came to a trembling halt when a woodpecker drummed a loud tattoo. Sunlight punched through the clouds, broke on the trees, and scattered a shadowy mosaic of Southern stained glass down the forest floor.

Panting, Beeman rasped, "Slow down, John. Talk to me. How should we handle it?"

"We get a look at the ground. Try to spot him first." Rane removed his cap and wiped sweat from his forehead. "If it is him, we lose in a long-range shooting contest. So we avoid the open and stay in the trees, fix him and then work in tandem. One drawing fire, the other shooting," he shrugged laconically, "make fewer mistakes than he does."

They cleared the underbrush, exited the woods, and walked across a broad field toward a triangular stack of black cannonballs. An earnest light now animated Beeman's face; part condemned man, part executioner. He swung the

Sharps off his shoulder and snapped it up, practicing his sight picture. Then he checked the cap on the nipple, his thumb caressing the half-cocked hammer. With a subdued pop, he unfastened the snap on his cartridge box. Then the cap pouch. Rotated his eyes back and forth.

They were out here all alone.

Rane slid his hand in his pocket and squeezed the card as he walked.

They jangled alert at a long, hollow roll of drums coming from the direction of the Confederate encampment. Rane's pulse quickened and then, spontaneously, they lurched into a run, crossed the highway, and ducked into the shade of the trees.

62

LASALLE PLUCKED THE CIGARETTE from Mitch's lips, pressed him back against the tree, and carefully removed the bandage from his cheek. Then he inserted something in Mitch's pocket. Cell phone, felt like.

"Didn't have to be this way," LaSalle repeated as he removed the blindfold.

For a moment, Mitch refused to open his eyes. Just the soft morning air on his face. The rattle of the drums echoing in his chest.

"You see," LaSalle said, "way it turns out you did your duty. You stood stud service for old Hiram after all. She was getting set to tell you. She's going on two months pregnant. No wonder she was so pissed . . ."

"What?" Mitch's eyes popped open. *"WHAT?"*

Oh what a sweet Jesus of a morning exploded fresh in his eyes—the green, sloping grass and the trees in spring feather and the clouds like warm rumpled silk sheets in burgundy and gold and the friendly rising sun could be an illustrated smile in a children's storybook.

The glorious second crumbled the moment he saw the stern set of LaSalle's face with its lumpy purple scars and the white rubber gloves on his hands. Standing there like a black nightmare, like duty itself.

Mitch blinked, panted, saw a solitary cannon sitting in the field. "Where?"

"Close to Shiloh. Hear the drums? Reenactors."

Mitch nodded, eyes fixed past the cannon, down the field. Three people walked toward the trees at the far end, two men in front and a woman in a loose raincoat bringing up the rear.

"Easy now," LaSalle said as a key appeared in his gloved hand. He unlocked the cuffs and slipped them from Mitch's wrists. "This is as far as my obligation to the Kirbys takes me." The black man stepped back. "You're free."

"Jesus," Mitch mumbled, massaging his wrists; squinting down the field, he isolated a flash of orange footwear. "That's Dwayne all right . . ."

"Yep, Marcy too," LaSalle said. "Don't know the other guy."

"I got to talk to Ellie, first thing," Mitch said earnestly, licking sweat from his lips. When he looked back, the trio had disappeared into the trees. "Where'd they go?"

LaSalle pointed to the right, to a trail that ran just inside the tree line. "You go down that path about a hundred yards and come to a big rock on the right. There's a tree down across the trail. You wait there. They'll meet you."

Mitch nodded. "Damn, LaSalle, you had me going," he gave a shaky grin, "with that pistol and all."

"In future I'd watch myself around the women, I was you," LaSalle said as he turned to leave, "especially the smart ones. 'Cause the smart ones, man, *first* they get directions, *then* they obliterate you."

LaSalle receded out of sight in the trees, then his footfalls faded. Mitch wiggled his fingers and ran them through his grubby hair. Satisfied LaSalle was indeed gone, he set off down the path.

Sonofabitch. A thought like bursting. Ellie being pregnant changed *everything*.

A few minutes later, he was sitting on the tree trunk that lay across the path by the rock. The drums had stopped. Faint at first, then louder, he heard the footsteps coming up toward him. Then he saw them. Dwayne in front, in his Day-Glo ostrich boots and a light Carhartt jacket so fresh it looked like it just came from the cleaners. Uh-huh, and ole fox-faced Jimmy Beal, Dwayne's driver and bodyguard, in back of him, wearing one of his Hawaiian shirts. Marcy bringing up the rear, hands plunged in her raincoat pockets.

"Shit man," Dwayne called out. "Lookit you, the fuckin' Missing Link."

"It's been crazy," Mitch said, standing up.

"You got that right, starting with you letting Beeman get away. Shoulda known you'd freeze when it came right down to it." Dwayne curled his lips as Jimmy Beal stepped to the side.

"Hey, Dwayne, man . . ." Mitch protested.

Jimmy drew a squarish black automatic pistol from under his shirt.

Mitch blinked. Now Dwayne reached around to his back and brought a pistol out too. Not as big as Jimmy's. Marcy sidestepped behind Jimmy, her face all wrong, dark-patched, and her hands coming out of her pockets.

White rubber gloves on her hands.

Same as LaSalle.

"Dwayne, what the hell, man? Wait a minute," Mitch blurted.

"You're a liability to me now, Mitch. Hiding out in the fuckin' woods . . . can't trust somebody pulls weird shit like that."

"Woods? Ellie had me locked up. Shit, Dwayne. I'm your cousin," Mitch protested.

The drums were going again but not so loud that Mitch couldn't hear Dwayne say, "You ain't no relation of mine. Not no more."

And then the whole world blew up with a muffled roar beyond the trees, which drowned out the tattoo of the drums, and Mitch's eyes spasmed as the sound swooshed right by his shoulder and knocked Dwayne over like a sledgehammer hit him in the chest, and at the exact same moment as

Dwayne tipped over, Jimmy Beal's eyes went wide and his head came apart in a smoky cloud and he pitched forward and where his head had been Marcy held a big Colt Navy in her white-gloved hand.

"Holy shit," Mitch yelped, jumping, unable to pull his eyes from Dwayne's feet that were beating on the ground.

Marcy cocked the hammer on the big pistol and leveled it at Mitch's chest. "Hold that thought, Sport, and don't even think of moving." Then Marcy took two steps and lowered the pistol and shot Dwayne once in the head and ended the twitching and it all was contained in the expanding echo of the cannons firing beyond the trees.

Mitch discovered that the astonishment of shock doesn't come from the outside, it comes from the inside when your heart and lungs turn to ice in your chest and you can't breathe anymore and you just get stuck with your eyes cranked wide open and what his eyes saw was Ellender Jane Kirby appear in wisps of white smoke, wearing the gray sweat suit and running shoes and a belt cinched around her waist with a holster, a cartridge box, and a cap box.

His belt. His rifle.

She held the Enfield in her hands and was wearing gloves, like LaSalle and Marcy, and she had a smear of black powder on her chin as she spit away the paper cartridge, yanked the rammer, and jammed it down the barrel.

She returned the ramrod, dug a cap from the pouch on her belt, stuck on the cone, and pulled the hammer back. Marcy cocked the pistol, loading another chamber. Ellie leveled the rifle at Mitch.

Another rattle of fire beyond the trees. Not as loud. Infantry.

Mitch swallowed and stared at what had been inside Jimmy Beal's skull and was now splattered on the leaves like something you find in the woods during deer season. Dwayne, eyes wide open, orange boots splayed out; and Marcy, not nervous or anything.

A sinking thought. Not so many moving parts. So this is how a pro does it.

He watched Marcy walk quickly to Ellie and stuff the pistol in the holster on her belt. Ellie never moved the Enfield off his chest.

Marcy's face looked terrible, bruises and swelling, but her eyes were still those witch-at-the-crossroads eyes.

"I told you not to do it and you didn't listen. Him either." She jerked her head contemptuously at Dwayne's body.

"That's all, Marcy. I got this. Go on," Ellie said in an icy voice, her eyes wild in her long Kirby face, like some red fury come down from the Highlands.

Marcy held up her hand, indicating her wristwatch.

Ellie nodded. Then Marcy just turned and walked back down the trail. Her footsteps faded off to nothing and there was only the sound of Mitch's breathing.

"What's going on?" he pleaded, dry-mouthed, studying the familiar rifle pointed at his chest.

Nothing. He was looking in dead, cold eyes.

"Jesus, Ellie. I'm your husband! LaSalle said . . ."

She cut him off. "You should have thought about that before you went off digging up other people's battlefields." She steadied the Enfield against her hip with her right hand and reached to withdraw the pistol with the other, having a little difficulty with the holster flap, so the Enfield jerked sideways and Mitch saw a tiny brass twinkle as the cap fell off.

Didn't crimp it down.

Suddenly spit came. Mitch's voice returned. A flicker of the old smile. "Set me up you two. Got it all figured out, huh?"

Fuck you, said her eyes, past talking now.

Raging, Mitch yelled and lunged forward.

Ellie pulled the trigger and would have shot him right in the chest, but the hammer fell on the naked cone. Click. Nothing. She yanked at the pistol but Mitch was on her, clawing at her hand, and the Colt discharged into the trees.

He swung his elbow through the white smoke at her goddamn Kirby chin. Stunned, Ellie staggered, eyes fluttering;
then rebounded, wiry as a wildcat, and they grappled for the
pistol. Teeth bared, eyes inches apart, they wrestled in the
mud and leaves, the Enfield trapped between them. Then he
rolled and mounted her and forced the Colt's muzzle down
toward her face. Their breath mingled and rasped into one
hysterical sob in the greasy smoke and spittle and Mitch was
bearing down, thinking I'm gonna stick this right in your
fuckin' mouth. Rearrange that goddamn jaw.

Ellie's eyes bulged, pushing back with all her might, with
both hands. Then she darted her head forward and clamped
her teeth on the knuckle of his trigger finger.

Mitch hissed in pain, the Colt went off, and he blinked,
coughing, blind from more smoke. The pistol pin wheeled
away from his hand and splashed muzzle down in a muddy
rut. Ellie squirmed, got her feet under her, surged up. Had
the rifle now. Raised it to club him. Mitch tore it from her
hands and gripped the leather belt around her waist to hold
her as he scrambled up. The buckle came loose, the belt
parted, and she broke free.

Shit.

Ellie was a gray flicker, dashing through the trees, and
Mitch started after her, fingering a cap from the pouch on the
belt and fitting it expertly on the nipple. Pregnant my ass!

"I GOT YOU NOW YOU LYIN' MURDERING
BITCH," he yelled.

63 THEY WERE THREADING THROUGH A grove of black gum and oak that ran aslant of the picnic area when they spied the cream-colored Caddy in the parking lot.

"Dwayne's car," Beeman said as the cannons went off on Hurlbut Field. They exchanged sweaty glances. More tense now, they padded toward the broad green field beyond the fringe of trees.

Beeman crouched against an oak and peered across the clearing. "There's the cannon," he said. Rane nodded, scanning the open space.

A shot popped in the trees across the clearing.

"Pistol. Black powder, by the sound. Okay." Beeman readied himself, wiping a sweat-slick palm along the stock of the Sharps.

Rane crouched, eyeing the rifle, opening and closing the fingers of his right hand. "If it comes down to black powder, remember, you got the better machine. You can load that thing on the move three times to his one."

Beeman nodded, blinking sweat.

Rane said, "We work up and around the north end. Keep inside the trees. You stay to my right, let me . . ." Rane froze in place. His right hand swept up, signaling silence.

"What is it?" Beeman whispered.

Rane squinted, angled his head, and then pointed. "Something in the trees across the field."

"What?" Beeman craned his neck. "Shit." He gripped the Sharps, bared his teeth.

"See that orange? Like shoes? Somebody down. Maybe two of them. Dwayne Leets wears those . . ."

They locked eyes. "Orange boots," Beeman said and then he shook his head. "We gotta go check it out."

"Stop thinking like a cop," Rane said emphatically, "not smart to cross that open ground, man. We have to work around."

A rattle of muskets beyond the trees put them more on edge.

"Can't do that, John," Beeman shook his head. "No time. They might need help. There's an ambulance up by the History Center at the landing. I can call it in." He lurched to his feet and stepped from the cover of the trees.

"Shit." Reluctantly, Rane rose, tossed the toy Enfield aside, and followed. Now that it was here he found he didn't really want it. But the way it worked he couldn't let Beeman go alone.

They were halfway to the trees when they heard a hoarse shout. Another muffled shot.

They ducked and dashed across the field. Pow. Another shot. Rane read the heave of rolling ground. They were leaving a section of hummocks that offered cover, on open ground now. The cannon stood a hundred yards off to the right, a solitary marker.

Panting in the shadow of the trees, they saw the two bodies sprawled on a trail. "That's Dwayne face up, other one looks like Jimmy Beal. Check 'em," Beeman said, swinging the Sharps, covering the end of the field.

Rane moved to the two bodies, careful of the red spatter, quickly felt for a pulse in the throats, and said, "They're gone." He started to pick up the 9-mm Glock next to Beal's stiff hand.

"Don't touch nothing," Beeman barked, then he muttered, narrowing his eyes, "Shit." He tore open the buttons of his gray jacket and reached for the radio attached to his belt. Before he could unclip it, a single shot boomed and echoed up the field. Louder than the other shots.

"Rifle. Muzzleloader," Rane said, gritting his teeth and bracing for the whiz of an incoming round.

Beeman crouched, swinging the Sharps, searching for a target. "Gotta go up there," he muttered. His whole body shuddered as he gathered himself, pushed to his feet, left cover, and started straight up the field.

CAN'T OUTRUN HER. NEVER HAPPEN. MITCH STUM-bled, hurdling a log. He had to turn her, get her out in the open. He made a snap decision, careened his shoulder against a black gum, raised the rifle, led the gray blur through the trees, and fired at a rock outcropping ahead and to her left. The rifle heaved against his shoulder and Ellie disappeared in a cloud of smoke. Mitch immediately was on his feet, running, reaching for another cartridge. Yes. Having the rifle in his hands was a source of strength.

A moment later, as he socked the charge home and returned the ramrod, he saw the ploy had worked. She'd changed direction when the round splattered off the rock and now was running with her hands waving around her head like she was shooing bees. Running to the right, toward the field.

Come to Daddy, darling. That's what I want. He slapped a cap on the nipple and ran for the edge of the trees. We'll go down together. You first.

"THERE'S COVER TO THE RIGHT," RANE CALLED, racing after Beeman. "Go right."

Beeman ignored him and continued to dash toward the cannon and then, oh shit.

"Beeman," Rane yelled, seeing Ellender Kirby sprint from the edge of the woods in gray sweats. White dots for hands? She slid, stumbled, fell, and rolled over on the slick grass. "Two o'clock, coming out of the trees! You gotta stop. Get in position. Get ready!"

Beeman changed direction and pumped his arms and legs, the rifle throwing off his balance. The Kirby woman had bounced back to her feet and was opening her stride.

Good. Rane sprinting himself now, one hand steadying the swinging camera bag. She was running on the broken ground. Had to shift her gait for footing. The zigzag would throw off a shooter. Good.

The shooter? Rane's eyes jerked at the blur of foliage. Where are you? "Get down, Miss Kirby," Beeman yelled, waving his arms to get her attention.

She saw him and started to skid to a stop.

"Keep running, *move*," Rane screamed.

"Stop. *Get down*," Beeman screamed, bearing down on her.

Rane was close enough to see the confusion on her face as she danced uncertainly from foot to foot, seeing Beeman coming straight at her, Rane not far behind. She swung her head back toward the trees.

Beeman slung the rifle on his shoulder and put out his arms to wrap her.

"No," Rane screamed as he saw the blur of motion in the trees, sunlight marking a face and a twinkle of steel. Now Beeman stretched out to tackle her, and as they hit the ground and rolled to a stop, Rane saw the puff of smoke and heard the boom.

Beeman sprawled over, covering her body with his own. Then the impact spun him.

"Enough of this shit," Rane shouted, cranking all-out the last few steps, vaulting over the two prone figures and peeling off the camera bag as he hit the ground. He rolled, turned, and grabbed the Sharps that had been flung from

Beeman's shoulder, checked the muzzle. Clear. The hammer lock. Still capped. His eyes flashed on Beeman. The cop's back was a rip of gray cloth, blood, and mangled flesh. But his eyes were alert with pain and he was functioning, checking the woman for wounds. "She's okay," he gasped. Rane looked once into Ellender Kirby's dazed eyes, then rolled over again, raised the Sharps, and fired immediately just behind the drift of smoke up the field. A second later he was on one knee, digging another round from his pocket, wracking open the lever, inserting it, capping the nipple. "Get down. Make yourself small. I'll draw fire," Rane yelled over his shoulder, then he snapped another shot.

"GODDAMN," MITCH GIGGLED, "IT'S A TWOFER." SEE-ing, no shit, that it was Kenny Beeman running across the field dressed in gray. Another guy behind him in blue. Don't matter. We'll all go down together, like it says in the song.

Ain't gonna miss you this time.

He knelt, grabbed a sturdy sapling with his left hand, extended his thumb as a shooting rest, and flipped the sights up for two hundred yards. For a long moment, he estimated the point of intersection between Beeman and Ellie, made a slight allowance for shooting downhill, and waited until Beeman and Ellie collided and rolled on the ground. When they lay still, he squeezed the trigger.

They disappeared in a cloud of smoke as he swiftly reloaded and primed the Enfield. For speed, he stuck the rammer in the ground, tulip up; scooped out three cartridges and placed them close to hand. Then he saw through a film of smoke that Beeman and Ellie were down in a tangle.

But the other guy? Bang!

A bullet clipped branches two feet above his head with a sickening whine. Shit. Mitch instinctively ducked as a sprinkle of punky wood bits fell on his sleeve. Shit.

He squinted, still ducking his head, and now the guy was up on one knee and—bang—a second shot sizzled right over Mitch's head.

For a long second Mitch was stunned by the spectacle of the man rising to his feet and dashing up the slope toward him. Lookit you: blue jacket and cap and sky-blue trousers with a rifle held out in front of your chest. Okay then . . .

He settled the sights on the brass twinkle in the middle of the blue chest and held his breath as the running figure approached the black cannon. Took a tiny space of time to steady down and reflect that the original rifle in his hands had seen this picture before.

Except suddenly the blue apparition swept up his rifle, set his feet, and fired again, and this time the round tore a white gash into the sapling he was using as a gun rest, just four inches above his head. A spray of wet sap and raw white splinters slapped his crusted cheek stiff as needles.

Mitch shivered as it dawned on him: *He's shooting at me.* And he's still coming, levering the breechloader on the run, and so let's finish this up. First this nut, then go back for Ellie. He leaned back to the sights and settled down but, damn, like waves of shock were still rippling off the bullet that passed close to his face, putting bends in the air, and it was a mighty effort to get his racing heart under control.

Then he settled down and shot the running fool in the chest.

RANE THREW HIMSELF UP THE HILL STRAIGHT AT the bullet coming from the white puff of smoke. He canted his right shoulder back, wrenching his torso sideways as he reached into his pocket for another round, and then the thing he had wondered about for all these years jumped out and found him and ripped a burning trough across his chest and shoulder, and a splatter of brass eagle tore up his chin and cheek and punched a crimson triangle into his right eye. He sagged, stumbled on, and fell against the hot black iron cannon wheel. Not pain so much as a great slowness.

His right eye was plugged with red, but he could see him now: a fuzzy, blood-veiled figure, kneeling in the trees maybe a hundred fifty yards, the long rifle held at a slant in a flurry of reloading. Not an image in a viewfinder.

Real this time.

His body continued to function with some difficulty, because the pulley system in his right shoulder was pretty much kaput and he had to keep his elbow tucked in tight to his side to lift his right hand. Best he could, he loaded the bullet and wracked the lever shut. Fumbled up the percussion cap. Saw blood trickle out under his cuff, down the crease of his thumb.

He cocked the Sharps, pushed off the cannon, and walked on, lead-footed, toward the trees, blinking blood from his right eye, trigger finger numb in his right hand. Methodically, he put the rifle stock to his shoulder, found the trigger. No magic left in his right eye. Little feeling in his right hand. The lethal Sharps clumsy as a two-by-four. Hopelessly awkward and muddling ordinary and you gotta keep walking forward and just club the fucker down.

Now he could make out the surprise on the man's dirty face. Same face from the picture.

So Rane stopped and took a stance and with every ounce of control and craft left to him he steadied the rifle and squinted through a tiny window in the red, right into Mitchell Lee Nickel's wide eyes. He was raising the Enfield up there, aiming; so Rane held a little low and pressed the trigger at a mere hundred yards and knocked Mitchell Lee loose from his life with a sloppy but effective shot in the heart.

64

RANE STOOD IN PLACE, LEANING ON the rifle. With his good left eye, he watched Beeman hunkered down, one hand on the woman's shoulder, talking, heads close. She huddled, knees drawn up, pillowing her head on her elbows. The day rushed in Rane's ears; locomotives of pain, shock, and adrenaline. Still, he noticed the white gloves had disappeared. Then Beeman pushed to his feet with difficulty and trudged up the hill, carrying the haversack that contained the Nikon.

"You look like shit," Rane said when the ragged Southern cop stopped next to him, left arm hanging limp, blood all down the left side of his back, more dribbling on his chin. "She okay?" Rane asked.

"Real shook. Was fighting for her life up there."

They staggered up the hill and stood over Mitchell Lee's gray-clad body that was torn and dirty and bearded. Sprawled on his back, both hands drawn up to his bloody chest, fingers arched like claws; he could have been a Confederate corpse photographed by Matthew Brady in a muddy trench at Petersburg.

Beeman turned and called out, "He ain't going to bother you no more, Miss Kirby." He sagged with the effort, fought for balance. Rane steadied him. Ellender Kirby raised her head, nodded, slumped back down on her elbows.

"What'd she say?" Rane asked finally, nodding toward the Kirby woman, who now had recovered enough to be talking on her cell phone.

"Says he snatched her this morning."

"What about the black guy nobody could get past?"

"Went to town. She was alone."

"Uh-huh."

Beeman toed the body. "Looks like he was gonna settle up with everybody right here."

"With a muzzleloader?"

Beeman grimaced. "She says he had a pistol. Saw him shoot those two then he turned it on her. They struggled and she got away . . ." After a moment, Beeman said with some difficulty breathing, "So how's it gonna be, John?"

Rane swept his good eye along the field. Wondered, what they said down there? Not my business. Let it go. You just have to live through this thing. You don't have to own it. So he turned, spit a bloody wad of saliva, and smiled at Beeman. "What about her? What'd she see?"

"She's in shock, was out of it."

"Uh-huh."

"Well?" Beeman asked.

Rane weighed it briefly, then said, "Looks like you got him. Hell of a shot, considering."

Beeman smiled slowly in acknowledgment and nodded. Then they gently helped each other remove their torn jackets and used the first-aid kit in Beeman's pouch to bandage their wounds. The ragged hole in Beeman's shoulder blade had bone splinters in it and he was coughing up blood. "How bad," Beeman wheezed.

"No exit I can see. From the angle I think it's lodged under the scapula. Some bubble action. You might have bone splinters in a lung. Sucking chest ain't good," Rane said as he taped a plastic bandage wrapper tight over the wound, and after that Beeman was breathing a little better.

Then Beeman saw to the plowed muscles across Rane's chest and shoulder, which looked like shivering red rubber bands, like when you tear apart a golf ball.

Rane cast around with his good eye and asked another of those rhetorical questions: "So the Kirby woman, she another confidential informant like Marcy?"

Beeman ignored the question, preoccupied with dabbing blood, gingerly working with a square of gauze over Rane's right eye. Then he lurched back with a wincing appraisal. "Stuff on your face is minor but I don't know about this eye? The way the eyebrow's torn and hanging down and the eye-ball all exposed under it, I can't tell. We got to get you to the hospital." With great deliberation, Beeman took his radio off his belt, tore away the clip-on mike, switched it on, and keyed the push to talk. "This is Beeman." He coughed pink froth.

"Jesus, Beeman, we copy. Where you been?" a voice came back. "He's here. We found his truck. Looks like he's been living in it . . ."

"He's here, all right. Start an ambu. I got three down, two wounded, and one real shook up woman. North of the picnic area across 22, west of the Old Cavalry Road. One's a pretty bad eye wound. And I ain't breathing so hot. Copy?"

"We copy. On the way."

Beeman let the radio drop to the ground. "Won't be long," he said. "They ain't that far." Weaving unsteadily, they continued to stare at each other.

Beeman raised the haversack with the camera in his right hand. He inclined his head at the Sharps Rane held in a death grip in his left hand. When they heard the sirens wailing on the other side of the trees, Beeman said, "Might be a good idea to trade."

Rane looked down the slope in the direction of the two bodies sprawled in the trees, then at the Kirby woman, head down on her knees. He parted his lips and spoke through red-stained teeth. "You figure out a way to make it come out right?"

"Never know for sure, will we, John?" Beeman said, laboring to breathe.

Rane thought a moment, then said, "Sometimes the chips fall where they been carefully placed."

"You just let me do the talking," Beeman said.

They could see the red-and-blue flashers through the trees, so they exchanged the camera bag and the rifle and Rane extracted the Nikon left-handed. Then he nudged Beeman in a shuffle around the corpse until he liked the light, and said, "Kind of let the Sharps hang in your good hand."

Rane staggered back and raised the camera with his left hand to his left eye with his fingers splayed awkwardly around the lens, one finger feeling for the shutter. Just before he tripped the button, he mumbled from old habit, "Pretend I'm not here."

Then he slung the camera and asked Beeman to borrow his cell. He walked off a few feet, made his call, and returned as Beeman gagged and coughed blood. Rane helped him to the ground, which was how the Hardin County deputies and the EMTs found them, sitting next to Mitchell Lee's body, propped up, leaning against each other.

"See to the woman," Beeman told the medics just before he collapsed.

A THOUSAND MILES DUE NORTH, AT THE BRADLEY Circle of Life Center off Highway 36 on the outskirts of Stillwater, Minnesota, Jenny Edin was greeting the last of the guests filing in for the service when her cell phone vibrated in her small clutch purse. She excused herself and opened the phone.

Mississippi prefix. Beeman's number. A text message.

IT'S OVER. ALL OK.

Think about that later.

She turned off the phone, returned it to the purse, and raised her fingers to her heart, to the brooch that closed the loosely crocheted, knee-length black cotton sweater she wore over a black linen dress. Then she turned back to the guests, smiled warmly, and extended both hands to Tom Dalton and

Davey Manning, who stood at the front of a delegation from the reenactors.

After everyone took their seats, the Reverend Brit Etzold raised his hand as a summons to Molly Edin to step forward, with Miss Vanni, to commence the service.

Molly squeezed her mother's hand and stood up in her black recital dress and walked with her chin lifted and her body erect toward the grand piano positioned next to an easel surrounded by flower arrangements. Mom had placed on the easel a large, three-by-five-foot, photo enlargement of a picture Molly had never seen before this morning: Dad running, smiling, behind her as she pumped her two-wheeler in the foreground.

Molly walked past the photo, took her seat on the piano bench, composed herself, nodded to Miss Vanni beside her, and together, counting under their breath, they placed their fingers softly on the keys.

65

LATE AUGUST IN THE QUETICO Provincial Park lake country is changeable, but the weather tends toward cool this season. So the mosquitoes and deer flies haven't been that bad on the four-day paddle. They've been living on trout and walleye to stretch the grub, because Rane has packed bare minimums into the one canoe, so it could carry a passenger in a pocket of gear in front of the aft thwart. It's a point-to-point speed trip, not a pleasure excursion. They're traveling light. With Jenny and Molly changing off in the bow, they pushed hard up through Tuck and McIntyre and Conmee and now they're hiking the rugged eight-hundred-rod portage into Poobah.

Sweat drips from John Rane's deeply tanned face. He wears shorts and a T-shirt. His muddy hiking boots crunch pine needles and gravel as he totes the eighteen-foot Grumman aluminum canoe on his shoulders. He carries a full Duluth pack on his back. This is the last leg of the rocky trail into Poobah Lake.

A lot has happened in the last five months.

He has had two surgeries on his right eye and one arthroscopic procedure on his right shoulder. After months of intense therapy, most of the strength has returned to his right arm but he may never get all the fine muscle control back in his fingers. The prognosis for the eye is better. Most of the damage was confined to the soft tissue and bone around the socket, and only a few tiny shards of brass penetrated the eyeball. Full recovery will require another year of eye exercises and possibly another minor operation.

He has been on extended sick leave, plans to take the buyout offered by the *Pioneer Press*'s new owners, and is discussing a book idea about Civil War reenactors with his publisher, but not urgently.

Finally, he clears the pines, arrives at the lake, lowers the heavy canoe off his shoulders, and sets it down on the granite shore. Then he wiggles out of the pack straps and stretches. He wears a black patch over his right eye to protect it from bright sunlight, his hair is longer, and a close-cropped piratical beard circles his mouth to disguise the scarring on his chin and cheek.

He lifts the patch, shades his eyes with his hand, and, for a moment, he peruses the remote wilderness retreat that will be Paul Edin's grave. Then he clears an area to set up the pup tent in which Jenny and Molly will spend the night. Once he's swept a sandy area free of debris, he quickly assembles the tent, stakes it down, and then repairs a fire circle left here by other campers. He gathers a supply of firewood from the abundant dead fall in the area and stacks it next to the fire pit. Lastly, he strings a rope over a high branch a hundred yards from the tent and ties off the food bag so they can hoist it after the evening meal.

His arms are deeply tanned from the last two weeks spent reroofing the dilapidated 1870s three-bedroom house Jenny Edin bought on Stillwater's North Hill after she sold the place in Croix Ridge. Next year Molly will walk to school.

Rane's relationship with the Edin women is evolving and he and Molly frequently find themselves side by side on the piano bench. Jenny has prepared a list of tasks to be accomplished in the new house, which resembles a mini Labors of Hercules: after the roof, there is the wiring and the plumbing and tearing out the floors, a couple of walls, and the old furnace. Rane keeps showing up with tools and his uncle Mike and she keeps letting him in. Jenny has never questioned the official story out of Mississippi about the shoot-out at Shiloh; just as Rane has never questioned that Paul is Molly's father.

Maybe someday.

For five months, he and Jenny have circled each other with elaborate reserve and have not so much as shaken hands. What their eyes do is a different story. Jenny insists that putting off this canoe trip until Rane's arm was strong enough to paddle and portage was Molly's idea. But he suspects she played a coaching role.

The campsite now complete, Rane kneels on the shore, cups his hand and dips it into the clear water, raises it, and drinks. This is one of the few places in the world where humans can still do this.

Then he turns and walks back up the portage toward the small puddle of a lake that serves as a rest stop in the long overland hike between Poobah and Conmee. For the last four days, he's slept like a guard dog by the fire in front of the tent. Tonight he'll camp alone. In the morning, Jenny and Molly will paddle out into Poobah and scatter the ashes that Molly carries in her backpack.

Halfway up the portage, he meets Jenny bent under the weight of the other Duluth pack.

Eyes lowered, he and Jenny exchange a curt smile and pass without a word. Molly has grown almost two inches and is lean and tan in Levi's cutoffs. As she swings by, she sweeps out her hand and their palms slap together in a low five.

Rane sticks his right hand in his pocket and squeezes the buckeye nut Beeman gave him when they released him from the hospital in Corinth and just before the Alcorn deputy named Del drove him to the Memphis airport. His Jeep is still down there, parked in Beeman's backyard. Beeman e-mailed that the Sharps rifle has been released by the Hardin County Sheriff's Office and now waits, oiled and spotlessly free of rust, in his den.

John Rane continues walking to his solitary campsite in no particular hurry. He has not brought a camera on the trip.

IN MISSISSIPPI, THE AUGUST HEAT DRAPES A GRAY haze over Kirby Creek. Kenny Beeman is pretty much healed up. He's agreed to sub for a friend on his day off, taking a deputy shift in neighboring Tishomingo County. He enjoys the break in pace, patrolling in a one-man car, away from his desk duties as chief deputy. Today is slow, so he varies his pattern: drives into Alcorn County and onto the Kirby property.

He hasn't been here since the week after the Shiloh shooting, when he attended, in a wheelchair, Hiram Kirby's funeral. True to his promise to Rane, he finessed the shooting incident during a testy hour-long meeting with the Hardin County prosecutor. Beeman had patiently but stubbornly explained from his hospital bed that he was acting on a last-minute tip from a confidential informant about Mitchell Lee Nickels. Proceeding to intercept Nickels, Beeman related, he lost his security detail in the bad terrain and developed radio problems. It was at this point that photographer John Rane produced a packet of live rounds for the rusty rifle he was carrying. Discovering that Mitchell Lee had already killed Dwayne Leets and Jimmy Beal, Beeman used the only weapon at his disposal to defend himself, the photographer, and Ellender Kirby, when they came under fire. The prosecutor tested the political climate, which was running heavy in Beeman's favor, and did not pursue the shooting; the informant's identity was never revealed and the shooting was ruled justified.

The saga of Mitchell Lee will fuel the border country gossip for years to come and includes an alleged plot to murder Kenny Beeman and Ellender Kirby. The scheme went awry and apparently precipitated a psychotic episode, during which Mitchell Lee attacked his girlfriend, Marcy Leets, killed his coconspirators, kidnapped his wife, and lured Beeman into an ambush. In the end, it was tied in a neat forensic knot when the rounds recovered from Beeman's back, Dwayne Leets's chest, and the bullet sent by the Ohio reenactor all matched the Enfield rifle Mitchell Lee was carrying at the time of his death.

The Hardin County investigation determined that the bullets that killed Jimmy Beal, and contributed to Dwayne Leets's death, came from the .36 caliber Colt Navy revolver found near the bodies. Ellender Kirby confirmed in direct testimony that Nickels used the pistol to kill Beal, administer a coup de grace to Dwayne Leets and then turned the weapon on her, a fate she narrowly escaped. Nickels's fingerprints were found on the pistol.

Finally, the Mississippi State Crime Lab identified the bloody thumbprint left at the scene of the attack on Marcy Leets as belonging to Mitchell Lee Nickels.

LaSalle Ector recovered from his Iraq wounds enough to attend nursing school. Marcy and Darl Leets have been seen more together in public, usually at their boys' sporting events. Margie Beeman is wearing her wedding ring again.

The photo John Rane took at Shiloh ran full front page in the *Daily Corinthian* and a hundred other papers. People think that picture will get Beeman elected sheriff. Billie Watts, sober and regularly back in church, has offered to raise money for the campaign.

Beeman eases the Tishomingo cruiser past the house and the monument, and the tires crunch on scattered branches as he parks in the shade of old magnolias. A storm came through this morning and knocked down some trees, so he looks around, assessing the wind damage. Down the other side of the hill, the lakeshore is being staked and measured. He can just see a group of surveyors talking with a man in a white hard hat, who holds a roll of blueprints. Soon they'll break ground for the Robert Kirby Memorial Research Center.

He leans over, picks up his mike, and calls in to dispatch. "T-sixteen out of the car."

Then he gets out of the cruiser, walks across the lawn, descends the slope, steps over the fence, and approaches the old Confederate burial trench. When he gets to the trench, he removes his cap and looks around. Up at the hill, he sees Ellender Kirby come out, stand next to the monument, and raise one hand to shield the sun. Her face is flushed and round, and she carries the baby high in her belly.

Beyond the necessary questions, they have never spoken about the tense minutes at Shiloh and probably never will. She waves to him and he waves back. Then he stoops and clears several ripped branches that have blown into the grave plot. He leaves one of them, heavy with magnolia blossoms, and then pats the warm red earth.

Up on the hill, Ellie Kirby watches Beeman pay his respects. She knows his great-great-grandfather was listed among the missing, that day long ago, at Kirby Creek.

Then Beeman stands up, replaces his cap, climbs the slope, returns to the Crown Vic, picks up the mike, and calls in. "T-sixteen, back in the car." The dispatcher tells him there is a semi wrecked out on 72, west of the Alcorn line. Beeman keys the mike. "T-sixteen direct," he says. Then he puts the car in gear and drives away. He doesn't turn on his flashers and really hit the gas until he's off the Kirby land.

ELECTRIFYING THRILLERS FROM
CHUCK LOGAN

HOMEFRONT
978-0-06-057021-7

Eight-year-old Kit Broker chose the wrong adversary when she triumphed over schoolyard bully Teddy Klumpe. Now Teddy's family has escalated a minor feud into a major offensive of intimidation, destruction, and terror.

AFTER THE RAIN
978-0-06-057019-4

Soon a panel truck and its terrible cargo will cross from one side of the U.S-Canada divide to the other. For retired law enforcement officer Phil Broker, his family, and America, the clock is ticking down—because doomsday is closer than anyone imagines.

VAPOR TRAIL
978-0-06-103157-1

A priest has been executed and a medal of Nicholas, patron saint of children, stuffed into his mouth. Now Phil Broker must stir up ghosts from his own haunted past to catch a killer who might be a cop.

LOG1 0109

ELECTRIFYING SUSPENSE
FROM #1 *NEW YORK TIMES*
BESTSELLING AUTHOR

ANDREW GROSS

THE BLUE ZONE // 978-0-06-114341-0

The Blue Zone: The state most feared, when there is a suspicion that a subject's new identity has been penetrated or blown. When he or she is unaccounted for, is out of contact with the case agent, or has fled the safety of the program. When there is no official knowledge of whether that person is dead or alive.

—from the Witness Protection Program manual

THE DARK TIDE // 978-0-06-114343-4

On the morning Karen Friedman learns that her husband, a hedge fund manager, has been killed, Detective Ty Hauck begins his investigation of another man's death in a suspicious hit-and-run. The two seemingly unrelated tragedies are about to plunge Karen and Ty into a maelstrom of murder, money, and unthinkable conspiracy.

And coming soon in hardcover

DON'T LOOK TWICE
978-0-06-114344-1

GRO 0209